To Dave –

With big

xx

Put Out The Light

By Guy Hale

Act III in the Shakespeare Murders series

A Bullington Press publication

ISBN 978-1-0683633-3-7 (paperback)
ISBN 978-1-0683633-5-1 (e-book)
ISBN 978-1-0683633-7-5 (special edition hardback)

For permission requests, please email: info@bullingtonpress.co.uk

Interior layout by Textual Eyes
Design for Print Services

Cover by Peter Adlington

Printed and bound by CPI Group (UK) Ltd, Croydon, CR0 4YY

www.bullingtonpress.co.uk

Praise for the Shakespeare Murders series

Absolutely superb. I loved the darkness of it.

Chris Lloyd (winner of the HWA Gold Crown)

Deeply satisfying, great writing. A dark tale and a cracking read.

David Penny (author of The Thomas Berrington Historical Mysteries)

Dark, twisted and hilarious. Hale's characters are so well drawn. A brilliant read. Get thee to a bookshop.

Heather Critchlow (author of the Cal Lovett Series)

Superb writing, a masterpiece. Crime, Shakespeare and humour. What more could you ask from a book?

Aimee Louise (@whataimeereads_)

This was a book I fell in love with from the opening pages and was totally hooked right up to the unexpected ending. Can't wait for the next in this highly original series.

Andy Wormald (@amwbooks)

Wildly entertaining, darkly funny. Hamlet as you've never seen it. Had me gripped and gasping. Outstanding!

Rob Parker (author of the Thirty Miles Trilogy)

Dexter meets Shakespeare in this dark and twisted tale of revenge.

Christie J. Newport (Joffe Books prize winner)

Masterful plotting, a dark and funny take on Hamlet.

Blair Kessler (The Birmingham Film Company)

I loved this book. Very atmospheric. This Hamlet is extremely good but also very bad!

Imran Mahmood (author of I Know What I Saw)

Fresh, funny and fiendishly clever. The Croaking Raven is an absolute triumph!

A.A. Chaudhuri (Amazon bestselling author)

By Guy Hale

The Comeback Trail Trilogy

Killing Me Softly
Blood on the Tracks
All the World's a Stage

The Shakespeare Murders

The Croaking Raven
All Our Yesterdays
Put Out The Light

To Fred and Kathryn
True friends and character fodder!

Chapter 1
The Coming Storm

The new diary lay open on the table: Tuesday the first of August, 1972. Oliver stared at the empty page. He picked up his pen and turned the pages until he reached Sunday the sixth. His hand hovered momentarily above the page and then he began to write.

Kill someone.

He sat back, read his entry and nodded his approval. Too much time had passed and vengeance is an impatient mistress. He stared at the words. As a statement it showed intent but lacked clarity. Who should he kill? He had a list of victims but who should be next? He started to write a fresh list and stopped after three. Was that all? There were so many that he could have included. He looked at the list again, every name was female; women he had loved, trusted, and all had betrayed him.

Did their betrayal warrant the death penalty he was imposing upon them?

A voice of caution sounded in his head. *O, beware, my lord, of jealousy! It is the green-eyed monster which doth mock the meat it feeds on.* He recognised the quote but this was not jealousy; he cared nothing for the affections of these women.

The weeks had passed and spring had turned to summer. Peace had descended, once more, upon Stratford. He had waited, allowed the storm to subside, all the time thinking, planning, allowing his mind to clear. It was time for the second act.

Oliver stood up and gazed into the mirror above the fireplace. The face that looked back at him was calm, focused … But the eyes? They blazed with intent. He raised his hands in front of him.

'"Put out the light, and then put out the light."' He smiled. 'Let the play begin.'

Chapter 2
Waiting

Toby Marlowe stood in the incident room at Guild Street studying the whiteboard. The faces of the dead stared out at him. It was hard to look at their photos. He had failed to save them; failed to catch their killer.

Nearly seven weeks had passed since Gerard Soames had been found beside the bandstand. Propped up in a seated position and tied in place, looking towards the theatre. There was a message there, he knew it. All of the victims were linked to the theatre. The killer was playing with them. Four murders in just a couple of weeks and then … nothing. This was not the end, it couldn't be.

'Searching for inspiration?'

Toby turned. Fred Williams was standing in the entrance to the room.

'What are we missing?'

Fred shrugged. 'The killer.'

Toby looked back at the whiteboard. 'We know who that is.'

'Do we?'

'Oliver Lawrence, it has to be.' Toby tapped the photo that was affixed to the top right-hand corner of the board. 'He's our man.'

'You think he is but what proof do we have? We don't even know if he's still alive.'

Toby couldn't argue with that. Nobody had even reported seeing him in Stratford. He tapped the photo again. 'This is the only picture we have of him and it's nearly sixteen years old. We have no idea what he looks like now.'

Fred sighed. 'We don't, all we can do is keep looking for whoever it is—'

'It's Lawrence, I know it.'

'You *think* it,' said Fred. 'You don't know it. He's a good candidate but we've made him fit the crimes. What if it's not him, what then?'

'It's him, I know it's him.'

Fred walked over to the kettle. 'Fancy a cuppa? Give you a chance to clear your head. You're letting this case get to you.'

Toby glanced at the faces looking out at him. Desmond and Tabitha Tharpe, Terry Fibs and Gerard Soames. All victims of the 'Shakespeare Killer'. That's what the press had christened him. He was out there somewhere, waiting.

'Staring at that won't bring you any answers.'

Toby turned his back to the board and headed over to where Fred was opening the biscuit tin. 'What will?'

'The next victim.'

For a moment, Toby didn't know what to say. Fred had said it so casually.

'Are you serious? That's our plan?'

'It's not our only plan but it is a plan. We can keep going over the details of each murder, checking and rechecking the evidence.' He paused for a moment and looked at Toby. 'I think we both know that's not going to bring us anything. Our murderer hasn't left any clues to his identity. He's not made a single mistake.'

'He's been lucky,' said Toby.

'Lucky is all he needs to be. The end result is we have four victims and we don't have a clue who did it.'

Toby went to protest but Fred silenced him with a raised hand. 'We have nothing tangible; we think it's Oliver Lawrence but, without any evidence, it might as well be Jack the Ripper.'

'So we just wait for him to kill again?'

'Can you come up with anything better? He's done nothing for six weeks now, maybe he's finished.'

Toby shook his head. 'You don't believe that.'

'No, I don't. He's planning, he's coming back for more. We

just have to be ready for him when he does.' Fred passed Toby a mug of tea. 'We are watching all of Sir Morris' players. At some point soon our murderer is going to show up and that's when we catch him.'

Fred's plan was a good one, there was just one flaw in it: they hadn't considered the director who had caused so many problems with her wild ideas. If Toby and Fred could have seen Oliver's list, they would have realised nobody was watching Lizzie Birchwood.

Chapter 3
Let The Fates Decide

Felix Richards stood outside Oliver's house on Trinity Street. Oliver had asked him to come around and that could only mean one thing: the calm of the last few weeks was about to end. He knew if he knocked on the door, he would be ushered into a new series of horrors the moment it opened.

Like a moth drawn to a flame, he knocked. He heard Oliver's footsteps approaching down the hallway and fought the urge to run. The catch clicked, the door swung open and there stood Oliver, wearing a pair of jeans, naked from the waist up.

For a moment, Felix was stunned by the sheer beauty of Oliver's body. His torso looked as if it had been chiselled from a piece of marble by Michelangelo himself, each muscle defined and honed like an athlete.

'You OK, Felix?'

Felix nodded. 'Yeah, I just wasn't expecting you to come to the door half-naked.'

'Thank your lucky stars it wasn't the other half,' Oliver chuckled. He turned and walked back down the hallway towards the kitchen.

Felix watched him. Those years of labouring in Morocco had turned Oliver into a powerful man. If he wanted to kill you … He dismissed the thought. He was Oliver's only true friend, surely it would never come to that. He followed him into the kitchen.

'Cup of tea or something stronger?'

'Depends what you're going to tell me.'

Oliver smiled. 'In that case, I'd better pour you a brandy.'

Felix sat down on the nearest stool; his legs suddenly felt weak. 'Well?'

Oliver locked eyes with him. 'It's time for the second act. The summer air has warmed my blood and I'm ready. I have a list and I have a plan.'

'A list,' said Felix. 'Are there many names on it?'

'Just three.'

Felix shuddered. 'You say three like it's nothing.'

Oliver shrugged. 'To me, it is nothing. Just three more steps towards the third act.'

'Do I know any of them?'

'All of them, you've even acted with one. Care to hazard a guess?'

'Not really, I'm not very good at this.'

'Nonsense, look how you set Soames up on the boat. You enjoyed watching me kill him, didn't you?'

Felix didn't answer. He stared at the kitchen floor. Oliver moved over to him and took his head in his hands. He gently tilted it back until they were looking directly at each other. Felix felt Oliver's warm breath on his face.

'You liked it, Felix, you told me. You and I are cut from the same cloth.'

Felix pulled away from him. 'No. I'm not a killer. You were wronged and I wanted to help you but—'

'Changed your mind? Got too real for you, did it?' There was a sneer in Oliver's voice.

'I'll never change my mind about the wrongs both you and your father suffered. Everyone you've killed was guilty, but where does it stop. How much is enough?'

Oliver leaned back against the worktop. 'Twelve, I think.' He paused for a moment. 'Over three acts. I think that will do it, don't you?'

'I'll take that brandy.'

Oliver grabbed the bottle from the shelf above the fridge. 'Large one?' Felix nodded. 'I'm sticking with tea, way too early in the day to start drinking the hard stuff.' He poured a double and passed it to Felix. 'I'm going to start on Sunday. Care to join me?'

The casual way in which he asked made Felix smile. 'You really are quite mad, Oliver.'

'Am I? I don't think so. Those of us that are driven by a purpose frighten those who lack the same drive. You're just worried about getting caught.'

Felix thought about that for a moment. 'Maybe, but another eight victims is pushing our luck. Stratford is a small place; sooner or later the police are going to catch up with us.'

Oliver nodded enthusiastically. 'That's why I need to get on with it. If I give them time to investigate, they'll have a chance but, if I hit them fast and hard, they won't know what's going on.'

Felix took a large gulp of his brandy. 'So, who are the victims?'

Oliver winked at him. 'They're all women.'

Felix's hand paused on the way back to his lips. 'All women.'

Oliver nodded. 'I believe in equal opportunities. I thought I would make act two a female exclusive. Put out a few lights.'

Felix understood exactly what Oliver meant. 'That sounds like jealousy, not revenge. Who are they?'

Oliver gazed out at the garden. 'I'll give you a clue. She can't act.'

'You'll need to narrow it down.'

'Cutting. Glad to see you still have your critic's head on.' He turned to face Felix. 'She's frightfully posh and very generous with her affections.'

Felix shrugged. 'Again, you'll have to narrow it down.'

'You don't have a very high opinion of some of our female actors, do you.'

'Most I do, but there are those that try to get by on their looks. It's lazy, entitled. They have no place in the theatre. I want to see talent, characterisation, emotion. Leave the window dressing to the set designer.'

Oliver stirred his tea thoughtfully. 'You still have the passion, Felix. I like that. I think you'll approve of my choice.'

'Go on.'

'Clarissa Pidgeon.'

'Clarissa. What did she do to you?'

'She dropped me like a stone. One word from Morris and she ended our affair.'

Felix was surprised. 'But you were going out with Tabitha.'

'Not then. She had dropped me two months before. Clarissa moved in the moment I was dumped; caught me when I was vulnerable.'

'And you want to kill her for that?'

'Of course not, I'm not a monster.'

Felix wasn't so sure about that but decided it would be best not to voice his opinion.

'She started leaving pauses in our scenes together, she even fed me wrong lines. She was deliberately sabotaging my performances. You must have noticed.'

'*As You Like It*?'

'You did notice. Why didn't you say something?'

'It just looked like you had missed your cue. She was a very good Rosalind.'

'I was a very good Orlando,' said Oliver.

Felix pursed his lips. 'Not that night, you weren't.'

'For good reason.'

'I see that now.' Felix put down his drink. 'I'd seen Desmond and Sir Morris do it to you but I'd never noticed it with anyone else. But now I think back, I see it.'

'That's why I have twelve names on my list, Felix. All of Sir Morris' inner circle was in on the plan.'

'I understand,' said Felix. 'But does she really deserve to die for it? Morris would have put a lot of pressure on her. She was a young actress; could she really say no?'

'Of course! They all could have,' snapped Oliver. He took a deep breath. 'But that's not the main reason. She did something inexcusable.'

Oliver fell silent and stared, unblinking, at Felix.

'What did she do?'

'She went to Lizzie Birchwood and told her I had assaulted her.'

Felix couldn't believe his ears. 'Are you sure?'

'I'm sure. Lizzie told me that Clarissa had complained about me.'

'Surely she didn't believe her.'

Oliver chuckled humourlessly. 'Lizzie didn't like me; she'd been waiting for a chance to put me in my place. When Clarissa came to her, she couldn't believe her luck.'

'Listen, you know I have no love for Lizzie, she's a terrible director. But why did she have a problem with you?'

Oliver grinned. 'If I told you, you wouldn't believe me.'

'Try me.'

'OK. Better pick that brandy up, this tale is crazy. I'd been cast as Orlando and the rehearsals were due to start the next day. Lizzie called me to a meeting in her office. I knew Lizzie thought I had been given leading roles too early in my career. She thought I was being given an easy ride because of my father. Things had been a bit tense between us the previous season, so I went to her office expecting some trouble. I just wasn't prepared for what kind of trouble.'

Felix listened intently.

'When I got there, she was on her own. "Come in and close the door, Oliver. I want to have a chat with you about how I see Orlando in this production." That got my alarm bells ringing. You know she had some pretty crazy ideas about settings and context.'

Felix nodded. 'Who could forget her *Tempest* set on Mars. A green Caliban, for God's sake! Woman's a menace.'

Oliver laughed. 'I'd forgotten about that one.'

'So, what did she propose?'

Oliver nodded towards Felix's brandy. 'I think you should take a sip, you're going to need it.'

Felix did as Oliver suggested.

'So, we exchanged the usual pleasantries and then she started. "Oliver, darling, I know you haven't played Orlando before but I am sure you have studied the text."

'I had, I was already word-perfect and looking forward to the start of rehearsals the next day. "Yes," says I. "I'm ready."

'She smiled at me in a very patronising way. "Well, that's lovely, dear, knowing the words is all very well, but understanding the subtext … that's quite another thing. What do you make of Orlando and his attitude towards Rosalind?"

'"He's a bit slow on the uptake," I said.

She nodded impatiently. "He is, but why?"

'I thought about it for a moment. "Because she's dressed as a man."

'She shook her head in disgust. "No, Oliver, it's because he's a homosexual."'

Felix spat out his brandy. 'What!'

'I kid you not, she asked me to play him as a closet homosexual.'

'How the hell did she justify that interpretation?'

'She told me Orlando was drawn to Rosalind when he thought she was a man. Once she revealed herself to be a woman, it was too late. He couldn't back out.'

'Jesus H Christ, the woman's mad! I'm all for new interpretations and settings but Lizzie Birchwood just goes too far. Can't you kill her, too?'

'Funny you should mention that. She's second on my list.'

Felix nodded his approval. 'Finally, something we can agree on.' He looked slyly at Oliver. 'You couldn't kill her first, could you?'

Oliver shrugged. 'I have no strong feelings on the matter, as long as she's dead before the end of Sunday.'

'Good, I think I have an idea you will approve of.' Felix drained his glass. 'Right, I'm off to make some plans. Let's meet tomorrow night at Kenilworth and I'll fill you in.'

'Do we have to meet there? Why don't you just come around here?'

Felix grinned. 'Frightened of the haunted tower, are we?'

'Not really. I'm in the business of making ghosts, not being scared of them.'

'Good, be there at midnight; the witching hour.' Felix turned and headed down the hallway, slamming the door behind him.

Oliver couldn't help but smile. Felix may be an old theatrical luvvie but it appeared that he was now fully on Oliver's side; at least where Lizzie Birchwood was concerned.

Chapter 4
A Results-Driven Business

It felt good to be away from Stratford. Since the last murder, the town had become calm. Like a yacht caught in the lull before the storm, he waited. Everyone waited. Without an arrest, surely it was just a matter of time before the next murder. It seemed that everyone was holding their breath; waiting to exhale but afraid to drop their guard and open the door to more horror.

Toby swung into the car park at Coventry HQ. He had been summoned by Chief Constable Wilson, the boss of all bosses in the Warwickshire constabulary. The call had come directly to his desk at Guild Street nick from Wilson's secretary, the indomitable Hilary Joy. Never was someone so inappropriately named. Toby remembered the call.

'DC Marlowe, can I help?'

'You can, this is Chief Constable Wilson's office calling.'

'Who would he like to speak to, DS Williams or Inspector Beeching?'

'Neither,' said an irritated voice. 'He wants to speak to you.'

'Me?! I'm just a DC.'

Hilary Joy harrumphed with irritation. 'If the chief constable had wanted to speak with either of them, he would have asked me to call them, not you.'

Her tone hadn't allowed any room for argument. Before he could say anything, she had put him through and Wilson's voice had slithered out of the receiver like a snake freshly moistened with oil.

'Ahh, DC Marlowe. How very good it is to finally speak with you.'

'Sir, yes, sir.' Even as he responded, Toby wondered where the hell this conversation was going and what it was leading to.

'I want you to pop over and see me at HQ tomorrow, be here for ten a.m.'

'I'll have to check with DS Williams, sir. We are under the cosh with this serial killer.'

There had been a moments delay and when Wilson had replied, his voice was cold. 'Last time I checked, DC Marlowe, chief constable outranked DC. Be in my office at nine-thirty sharp.'

The line had clicked dead. There was no mistaking the intent in Wilson's voice. He was on the warpath, and he had just moved up their appointment by thirty minutes, probably as a rebuke for being questioned.

Had Chief Wilson discovered Inspector Beeching had information that would link Wilson to Tommy Vaughan and his illegal money-lending scheme? Like a caged tiger, he needed to be approached with caution.

Toby had gone straight to Fred Williams and told him what had occurred. Fred had nodded slowly.

'What's the old devil up to? He clearly wants you alone. I think he wants to find out if you know anything about Beeching's blackmail. He's probably assumed that I'm in on it. Beeching's not a good enough copper to have worked it out for himself.'

'Maybe Tommy has told him it was you and me that got the confession out of him.'

'No, Tommy Vaughan would never let on to grassing. You go there and pretend ignorance.' Fred winked at him. 'That shouldn't be too hard for you.'

Chapter 5
Summoned By Joy

The next morning, Toby climbed reluctantly out of his MG. He really wasn't looking forward to this meeting and he resented being summoned to HQ when there was a serial killer running loose. Politics, he thought. Everything's political these days.

He walked into the nick and there, in the foyer, was a familiar face: Sergeant Frank Godiva.

Godiva smiled in recognition. 'DC Marlowe, to what do we owe the pleasure?'

'I've been summoned to see Chief Wilson by Mrs Joy.'

The smile left Godiva's face. 'Bad luck, son. You got time for a cuppa?'

Toby shook his head. 'No, he wants me at nine-thirty sharp.'

'Better get up there. The old boy is a stickler for timekeeping.' Godiva gave him a friendly tap on the back. 'Pop into the canteen after. If you've still got a job.' He winked at Toby and then hurried off towards the custody suite.

Toby turned and headed up the stairs to Wilson's office. When he reached the door, he knocked almost apologetically.

'Enter.'

The voice was unmistakable. He pushed open the door and there, seated at her desk outside the door to Wilson's office, was Hilary Joy. She looked as welcoming as the gatekeeper in hell. 'DC Marlowe?'

'Yes, Mrs Joy.'

A muscle below her left eye twitched. 'It's Miss Joy,' she hissed through pursed lips, forcing a smile that had been strangled at birth. 'Take a seat, DC Marlowe. Chief Constable Wilson will see you shortly.'

'He said nine-thirty sharp.'

She gave him a look so cold that he felt his testicles retracting. The woman had presence. He gazed at the floor but could still feel the polar chill of her stare on his head.

After what seemed like an Arctic winter, her phone buzzed. 'Yes, sir. I'll show him in.' She replaced the receiver. 'The chief constable will see you now.'

There were two doors on the far side of the office. He looked at her for direction but it was clear all conversation was over.

Toby took a deep breath, straightened up and strode across the office. He knocked firmly on the door and, without waiting to be summoned, walked briskly into the stationery cupboard.

He emerged sheepishly to be greeted by the unblinking stare of Miss Joy. The trace of a smile played at the corner of her mouth, almost as if she couldn't remember how to do it.

'Plenty of paper,' said Toby.

'It's a stationery cupboard,' came the reply, in a voice so full of condescension he felt like he was back in school. Toby moved to his left and knocked on the next door. To his relief, his knock was answered.

'In.'

It was a command, not an invitation. Toby entered.

'Shut the door behind you, this isn't a barn.'

'Yes, sir,' Toby did as he was told and then turned and moved towards Wilson's desk. He reached for a chair that was off to the side.

'What do you think you are doing, DC Marlowe?'

'Sitting down, sir.'

Wilson leaned back in his chair and looked at Toby. 'Did I ask you to sit down, Marlowe?'

'No, sir.'

'Then don't.'

'Yes, sir,' said Toby, now wishing he was back in the office with the gatekeeper from hell.

'I've been hearing good reports of you, DC Marlowe.'

'Thank you, sir.'

'Never believed them though.'

'Sir?'

'DS Williams is not a good role model, not a team player. It seems that you and he are thick as thieves.'

Toby wasn't sure how to respond so he stayed silent.

'You and I know that Fred Williams is one cock up away from being fired. If one more suspect falls down the stairs or slips on some soap in the showers, he's gone. Do you think being on his team will do your career, such as it is, any good?'

'He's a fine officer, sir. His arrest and clear-up rates speak for themselves.'

'A parrot can speak for itself but that doesn't make it Larry Olivier, does it?'

Toby had to agree. 'No, sir.'

Chief Wilson looked him up and down distastefully. 'I don't like your attitude, I don't like the company you keep but, most of all, I don't like you.'

'With respect, sir, you don't really know me.' Toby was surprised by his response.

Wilson looked a little surprised too. 'Are you trying to be funny, Marlowe? Because if you are, I have to inform you that you are failing miserably.'

Toby didn't trust himself to reply. There was a rage building inside him that threatened to explode. How could this idiot be talking about not liking him when they had a serial killer on the loose?

'DC Marlowe, there are a few ground rules that you need to understand. Firstly, I am your boss. I don't care what Fred Williams or Inspector Beeching say, they all answer to me, and so do you.'

He glared at Toby, daring him to answer. Toby just stared

back.

Wilson seemed to be considering his next move. 'Are you ambitious, DC Marlowe? Would you like to rise through the ranks?'

'Yes, sir.'

Wilson nodded. 'Then let me give you some important advice. Choose your friends carefully and don't overstep the mark. There are those in the force, like Fred Williams, who will lead you astray. They don't play by our rules, they drive a coach and horses through protocol. That's why Williams is the longest serving DS in the country. He's stuck in a limbo of his own making. You don't want to be stuck in a limbo with Williams, do you?'

'No, sir.'

'Good. So tell me, DC Marlowe, are DS Williams and Inspector Beeching doing anything that would concern me?'

There was an accusation in Wilson's question. This was the moment, thought Toby.

'No, sir. They are so tied up with the murders that they aren't thinking about anything else. I don't think DS Williams went home last night.'

This seemed to satisfy Wilson but he pressed on, trying to appear casual but unable to hide the concern in his voice.

'And, er, what about our friend Tommy Vaughan?'

'What about him, sir?'

'Are you still looking into his assault and robbery?'

'No, sir, we have far more important things to worry about than Tommy Vaughan.' Toby saw Wilson's posture relax. 'I think Inspector Beeching has closed the file, it's not deemed worth spending any time on, given the lack of information and the serial killings.'

'Good, that's very good. One less thing for you to worry about.' Wilson stood up and held out his hand. 'Thank you, DC Marlowe, I feel more comfortable letting Stratford get on with the job now that we have spoken. I'll be monitoring your progress closely.'

I bet you will, thought Toby. He made a mental note to stick a metaphorical knife into Chief Constable Wilson the first chance he got.

Wilson squeezed his hand with a firm grip. 'Looking forward to working closely with you, Marlowe.'

'Feeling's mutual, sir,' lied Toby. He stood there for a moment, unsure if the meeting was over.

'Shut the door on your way out, Marlowe,' said Wilson.

As Toby closed the door behind him, he breathed a sigh of relief and then saw Hilary Joy. Her face was a mixture of dislike and contempt, not an easy look to pull off. Her features contorted like an uncoupled bull; full of emotions, none of them positive. Toby watched, waiting for her apparent frustration to subside.

She pursed her lips. 'That will be all, DC Marlowe.'

Toby nodded. 'Thanks, Mrs Joy.'

'It's Miss!'

Chapter 6
Escaping Cerberus

Toby walked into the canteen and there, behind the counter, was Mavis Blunt. She smiled at him as warmly as her few remaining teeth would allow.

'Hello, Mavis, how are you?'

Mavis twitched. 'You remembered my name.'

Toby grinned. 'Never forget a pretty face.'

She leered at him like the runner-up in a gurning contest. 'This face?'

'Yes, that's the one.' He felt a warm affection for Mavis. Life had not been kind to her and yet she still embraced the world with warmth and hope.

'What can I get you? Still got some bacon on the go.'

'You know the way to a man's heart. Can I have it on brown bread?'

Mavis gave him a look that implied he was some kind of pervert. 'Brown. What do you want that for?'

'It's supposed to be healthy.'

Mavis didn't look convinced. 'I could toast some white. That be brown enough for you?'

Toby knew when he was beaten. 'Close enough, thanks.'

'Do you want me to fry the bread?'

Toby felt his arteries shudder. 'No, toasted will be fine. Please can I have a cuppa too?'

Mavis beamed a smile that could only come from the heart. 'Of course you can. It's always a pleasure to have you Stratford boys over, makes a nice change from the apes we have here. No manners.'

Oliver pulled out a pound note and passed it over to Mavis.

She winked and pushed it back to him.

'This one's on the house, old Wilson has a big enough budget to cover it.'

Toby smiled. 'You sure, Mavis? I don't want to get you into trouble.'

'No trouble, that bacon's been in the pan since half past seven. If you don't have it, it'll be cremated.' She laughed.

Toby put his money back in his wallet and headed for a table to do his chewing exercises.

When the toasted bacon sandwich arrived it was surprisingly digestible but, just as he was beginning to relax, the canteen door swung open and in came Detective Inspector Mel Townsend. The Blonde Bombshell was looking particularly explosive this morning.

She made a beeline for his table. 'Mind if I join you?'

It was clearly a rhetorical question and Toby watched as Mel slipped her athletic frame into the chair opposite. She was a classy lady and somehow, despite a very vivid imagination, he could not imagine Fred and Mel ever having been a couple.

'So, Toby, what are you doing here?' Again, a rhetorical question; nothing got past Mel Townsend.

'Wilson's digging,' said Toby.

'His own grave hopefully. He grill you about the Tommy Vaughan enquiry?'

'Yeah, he managed to do it without really mentioning it, just slipped it in at the end of our meeting.'

Mel nodded. 'Does Fred know you're here?'

'Of course. I told him that I'd been summoned to see Wilson the second I got the call from Cerberus.'

'Who the hell is Cerberus?'

'Mrs Joy.'

'It's Miss.'

'I know,' grinned Toby. 'Drives her mad.'

Mel chuckled but looked confused. 'So, who is Cerberus then.'

'Greek Mythology. Cerberus was the gatekeeper in Hades. I just thought Mrs Joy would make a very good gatekeeper for hell.'

Mel nodded her approval. 'I like it. Mind if I call her Cerberus too?'

'Be my guest.'

Mavis came over to their table. 'Anything l can get you, inspector?'

'Black coffee, please, Mavis.'

Mavis leaned towards Mel. 'Are you and Toby here at it?'

Toby nearly choked on his bacon but Mel just smiled.

'Not yet, Mavis, I'm working on it.'

'Good for you, inspector.' Mavis gave Toby a knowing smile and headed back to her counter.

Mel looked at Toby's expression with amusement. 'What's wrong, DC Marlowe?'

'Nothing, inspector, nothing at all.'

Now that she had got Toby off guard, Mel began to question him. 'Where are you with the Shakespeare Killer? Any sign of this Oliver Lawrence character?'

'No, he's nowhere to be found. Trouble is, we don't even know what he looks like or where he came from.'

'I think you're right though, Toby, this Lawrence chap is our best bet. Just got to find him.'

'Yes, ma'am, we are doing everything we can but he's just stopped. Four murders in a couple of weeks and then nothing for over a month.'

'You think it's over?'

Toby shook his head. 'No, it won't be over until we catch him, he's enjoying it too much.'

'What makes you say that?'

'It's a performance … The way he laid out Terry Fibs. It's Gloucester from *King Lear*. Tying Gerard Soames to the bandstand so that he was gazing across the water towards the theatre, pure staging.'

Mel smiled. 'This is all to do with your *Hamlet* theory.'

Toby looked at her questioningly.

'Fred told me.'

'Pillow talk?' The words were out of Toby's mouth before he could stop them.

'No, Toby, shop talk.'

Toby blushed with embarrassment. Mel leaned towards him. 'Learn to think before you speak, might save your career.'

'Here's your coffee, inspector,' Mavis plonked it down on the table breaking the tension. 'You want another cuppa, Toby?'

Toby nodded. 'Please, Mavis.'

Mel raised the cup to her lips and took a sip. Her eyes never left him, piercing through the steam that rose from the coffee and freezing him into silence. 'I think your theory is a bit far-fetched but, if it is Oliver Lawrence, it sounds like just the sort of thing he would do.'

'It is,' said Toby, 'I'm sure of it.'

Mel nodded. 'If that's the case, why has he stopped? In *Hamlet*, the king and queen die. That begs the question, why are Sir Morris and Lady Oxford still alive?'

'Because Hamlet dies too. Oliver isn't planning on dying, he wants to revenge himself on everyone he thinks betrayed him.' Toby's passion for his theory was infectious.

'Then what?'

Toby leaned towards her. 'Move to another play, use that as the vehicle for the next lot of murders.'

'Which play?'

'Well, it won't be one of the comedies,' quipped Toby.

'You're supposed to be the Shakespeare expert, what do you think?'

Toby leaned back and shook his head. 'That is the question.'

Mel smiled. 'Funny, but what do you think?'

'It's got to be a tragedy. If I'm right, we've already had *Hamlet*.'

'How many are there?'

'Twelve.'

Mel slammed her hand down on the table. 'Twelve! How the hell are we going to work out which one is next?'

Toby held up a hand. 'It's not as bad as it sounds. There are twelve but only five are regarded as the major tragedies, the others are more historical, like *Julius Caesar* and *Coriolanus*.'

'So what are the five? I'm more of a musicals girl.'

Toby tried to hide his distaste but Mel saw it. 'Don't judge me, I love a song and a dance after a tough day. We see enough tragedy in this job, I don't need to see it in the theatre.'

Toby gave her a sickly smile. 'Musicals?'

'Focus,' she warned. 'What are the five major tragedies?'

Toby closed his eyes and counted them off. '*Hamlet*, obviously. *King Lear*, *Romeo and Juliet*, *Othello,* and the Scottish play.'

'What's the Scottish play?'

'Begins with an M; it's bad luck to use its name in a theatre.'

Mel looked around the canteen. 'We're not in a theatre.'

'I know, I just don't want to risk it.'

'For God's sake, Toby, you're a detective. Forget all this mumbo jumbo and crack on.'

Toby spoke reluctantly. '*Macbeth*.' He grabbed the salt from the table, threw some over his shoulder, stood up and turned around three times.

Mel watched him; an amused smile on her face. 'What was that? You a morris dancer?'

'Funny, ma'am. I was just un-cursing myself.'

Mel shook her head sadly. 'You theatre types are all slightly mad, aren't you?'

'Eccentric maybe, but these superstitions are hundreds of years old, you have to respect them.'

'You can but they're not for me. If *Macbeth* is the name of the play, that's what I'm going to call it.'

Toby winced but said nothing to contradict her.

'OK, so we have *Macbeth* as a possible candidate, who dies in that?'

'Pretty much everyone,' said Toby.

'Well, that sounds more like a finale to me. What about *Romeo and Juliet*?'

Toby thought for a moment. 'That's a story about doomed love, and he's already killed his ex-fiancée.'

'Tabitha?'

'Yes.'

'Come on, Toby, you're our resident Shakespeare expert. What do you think?'

'*King Lear* could be made to fit and he could cast himself as the king. He's been betrayed by his daughters. Well, two of them.'

'And *Othello*?' pressed Townsend.

Toby nodded. 'That could be the one. *Othello* was lied to and betrayed by those closest to him. That's how Lawrence is feeling.'

'That's a bit of a stretch. He, if it is him, could just be a nutter. It might have nothing to do with the plays. I think we, and by we, I mean you, are in danger of creating a whole scenario around a character we don't even know is alive and giving him a modus operandi to fit your plot.'

Toby looked at Mel and shrugged. 'You could be right, but what else do we have? I have a feeling about this and Fred told me always to follow my instincts. Right now, there's nothing else to follow.'

Mel leaned back and took a sip of her coffee. 'I guess we will just have to work on that assumption until we know better.' She finished her drink. 'What's the plan?'

'We have an artist doing a new drawing of Oliver Lawrence based on his last programme photographs. He's going to try and age him fifteen years. Then we will put it out there and see what happens.'

Mel nodded. 'Makes sense. Problem is, we don't know if he's

got fatter or thinner, long hair or bald … It's just a guess.'

Toby nodded. 'It's all we have. We can't find any record of him arriving in the UK in the last year, or moving through European borders. He disappeared over fifteen years back and hasn't been seen since.'

Mel Townsend had listened intently to Toby. She took in every piece of information and dissected it in her head. It led her to only one conclusion. 'We don't have a hope in hell of catching this guy until he commits another murder, do we?'

Toby looked at her sheepishly. 'No. Until he makes a mistake, or we catch him in the act, we're flying blind.'

Mel finished her coffee and stood up. 'Well, that's just dandy. Call me when you have something I can work with.' She smiled at him and walked out of the canteen without a backwards glance. He and Fred were on their own now.

Chapter 7
'Tis Destiny Unshunnable

Despite not wanting to meet at Kenilworth Castle, Oliver was enjoying the drive through the midnight lanes of Warwickshire. It was now August and the evenings were warm. He preferred the night lately, the comforting blanket of darkness that it wrapped around him made him feel invisible, and invincible. Without realising, he had become a creature of the night; lurking in the shadows and watching, waiting for his moment.

So different from his life in Morocco where he had lived outdoors and embraced the sunlight. Back then, he was an innocent; guilty of nothing, save fear. He had run away, too scared of failure to stay and fight.

Maybe he was just like his father. Weak. It wasn't a thought he wanted to consider. His father had always seemed so wonderfully self-assured, admired by all, a king in waiting. How did he go from that to throwing himself in front of a train? It didn't seem possible. Oliver was his father's son, but that was where the resemblance finished. He would not kill himself; he had come back to do that to others, those that deserved it. It was his destiny.

From the top of the Mortimer Tower, Felix saw the lights of Oliver's Morris Minor van as it pulled up on the south car park. He would be here in five minutes. Felix knew what he wanted to say, he had planned it out yesterday. If Oliver accepted his proposal, he would be complicit in everything Oliver would do. He was already, but now he was ready to become the instigator.

The realisation horrified him; how easy it had been to slip from decency to evil.

The death of Gerard Soames had shocked him, not by its terrible nature but by the fact he had enjoyed it.

Watching Oliver build towards it and then commit the murder was … thrilling. It was Shakespeare's darkest tragedy brought to terrible life. Oliver's acting was amazing; only it wasn't an act, it was real. He knew now that there was to be no happy ending to this story. He and Oliver were doomed, to jail or death. Both were options. This would not end well, and yet he had decided to play the scene out until the very end.

Oliver's footsteps came pounding up the stairs and Felix sat back in his deckchair trying to display a calm he did not feel.

'Evening, Felix. Hope you've brought a snack, I'm bloody starving.'

Felix pointed to the other deckchair. 'Of course, I made some cheese and pickle sandwiches and a flask of tea.'

'Good man, I knew I could rely on you.' Oliver did not sit down but made instead for Felix's hamper.

'You packed a picnic hamper,' said Oliver, an amused smile spreading across his face. 'We must have the best catering of any serial killers in the county, did you bring napkins?'

'Of course, I'm not an animal.'

Oliver snorted with amusement. 'True, animals wouldn't do what we are doing.' He flipped open the lid, took half of the sandwiches and placed them on a plate he took from the hamper. 'Where's the tea?'

Felix reached down and picked up the flask. 'You want me to pour you one now?'

Oliver nodded. 'These sandwiches will be too dry without it.'

During the course of the next ten minutes, Felix watched Oliver devour most of the sandwiches, half a Battenberg cake, a whole packet of Jammie Dodgers and two mugs of tea.

Finally, Oliver leaned back and stretched contentedly. 'That was lovely, Felix.'

'Really, you surprise me.'

Oliver folded his arms. 'Very well, you've wined me and dined me. Now tell me what you really want. I'm intrigued by the notion that you have a plan for murder. It doesn't seem your thing.'

'I didn't think it was until I witnessed you killing Gerard.'

Oliver nodded approvingly. 'Yes, I seem to recall that you confessed to enjoying that.'

'To my shame, I have to concede, I did. It was the most thrilling piece of theatre I have ever seen. Shakespearian in its bloody tragedy.'

'I think you're giving me too much credit, what you watched was a snuff movie. A classy one, I grant you, but a snuff movie nonetheless.' Oliver got up, walked across to the battlements and looked out over the sleeping roofs of Kenilworth. 'Do you remember the first time we met here?'

'Of course, it was only a couple of months ago.'

'Is that all, it seems like a lifetime ago. So much has happened,' Oliver turned back to Felix. 'You've changed; you were my voice of reason. Despite what you may think, I listened to you.'

'Didn't feel like you did.'

Oliver smiled. 'No, it probably didn't but, without you, there would have been many more bodies in the mortuary. You curbed my excesses, made me less reckless. When my blood is up, reason takes a backwards step.'

'I've noticed.'

Oliver nodded. 'Don't you think it's ironic that you, of all people, are now the one planning the murders.'

Felix thought about this for a moment. 'Only because I want you to kill those that deserve it. This only works if your revenge is against the right people.'

Oliver shook his head. 'I feel bad about this. You are a good man, Felix, and I have turned you into something else.'

'I haven't changed.'

'You have. You're a different man than you were before I started this. What happened?'

'I've just entered into the spirit of it.'

'No, I've dragged you down this dark hole. I'm responsible.'

'You wouldn't be here if I hadn't written you that letter,' said Felix.

'True, but you did. You're a good friend, Felix. The road I'm on is not going to end well. I'm headed for a crash and I don't want you to be with me when it happens.'

'If it happens.'

'Oh, it will happen. Why not let me finish the journey on my own? This is a crazy ride, get off now before it's too late.' Oliver studied Felix's face. He moved over to his friend and put his hand on his shoulder. 'Walk away, Felix, while you still can.'

Felix shook his head. 'I don't want to.'

Oliver squeezed his shoulder. 'Walk away, my old friend. I don't know what I will do next. When the moment comes, I am not myself; I'm playing a part but it's not me acting. The character takes over. I'm out of control.'

'What do you mean?'

'Don't you see it? When I became Prince Hamlet, I wasn't acting, I *was* Hamlet.'

'That's method acting for you,' quipped Felix.

Oliver stood up and walked back towards the battlements. 'Walk away now, Felix. If you stay, I cannot guarantee your safety.' He turned and looked at his old friend, who held his stare. Neither said a word for what seemed like an hour but was only twenty seconds.

'I'm staying,' said Felix. 'Without me, you will be in a jail cell or dead within the week. This thing, let's see it through together. I've come too far, have too much blood on my hands to walk away now.'

'You have no blood on your hands! Walk away, man,' urged Oliver.

'No, I was the catalyst for this, all of it.'

'Don't be stupid, man, you didn't know where this was going to go. What I was going to do. Hell, I didn't know.'

'And yet, here we are, trapped by our past, condemned to write a bloody chapter of the future.' Felix held out his hands. 'I didn't kill anyone but there *is* blood on these hands. I took the gun and loaded it. I passed it to you. I'm steeped in the same blood, Oliver. Let's play this out until the end, whatever that is.'

Oliver nodded slowly. 'Is that your final word?'

'It is.'

As Oliver strode back to his chair and slumped down, a huge grin spread across his face. In a moment, his mood had changed from darkly introspective to one of levity. 'Very well, Felix. If you are still in the cast, let us continue. *The play's the thing.* So, what is this great idea of yours?'

Chapter 8
Look Like The Innocent Flower

As Beatrice Oxford approached the Clopton Bridge, she glanced across at the theatre. Once it would have filled her heart with joy, but not now. It stood like a monument to her failure, a permanent reminder that beauty, on its own, was not enough. She had dreamed of taking the stage by storm, fulfilling her destiny. Ambition is a double-edged sword, it can drive you to achieve, reach amazing heights, but … ambition without talent? That's the cruellest dream of all. Beatrice was wise enough to realise that she didn't have what it took. In her first season, she was overshadowed by every actor, and even the scenery. To compensate for this, she became popular. For a beautiful woman, that's not too hard.

There had been no murders for six weeks but Stratford would hardly be on anyone's list of desirable holiday destinations at the moment. As she drove onto the bridge, Beatrice noticed DC Marlowe leaning on the railing, gazing at the water, lost in thought. She resisted the urge to swerve into him and send him flying off the bridge into the Avon.

When he had questioned her in Woodstock, he had been aggressive, had even suggested that she was not telling him the full truth. She wasn't going to be spoken to like that. She had spent too many years protecting her position, climbing the greasy pole to become Lady Oxford.

She had found her place in the hierarchy of British stage acting; not by talent but by association. It had been a longer, more ingratiating climb. Moving from one stepping stone to another until she had become Lady Oxford. There was evil afoot, she had sensed it. Instead of running from it, she had been drawn towards it, knowing in the deepest darkest part of her heart she was the spark from which the flame of death had been ignited.

She slowed and turned the Rover left onto Waterside; drawn inexorably to the one thing she could not control. Fate.

'Morning, Toby, thinking about jumping?'

Toby hadn't seen Fred Williams approach. For a big man he was light on his feet.

'Not until I saw you, boss.'

'I have that effect on people.' He leaned on the parapet beside Toby. 'Looking for passing bodies?'

'I suppose I am, can't help thinking we're due one.'

'You don't think it's over?'

Toby shook his head. 'No, do you?'

'Nope. I just think its half-time. When our killer has had a rest, sucked his orange segment and had a cup of tea, he'll be back.'

'Is that from the press release.'

'No, it's from the Fred Williams play book. This bugger is in it for the long haul. If it is Oliver Lawrence, well, he has a lot of scores to settle.'

'You agree it's Lawrence.'

Fred sighed. 'It might be but how do we prove it? There's only one way. Catch him in the act.' Fred paused. 'Actually, there are two ways. He could make a mistake and leave some evidence.'

'He could, but how would we link the evidence to him if we don't know how to find him, or what he looks like. We don't even know if he's alive.'

'I agree, those are minor obstacles.'

'Minor?' Toby laughed. 'We've put those posters out of Oliver's old pictures, the ones we had aged.'

'And?'

'Nothing. It's almost as if the guy doesn't exist.'

'Oh, he exists all right, we have the bodies to prove it.' Fred looked reassuringly at Toby. 'Mark my words, when he commits his next murder, we'll have him.'

'I'm sure that will be a comfort to the next victim.'

'Can't make an omelette without breaking eggs, son.'

With that, Fred eased himself up. 'I'm going to the theatre to have a little chat with Sir Morris. Want to join me, see if he's still alive?' Fred winked at Toby and marched off into town.

For a moment, Toby watched him go. They broke the mould when they made Fred Williams, which was probably a good thing. But, right now, there was no one Toby would rather have at his side. He chased after him.

As Toby and Fred approached the stage door there was no mistaking the Rover P6 parked outside the theatre.

'That's Lady Oxford's car,' said Toby.

'You sure? Big car for a lady.'

'She's stronger than she looks.'

Fred gave Toby an amused glance. 'Give you a tough time when you interviewed her, did she.'

'Don't let the airs and graces fool you, boss, she's as hard as nails. She may look like an innocent flower but she's a serpent under the petals.'

Fred pushed the stage door open. 'Nails get hammered, son.'

The stage door keeper did not seem thrilled to see them. 'I'm sorry, officers, but Sir Morris isn't available at the moment, Lady Oxford has just arrived.'

'Even better,' said Fred. 'Two for the price of one.'

'No, I don't think you understand—'

'I don't think you understand, my friend. If you don't let us in, I will nick you for obstructing a police officer in the course of his duties.'

'You wouldn't.'

'He would,' said Toby as he pushed past. 'They in Sir Morris' dressing room?'

The doorman looked flustered. 'Yes, it … it's that way.'

Toby didn't acknowledge the directions; he knew where he was going and he wanted to question Lady Oxford again.

Fred winked at the doorman as he squeezed by. 'Better keep up with my DC, this could be interesting.' When Fred reached the corridor where Sir Morris' dressing room was, he could hear an outraged voice.

'How dare you charge in here unannounced, DC Marlowe. My wife has only just arrived.'

'Toby nodded and gave the couple a curt smile. 'The door was open, Sir Morris and, if I need to remind you, this is a multiple murder inquiry.'

'We are well aware of that,' said Beatrice, her voice full of condescension.

'Excellent, then you won't object to answering a few questions, will you?'

Beatrice turned to her husband. 'Can't you get rid of this tedious little man.'

Sir Morris held up a placatory hand. 'Now, dear, DC Marlowe is just trying to help, maybe we should hear him out.'

'He's just an upstart who doesn't know his place. Get rid of him.'

Fred stood back, fascinated to see how Toby would handle the tense situation.

'Maybe we could do this back at the station, Lady Oxford. The tea's very good and I think the cells are pretty clean.'

Anger flared in Beatrice's eyes and she took a step towards Toby. Sir Morris grabbed her shoulder.

'Steady, darling, I think DC Marlowe is having a bit of fun with us.' He looked beseechingly at Toby. 'Aren't you?'

Toby hesitated for a moment, as if deciding which way he was going to play it. He smiled. 'Of course I was, Sir Morris. The cells are actually pretty dirty.'

Fred choked back a laugh and eased his way into the room. 'He's a bit of a joker, our DC Marlowe. Why don't you order some tea and we can have a sit down and make this as comfortable as possible.'

Sir Morris nodded and picked up his phone. 'Hello Raymond, it's Sir Morris. Could we have a pot of tea for four, please.'

'With biscuits,' said Fred.

'Oh, and some biscuits, please.' Sir Morris put down the phone. 'Be about five minutes.'

'Excellent,' said Fred. He took a seat from the side of the room and pulled it up in front of the couch. 'Why don't we all sit down and let DC Marlowe bring you up to date.'

'Don't you want to question Sir Morris first, sir.'

'I do, but I think you should share your theory with Sir Morris and Lady Oxford, don't you?'

Toby didn't but Fred had left him no choice. Before he could begin, Beatrice Oxford spoke.

'Never mind your stupid theories, constable, how about just catching the killer.'

'That's what we are trying to do. We are working on the theory that Oliver has returned.'

Beatrice snorted with derision. 'Is that the best you can come up with? You know he's dead.'

'We don't know that,' said Toby.

'I'm his mother, I know.'

'I disagree.'

The atmosphere in the room had become tense. Fred tried to calm the situation. 'DC Marlowe's theory is shared by me. I think we should hear him out. What have you got to lose?'

Sir Morris squeezed Beatrice's knee. 'Let's hear him out, my dear, you never know …' His sentence trailed off under the hard stare she gave him.

'Very well, constable, let's hear it.'

Toby looked at Fred, who nodded. He cleared his throat. 'The killing stopped six weeks ago. The papers have declared that the killer has gone, he's finished, but I don't think he has. He's been planning, waiting for the moment to start again, trying to find a way to launch a new series of killings.'

'Oh, here we go again. He's acting out *Hamlet*, is he.' Beatrice's voice was full of accusation and cynicism.

'No, Lady Oxford, we think it may be *Othello* this time.'

Beatrice burst into laughter; out of control, slightly crazy sounding laughter. It was totally inappropriate. 'But Oliver isn't a Moor and I don't think he has a wife to smother.'

Toby pressed on. 'There are five major tragedies in Shakespeare's works. We believe he has already done *Hamlet*. *King Lear* doesn't seem appropriate.'

'None of this is appropriate, you fool.'

Sir Morris didn't appear to share his wife's scorn for Toby's theory. 'Go on, DC Marlowe, I'd like to hear your reasoning.'

'These murders are about revenge. Oliver feels that you and your colleagues ruined his career, ruined his father's career and caused his death.'

'He killed himself. Nobody made him jump in front of that bloody train.'

All three of them looked at Beatrice; she was angry, emotional.

Toby stayed calm. 'Your husband's death would be seen by Oliver to be a consequence of his sacking by Sir Morris. He is looking for revenge.'

'He. He!' Her voice had become shrill. 'You don't even know if he's alive and yet you are building a whole theory based on this … this fiction.' Beatrice was on her feet now, all pretence of self-control gone. 'Why don't you prove he's alive first, then prove that he's here and then, and only then, share this madness with me.' She stormed out of the room, slamming the door behind her.

The three men remained seated, looking at each other in silence.

Fred was the first to speak. 'That's a shame.'

'I know,' said Sir Morris. 'All this has become a bit too much for her.'

'No,' said Fred. 'It's a shame she's gone, she's going to miss the tea and biscuits.'

Right on cue there was a knock on the door and Raymond, from catering, entered the room with the tea. 'Tea for four,' he said cheerfully.

'Just three now,' said Fred, greedily eyeing the biscuits. He picked up the teapot. 'Shall I be mother?'

An hour later, they were back at the station sitting by Fred's desk. 'What did you make of that, Toby? Quite an outburst. Methinks the lady doth protest too much.'

Toby nodded. 'Not the action of a rational person; it's almost as if she knows that the sins of her past are about to catch up to her.'

Fred nodded. 'I agree, walk me through it again.'

Toby moved over to the large whiteboard and picked up a marker pen. 'OK, we're working on the assumption that it is Oliver Lawrence and he's come back to revenge himself on those he feels betrayed him and his father.'

Fred nodded. 'Agreed. He's already knocked off four of them. The question is how many more and who are they? Let's go through that list again.'

Toby began to read the other eight names he thought could be in the firing line. There were two options missing that would soon come back to haunt him.

Fred read down the list. 'You're confident that this is all of them.'

Toby shook his head. 'No.' He reached up and wrote a new name on the board.

Fred couldn't believe what he read. 'Seriously?'
The name on the board was Beatrice Oxford.

Chapter 9
Felix From The Ashes

The boat rocked gently as Felix sat on the deck looking out across the fields towards Alveston; it soothed him. Last night he had taken a decision that he knew would change his life forever, maybe even end it. He had given Oliver a plan to murder Lizzie Birchwood. He was in this up to his neck. Complicit. He needed to control the narrative to keep Oliver from being careless, but that wasn't it. He was caught up in the sheer exhilarating drama of the whole thing, a witness to a real tragedy as dark and twisted as anything the Bard had written.

The decision had been a hard one until the moment he had witnessed the death of Gerard Soames. It was … wonderful. No other word for it. Never before, in all his years in the theatre, had he witnessed a moment quite like it. Seeing the recognition slowly dawn in Gerard's eyes that the man in front of him was Oliver; back from the dead to send him there in his place. Watching his growing terror as Oliver had quoted the Bard and he realised that he was going to kill him. It was drama, heightened to a level that was not possible in the theatre, because it was more than drama. It was real, it was death. From that moment, he knew he had no way out. Whichever way this tragedy progressed, he was there until the final curtain.

Felix didn't like Lizzie Birchwood; hate would be nearer the mark. The way she had treated the sacred text, the belittling of actors and crew. She was a dictator who crushed the life out of the play and forced actors to submit to her stifling direction. Death would improve her.

Felix felt he knew everything there was to know about Lizzie Birchwood. He didn't. There were secrets so dark that virtually nobody knew them. The plan to kill her was creative, a gradual build-up of tension, a breaking down of reason. It was an elegant solution, stolen, he had to admit, from the player king in *Hamlet* but he had put a twist on it. Shakespeare, if he was a killer, would have been proud of him.

Oliver had been impressed. As he finished listening to the proposal, he had nodded approvingly. 'My, my, Felix, you are a dark horse. It may lack spontaneity but it certainly has class. Do you want to write the soliloquy or shall I?'

'You do it,' Felix said. 'I'm sure your words will rise to the occasion.'

Oliver laughed. 'Oh, they will, Felix, they will.' He leaned forward and clasped Felix's hands in his. 'We are now in this together, to the end. Win or lose, live or die.' As he looked into Oliver's eyes, he knew that both were an option. If he was to die, he had to tell his story. His truth.

Back on his boat, Felix's journal lay open before him. The empty page daring him to fill it, to condemn himself and Oliver in writing. If he died, this would be his epitaph, a justification of sorts. But how could he justify something so immoral? He couldn't; this was merely his story. A witness statement of a revenge that had taken fifteen years to fester and explode. A wildfire that had burst out in Stratford after fifteen years of smouldering, he had fanned the flames and no amount of blood could put them out.

Sitting in his kitchen in the house on Trinity Street, Oliver couldn't help but smile. Felix would have made a great director. Still could if this went well. But that was in the future, right now he had a soliloquy to write. Next to the empty notepad were Felix's hand-written notes on how to murder Lizzie Birchwood.

There was even a little diagram showing the layout of the apartment she lived in. It wasn't really an apartment, just a room above the bar in the Windmill on Church Street.

The landlord had given Lizzie a special deal because she brought a lot of the actors and theatre folks back there for late-night drinks. Oliver smiled. Felix had put in a lot of work. Lizzie's room was at the back of the pub overlooking the courtyard. After midnight the courtyard would be deserted and hidden from the street. There was even easy access from the car park behind. Oliver read Felix's instructions.

You can see from my diagram that LB's bedroom is at the rear of the Windmill. This will make the implementation of my plan simple. I am going to rent a room there and plant a walkie-talkie in the void, where the air vent is on the rear wall. I have stayed there before and the maid leaves the doors unlocked when she is doing her cleaning rounds. It will be easy for me to plant it in there. I have had a special battery pack added which will give it several days before it runs out.

I have a second walkie-talkie tuned into the same frequency. All you will have to do is walk round from Trinity Street. Anywhere on the car park with a clear line of sight will do, then just turn it on and deliver your soliloquy.

As she lies in her bed, no doubt dreaming of new ways to ruin the Bard's plays, you can enter her dreams. Choose your words carefully, my friend, you need to slowly drive her mad. If you have seen her productions of late, it is clear she is already well on the way, but you must slowly drive her crazy. Speak to her innermost fears. Render unto her the final soliloquy before you put out her light.

It was a simple plan but rather brilliant. Play with her mind, drive her crazy, and when she is at her most vulnerable, end her. He would enjoy writing these words, he had several nights to build to a finish before the batteries died; hopefully, she would be dead before that happened.

Back on his boat, Felix had been busy. The journal had its first entry. He reread his words, it was August thirteenth; unlucky for some.

August 13. As I sit here aboard the Styx, I realise that my quest for justice has become something darker. Revenge, at any price. When I look back over fifteen years and remember the wrongs that I witnessed, the destruction of a young actor's career, I burn at the injustice. Oliver Lawrence, like his father many years before, has been destroyed by the jealous actions of others. When I discovered, by chance, that Oliver was still alive, I had no choice but to tell him who had destroyed his life. I didn't know what he would do. Whatever it was, I swore I would help him. I was naïve, I misjudged the depth of his anger and his need for revenge.

On his return, it soon became clear that a mere confrontation would not suffice; Oliver had a more final solution. At first, I tried to dissuade him, it was useless. I had loaded the gun and aimed it, and now the bullets were flying and I could not stop them. I was appalled, horrified by what I had set in motion, but then something very strange began to happen. As the victims fell, one by one, it dawned on me that these people were terrible, a cancer of the stage upon which they strode. A disease that permeated the fringes of the theatre and was rotten to the core. There needed to be a cleansing, and Oliver would be the means by which that happened.

Am I now using him for my own ends? I don't know. All I do know is that witnessing him killing is the most thrilling theatre I have ever seen. The best seat in a very dark house. I am complicit, I am his enabler. I have become death. When will this stop? Who knows. Probably when he is caught, more likely when he is dead. This will not end well: if you are reading this, I am already dead, at Oliver's hand. Who can tell the future? What's written in a man's stars? That is for history and the gods to know.

All I can say is that this started out as a quest for justice. What it became, well, only time can judge. I regret nothing and everything. It has been the most terrible experience of my life and yet, there have been moments when I have been more alive than I ever thought possible. A strange conundrum. Where and when this ends is an unfinished tale, but know this: when injustice has no remedy, there will be a reckoning. There will be blood … and reason, like hope, will disappear with the fading of the sun.

Chapter 10
The Allure Of The Deep Fat Fryer

No matter how long they looked at the incident board, the only answer that Toby and Fred could come up with was Oliver. It had to be him.

'We need to place him in Stratford, there has to be some record of him coming back into the country,' said Fred.

'We've checked all ports and flights from everywhere for the last three months.'

'Under his real name.'

Toby shrugged. 'It's the only name we have.'

'Perhaps he's using a false identity.'

'Such as?'

Fred thought for a moment. 'What about something from Shakespeare?'

'It's possible, but unlikely. Most Shakespearian names would stand out like a sore thumb these days. Mister Malvolio arriving from Lloret de Mar.'

'The cross-garters would give him away.'

They both chuckled. Toby scribbled a name on the whiteboard: Richard Jenkins.

'Who's he?'

'Oliver's father, remember?'

Fred nodded.

'What if he is using his real name, the one his father gave him.'

'Worth a try, Toby. Put it out there and see if we get a hit.'

'How far back … Three months, three years? We have no way

of knowing when he returned, we don't even know if he returned. This is hopeless.'

'He'll make a mistake.'

Toby wasn't so sure. 'He hasn't made one yet.'

'He will.' Fred walked over to his desk and sat down. 'How do we know that he hasn't finished? Nothing for six weeks now.'

'You don't believe that, boss. Oliver won't leave Sir Morris alive.'

'No, he won't.' Fred dropped his pen onto the desk and stood up. 'Look, we have surveillance on all those we feel are at risk, all we can do is wait and if we are going to wait, why don't we do it constructively. I hear that the Green Dragon has just got a deep fat fryer.'

'And how is that constructive, boss?'

'Can't think on an empty stomach, can we. Maybe Whomper will be there and have some juicy information.'

'Of course he'll be there, it's open.'

'Come on, Toby, let's go and follow a lead and see what we can find.'

'You're hoping for Scampi and chips in a basket,' said Toby, as he followed his boss out of CID.

Chapter 11
Subtext, The Unspoken Word

Oliver sat looking at the soliloquy he had just written, it was good. The words flowed and, if delivered properly, would have the desired effect. He needed to be ready the moment that Felix planted the walkie-talkie.

Lizzie Birchwood; just saying her name made him shudder. He was only twenty-three when they first met. He was cast as the understudy to Romeo and she was the director. She had summoned him to her office.

He knocked on her door. 'Come.'

Lizzie was reading something on her desk. She looked up as he entered. 'Ah, Oliver, take a seat over there.' She pointed to a settee by the window.

Oliver sat down and waited. Lizzie was a powerful woman in Stratford, but she was divisive. Her settings and interpretations of Shakespeare's plays had been controversial; praised by some, condemned by others. She was something of an *enfant terrible* amongst directors. She looked up at Oliver. 'I expect you're wondering why I asked you to come here.'

'Yes, I am.'

'Do you know your lines?'

'Yes, I played Romeo when I was at university.'

Lizzie sighed. 'And how did you play him?'

'Very well, I think. The reviews were good.'

'Not how did you play him, but *how* did you play him?'

Oliver was confused. 'In love?'

Lizzie seemed annoyed. 'How did you interpret his character?'

'I just said the lines.'

Lizzie threw down her pen. 'What is it with you young actors? All you want to do is learn your lines and say them. What about the subtext?'

It was a good question but Oliver wasn't sure how to respond.

Lizzie had no intention of letting him off. 'Well?'

'Well, I think he knows that falling in love with Juliet is going to be a problem because of the family thing.'

'The family thing? Would you care to elaborate?'

Oliver didn't but Lizzie was now on her feet and moving towards him with all the warmth of a hissing cobra.

'He's besotted with her.'

'Why?'

'Because he, well, he's in love,' mumbled Oliver.

'He's a berk,' shouted Lizzie. 'Ruled by his gonads like most young men.'

'Yeah, that's one way of looking at it.'

She took a deep breath. 'It's not your fault, Oliver.'

'What's not?'

'Ignorance. You've trained for years to follow the text and interpret the words but never explored the subtext and how it relates to today. For Shakespeare to thrive it must be relevant, reflect the period in which it is being performed.'

Her words made sense. 'Then how do we make *Romeo and Juliet* relevant to the fifties?'

'She's a lesbian.'

Oliver was stunned. 'She's a—'

'Lesbian. Don't you see it?'

Oliver didn't.

Lizzie sat uncomfortably close to him on the settee, her eyes ablaze. Just as the set had been at the theatre when she had tried to stage *Henry V* with flamethrowers instead of archers. 'Juliet is a Capulet; she hates the Montagues.'

'But she falls in love with Romeo.'

Lizzie laughed. 'No, she doesn't. She's a woman, she knows how to fake it. More importantly, she's a lesbian and there's no way she is going to marry that idiot Paris. She uses stupid, love-struck Romeo and plays him like a fool. Revs him up to kill Paris and fakes her own death to get the idiot to kill himself. Do you see it?'

Oliver did see it and he didn't like it. 'It's a bit of a stretch. Juliet, a lesbian?'

'Why not?'

'Did they have lesbians in Tudor England?'

'Of course they did, they have everything we have today.'

'Even the comfy shoes.'

Lizzie actually smiled. 'Funny, now you are getting into the spirit. So, what do you think?'

'Will my lines change?'

'No.'

'Will I have to say them differently?'

'Jesus. Of course you will. I need you to play Romeo as a dumb teenager who is being dragged around by his libido instead of his brain.'

'So, not sympathetically.'

'No. He is a fool. A young man so besotted that he tries to date the daughter of his family's number one enemy. He's an imbecile, that's how you need to play him. Dumb. Dumber than dumb.'

Oliver wasn't sure. 'How does Sandy feel about this?'

A pained expression crossed Lizzie's face. 'He's not keen.'

Neither was Oliver but he stayed silent. 'I've given him an ultimatum, either he plays it my way or he's out.'

'Sandy out?'

'Out!' She stared at Oliver defiantly.

'Then I would be—'

'Romeo.' She let that sink in.

'Can I think about it?'

She shook her head. 'No, you are either in or you're out. Make your choice.' There was no choice. 'Could I butch him up a bit.'

'No, dumb is what I want. I don't know you well, Oliver, but you strike me as an actor who could do dumb.'

'And what about Tabitha, is she happy to play Juliet as a … feminist?'

'Tabitha is open to anything, she was in my *Tempest* set on Mars, remember?'

He remembered; no one who saw it could ever forget.

Lizzie Birchwood had been pushing the envelope of theatre for the last twenty years. There were moments of genius and long hours of crazy. For some reason, she kept getting hired. Now she was at Stratford, they had reined her in a little but she was still pushing the text to discover new meanings; it didn't seem to bother her whether they were there or not.

'If you are prepared to give it a try, I will let Sandy know that he can step down.'

He wasn't sure about this. Sandy Banks was a star; it would not look good if Oliver stole his part. 'Won't this create bad feeling; people will think I'm sleeping with you or something.'

'Do you want to?'

Oliver was shocked. 'No.'

'Why not?' Lizzie stared directly at him.

'It wouldn't be appropriate, you're the director.'

'I could direct you in bed. Maybe sex with a real woman would improve your acting.'

'You do know that I'm engaged to Tabitha.'

Lizzie shrugged. 'And that affects me how?'

'Listen, I'll play Romeo as a randy idiot if that's what you want, but I'm not sleeping with you.'

Lizzie was unfazed. 'Excellent, we start rehearsals next week. Congratulations!'

Oliver had walked numbly from her office; he should have been over the moon but all he felt was shame. Shame at the way he had agreed to take Sandy Banks' role and shame at the way he had agreed to play it. From that moment on, he had disliked Lizzie Birchwood. During the course of rehearsals, he had grown to hate her.

When *Romeo and Juliet* opened, he'd decided to play it straight. Tabitha's Juliet was strident, unyielding. Every night, Oliver tried so hard to win her over using guileless charm, falling at her feet like unwanted pearls. The critics loved him, as he proved to be the most sympathetic of Romeos.

Lizzie had screamed at him every night for the first week until the reviews came in. They were sensational; she had accidentally created a *Romeo and Juliet* for a new age. A strong, assertive Juliet wooed by a gentle, caring Romeo.

It wasn't long before Lizzie was claiming that it had been her intention all along and Tabitha, well, she enjoyed the acclaim and nobody, especially her, ever let on she was meant to be a lesbian.

As he sat at the table remembering, Oliver realised that he could make a case for sparing Lizzie; inadvertently, she had helped to make him a star. Then he remembered all the other terrible things she had tried to get him to do and the way she had attempted to blackmail him. When he added up the pros against the cons, there was only ever going to be one winner.

Chapter 12
Whomper And The Three-Legged Chicken

As they walked into the Green Dragon, Fred and Toby slowed. They needed their lungs to adjust to the oxygen-depleted atmosphere within. Regulars at the Green Dragon were a rare species; they could survive on forty per cent of the oxygen a rational human needed. The smoke had reduced their lung capacity and the lead in the water pipes their mental capacity. This enabled them to operate at lower metabolic levels than a sloth. The alcohol helped too. Fred and Toby headed for the back of what was optimistically called The Lounge. It was shrouded in dense clouds of second-hand cigarette smoke and smelled of decomposing humans. They weren't dead yet but their shuffle off this mortal coil had surely begun.

A face peered out from the gloom. 'Greetings, gents, and to what do I owe the pleasure of this visit. Has there been another murder?'

'Only of the food hygiene laws,' muttered Toby, looking across the table at the debris that had once been a chicken.

'You had the chicken and chips in a basket, Whomper?'

'Yes, I fancied an appetiser before the main course.'

'Was it good?

Whomper considered this for a moment. 'Not bad. The chips tasted of chicken though. I think he put them all in the same fryer.'

Fred inspected the remnants of the culinary carnage. 'This chicken appears to have had three legs.'

'I'm a regular. Chef threw in an extra leg free. Gratis!'

'And what are those?' Toby shuddered, looking at some tiny, golden, almost black balls.'

Whomper leaned forward and inspected them. 'I think they are, or were, garden peas.'

'What happened to them?'

'Fallout Phil deep-fried them with the chicken and chips.'

'Who's Fallout Phil?'

Whomper looked surprised at Toby's question. 'He's the chef.'

'There's a chef?'

'Of course. How do you think they manage such a varied cuisine?'

'I wasn't aware they did,' said Toby.

'So what would you recommend today, Whomper?'

Whomper considered Fred's question. 'Well, anything fried is good, just don't have the peas. You could also consider anything nuked as being pretty safe.'

'That's a nice recommendation; eat at the Green Dragon, some of our meals are safe.'

'Better than safe, the scampi and chips in a basket is a triumph.'

'That'll do for me,' said Fred. What about you, Toby?'

'I'll have a ploughman's.'

'Deep-fried?'

Toby gave Fred a sickly grin which clearly meant no. 'What about you, Whomper, care for a dessert? Deep-fried sticky toffee pudding.'

Whomper considered it. 'You know, that would probably work, but I don't want too much sweet stuff, I'm watching what I eat.'

Toby laughed. 'Anything green?'

'Those peas were green once.'

Toby shook his head and looked at Fred. 'Three beers?'

'And I'll have another chicken and chips,' said Whomper. 'But ease back on the legs and leave the peas.'

Fred nodded and headed for the bar.

Whomper smiled at Toby. 'Gone quiet, hasn't it.'

'It has,' agreed Toby. 'Disturbingly quiet.'

'Not for long, I can feel it coming. The avalanche has started at the top of the mountain, it's on its way down, and you can't stop it.'

'No, I can't.'

'What's the plan?' I assume you have one,' said Whomper.

'We do, but it's not much of one.'

Whomper grinned. 'I didn't think it would be, want to share it?'

'We are covertly watching all the actors we feel are likely victims. If Lawrence comes anywhere near them, we'll catch him.'

'Not much of a plan, is it, using your potential victims as bait to lure him out. You going to tether Sir Morris to a tree and wait?'

'We're not shooting a wildlife documentary, Whomper. Apart from the fact that we can't prove Oliver Lawrence is still alive, or in the country, he's our main suspect.'

'Sounds like an open and shut case.' They both laughed.

'Maybe I can be of some help to you.'

'How?'

Whomper noted the caution in Toby's voice. 'My twin sisters are coming in shortly; we could join together and do a psychic scan.'

'And what the hell is that.'

'It's like a radar scan but psychic. We can feel bad vibes, pick up on evil.'

'Crazy as that sounds, Whomper, I'll give it a go. Your little Greek chorus with your twin sisters was right last time.'

'First time for everything,' chuckled Whomper.

Chapter 13
The Course Of True Love

Chief Constable Wilson had got home early. He would have preferred figuring out how he was going to put Inspector Beeching back in his box, but duty, in the shape of Heather, had called. Apparently, it was their eight-month anniversary and she expected dinner.

Before the engine on his Rover had started to cool, the lovely Heather appeared at the door. She was wearing a beautiful red dinner dress, with diamonds and pearls scattered liberally about her person.

'Come on, Big Daddy, I have a table booked at seven-thirty.'

'Could you not call me Big Daddy while we are out, darling, it's a bit embarrassing.'

Heather looked hurt. 'But I always call you Big Daddy. You like it.'

'I do, in the bedroom or when we are alone, but in public, perhaps you could just use my name, lends a bit of gravitas.'

'Gravel what?'

He shook his head sadly; he hadn't married Heather for her intellect. 'Nothing, dear. Where are we going?'

'La Revolta, it's the new Italian place near Warwick.'

'Surely you mean French?'

'No, it's Italian, they even do tapas.'

Chief Wilson wasn't sure but he could have sworn that tapas was Spanish. 'Well that's sounds very European, dear.' She pecked him on the cheek and he smelled her sweet aroma. 'You smell nice, something French?'

'Yes, it's called Seville.'

He thought for a moment and decided against further

questions. Heather was beautiful but limited in the conversation department. She would be his Eliza Doolittle; the name suited her, she did little but she cost a lot.'

Fate is a complex thing, unpredictable, unwritten. And yet, it is inescapable. For Heather Wilson, the bonds of fate were being invisibly drawn around her, pulling her towards her destiny. Chief Constable Wilson could not know that his new love would not last. All things must end; some sooner than others.

He kissed his wife and headed upstairs to change. She was young enough to be his daughter. He knew they laughed at him behind his back but he didn't care. He had Heather. She was young and beautiful, just being close to her reminded him of his youth and the times when his blood had run hot. These last few months had been the best of his life. He may be an old fool but he was grasping the moment, clinging to the wreckage of late middle age. Holding on to a dream while it was still within his grasp.

He didn't know it, but the bonds that bound them were unravelling. His new life was built on sand. In Stratford, a chain of events, seemingly unrelated, would draw them into its web and undermine their future. Sooner or later, everything comes to dust.

Chapter 14
When The Night Comes

It had been a close-run thing, but Felix had managed to sneak into Lizzie Birchwood's room at the Windmill. He had waited for the maid to disappear from view with the dirty linen. He slipped into the room; he would have a couple of minutes while she loaded the washing machine. The plastic vent on the wall was secured by four screws.

He grabbed the chair from the dressing table and dragged it over to beneath the vent. His heart was pounding in his chest. What if she came back? He worked quickly and had the cover off in under a minute. There was an eight-inch gap between the inner vent and the airbrick on the outside wall. He slipped the walkie-talkie from his bag and slid it into the gap, pulled out the battery pack, placed it next to it and plugged it into the walkie-talkie. He switched it on and made sure it was tuned to the same frequency as the one he had for Oliver. The green light came on.

As he raised the vent cover back up to the hole, he heard a creak on the stairs. The maid was coming back. For a moment he froze in panic: what could he do? Feverishly, he started screwing the cover back in place. He wasn't going to make it. Then, from somewhere below, there was a call.

'Sandra, you fancy a cuppa?'

The footsteps on the stairs paused. 'Please, Phil. I'll just grab some more washing first.'

Felix glanced at the bed; it still had the sheets on. The linen Sandra had been carrying down to the laundry wasn't from Lizzie's room. Felix felt all his muscles start to tense. He'd only managed to get two screws in and there was nowhere to hide.

'There's chocolate digestives.'

'Why didn't you say, the laundry can wait for a bit, I'm starving.' Sandra started back down the stairs.

Felix stood motionless and felt relief wash through him. He took a couple of slow, deep breaths and got back to the task at hand. Within a minute, he had finished. He climbed off the stool and looked up at the vent. From below, you couldn't see the glow from the green light. He dragged the chair back to the dresser and walked slowly out of Lizzie's room. He looked back once more before he pulled the door shut. 'Sweet dreams, Lizzie.'

He hurried from the room and went to the reception area by the bar. There was a bell but he didn't need to ring it; Phil Townsend was already there.

'Was that OK for you, Felix?'

'Yes. Great, thanks, Phil.'

'We haven't seen you in here for a while.'

'I know, I have a cottage in Welford but I had a few glasses of beer last night after the theatre. Thought it best not to drive.'

'Very wise. Hopefully, we'll be seeing you again soon.'

Felix nodded. 'Definitely.' He'd paid for the room when he'd arrived the night before. He pushed his room key over to his host. 'See you soon, Phil.'

'Cheers, Felix.'

Phil watched him go, pleased to have seen Felix again but wondering why he hadn't just got himself a cab, would have been much cheaper. Phil Townsend was a curious chap, just like his sister, DI Mel Townsend.

Twelve hours later, Felix was knocking on Oliver's door on Trinity Street. The door opened within seconds.

'Come in,' said Oliver. He hurried down the hallway in front of him. 'I trust you come bearing glad tidings.'

'I do. The walkie-talkie is installed in Lizzie's room.'

Oliver beamed with pleasure. 'Was it tricky?'

'Just a bit, nearly got caught when the maid decided to come back up from the laundry for some more washing.'

'What happened?'

'I was saved by a chocolate digestive.'

'Of course you were,' said Oliver, without asking for an explanation. 'So, tonight dear Lizzie will be serenaded in her bed.'

'Lucky girl, let me guess. "But soft, what light through yonder window breaks?"'

Oliver shook his head. 'Nothing so romantic. The only thing breaking through the window will be Lizzie when I chuck her out of it.'

'Not very romantic, or fatal. It's only about a twelve-foot drop.'

Oliver shook his head slowly. 'Lizzie isn't dying tonight or tomorrow or tomorrow or—'

'I get it,' said Felix. 'So when?'

'I think at least three nights of my serenading will do the trick, maybe more. I want to enjoy this. I'm going to build to a big finish, take my time. Did you put those fake sleeping tablets I gave you in her room?'

'I did,' said Felix. 'Will they kill her?'

'No, but the magic mushrooms they're made from will give her some very intense dreams.' A satisfied smile settled across Oliver's face.

'You won't do anything without letting me know beforehand, will you?'

Oliver looked at Felix slyly. 'You want to watch?'

To his shame, Felix felt himself nodding his head. 'I do.'

'Felix, Felix, Felix. What have I done to you. Are you sure about this?'

Again, Felix nodded.

'Yes, though this be madness—'

'There is method in't.' Oliver finished the sentence for him. 'Then you are, my Cassio.'

'Are we doing *Othello*?'

'Might as well,' shrugged Oliver.

'But this isn't really the plot.'

'We're killing women; I reckon that's close enough.'

'I guess that makes you Iago and Othello.'

Oliver laughed. 'Yes, I suppose it does. I'm whispering lies in my own ears. Does that make me schizophrenic?'

'No, just a bit crazy, we both are.' They looked at each other and started to laugh. The second act was about to begin.

Two hours later, Oliver was heading past Holy Trinity. It was only a short distance to the building site that would soon become The Other Place theatre. There was a walkway through into the car park at the back of the Windmill. From there, he would be able to broadcast his dark soliloquy to the unexpecting ears of Lizzie Birchwood. It was nearly three a.m. and the streets were empty. Only the cry of a lone raven on the roof of the church broke the silence.

Oliver grinned. '"The Croaking Raven Doth Bellow for Revenge."'

Hamlet knew a thing or two about revenge, the portents were good. He headed towards the Windmill and stood beneath the window of Lizzie's room.

He had thought long and hard about the soliloquy he would deliver. There were over fifteen years of hurt and pain contained within its verses. Feelings and emotions he had suppressed for years, pushing them down to a dark place but, like molten lava, they had bubbled away waiting for the moment they could erupt. Release the pressure of hate. For Lizzie Birchwood, that moment had come; the monster she had helped to create was now knocking at her window. Fate will always find you.

At the far side of the car park, there was a figure lurking at the bottom of the garden of Hall's Croft. It moved furtively, getting into place. Felix had arrived for his front row seat. It was time. Oliver clicked on his walkie-talkie, made sure it was tuned to the right frequency and began to speak.

'You Reap What You Sow'

'You sleep the sleep of innocence
hoping time has you forgot,
but in the memory of the injured
lies the ticking of the clock.
The slowly moving hands
that have tracked you through the years,
have found you in the darkness
to fulfil your every fear.'

The voice floated into Lizzie's bedroom through the vent. It sounded detached and far away. Lizzie was asleep but, as the words fell across her like a fatal mist, she stirred. Its words gently permeated her slumbers.

'I have waited for this moment
when we can be as one,
Short our time together;
your ending is begun.
The sun will rise tomorrow
and you will see its glare,
taking it for granted
until it isn't there.'

Lizzie awoke. 'Who's there?' There was no answer. She stared anxiously around her dark room. She could have sworn she'd heard a voice; and then she did.

'When you sleep you will hear me

for I am your unconscious mind,
waiting to destroy you
a future soon denied.
Did you hear me calling
like a memory of the past,
trapped in a sea of solitude
in to which I was cast.'

Lizzie had heard every word of the last stanza and it chilled her to the bone. She wasn't sure exactly what it meant but … that voice … she recognised it.
'Who's there, who are you?' She reached for the bedside lamp and switched it on.

'Awaken to your destiny,
the sands of time move fast
but for you, Lizzie Birchwood,
the future has passed.'

Oliver chuckled as Lizzie let out a shriek at the mention of her name. She appeared at the window, looking out at the darkness. Her eyes scoured the shadows but Oliver wasn't worried; he and Felix were well hidden. She opened the window and peered below it. This was working better than he had hoped. Time to gild the lily. Lizzie closed the window, and he waited for the right moment. After about five minutes, the bedside light went out. Lizzie looked out of the window one last time before closing the curtains.

'Goodnight, Lizzie Birchwood. I'll see you in your dreams.'

Lizzie's screams could be heard from the car park and, judging by the amount of lights that had come on, they could also be heard in the other rooms above the Windmill pub. Oliver walked towards the pathway that led to Southern Lane. As he turned the corner, he called back over his shoulder. 'You coming, Felix, or are you going to hide behind that wall all night?'

Chapter 15
No More Cream In Your Coffee

Theo Cumberbatch had been expecting this call. With the death of Desmond Tharpe, Inspector Cream to his Sergeant Coffee, the future of Coffee and Cream, the TV detective series, was in doubt. It was popular and had completed six series without ever troubling the awards system or, indeed, the intellect of its fans. Safe early evening detective drama to ease the audience towards The Black and White Minstrel Show. Theo cringed inwardly; he had once been accused of being an Uncle Tom character. Compared to the blatant racism of the Minstrel show, he felt partially vindicated; at least he was Black.

The door to the Windmill pub swung open and in swept Basil Powell, the producer of *Coffee and Cream* and one of the owners of Argon TV. He looked across the bar and spotted Theo. He threw open his arms and strode towards him.

'My dear Othello, how are you?'

Theo cringed inwardly. 'Fine. How are you, Basil?'

'All the better for seeing you, dear boy. Have you reserved a table for luncheon?'

'This is the Windmill. I don't think reservations are required.'

'Of course, of course. I forget when I am outside of London that the normal rules of civility do not apply. What would you recommend?'

'The cheese and tomato cobs are pretty good.'

Basil looked at him, askance. 'Cob? What on earth is that?'

'It's a sort of crusty roll.'

Basil rolled his eyes. 'What fresh hell is this. Do they not have any smoked salmon or quails' eggs?'

Theo pursed his lips, trying to suppress a smile. 'This is Stratford, Basil, there is more demand for fish fingers than smoked salmon.'

Basil shook his head, a look of dismay spreading across his fox-like features. 'How do you survive.'

'I like it here. It's a small town and people are friendly. There's a sense of belonging.'

Basil didn't look convinced. 'Maybe a nice glass of red would help.' Before Theo could demur, Basil looked over to Ted, the landlord. 'Could I have your wine list.'

Ted nodded. 'Red or white?'

'Red, I think. Do you have a Montepulciano?'

Ted looked confused. 'I thought you wanted red.'

'Montepulciano is red.'

'Well, we've got red.'

Theo sat silently watching the clash of cultures. They spoke the same language but the meanings didn't match.

'What type of red is it?' Basil could not hide the rising irritation in his voice.

'Red red,' replied Ted, his features deadpan.

'Does it have a name?'

'It's the one that comes in the bottle you can make lampshades from.' Ted was never going to be a sommelier.

Basil looked to Theo. 'Do you have the slightest idea what he is on about?'

'I think Ted's referring to Mateus Rosé.'

Basil swayed for a moment, struggling to comprehend the information. 'People actually drink that stuff.'

'It's nice with lemonade,' suggested Ted, calling upon his vast experience within the wine trade.

Basil turned to Theo. 'How do you survive in this wasteland?'

'I try not to drink the wine.'

Basil was not to be defeated. 'Dare I ask you about your range of white wines?'

'White or fortified?'

Basil fell silent but Theo could almost see the cogs turning in his head. 'White,' he ventured.

Ted smiled. 'White it is.' He pulled up a bottle from beneath the bar. It was a third full and had a broken cork rammed in the top.

Before he could pour, Basil raised his hand. 'What is that and how long has it been open?'

Ted read the label. 'Liebfraumilch.'

'Dear God,' moaned Basil. 'What year?'

'This year,' said Ted. 'I only opened it last month.'

Basil's eyes met Theo's, they seemed to be asking for help.

Theo turned back to Ted. 'Could we have two teas, please, and a couple of cheese and tomato cobs.'

Ted nodded. 'No wine then. I was looking forward to serving that. I was going to put a glacé cherry in to make it special.'

Basil muttered something about a cultural desert and turned back to Theo. 'I suppose you're wondering what bought me here.'

'Not really. With Desmond gone, I'm guessing you are cancelling the show.'

Basil was no actor and the expression of regret that crossed his features looked as sincere as a politician's promise.

'Terrible business, a great man, a giant of the theatre.' He paused but in a moment he was back in business mode. 'Time waits for no man, Theo, and *Coffee and Cream* was approaching its sell-by date.'

Clearly Desmond's eulogy had ended. 'This is 1972, Theo, times and tastes are changing and Black is hot.'

Theo wasn't sure he had heard Basil correctly. 'Did you say Black?'

'I did. Sidney Poitier, *Heat of The Night*; Richard Roundtree,

Shaft. The Black thing is happening and we need to be in on it.'

For once in his life, Theo really was speechless.

Basil misinterpreted his silence for awe. 'I know, it's amazing. We have a new pilot written for you.'

'For me?'

'Well, you're Black and an actor.'

Theo couldn't disagree with the statement; he was Black and he was an actor. 'When you say "written for me", what does that mean?'

'You! We wrote it for you! You're a great actor, Theo. We know you were capable of being so much more than Desmond's sidekick. That's why we wrote the show with you in mind.'

Theo had not expected this; he was stunned. He was expecting to hear that his TV career was over and now he was being told there was a leading role for him. 'What kind of show?'

'Detective, but real kick-ass. You break all the rules, sleep with all the women, but you always get the bad guy.'

'What's it called?'

Basil leaned towards him triumphantly. '*Othello Jones*!'

Theo was stunned into silence. What could he say to that?

Basil said it for him. 'I know, stunning title, isn't it. A nod to the Bard and a reference to the common man. We were going to call it *Romeo Jones* but that wasn't manly enough.'

'And you think *Othello Jones* is?'

'Of course. He's big and he's Black, he's a lover and a killer but he's a good guy.'

'A good detective who's also a killer.'

'I never said he was perfect. We need an anti-hero. But we need him sexy and tough to appeal to the ladies. And single. That's why he kills his wife.'

'Yeah. Ladies love a wife killer, don't they, Basil.'

Basil leaned back on his chair and looked at Theo with dismay. 'I'm sensing you are not as keen on this as the rest of the team are.'

Theo nodded slowly. 'You would be right. It sounds ridiculous, exploitative and it's using my colour as a badge.'

Basil slid a sheet of typed A4 paper towards him. 'That's what we would pay you per show. Twelve episodes and we are so confident that we would pay you for two series up front with an option for a third.'

Theo glanced down at the figures on the sheet and decided that he had no problem with the script after all. His fee for one episode was more than he was getting for a whole series of *Coffee and Cream*. 'Where do I sign?'

A smile erupted on Basil's face. 'Change of heart, Theo?'

'Need of money, Basil. I can't pass up a payday like this. Will I still get time to do some theatre?'

Basil grimaced. 'Probably not, but if all goes well you could probably buy one.'

Theo nodded. 'Pass me the pen.'

'You won't regret this, Theo.'

'Maybe but, if I do, I'll be regretting it from a large, detached house.'

Chapter 16
Domestic Bliss

'Look, dear, I think you need to calm down.'

Beatrice Oxford glared angrily at her husband. 'What is there to be calm about? Half of your company have been murdered!'

Sir Morris raised a placatory hand. 'No, dear, it's only four. That's barely ten per cent.'

'Listen to yourself, Morris. You can't make light of this, it's serious. Oliver is back, I know it.'

He tried to lay a hand on her shoulder but she shook it off. 'It's not Oliver, he's dead.'

'He's not. I can feel him, like an evil spirit come back to haunt us. He knows what we did and he wants revenge.'

Her voice was rising and other diners in the Garrick were beginning to look at them. They were a well-known couple in Stratford and a scene was the last thing they needed.

'You need to calm down.' There was steel in his voice as he leaned towards her. 'We have been saying that Oliver is dead for years. You can't go shouting that he's alive, especially when other diners can hear you. Imagine if that got back to the police.'

Beatrice stared at her husband sullenly. She knew he was right. The problem was that she could feel a rising sense of dread. Things she had done, so many years ago, seemed to be rising from the graves in which her memory had buried them. Morris had played the game and won her hand. She had wanted that, but at what cost? The loss of a child, the loss of her one true love. If she had had the talent everything could have been so different, but ambition is a ruthless taskmaster. It takes talent to fulfil it and she had none. Destined to conquer the catwalk but never the stage, she had done what she had to do to survive; finding her place by clawing and punching, scheming and planning. She had landed her knight and secured her castle but, as with all compromises, there was a bill to be paid.

She calmed herself, with great effort, and Sir Morris gazed at her with the deep love and affection that he had always held for her, even when she was married to Richard. We are such things as dreams are made of, but for Beatrice Oxford those dreams were rapidly becoming a nightmare.

'Do you fancy the spotted dick?'

Beatrice looked at Morris' questioning face. He resembled a Labrador at feeding time. 'I couldn't eat another thing after that pie.'

He looked crestfallen. 'Oh, that's disappointing.'

'You have some if you want to, dear.' She glanced across at his corpulent form; the once athletic body had grown bloated with age and overindulgence. His success could be measured by the ever-expanding number of holes on the belt of his trousers. He still had star quality, but the fine thoroughbred she had bound herself to was a mere shadow of his former self. A very big shadow but a shadow nonetheless.

'Should I have it with custard and cream?'

'Have it with lard for all I care, darling. Fill your boots, you've filled everything else.'

Sir Morris looked sadly at his stomach, but that was soon forgotten when a waiter passed by with a tray of desserts. 'An actor is like an athlete, dear; he needs to fuel the engine to enable it to perform.'

Beatrice nodded. 'Are you going to run a marathon then?'

'No.' Sir Morris shook his head. 'But I may take a stroll down to Holy Trinity after dinner. It's so peaceful there.'

'Of course it is, it's full of dead people, including Desmond and Tabitha.'

'I'm sure that there is nothing to worry about, my dear. Things have been quiet for weeks.'

'You are such a fool, Morris. Being famous won't stop a knife.'

'But I am a national treasure.'

Beatrice looked at him with despair. 'You live in this little bubble, don't you. Sir Morris Oxford, the greatest-living Shakespearian actor. Feted by the theatre-going masses. Critics fall at your feet; the world must be a very simple place from your point of view.'

Morris shrugged. 'It is, darling. I have worked my bottom off to get where I am, I've worked even harder to stay there.'

'What about those you trod on to succeed, do you think they love you?' Her words were cold. Bitter.

Sir Morris looked genuinely hurt. 'I never did that.'

'Really. What about Richard?'

'Oh, dear Richard, he was such a troubled soul.'

'Not before you and your toadies decided to destroy him.'

'That's a little harsh, dear.'

'He was becoming too good; you felt threatened by his talent.'

Sir Morris narrowed his eyes. 'Need I remind you that your hands aren't exactly clean in this matter. You made it pretty clear to me that your marriage wasn't working. It takes two to have an affair.'

'You didn't exactly back away, did you. I was vulnerable and you took advantage.'

Morris laughed. 'Nobody took advantage of you, dear. You may not be able to act but you sure as hell know how to exploit a situation. It was you who pushed me to get rid of Richard from the company.'

'There, you've admitted it, you never thought I could act.'

Sir Morris shrugged. 'You couldn't, everyone knew it but being Richard's wife and being beautiful conferred a level of protection, which you exploited. You must have known you were terrible?'

Beatrice looked at him, all pretence now gone. 'So why did you marry me?'

'Because I love you. We don't choose who we fall in love with, it just happens. From the moment I first saw you, I was in love. Seeing you with Richard every day was torture. I tried to force my feelings back; Richard was my friend, my protégé. Imagine what it was like to see you with him every day while his star was rising and mine was dimming in comparison. He had everything I wanted and there was nothing I could do about it, until …' His words dried up and he gazed into the eyes of the woman he loved. The woman for whom he would do anything.

Beatrice reached out and laid her hand tenderly upon his. 'I know, Morris, I know. We have a past and secrets to keep.'

'You do love me?' There was a quiet desperation in his voice.

She nodded slowly. 'Yes.'

The back bar at the Garrick was full of oak beams and columns. Sitting on a stool at a tiny wall-mounted table, within earshot of the Oxfords, was Whomper. He hadn't been in the Garrick for quite some time but, today, the toxic charm of the Green Dragon had failed to draw him across the threshold. Life is so much about fate, and fate had bought him here today to hear the confessions of Sir Morris and Lady Oxford. What should he do with this information?

He could walk around to Guild Street and find Toby. He dismissed the idea. The last time he had gone voluntarily into a police station, he had broken out in a rash. Whomper was a philosophical man. Fate had brought him here to witness this conversation, he would let fate bring Toby into his orbit. Actively seeking out the police was anathema to him. Whomper would keep his lips sealed until the moment he bumped into either Toby or Fred. Sir Morris and Lady Oxford's secrets were safe for now.

Chapter 17
Passing The Torch

Fred put down the phone and stared at Toby.

'Who was that?'

Fred didn't respond; he just looked back at the receiver.

'Everything all right, boss?'

'No, Toby, everything is not all right. The Earth has moved on its axis, it is out of kilter.'

'Who was that on the phone. NASA?'

'No, it wasn't NASA. It was madness, a world that has lost its compass. All things we thought of as normal are now discarded, thrown aside and left to pollute all reason.'

Toby leaned back and looked at Fred. 'Have you let your blood sugar drop again.'

'Why?'

'You seem … prosaic, lyrical almost.'

'Don't I always.'

'No, you usually sound blunt and sarcastic.'

'Sometimes blunt sarcasm just can't fill the void in a man's heart.'

Toby put down his pen and turned to Fred. 'What's wrong, boss? Who was on the phone?'

'Mel Townsend,' sighed Fred.

'Well, that's a good thing, isn't it?'

'There was a time when I would have agreed with you, but not today.'

'What did she want?'

Fred shook his head sadly and then looked up at Toby. 'She wanted to know if you have a girlfriend.'

'Sorry?'

'Don't make me say it again.'

Toby needed him to say it again. 'What?'

'She wanted to know if you have a girlfriend.'

'Why would she want to know that?'

'For a detective, you're not very good at putting things together, are you. There is only one reason that Mel Townsend would be asking that question.'

'Which is?'

'Cassandra has moved her favours from Apollo.'

'Eh, who are they?'

Fred sighed. 'Mel is Cassandra.'

'From Greek mythology?'

'The very same.'

'So, who's Apollo?'

Fred looked hurt. 'Me, obviously.'

Toby tried not to smile as he looked Fred's rumpled body up and down. There was little evidence of Apollo's abs or indeed any clear definition of a godlike physique. Apollo had clearly let his fitness regime lapse.

'Why are you staring?'

'I'm not staring, I'm trying to visualise.'

'What?'

'You as a god.'

'Sod that, it seems you may have greater things to visualise. Cassandra has taken an interest in you.'

'Cassandra?'

'Mel Townsend. She wanted to know if you are …' Fred paused for a moment, the words he was about to say were clearly distasteful to him. 'Available.'

Toby wasn't sure how to respond, then he thought about the things she had said in the canteen in Coventry. A smile spread across his face.

'What is it?' demanded Fred.

'When I bumped into Mel at HQ, Mavis, the canteen lady,

asked her if we were an item.'

'The poor lady is obviously very sick. What did Mel say?'

'She said she was working on it.' Toby chuckled; he couldn't help it.

'That's disgusting, she's old enough to be your mother.'

'She's not that much older than me.'

An uncomfortable silence fell between them. Fred seemed in a state of melancholic shock, if indeed that were possible.

Toby tried to lighten the mood. 'There's nothing happening, boss.'

'It will, Toby, it will. If Mel has decided she wants you, she will have you.'

'Don't I get a say in this?'

'Do you want one?'

Toby considered it for a moment. 'Well, no, not really.'

'Exactly. Why do you think she looks so young? Mel selects her victims carefully, drains their life force and then moves on. She lives life on her own terms, no man will ever own her.'

Toby considered Fred's warning. He was very fond of his life force but he was sure he could spare some for DI Mel Townsend. Toby weighed up the ramifications of a dangerous liaison with Cassandra. He was certainly more Apollo than Fred was these days.

Fred got up and held out his hand. Toby took it hesitantly.

'Time for me to pass the baton to you, young Toby. You may be the next Apollo.'

'How will I know?'

Fred smiled. 'You'll know. For a while you will be the happiest man in Warwickshire, and then …' he gazed wistfully out of the window at the Loxley Dairies milk float on the car park. 'Then, it will be just a memory. A fleeting moment of promise, a brief image of the possibilities that life can hold. A memory to cherish and cling to, until the soil falls across your coffin, shutting out the light of life forever.'

Toby took Fred's hand; clearly, he hadn't moved on.

'You may be reading too much into this, boss.'

'No, I know my Mel. She has set her mind on you and she will have you. She will never be mine again.' Fred bit his lip.

'I thought you were dating the barmaid from The Railway.'

'I am.'

'Then why are you so worried about Mel fancying me? You've got your hands full.'

'I have big hands, Toby.'

Toby smiled weakly at Fred. He did have big hands but, sadly, he didn't appear to have the ability to juggle.

They fell silent again and turned their attention back to the stacks of papers on their desks.

When Inspector Beeching came sweeping in, he was shocked to see them working. 'Now there is a sight for sore eyes.'

'Sir. How did the meeting go?'

'Not bad. Wilson was seething but, with what we have on him, he couldn't really say anything, could he.' Beeching sat down on the end of Toby's desk. 'Kipper was there.'

Fred looked up. 'Kipper of the Yard? I thought he'd retired. He hasn't been up this way since the Meon Hill murder.'

'He was only thirty-two when they put him in charge of that one.'

Fred did the maths. 'Fifty-nine, you'd have thought he would have retired by now.'

'No such luck, he only had one murder that he failed to solve and, sod's law, it was ours.'

Toby looked up. 'What happened?'

Fred leaned back in his chair. 'It was the winter of forty-five, I was still at school. You know Meon Hill?'

Toby nodded. 'It's the other side of Long Marston airfield, isn't it?'

'Yeah. Sometime in mid-February the body of Fred Marston was found on the lower slopes of Meon Hill. He'd been pinned down by a pitchfork round his neck and his throat had been slashed open with a pruning knife.'

'Nasty,' said Toby.

'It gets worse. Reports say that a cross had been carved on his chest. There was talk of a ritual killing; always been a rumour about witchcraft in Quinton.'

'Who did it?'

'That's the thing, Kipper never found the killer. A wall of silence descended and the people of Quinton let poor old Fred take the secret to the grave. Kipper never got over it. Kept coming back year after year on the anniversary of the murder and standing vigil all through the night waiting for the culprits to return. He did it right up until 1965. Twenty years. He just couldn't let it go.'

'Sounds gruesome,' said Toby.

'It was. Kipper was convinced it was black magic but nobody would listen to him.'

'Quite right too,' said Beeching. 'There's no such thing.'

Fred looked questioningly at Beeching. 'I'm not so sure, sir. I've been up on Meon Hill at night. It's a creepy place. There's something very wrong with it. Made my flesh creep.'

'What were you doing up there?'

Fred shrugged. 'It was back in fifty-nine. I was a young detective and thought I would reopen the case to see if I could uncover the truth. It's the only unsolved murder we have on the books.'

'We have a growing pile of them now,' said Beeching bitterly.

'I worked with Kipper; he came up for a week when he heard I'd reopened the case.'

'What was he like?' asked Toby.

'Seemed OK to me. Decent bloke and sharp as a knife, not sure what he will make of our Shakespeare murders.'

'You try and keep him in check, Fred. I don't want Scotland Yard catching the culprit and stealing our glory. It'll make us look incompetent.'

'Surely we should welcome any help we can get.'

Beeching looked at Toby pityingly. 'You have so much to learn about the modern police force, Marlowe.'

Fred nodded in agreement. 'It's our problem, we need to clear it up. There's only one thing worse than an unsolved murder.'

'What's that?'

'A murder that's solved by an outside force. Those are career killers. Luckily, mine's already dead but for you and Inspector Beeching, it will go as a little black mark on your records.'

'And I will never get back to the Met,' sighed Beeching. 'Unless …' he slapped his thigh. 'Yes!'

'Everything all right, sir?'

Beeching nodded. 'Yes, I think it could be. I've just had an idea that will get Kipper off our backs. Why don't you go and see him, Fred? Fill him in on the case and then suggest you think there may be a link to the Meon Hill murders.'

'Do you think there is?'

'No, of course not.'

'Is that ethical?' asked Toby. 'We need Kipper's help; we need all the help we can get.'

'No, we need to sort this ourselves, anything else is a disaster.' Beeching turned to Fred. 'He's at Coventry right now, why don't you give him a call and catch up on old times.'

He winked at Fred and Fred nodded back. 'I'm on it, sir.'

Beeching turned and strode back into his office, shutting the door firmly behind him.

Toby leaned back in his chair. 'I can't believe you're going along with this, boss, it's wrong.'

Fred held up his hands. 'Listen, I know Beeching is a career-obsessed idiot but, in this instance, he's right. If Kipper comes in and catches our killer, it's going to make us all look bad. Me, I don't care. I've had so many disciplinaries that my career has hit the buffers. The only reason they haven't sacked me is because I catch a lot of villains. But you, there is a great career in front of you, Toby. You could be a DI by the time you're thirty. Don't bugger it up by having integrity.'

'Isn't that a minimum requirement in this job?'

Fred shrugged. 'Some integrity is fine, but if you have too much it just gets in the way. You can do it by the book if you want but the bloke who wrote the book never caught any criminals, that's why he wrote the book.'

'But we need you working the case.'

'What case! Look at the board. Four dead bodies and not a single lead or clue. We think it's Lawrence but we have no proof. Right now, we don't have a thing. Our plan, and it's not much of a plan, is to use potential victims as bait to lure him out. We're stuck, Toby, just hoping that he makes a mistake. I might as well steer Kipper towards a link with Meon Hill while we're waiting.'

Toby shook his head. 'It doesn't seem right to me.'

'We've got Ginger and Kinky looking after the observations. Check in with them and make sure they are on high alert. It's coming, we can all feel it. It's just a matter of time.'

And they could feel it; everyone in Stratford could feel it. The air was heavy with expectation and fear. Something terrible was about to happen. The tourists were staying away and the newspapers were full of stories about the killer lying in wait for his next victim. Who would it be? Only one person knew the answer to that question.

Chapter 18
What Dreams May Come

When the voice had come there had been no escape; it had been a waking nightmare. The darkness had closed in on her like cold, impenetrable walls. Lizzie had been imprisoned by the night but, like a jailor's key unlocking a cell door, the sunlight filtered through the window and she finally dared to move.

At first, Lizzie hadn't been sure whether she had dreamed it, then she had remembered. After she had got up and looked out of her bedroom window, she had gone back to bed, put out the light and the nightmare had returned … and spoken her name. That's when she had screamed.

Phil, the landlord, had rushed to her room. She had told him everything but he thought she'd had a bad dream. He'd tried to reassure her.

But it wasn't a bad dream, she knew it had happened. And that voice. She recognised it, but from where?

Two hours later, Lizzie sat in her office at the Royal Shakespeare Theatre. She had a rehearsal to take in one hour and should have been compiling her notes, but she just couldn't get the previous night out of her head. There was something so familiar about that voice despite her memory of it being confused; the voice had changed: deeper, stronger, more confident. She had heard so many fine voices over the last twenty years but this had been one of the finest. It had also been full of menace. If she didn't know better, the words could be construed as a threat. When she really thought about it, she realised that it was a threat. But from who, and why? So many questions. There was a knock on her door. She welcomed the distraction.

'Come in.'

The door swung open and there stood Theo Cumberbatch. He had always been one of her favourite actors.

'Hi Theo, come in.'

He smiled and entered her office. 'Hi Lizzie, could you spare me a few moments?'

'Of course,' she pushed her unfinished notes to one side. 'What can I do for you?'

Theo sat down opposite her and placed his elbows on her desk. She was struck by just how good looking he was. Why had she never slept with him?

He stared at her intently. 'If I tell you something, will you promise to keep it a secret?'

'Sounds intriguing, what is it?'

'No, you have to promise to keep it between us.'

He was serious, this wasn't a trivial matter. Lizzie nodded. 'Of course, you have my word.'

Theo looked around to make sure the door was closed behind him. 'I've been offered the lead role in a new police drama starting next year. They've offered me a guarantee of two series with twelve episodes in each.'

'Wow.' Lizzie leaned back in her chair. 'The, er, the lead role?'

'Yes, the lead.'

'OK. What's it about?'

Theo sighed and leaned forwards, resting his elbows on the desk. 'You need to keep an open mind, Lizzie. Wide open.'

Lizzie laughed. 'You're talking to the lady that did the *Tempest* on Mars, and burned down a bloody theatre doing *Henry V* with flamethrowers. I'm the queen of crazy.'

Theo smiled. 'Yeah, I guess you are.' He hesitated.

'Well, get on with it. I've got a rehearsal in fifty minutes.'

'You familiar with Shaft?'

'You mean the Black detective?'

'Yes, Richard Roundtree.'

Lizzie was intrigued. 'Go on.'

'Imagine a character like him … but English.'

'I'm trying.'

'He's a kick-ass detective who breaks all the rules, but gets results.'

'And he's Black?'

'Yeah, that's my part.'

'You are going to play a Black English detective who doesn't play by the rules but still gets results?'

'That's right. Imagine Shaft in England.'

'I'll try. This is hard to visualise, Theo. Does he wear a suit?'

'No, he wears a leather coat with a tie-dye T-shirt and flares.'

Lizzie nodded thoughtfully, trying very hard to conceal a smile that was cracking the corners of her mouth. 'And is he, perchance, sporting an Afro?'

Theo nodded. 'He is.'

The corners of Lizzie's mouth began to ripple. She took a deep breath, composed herself and asked one last question. 'Does he have a name?'

Theo pursed his lips. 'Othello Jones.'

That was the final straw for Lizzie; she burst into hysterical laughter. Theo had expected this and sat patiently waiting for her laughter to subside; it took a while.

Finally, Lizzie wiped her eyes and dragged herself back to her desk from the position she had slid to on the floor. 'Sorry about that, Theo, it's a lot to take in.'

'So, what do you think?'

Lizzie stroked her chin as she considered her response. 'We agree that I'm the queen of crazy, don't we?'

'Undisputed,' said Theo.

'Well, that's too crazy, even for me.'

'Why?'

She looked into Theo's eyes. 'Theo, darling, they are using you to jump on some Black bandwagon. If it doesn't work, and it probably won't, it's a career wrecker. Have you ever seen any Black detectives? And, if you have, do they wear leather jackets and sport an Afro? It's tokenism of the worst kind, and to call him Othello Jones … It's like a bad musical.'

Theo pulled the contract from his pocket and slid it across the desk to her. 'Look at the bottom paragraph.'

Lizzie took the contract, read the final paragraph and saw the numbers. She looked up at Theo in shock. 'Is this for real?'

He nodded.

'It's a fortune.'

'I know, it's too much to say no to, but …' Theo couldn't finish his sentence.

'You're worried it will damage your reputation?'

He nodded. 'I don't want to do it, I need to do it … but how can I?'

Lizzie leaned back and closed her eyes in thought. Theo waited; he knew Lizzie was crazy but she also had moments of brilliance. She was just about to have another.

'Ask for the right to revise or comment on the scripts.'

'Why?'

'Because, dear Theo, you are going to play this part for real. Sounds to me like they are trying to just put Shaft in England without any assimilation but you're not going to play him like an American cardboard cut-out. You're going to play him for real.'

Theo looked confused. 'I don't understand.'

'Where are you from, Theo?'

'Birmingham.'

'Well, play him from Birmingham, just without the accent. Somehow you have managed to become an undercover detective, despite the prejudice. There's a glass ceiling and you have gone so far but you can't go any further. You know their game and you are playing them at it. People underestimate you.'

'Because I'm Black?'

'Of course. Use that to show how clever your character is. I haven't seen those scripts yet but I have a pretty good idea what they will be like.'

'You think?'

'I know. They'll be a pile of crap, facile words written like slogans … but here's the thing,' Lizzie held up an index finger. 'You're a great actor. Make him human, give him a soul. Show his intelligence. Make the audience believe you.'

'What if the script writers won't let me do it?'

Lizzie winked conspiratorially. 'Change a word, add a sentence, there are so many ways to say something, to alter its meaning with an inflection. This is your chance to show that you are the equal of any other detective, better than most. You have the acting chops to do this.'

'That's great in theory but what if they sack me?'

Lizzie chuckled. 'No offence, Theo, but they wouldn't even consider that until you were several weeks into shooting. And not to be too indelicate—'

'It's never stopped you before.'

'True, but how many Black English actors do you know who have had a TV show for six series?' Lizzie stood up and walked around the desk. She leaned down behind Theo and whispered in his ear, 'I think you are just about irreplaceable.'

Everything that Lizzie had said made sense. He had seen the first few scripts and they hadn't been very good, but he could improve them. Lizzie turned his chair around so she could look directly at him. 'Nobody ever fell in love with a plot. They fall in love with a character, Theo. Make him real, make them care.'

'But what about the name?'

She grimaced. 'You won't be the first person to be given a terrible name. Make a joke of it; let it be your cross to bear, a burden given to you by the parents that named you.'

Theo nodded. 'I get it, Lizzie. I'm going to play it my way. I don't care what they say.'

'Good. Was that all?'

'No.'

'I've just given you advice that will make you a star, what more can there be?'

'Othello,' said Theo.

'Make a joke of it, just like I said.'

Theo shook his head. 'Not *Othello Jones*, your Othello. I want to play him.'

Lizzie took a step back. 'How did you know that I was doing *Othello* next season?'

'Pierre Corridor told me.'

'He did? We weren't going to announce that until I had cast it.'

'That's why he told me. He wants Othello to be played by a real Black man, not some White actor pretending to be Black.'

'I understand that, Theo, but there's a tradition of great White actors blacking up to play Othello, a bit like men playing pantomime dames.'

'It's hardly the same, Lizzie. It's 1972, for God's sake.'

'Look, the company was casting Paul Robeson as Othello back in fifty-nine; it's not a race thing, it's a theatrical tradition thing. All great actors like to take a shot at it.'

'That's fine, just don't black them up.'

Lizzie held up her hands. 'Hold on, Theo, you're having a go at the wrong person here. I'm a massive believer in reinterpreting the classic texts. I would love to see you play Othello. Have you ever played him with Sir Morris?'

'No,' said Theo tersely. 'I asked him to let me play it four years ago. Told me I wasn't Black enough.'

Lizzie grinned. 'You're kidding?'

'No, not only that, he told me that I'd have to black up because I wasn't Black enough. There was no way I was doing that.'

'What happened?'

'Sir Morris blacked up and I played Cassio.'

'I can see how that would piss you off.'

'Don't you think it's unfair?'

Lizzie slumped back down in her chair. 'It's a hard one to call. Stratford has had Black Othellos before. There was Edric Conner and he was followed by Robeson. It's clearly not an issue of race. Go back as far as 1825 and Ira Aldridge played Othello on the London stage to great acclaim. I just think that it's one of the great parts so it stands to reason that great actors want it. Would you have denied Olivier, Burton, Gielgud the chance?'

'No, I just want the chance to play it too. Do you think I could?'

Lizzie nodded. 'I think you would be an amazing Othello; will you be available, though? When will filming for *Othello Jones* begin?'

'June next year.'

'And how long will it take?'

'It's slated for twelve weeks.'

'Lizzie noted down the dates. That could work. The Stratford run ends in May and the London transfer is for early September.'

'I'm going to be getting a lot of publicity from the TV, that's going to cross over to the theatre audience.'

'It won't hurt.' Lizzie seemed to consider the idea for a moment. Let me speak to Pierre. If he really is as keen as you suggest, I won't have any objection.'

Theo ran around the desk and hugged her. 'Thank you, Lizzie, you don't know how much this means to me.'

'Go easy, Theo, I'm feeling a little delicate this morning.'

Theo stood back and looked at her. 'Are you all right? You look tired.'

Lizzie ran a hand through her hair. 'I'm not sure.'

'What's wrong?'

She shot him a nervous smile. 'I had a bad dream last night.'

'Go on.'

'Seems I've started hearing voices in my dreams. Voices that speak in iambic pentameter.'

'Isn't that normal for someone who is producing Shakespeare plays?'

'They don't normally call my name out in the speech though.'

'Dreams are funny things.'

'This wasn't just in my dream though, Theo. I woke up but the voice didn't stop. I went to the window and looked out. I was convinced there was someone outside.'

'And?'

Lizzie looked at him through eyes framed with dark creases. 'There was no one there. I went back to bed and tried to go back to sleep and then …' her words dried up as she remembered.

'What happened?'

'The voice came back, and I was most definitely awake.'

'Can you remember what it said?'

'I can. "Awaken to your destiny, the sands of time move fast but for you, Lizzie Birchwood, the future has passed."'

Theo looked concerned. 'That sounds a little menacing. Are you sure you weren't dreaming?'

'I wish I had been. There was something else … I recognised the voice.'

'Whatever happened it was obviously disturbing. Do you think someone's playing a sick little prank?'

Lizzie shrugged. 'Who knows, I've upset enough actors over the years.'

'You think it's an actor?'

'Yes, his diction was precise and the lines were delivered impeccably. All the intonations were perfect.' Lizzie looked up at Theo. 'At least my nightmares are splendidly performed.'

'You said you recognised the voice. Can you put a name to it?'

She shook her head. 'No, it's so familiar and yet … I just can't quite pin it down. I've been trying all night.'

'Maybe you should report this to the police,' said Theo.

Lizzie grinned. 'And what do you think they would make of

that, a middle-aged luvvie reporting on a nightmare. I'd be laughed out of the station.'

'Given what's been happening in town recently, I think they would probably want to know about it.'

Lizzie looked at Theo; he was serious. 'No, I'm not giving the local plod a laugh at my expense.'

'You need to take this seriously, Lizzie. There is a serial killer in town and he's killing actors and critics associated with Sir Morris and the theatre.'

Lizzie waved his fears away. 'I'm not an actor or a critic. As for Sir Morris, well, you know what I think of that old windbag. If they were going to kill him, I would probably open the door for them.'

'Look, I won't bother trying to defend him. Your opinions of Sir Morris and his productions are well known and you're not likely to be going to the pub together any time soon.' 'No, we're not,' Lizzie chuckled.

'That being said, if it happens again I really think you should reconsider.' The concern on Theo's face was clear.

'Bless you, Theo, you're a real sweetie.' Lizzie glanced at her watch. 'Oh, bugger, I need to be off to rehearsal.' She started throwing her papers into a shoulder bag. 'Let me speak to Pierre and then we'll get back to you.'

Theo smiled. 'I really appreciate this.'

Lizzie waved him away. 'Nonsense, you'll be a great Othello. You're going to make me look good.' She picked up her bag and made for the door, giving him a brief peck on the cheek as she swept by. 'I'll give you a call in a couple of days.'

He watched her go. A lot of people didn't really care for Lizzie Birchwood; she was seen to be too opinionated, too controversial. Theo had none of those reservations. Lizzie took risks, she was an innovator; sometimes it didn't work. On other occasions, it was glorious. He fought the urge to run after her and tell her how much he admired her. If he had known that he would never see her alive again, he probably would have.

Chapter 19
The Waiting Game

Kinky Bernstein was sitting doing nothing; he was good at it. Evolution had shaped him. His movements, or lack of them, meant his bottom had come to resemble two watermelons trapped in a pair of boxer shorts.

Ginger Dalton had once suggested he was suffering from a rare melanoma; the non-dangerous comfy kind. It didn't concern him; his body had adapted to the demands of his job. Darwin would have been proud of him.

'You comfortable, Kinky?'

Toby had crept up behind him, trying to make him jump but Kinky, despite his sloth-like nature, was a bloody good detective. He'd spotted Toby sliding up the far side of Old Town Road, coming from the direction of Holy Trinity, slipping behind trees and crouching near cars. From his bench in the Garden of Remembrance, he had watched with amusement. He liked Toby but the kid still had a lot to learn.

'Try walking normally when you're trying to creep up on someone; crouching around like a gorilla with trapped wind catches the eye every time.'

Toby frowned. 'That was my stealth approach.'

'Good job I'm not a sniper then, isn't it.'

Toby slumped down on the bench next to Kinky. 'Anything to report?'

'Ted Heath is still prime minister.'

'Good to know. What about Sir Morris and Lady Oxford?'

'Still inspecting the renovations at Hall's Croft, been in there nearly two hours. I think the old boy likes to imagine that he's sitting around the kitchen table with Susanna, having a cup of tea.'

'Who's Susanna?'

Kinky sighed. 'I thought you were our resident Shakespeare expert. Susannah was Shakespeare's daughter and she used to live there with her husband.'

'I never knew that.'

'Lots of history in this town, son.'

'Anyone else in there with them?'

'Just the guy from the Shakespeare Trust.'

'What happens if they go their separate ways when they come out?'

Kinky pointed to a brown Ford Cortina parked fifty yards down the road. 'Kerby is waiting just in case Lady Muck drives off in her Rover. If she does, he's going to follow her all the way back to Woodstock, if necessary.'

Toby nodded his approval. 'You've got this covered from every angle, Kinky.'

'This ain't my first observation, son. I'm a finely-honed detective, poised and ready to pounce.'

Toby glanced at the large stomach hanging over Kinky's belt, like an avalanche in waiting. 'Was that pounce or bounce?'

'Bugger off, Toby, I've got work to do.' Kinky opened his paper. 'Nobody's going to get to those two, why don't you go and check on somebody that really doesn't know what they're doing, someone like Ginger Dalton.'

Toby glanced down at Kinky's paper; concealed inside it was a copy of Playboy magazine. 'Kinky by name, Kinky by nature?'

Kinky looked up at him disdainfully. 'I bought it for the article by Gore Vidal.'

'Course you did, Kinky.' Toby pointed towards the open page. 'Gore's breasts are bigger than I remember.'

On the other side of town, Ginger Dalton was following Clarissa Pidgeon down Bridge Street. She was in shopping mode and her purse was working overtime. Ginger was thankful that he wasn't married to her; she had spent more in the last two hours than he earned in three months. That said, she did look pretty good. Kinky had said Ginger could follow her because she looked too energetic, there were times when Kinky failed to live up to his nickname.

Clarissa came out of the store, crossed the high street and made a beeline for him. He pushed himself up against the doorway of the shoe shop but, as an invisibility cloak, it failed abysmally.

'Morning, officer.'

Ginger nodded awkwardly. 'Morning, miss.'

'Are you my protection for the day?'

'Yes, miss.'

'Great,' she thrust her bags towards him. 'Carry these for me then. My arms feel like they're about to fall off.'

He took them from her. 'I'm not sure I should be doing this, miss, I'm here to discreetly observe and protect.'

'Well, you weren't as discreet as you thought. You've spent forty minutes watching me, now you can observe how heavy my bags are and protect me from a hernia. That's your motto, isn't it, "To serve and protect"?'

'Sort of but you're taking it too literally.'

The conversation had ended. Clarissa was off down the Street. 'Come on, officer, I'll buy you a coffee.'

Fred Williams had seen all of this happen as he stood at the bottom of Bridge Street where it meets Waterside. He moved to the middle of the pavement so that Ginger couldn't miss him as he trailed past in Clarissa's wake. Poor old Ginger never stood a chance. 'Finally found something you're qualified for, eh, Ginger.'

'Sod off, boss. I'm just helping her to move faster so it's harder for a sniper to hit her.'

'How thoughtful of you. Careful when you get back to her place, I've heard she's a bit of a man-eater.'

The thought hadn't occurred to Ginger. Now he considered it, it wasn't unappealing; then he looked at the amount of stuff he was carrying. He could never afford a girlfriend like Clarissa Pidgeon.

Clarissa turned left and went into the tearooms on Waterside. Ginger followed her in, squeezing the bags through the door with difficulty. She was already seated at a table. 'Are you allowed a cup of tea and a bun, Constable?'

'As long as there is no alcohol involved.' He piled the bags of shopping up against the side of her table and sat down. 'Planning on going somewhere special, miss?'

Clarissa looked at the bags. 'No, just a few essentials. I'm going to be in Stratford for the next four months. I thought I had better replenish the wardrobe.'

'You might need a bigger one.'

Two tables away, Oliver sipped his tea and watched the performance. The detective who was supposed to be protecting Clarissa had followed her straight to him. Now he knew their plan: watch the potential victims and wait for him to pounce. It was simple but effective. Clearly the police had run out of ideas. He smiled to himself. They hadn't put a tail on Lizzie Birchwood; he'd been following her for the last few days and seen nothing. Nobody even realised that she was on his hit list. This was going to be easy. As for Clarissa, she would keep. Her time would come and she would give him ample opportunity.

Chapter 20
Close To The Edge

The day had been a long one and Lizzie Birchwood was exhausted. She needed a decent night's sleep. Rehearsal had gone well until she had nodded off in the middle of a scene. Only for a few moments, but when she awoke the cast were all looking at her, giggling.

'What was I saying?' said Lizzie, pretending she had been listening and momentarily resting her eyes.

'You've been asleep for about ten minutes, Lizzie,' said Dame Suzy.

'No, I haven't.'

'Your snoring was drowning out the dialogue.'

The cast were all smiling and Lizzie realised denial was pointless. She held up her hands. 'Guilty as charged. I had a very rough night last night, only got about three hours sleep. Why don't we wrap it up for today and make up time tomorrow.'

The sun was out and the bars were open, so she got no argument from her cast.

Dame Suzy had watched her go and then turned to Theo. 'Fancy a drink at the Dirty Duck?'

Theo nodded. 'Be a shame not to.' Ten minutes later, they were seated outside watching the river through the trees and hearing the bells of Holy Trinity.

'The bells are calling the faithful to the bar,' said Dame Suzy.

'Amen to that,' replied Theo, as he raised his pint to his lips.

They drank for a moment in silence, savouring the cathartic action as the sun warmed their skin and the gentle breeze wafted up the river from the south.

'You know, Theo, there are times when I think this is the most wonderful place in the world.'

Theo nodded. 'I know what you mean, I'm going to miss it.'

She picked up on his comment. 'What does that mean?'

Theo leaned forward. 'Can you keep a secret.'

Dame Suzy's eyes twinkled. 'Of course not, but I am a national treasure so you're going to have to tell me anyway.'

'I've been offered the lead role in a new prime-time TV show.'

'That's wonderful, Theo! What's it called … no, don't tell me. Let me guess.' Dame Suzy scrunched up her face in concentration. '*Coffee, No Cream*?'

'You are bad, Suzy.'

She smiled. 'I know.'

'No, *Coffee, No Cream* would be a bit insensitive given the nature of Cream's demise.'

Dame Suzy shrugged. 'That's a pity. *Black Coffee* would have been a great title.'

'It's nothing to do with *Coffee and Cream*, this is a brand-new show with a big budget behind it.'

Suzy put down her gin and tonic and leaned towards him. 'This sounds exciting, what's going on?'

'Have you seen the *Shaft* film with Richard Roundtree?'

'Course I have. I met him when I was doing a film in Hollywood last year. Is he in it?'

'No, it's a British series. Just imagine a Shaft-style detective, but English, in England.'

Dame Suzy leaned back thoughtfully in her chair. 'I'm trying. Are you the lead?'

Theo nodded. 'The show's called *Othello Jones*.'

'And … you're Othello?' She cleared her throat. 'Have you read the scripts?'

'No, but I've seen the contract and it has a guarantee for two series, so even if they don't make it I'll get paid.'

'Is it good money?'

Theo chuckled. 'Enough to buy a couple of houses and stash a load in the bank.'

'It sounds too good to be true.'

'You seem concerned. Do you think I'm making a mistake?'

'No, it makes sense to become financially secure in this game, it's just that …' she hesitated for a moment. 'You have a great name in the theatre, Theo, and nothing but praise for your performances in *Coffee and Cream*, I'd hate to see you damage it in any way.'

Theo winked at her. 'I've got another secret, sort of a back-up plan.'

'Oh, do tell.'

'I'm going to play Othello; the run in Stratford falls nicely before we start filming series one of *Othello Jones*. The filming finishes in time for me to go straight to the transfer to London.'

'Othello? You have the part?'

'Yes, I think so. Pierre Corridor told me he wanted me to have it and Lizzie says she is happy as long as he approves.'

'Sounds like you're a shoo-in then.' Dame Suzy leaned forward, took his head in her hands and kissed him. 'You deserve this, Theo, you're a great actor. It's time you were out from under Sir Morris' constraints.'

Theo savoured the kiss and then smiled. 'You don't think much of Sir Morris, do you?'

'Not really, I think he's trading on his past glories. Shouting out the lines to show he still has it, but theatre's changed. He has no nuance, no inner monologue, there's nothing on show but the hulking shell of a once great artist.'

Theo didn't respond to Dame Suzy's comments. He agreed, but Sir Morris was his employer, he had given him regular work for nearly twenty years. It was going to be hard enough breaking the news to him that he was leaving for a starring role on prime-time TV, something that had eluded Sir Morris. When he discovered that he was going to be Othello, a role that Sir Morris thought would be his by right, things would become tense.

'Do you think Lizzie is OK,' he asked, deftly changing the subject.

'Of course. You know Lizzie; burns the candle at both ends and then in the middle.'

'She's a wild one all right, but I like her. As a producer, she has had some brilliant moments.'

'And some terrible half hours,' sighed Dame Suzy.

'You're not a fan?'

Dame Suzy considered his question. 'To a point. As you say, some of her interpretations have been stunning, but others …'

'Her Martian *Tempest*?'

She shook her head. 'Good God, did you see it.'

'I was in it,' admitted Theo.

'No. Oh, you poor thing. Who were you?'

'Trinculo.'

'You were the jester? I never noticed.'

'It was a long time ago.'

'I was too busy crying with laughter. Poor Lizzie really did go out on a limb with that production. Nothing the jester did could have been funnier than Lizzie's staging.'

Theo cringed inwardly at the memory. 'True, but sometimes you have to take a risk to move things forward, make them relevant.'

'This is Shakespeare, Theo, you can't bugger about with it, it's too precious. No one has ever understood the human condition better, it needs to be treated with reverence.'

Dame Suzy's passion was clear. He shared it, but he also thought that varying interpretations could add to the impact.

'The key is to always respect the text, don't you think?'

Dame Suzy nodded approvingly. 'Always.'

Chapter 21
As Good As A Five-Mile Run

Oliver had followed Clarissa and Ginger Dalton as they left the café, he wanted to see where the detective positioned himself when he left her. If he knew where they were watching her from, he could always find a way of getting into her building from another side, hidden from the prying eyes of the police.

They walked down to the end of Southern Lane and crossed the road, walking along the side of the Memorial Garden before turning left onto College Street. The first house on the right-hand side was a large redbrick, double-fronted with limestone lintels. It was a big house with a walled garden that curved along to the end of the road and around the corner to the left onto Old Town. Oliver knew that Clarissa came from a wealthy family but how had she ended up here?

Clarissa pulled out a key and inserted it into the lock of the big blue door.

'This looks expensive,' observed Ginger.

Clarissa winked at him. 'Good job I'm not paying for it. God bless Uncle Derek.'

Oh, your uncle's place, is it?'

'One of them. He has houses all over the world, don't think he's been to this one for about two years. Let's me use it whenever I'm in Stratford.'

'It's a big place for one person,' said Ginger.

'I'm seldom alone,' Clarissa looked at him coyly. 'Care to come in, officer?'

Her flirtatious tone was unmistakable. Ginger hesitated. 'Er, better not, Miss Pidgeon. I'm still on duty.'

Clarissa walked up to him until she was almost standing toe to toe. Ginger was rooted to the spot, both hands full of Clarissa's shopping. 'Well, if you're my bodyguard, surely the closer you are to my body, the safer I'll be.'

Ginger swallowed hard. 'Safer for you, perhaps, miss, but if my boss caught me in there with you, I don't think my job would be very safe.'

Clarissa pouted with fake disappointment. 'Never mind, officer, maybe another time when you're feeling braver.'

Ginger stepped past Clarissa and placed her bags in the entry hall. Before he could straighten up, Clarissa gave his bum a playful tap. 'Ooh, that's a nice firm bum, do you work out?'

Ginger jumped up as if a hot poker had been inserted. 'Yes, Miss Pidgeon. I train most days, running or badminton.'

Clarissa looked him up and down like a hyena assessing its next meal. 'They say sex is as good as a five-mile run … how far do you run?'

'Er, four miles.'

'Close enough,' sighed Clarissa.

She made a grab for Ginger but he was too quick. With an agility born of years of club badminton and enhanced by fear, he leaped backwards, almost reaching the road. He paused for a second, teetering on the edge of the pavement, but Clarissa had not given up on her prey. She kept coming at him, her nostrils flaring and a long low growl issuing from somewhere deep in her body. Ginger Dalton abandoned his manly posturing and fled in abject terror down Old Town until he disappeared into the park that ran down to the Avon.

Oliver had watched them from a covered bench in the Memorial Garden. The same bench where, just thirty minutes before, DC

Kinky Bernstein had been seated as he waited for Sir Morris and Lady Oxford to emerge from Hall's Croft. Oliver looked across at the pantomime playing out on the other side of College Street; the poor detective was being made to look a fool. Clarissa was standing on the pavement watching him retreat, laughing her head off. She had been playing with him. Oliver had laughed too. Clarissa Pidgeon was a force of nature; she would take a lot of killing.

Oliver had settled in and waited, his eyes never leaving the house on College Street. There had been a succession of people sitting on the bench. The latest was an old boy, who had lit up his pipe and smoked what smelled like sweaty socks. Oliver's gasps were noticed by the old boy, who mistook his writhing for pleasure. He smiled between puffs. 'I know, you just can't beat the aroma of a pipe, can you?'

At that moment, Oliver would have loved to beat him unconscious with his pipe, but that was not in the plan. He smiled weakly. 'One man's meat,' he whispered.

The man drew deeply on his pipe and gazed across the rooftops of Old Town Stratford; he seemed very content. Downwind of him, Oliver was not at all content. He had an overwhelming desire to help him towards his maker. He bit down hard on his lip, random acts of violence were not in his plan. Finally, the old boy finished and then without hesitation, leaned forward and began to casually knock the sooty, tobacco remnants of his pipe onto the pavement between his feet.

'You can't do that,' protested Oliver. 'People have got to sit here; their shoes will get filthy.'

'Well, I can't put it back in my pocket, can I.' He wasn't aggressive, he said it matter-of-factly.

'But … but people are going to sit there.' Oliver pointed to the mess.

The old boy shrugged. 'I fought in a war to have the right to do that.'

'Oh, and there was me thinking it was about Nazi expansionism.'

'I don't like your tone, young man. I fought for the freedom to do that.'

'What in, the catering core,' said Oliver sarcastically. He instantly regretted his words. He couldn't afford to be getting into an argument, he needed to be invisible.

The old boy pocketed his pipe and straightened up to his full height. He looked down at Oliver with contempt. 'As it happens, I was in the catering core,' he leaned in. 'And I killed more people than you'll ever know.' He winked at Oliver and headed out of the memorial gardens.

Oliver watched him go, unsure whether he had been joking or not. Before he could ponder the matter further, the tall, red-headed form of DC Ginger Dalton entered the gardens from Southern Lane.

He went to sit down but Oliver warned him.

'Careful, an old boy just emptied his pipe there.'

Ginger stopped and looked down, his left shoe just an inch short of the soot. 'Dirty old sod.'

Oliver slid down the bench. 'Here you go, plenty of room at this end.'

Ginger nodded his appreciation. 'Thanks, I don't want that muck on my new Hush Puppies.'

Oliver glanced down at the pristine suede of Ginger Dalton's shoes. 'Is that what you call them?'

'Of course, really comfortable. You must have heard of them?'

Oliver shook his head.

'Been over here since about 1960.'

Oliver shrugged. 'Must have missed them.' He stood up and nodded to Ginger as he left. There was no need to stay, because now he knew where the police were watching Clarissa's house from.

Chapter 22
The Traps Are Set

As the clock approached six p.m., Fred leaned back from his paperwork and stretched. 'You fancy a pint, Toby?'

Toby glanced at the clock. 'Where you thinking?'

'How about the Garrick for a change.'

'Yeah, why not. Just got to finish my notes and I'll be with you.'

'What notes?'

'My observation notes. I've collated them all onto this diagram. I know who's going where and when. Every possible victim is being observed. The second that Oliver Lawrence makes a move, we'll have him.'

'If it is him,' cautioned Fred.

'It's him, I know it is.'

Fred scratched his head. 'Maybe, but best not to say it out loud. Let's just say, "our killer" for now. At least if we're wrong, we won't look like total pillocks.'

Fred had a point. 'Fair enough, boss. The traps are set, we just need him to take the bait.'

As they walked down Waterside, Toby glanced across at the theatre. 'What do you think William would have made of this?'

'Shakey?'

'What other William is there in this town?'

'I reckon he'd be amused.'

'Really?'

'Big time. Just imagine, you write a load of plays and then three hundred and fifty-six years after you die, some bugger's using one of your plots to knock folks off. Plagiarism, it's the sincerest form of flattery.'

Toby stared at Fred. 'Anyone ever told you that there is something not quite right about you, boss.'

'Son, if I had a pound for everyone that's told me that over the years, I'd probably have about eighty-four pounds.'

They reached the bottom of Sheep Street and turned right towards the Garrick.

They went to the little bar at the front but it was full.

'This way,' said Fred.

Toby followed Fred round to the other side of the bar that opened into the back room. He went straight up to the barman and ordered. Toby glanced around; in the far corner he spotted a familiar face. He tapped Fred on the shoulder. 'You'd better get another pint in, boss, Whomper's over there looking dehydrated.'

Fred turned and peered into the room; Whomper was indeed there. Clearly the allure of the Garrick was not irresistible.

Fred put down the tray and Whomper eyed the three pint glasses. 'One of those for me, gents?'

'Just the one, Whomper. What brings you here?'

'I could ask you both the same question.'

'I asked first,' said Fred curtly.

'You did,' admitted Whomper. 'Fate would be my answer. I was in here yesterday when a piece of information fell into my lap.'

Toby sat up straight. 'Is it to do with the case?'

'It is.'

'Well?'

'All in good time, I just need a sip first.' Whomper took a sip and half of his pint disappeared. He burped. 'Beg pardon, gents.'

'Come on, get on with it,' said Toby.

Whomper leaned back and waited for Fred and Toby's undivided attention. 'Very well. I was in here yesterday, standing at the bar. Who do you think was seated at the table next to me?'

'Just tell us, Whomper, we've had a long day and we don't want a quiz.'

'Sir Morris and Lady Oxford.'

Toby and Fred exchanged glances.

'What they were discussing was interesting, very interesting.' He took a second sip from his pint and the glass was miraculously empty.

Toby pushed his own untouched pint over to Whomper.

'Are you sure, DC Marlowe?'

'Just tell us what you heard, Whomper,' replied Toby.

'Well, where do I begin?'

'Try the beginning,' snapped Fred.

'We are a bit touchy today, gents, I'm only trying to help.'

Fred tilted his head menacingly to one side; Whomper got the message.

'They were having a bit of a tiff. Sir Morris told her that she couldn't act, it all got a bit heated.'

'What did they say?'

'They discussed Richard and his rising star. Sir Morris revealed he'd felt threatened by his talent.'

'And?'

'They more or less admitted that ruining Richard's career had been planned between them. She wanted out and Sir Morris wanted her. Seems like these two were capable of anything to protect their careers and reputations.'

Toby looked at Fred. 'If they could do that to Richard Jenkins, they could do it to Oliver Lawrence.'

Fred didn't look so sure. 'Couples can fall out of love, but can a mother actively plan to sabotage her own child's career? I'm not a parent but that sounds pretty mucked up to me.'

'Beatrice Smallman was a very ambitious young lady by all accounts. I think she is capable of anything.'

'You a psychologist now, Whomper?'

'I can be anything you want me to be.'

'How about quiet,' said Fred.

'I think Whomper's right, boss. Beatrice realises she's not going to make it and that Richard, though brilliant, likes a drink a bit too much and is fragile. Sir Morris, on the other hand, is already established, has money and a reputation. She could marry him and they'd become the power couple of British theatre. It makes sense.'

Fred shook his head. 'I can't believe a mother would do that to the father of her child, and then do the same to her own child, just to get on.'

'I can,' said Toby. 'That day when I went to Woodstock to interview her, she was chilling. I swear that woman has a heart filled with darkness, there is something of the night about her. I believe she is capable of doing anything to protect her position.'

'You got all that from one meeting?'

'I did, boss. If you'd been there, you would have to. Beatrice Oxford is bad to the bone.'

'I agree with Toby,' said Whomper.

Fred didn't look happy. 'Let's say I believe you both. How do we progress? We've already interviewed her at her home, and with Sir Morris in Stratford on at least two occasions. If we don't charge her with something, we are never going to be able to get her in for another interview.'

'Maybe the killer will knock her off and save you the trouble,' suggested Whomper.

Fred looked at Toby. 'You think that's likely?'

Toby paused for a moment before answering, he was trying to weigh up everything he knew against the character of the person he had interviewed in Woodstock. 'It's possible. If our killer is Oliver and his mother has betrayed him, who knows what he could do? We've all seen what he's capable of.'

The three men fell silent. The walls were slowly closing in and all they could do was wait. They had nothing except a theory. Fred broke the silence.

'How long's it been since Gerard Soames copped it?'

'About six weeks.'

'Maybe he's finished.'

'Do you believe that?' asked Toby.

Fred shook his head. 'No, our killer is very far from finished. He's building his masterpiece. I think you're right, Toby, the killer was following the plot of *Hamlet*, but who knows what will be next. He's using the Bard's plays as a backdrop to his revenge. He's enjoying himself, playing a part. The only problem is we won't know what part he's playing until the next victim dies.'

'He's got to get to them first,' said Toby. 'We've got eyes on every probable victim. If he makes a move, we'll have him.'

'What if it's someone you're not watching, what then?'

Fred looked at Toby. 'Yeah, what do we do then?'

'Reassess our list, that's all we can do.'

There was an air of helplessness that surrounded them, they knew they were prisoners of fate, waiting helplessly for something to happen.

'We could put the screws on Lady Oxford and Sir Morris, confront them with Whomper's information.'

'They would just deny it,' said Fred. He grinned. 'But while we are waiting, I can't see what harm it would do.'

They didn't have long to wait. Lizzie Birchwood was already in bed, and Oliver and Felix were sitting at the kitchen table in Trinity Street planning the evening ahead. The police had set their traps but Lizzie wasn't on their list.

Chapter 23
Where The Wild Thyme Blows

Oliver looked up at the clock. It was dark outside and he had been writing for at least three hours. Opposite him, Felix had fallen asleep in his chair. All this excitement had worn him out.

'Felix, wake up.'

Felix began to stir but then settled back into sleep.

Oliver moved closer. 'Wake up!'

Felix's eyes snapped open. He ran his hands over his face and stretched before looking from side to side. He focused on Oliver and sat up straight. 'Is it time?'

'The witching hour has been and gone, darkness has descended and soon, all of Stratford will be asleep.'

'It's definitely happening then.'

'Of course.'

Felix swallowed hard. 'Do you really think this is necessary. I keep replaying her screams of terror … I thought I would enjoy this, but Lizzie never plotted with Sir Morris to ruin you, why kill her?'

Oliver raised an eyebrow. 'She wasn't very nice to me, Felix, you know that. She made sexual advances.'

'Most young men would love that.'

'She undermined my acting and made me play characters that weren't real.'

'Of course she did, Oliver. She's a director, that's what they do. Sometimes they are inspired and other times they get it wrong. It's not a crime, there is no vengeance to be had here.'

Oliver looked at Felix sadly. 'You don't understand, do you? This isn't just about revenge, it's about clearing out all the dead wood so that we can make a fresh start. Lizzie has two seasons to go on her contract, imagine the stuff she could dream up in that time. There is also the problem that I don't think she would ever choose me.'

'You really believe you can make a return to Stratford, after all this time?'

'Of course I can. Nobody knows who I am, I can get myself an audition.'

'Without a CV? Good luck convincing Pierre Corridor of that.'

Oliver chuckled. 'Have faith, Felix. I already have the ear of Dame Suzy and she's promised to put in a good word for me. All I need is an audition. Once Pierre witnesses my Macbeth, he will be putty in my hands.'

'I'm not so sure, everything is cast for next year. There won't be a place for you.'

'Are you forgetting how many I've already killed and how many have yet to die? There's going to be plenty of opportunity.'

'When you put it like that, it's hard to disagree.' Felix sighed. 'Trying to talk you out of it is pointless, so let's push on. How are you planning to kill her?'

'I'm not exactly sure.'

'Don't you think you should be?'

Oliver bit his lip. 'In an ideal world, yes, but this is so far from ideal. She's sleeping in a room above a pub surrounded by other guests and staff. If I try to kill her there, it's going to be too risky.'

'Then how are you going to do it? Osmosis?'

'Now, now, Felix. This is no time for sarcasm. I do have a plan of sorts.'

'Which is?'

'I'm going to try and lure her outside.'

'How?'

'With the power of words and brilliant acting.'

Felix didn't look convinced. 'You don't have a plan, do you?'

Oliver shook his head. 'Nah, just going to have to make it up as I go along. Mind you, if she's taking those magic mushroom sleeping pills you planted in her room, I'll have a good chance. You coming along to watch?'

Felix smiled sadly. 'Yes, I fear I am. Promise me one thing?'

'What's that.'

'Don't hurt her.'

'I'm going to kill her, Felix. That usually hurts.'

'Then make it as painless as possible. Promise?'

Oliver looked at his friend. 'You're not enjoying this, are you?'

'I don't like Lizzie but I don't think she deserves to die; she isn't guilty of plotting with Sir Morris. This feels wrong.'

'Don't you see, this will help me kill the others. The police are watching everyone in Sir Morris' company that was around when I was ruined. When I kill Lizzie, it's going to throw them into total confusion. Nobody is watching her, they don't think she's at risk. It really is quite beautiful in its simplicity.'

'Man, that's cold.'

'Listen, Felix, this is about more than just revenge and a fresh start. This is about me getting back on the stage … becoming the star I should have been. Nothing, and I do mean nothing, is going to get in the way of that happening.'

Thirty minutes later, Oliver was in position in the car park behind the Windmill pub. He'd told Felix to hide behind the wall in Hall's Croft, ensuring he was too far away to try and stop what was about to occur.

Oliver looked towards Lizzie's bedroom window. The whole pub was in darkness. He glanced at his watch: two forty-four a.m. He had another two hours, maximum, before the first rays of daylight would illuminate his presence. He took a deep breath and pressed the send button on his walkie-talkie.

Lizzie Birchwood lay in a deep sleep. She had taken the sleeping tablets Felix had planted, and her dreams were wild and deep.

'Awaken, Lizzie Birchwood,
awaken from your sleep.
The creatures of the night,
your company do seek.'

The words came wafting through the airbrick and into Lizzie's bedroom, descending like a silken web in which they would trap her. She twitched and turned over. She was deep in sleep; flying through endless clouds of purple custard, while seated on a pogo stick.

'In darkest night,
what dreams may come,
their shadowed presence
seen by none.'

From somewhere deep in her subconscious, Lizzie began to stir. She had heard the words as if submerged in deep water; she fought to resurface from her drug- and brandy-fuelled slumber. It was that voice again; warm, insistent yet menacing. Her eyes opened and the dark room slowly swam into focus.

'My words will find you
and dreams subside,
leave just a memory
of a life denied.'

Lizzie was awake now, hearing every word as it floated into the room. She was still drowsy but able to understand. The voice was beautiful but oh so cold. There was a terrible deathless quality hidden behind those liquid tones. She thought back to the last line

– *a life denied* – and instinctively knew that whatever it meant, she wasn't going to like it. Before she could rise from her bed, the voice returned.

'Lizzie Birchwood, Lizzie Birchwood,
we wait for you in moonlight.
We creatures of delight,
let us take you from the shadows,
come dance with us tonight.'

Oliver prepared himself. Not only was he trying to frighten Lizzie, he also had to draw her from the safety of her room and out into the night. His tone and delivery really were quite masterful. If he were Lizzie, he would be climbing out of the window already.
The window of her room slowly creaked open and Lizzie leaned out into the terminal night. 'Who's there, what do you want?'
Oliver stayed in the shadows but spoke again. 'This is just a dream, Lizzie. A midsummer night's dream. Come with me.'

'I know a bank where the wild thyme blows,
Where oxlips and the nodding violet grows.'

'*A Midsummer Night's Dream*,' said Lizzie. A smile softened her features, erasing the worry that had creased her brow.

'What angel wakes me from my flow'ry bed?'

Oliver looked over to Felix and gave him a thumbs up. Lizzie Birchwood, in her sleep-deprived, drugged state, was being drawn into the world that Oliver was creating. The two double brandies she had each evening, plus the doctored sleeping pills, were doing their job. He turned back towards Lizzie and spoke once more.

'I have had a most rare vision.

I have had a dream
past the wit of man to say what dream it was.'

Lizzie rubbed her eyes and leaned further out of the window. Oliver smiled. She was becoming enraptured by these words she knew so well.

'The eye of man hath not heard,
The ear of man hath not seen,
A man's hand is not able to taste,
His tongue to conceive,
Nor his heart to report,
What my dream was.'

Oliver pushed the walkie-talkie into his back pocket and stepped out of the shadows. He had a halo of golden flowers upon his head and they sparkled in the light of the moon that shone above him; the Hunter's Moon. He made a striking figure and Lizzie's mouth fell open when she saw him.
'Oberon?'
Oliver bristled. His words were from Oberon, Puck and Bottom.
'Yes, dear Lizzie, I am Oberon and everyone.'
'You are!'

Oliver's woven dream was drawing her into his web of deceit. He moved beneath her window and looked up at her, holding out his arms beseechingly.

'If we shadows have offended,
think but this, and all is mended,
that you have but slumbered here,
while these visons did appear.'

'Will you come with me, Lizzie, to the bank where the wild thyme

blows.'
She nodded. 'I'll follow thee and make a heaven of hell.'

As Lizzie disappeared from view, Oliver looked over at Felix. 'Do you think she bought it?' The clicking of the back door gave him his answer. It opened and Lizzie peered out into the moonlight. He smiled at Felix in triumph. '"Lord what fools these mortals be."'

'If she had continued, spoken the next line—'

'"To die upon the hand I love so well,"' said Oliver.

'Yes, if only she had carried on, she may have realised, been more cautious.'

'Come on, Felix. You know it's far too late for that.'

Lizzie stepped out into the backyard of the Windmill and Oliver moved towards her like a panther, flowing across the ground between them; his movement liquid and rapid. As he reached her, he dropped to one knee. 'Dear sweet, Helena, let me take you to where the oxlips grow, and there will be your true love.'

Oliver was using the fact that Lizzie was tired, drugged and confused against her. It had seemed outrageous at first, the idea that he could ever draw her into this fantasy, but it was working. Lizzie's knowledge of *A Midsummer Night's Dream* would be her downfall. She was embracing the role he had cast her in, sure that he would lead Helena to her true love, Lysander. If only she knew where that would lead …

Lizzie reached out her hand and he took it tenderly.

'Will you come with me?'

'I will.'

Oliver stood. 'Let us go to the river and hear the current sing its lullaby.'

He led her across the car park and down the alleyway that emerged onto Southern Street. He paused and looked both ways, checking for police. The street was empty so he urged her forward. 'Come, we must make haste before the dawn's light disrupts the enchantment of the moon.'

'Yes,' said Lizzie. 'Where are we going?'

'"I know a place where the wild thyme blows."'

'"Where the oxlips and the nodding violet grows,"' whispered Lizzie.

Oliver smiled at her. 'You have it, you understand.'

He led Lizzie into the park and moved into the shadows of the trees that sheltered it from the quiet lane. They moved silently, swiftly, deeper into the dark recesses, moving inexorably towards the river.

Oliver looked back as they walked. Felix had voiced mixed feelings about the murders so far, yet he still hadn't heeded Oliver's warnings to stay away. They were bound by more than years now; they were bound by blood. Felix would always be drawn to him, horrified and thrilled by the performance he was witnessing. When Oliver turned it on, he could charm the very stone of Shakespeare's statue to life.

Oliver and Lizzie made their way towards the hollow where the wall that marked the graveyard of Holy Trinity ran atop a high grass bank. Down to the left, within yards of the river, there were steps that climbed the bank and led to a small gateway through the wall into the graveyard.

On the other side was the bench where Oliver had stabbed Desmond Tharpe and then, just a day later, convinced Desmond's daughter, Tabitha, to throw herself into the river. This was familiar ground; his killing ground. Oliver felt a surge of elation swell within him. The desire to kill was strong, anything and everything that had thwarted him must die. He was about to break into a jog when he saw something that made him stand stock still: a beam of light illuminated the gateway.

For a moment he was confused and then he saw someone carrying a torch. He grabbed Lizzie's arm and gently placed his finger on her lips. 'Be quiet,' he whispered. 'There are devils that walk the night, we must hide.'

In her confused state, Lizzie did not resist him as he dragged her towards the trees. They took shelter behind the branches as the figure walked down into the hollow. He paused and played his torch back towards the gateway to the graveyard, as if nervous that he was being followed by the dead.

In the glow of the torch, Oliver could see that its owner was wearing a pointed helmet. The police! He looked over his shoulder and saw Felix crouching down in some bushes. He looked again at Lizzie. 'We must be quiet.' He needn't have worried. Lizzie's eyes were now wide with wonder and excitement, she wasn't sure if this was real or a dream, *A Midsummer Night's Dream.* She nodded and crouched down a little further.

The policeman made his way up the bank, emerging from the hollow twenty yards from where they were hiding. He looked to the left towards Southern Lane and then turned and followed the path that hugged the bank and led to the back of the theatre. As he passed by, he muttered under his breath, 'This place gives me the bloody creeps.'

He walked away slowly, casting the light of his torch into every dark corner, lest any of the creatures that inhabit the night were creeping up on him. Oliver had been saved by an ancient fear of the dark, one that had inhabited man's mind since the beginning of evolution. The policeman should have walked all the paths.

Oliver watched him go, realising that, had he been just ten seconds earlier, he would have walked straight into the officer at the gateway into Holy Trinity's graveyard. It had been close, too close. The desire to go through the gate and into the graveyard deserted him. He had no time to put on a show, he needed to end this and end it now.

'Come, we must go.' He pulled Lizzie up roughly and led her back towards Southern Lane.

Lizzie resisted. 'But the river, the place where the wild thyme blows.'

Oliver stopped and looked at her. All pretence now gone from his voice, his words cold with finality. 'There is no place "where the wild thyme blows". It was all deceit, Lizzie, a pretence to get you to come with me. This is not a dream.'

Lizzie looked at him, confusion covering her face. 'But Lysander?'

He let out a harsh laugh. 'Is just a character in a play.' He waved his hand at their shadowy surroundings. 'This is real.'

Felix watched from the bushes, every muscle in his body tense. The moment was approaching, he could feel it. Above them an owl hooted; its voice rippled through the trees like a warning that had come too late.

Lizzie shook her head. 'What are we doing here?'

Oliver moved towards her so that their faces were just inches apart. 'Do you know who I am?'

Lizzie peered at him, she seemed confused.

'Look closely, cast your mind back over fifteen years.'

She shook her head. 'I don't know you.'

'*Romeo and Juliet*, sixteen years ago on that very stage,' he pointed towards the theatre. 'Tabitha Tharpe was my Juliet,' Oliver waited for his words to register, when Lizzie did not respond he added another clue. 'The lesbian Juliet …'

The only sounds from the shadows of the trees was the plaintiff call of the owl and the gurgling of the Avon as it fell across the weir. Lizzie swayed slightly. Oliver could see her confusion slip away, as slowly, very slowly, the memories spilled out of the dark recesses of her mind. He gazed deeply into her eyes and, like a safe-breaker hearing the tumblers drop into place, he saw the memories coalesce in her mind and translate into words.

'Oliver?'

'Yes.'

She didn't run, just stood there, staring at him. 'We thought you were dead.'

'Thought or wished?'

Lizzie shook her head. 'No, none of us wished you dead, Oliver. You were loved.'

He snorted derisively. 'Really, no one looked very hard to find me. Seems like I was forgotten after just a few weeks. An awkward memory, his father's son!' There was a harsh bitterness in his voice. He grabbed Lizzie by her arms. 'Do you know why I am here, why I have brought you to this place?'

Lizzie shook her head. When she spoke, her voice trembled; finally, she was afraid. 'No.'

'You betrayed me, Lizzie. You forced me to do terrible things. Take something beautiful and turn it into a joke, a sick pastiche of what it should have been. *The Tempest* on Mars, Juliet a lesbian. What the hell were you thinking?'

'I'm a director, we interpret the text, we visualise modern adaptations, give a relevance to the modern world.'

'Agincourt with flamethrowers? Don't make me laugh.'

The penny had finally dropped with poor Lizzie Birchwood. The fog of sleep, too much brandy and doctored sleeping pills had lifted; she knew that Oliver was the killer.

'Why would you want to hurt me, Oliver? I gave you leading roles, I made you a star.'

'I made myself a star,' he snapped. 'I ignored your direction to play Romeo as a simpering fool and let his frailty show. I made that show work despite you, not because of you.'

His words hot with anger, he pushed her away in disgust and Lizzie, now free, didn't hesitate. She ran like the devil was behind her, and he was. Oliver cursed and went after her but she was surprisingly fast. As she sprinted towards the perimeter wall of the park, she would have two choices: left towards the gateway that came out near the entrance to Holy Trinity, or right towards the entrance by The Other Place. Both were too far; Oliver would catch her.

Between the two gateways was a passage, open to the sky but hemmed in by walls that rose as you descended the slope. She was heading for the steps. There was a tunnel that ran under Southern Lane and she could lose him in the gardens beyond. She fled down the path and he followed, the sharp edges of the ridged stone drawing blood from her bare feet. She reached the bottom ahead of him and turned left under the road. There was a gate; he couldn't let her get away.

She reached the gate first and pulled it but it held fast. Oliver was gaining on her. She let go of the handle and turned, her back pressed up against the cold stone wall that would become her tomb. He walked slowly towards her, relishing the moment. The fifteen wasted years were almost worth it just to see the terror on her face. Oliver stopped two feet away from her. He took some leather gloves from his pocket and slowly began to pull them on.

'I'm sorry it had to end like this, Lizzie, but I'm cleaning house. Getting rid of the dead wood. Preparing for greatness.'

'You're mad.'

Oliver shrugged. 'I prefer misunderstood.'

'What are you going to do?'

'Oh, Lizzie, you know what I am going to do.'

'Don't kill me, let me live just one more night.'

'Why would I do that when you betrayed me.'

'I never betrayed you. Never.'

With lightning speed, Oliver shot both hands up and grasped her firmly around the throat. He squeezed hard. Lizzie struggled, her hands and nails digging into his arms, but Oliver had prepared. His tweed jacket was thick and her nails could not penetrate the material. He watched as her eyes bulged and her lips darkened as the purple pallor overtook them. He saw the realisation of death in those windows to her soul.

He felt the grip on his arms slowly loosen as he leaned forward and whispered in her ear, 'There is no place where the wild thyme blows, there is no place where the oxlips and the nodding violet grows. There is just darkness, where you must go.'

Chapter 24
Act Two

Julia Bouquet was breathing hard; this running lark wasn't as much fun as it looked on TV. Since separating from her husband, the landlord at the Dirty Duck, she had decided to get fit. When Dick next saw her, she wanted him to see what he was missing. With all the murders recently, she had given up on her morning runs; she didn't want to be mistaken for an actor. But they seemed to have stopped, nothing for over six weeks, and she, like most of the population of Stratford, hoped that it was all over.

She jogged along the riverbank, past the theatre and over the footbridge to the boathouse. When she reached the other bank, she turned right and headed down towards the bandstand, on to Lucy's Lock and back again. As she passed the Chain Ferry, she took the path away from the river. Up ahead she saw someone crouching down, his shoulders heaving. He was being sick. There was a boxer dog on a lead clutched in his right hand; she recognised the dog, it was Chris. But if that was Chris, the man throwing up had to be …

The man looked up, wiping his mouth with the back of his hand.

'Dick?'

He held up his hand. 'Stay back, Julia, you don't want to see this.' He was pale, his skin almost translucent.

'See what?'

He pointed to the wall behind him. 'It's started again.'

'What's started?'

'The killing, there's a body in the passage.'

'You're kidding?'

Dick got slowly to his feet; he looked shaken. 'Do I look like

I'm kidding?'

Julia moved towards the wall. Dick watched her without a word; he never could get Julia to do what he wanted. He sighed and stepped towards her, he couldn't ask her do this alone.

There was the body of a woman crumpled at the foot of the slope. She was propped in a sitting position where the angle of the wall met the gate … and she was dead. Very dead.

'Oh, my God.'

'I told you not to look.'

'No, I know who it is.'

Dick turned to face her. 'Who?'

'Lizzie Birchwood, the director.'

Dick couldn't believe what he was hearing; Lizzie Birchwood was one of his customers. He steeled himself and looked down. The sight before him was as terrible as it had been two minutes ago. Lizzie's eyes were bulging, her lips purple and distended. Her tongue lolled out from the corner of her mouth. She had been a good-looking woman, but her death, and the nature of it, had robbed her face of those good looks. Now it was a twisted parody; a mask of death. Julia was right. Now he looked, really looked, he could see that it was Lizzie. An uncharitable thought passed through his mind: had she paid her bar bill? He dismissed it, he was better than that.

'I'm right, aren't l,' said Julia, seemingly unfazed by what she was witnessing.

'Yes, you're always right.' Dick turned away; he couldn't look at poor Lizzie any longer.

'Looks like our killer is back off his holidays.'

It was a poor joke and Dick looked at Julia disapprovingly. 'That's a dead woman right there, how can you make jokes about it?'

She shrugged. 'It wasn't really a joke, more an observation.'

Dick nodded. Julia never had been an overly sensitive person, maybe those years working in her father's abattoir had desensitised her.

'Have you called the police?'

Dick shook his head. 'I've been a bit busy throwing up.' He wiped his mouth with the back of his hand. 'I'll call from the pub, you stay here and don't let anyone go down there.'

'Why not?'

'It's a crime scene, Julia.'

She nodded. 'Oh, OK. You won't be long, will you? I'm having coffee with Samantha this morning.' Dick walked briskly away shaking his head.

'Who's that?'

'Who's what?' asked Dick, turning back to Julia.

'That bloke up there by the trees.' Julia nodded discreetly in his direction. 'I think he's watching us.'

Dick turned slowly and, as he pretended to go back over to the wall to look down at Lizzie's body, he glanced furtively over towards the trees. There was a man there. He turned back to Julia. 'I think you're right.'

'Don't they say killers always return to the scene of their crime?'

'No, the killer will be long gone, but we still need to call the police.'

Julia shook her head. 'You can't leave me here with a killer in the trees.'

'We don't know he's the killer.'

'You want to take that chance?'

Dick smiled. 'I'm game if you are.'

'You can sod right off, Dick Mayrick.' She looked back towards the trees but the man had gone.

'I'd better go and call the police,' said Dick, and headed back towards the Dirty Duck.

It was the call that they had all feared. Sergeant Frank Whittall took it.

'There's been another murder.' The voice was clearly agitated but trying to stay calm. Frank felt his gut drop like a broken lift; they had all been dreading this moment.

'Can you give me some details, please.'

'Yes, you know the tunnel under Southern Lane, the one that comes from the park?'

'Yes.'

'There's the body of a woman down there, leaning on the gate that leads under the road.'

'Are you sure she's dead?' asked Frank, as he rapidly scribbled down the information.

'She's dead, been strangled.'

'How can you be sure?'

'I can't, but her tongue's hanging out, her face is blue and there are bruises around her neck.'

'You haven't touched the body, have you, sir?'

Dick shuddered. 'No, I couldn't face it. I've left someone there to make sure nobody goes near.'

That concerned Frank: they couldn't afford to have the scene tampered with. 'Could I ask you to get back there, sir, we can't have anyone touching her until SOCO arrive.'

'Don't worry, officer, nobody will get past Julia.'

'Could I take your name, sir?'

'Dick Mayrick.'

'The landlord at the Dirty Duck?'

'Yes. That you, Frank?'

'Yes, it is, Dick,' he paused for a moment. 'I thought you and Julia had split up.'

'We have, I'd just found the body when Julia found me, she was out on a run.'

Frank nodded to himself. If Julia was getting fit she had to be having an affair. On the upside, if Julia was guarding the crime scene, Dick was right; nobody would get past her.

'OK, Dick, can you get back there now and I will get a car

there straight away?'

'No problem, Frank, on my way.'

Frank hurried into the office. Fred and Toby were having a chat over a cup of tea and staring at the incident board. They turned to greet him, but the look on his face stifled their greetings.

'It's started again, hasn't it?' said Toby.

Frank nodded. 'Body of a woman at the bottom of the passageway that goes under Southern Lane.'

Fred slammed down his cup and headed for the door, grabbing the keys to his Cortina from his desk. 'Call SOCO and get Alf Butcher down there.' He stopped for a moment at the door. 'Call Inspector Beeching, let him know what's going on. I want four uniforms down there now. They need to close Southern Lane from Old Town, and I want the park closed from the back of the theatre all the way to the graveyard wall at Holy Trinity. Get hold of Kinky and Ginger and get them down there as soon as you can.'

'Will do, Fred.'

Frank watched Toby and Fred charge down the stairs and out onto the car park. As they ran to the car, he turned back towards his desk; he had a lot of calls to make. He dialled up the number for SOCO just as Fred's car tore from the car park. Things were about to get intense.

Chapter 25
Why?

Fred screeched to a halt, leaving his car angled across the road so no other vehicle could pass. Toby was out and running before he turned off the ignition. He ran through the entrance and in just a few yards he could see Dick Mayrick standing there with a woman he didn't recognise.

'Morning, Dick.'

Dick nodded, he looked pale. 'Morning, Toby.'

'She down there?' Toby nodded towards the gateway that led to the tunnel.

'Yeah,' he hesitated. 'It's Lizzie Birchwood.'

Toby stopped in his tracks. 'Are you sure?'

'I'm sure.' He glanced at the woman. 'We both know … knew her.'

Toby tried to absorb this information. Lizzie Birchwood wasn't on their list of people to watch. He walked up to the wall, took a deep breath and looked down: it was Lizzie. She was propped up in a sitting position, her arms and legs splayed out like a discarded rag doll. How had he missed this?

Fred arrived at his side, panting. 'Jesus!' He stared down at Lizzie's crumpled body. 'She wasn't on the list.'

Toby nodded. 'I know. How do we explain this?'

Fred chewed his lip before slowly shaking his head. 'I can't, she's not in the picture. She's never been linked to Sir Morris and his merry band.'

'So why is she dead then?'

The two detectives looked at each other. Their whole theory had been thrown into the bin with this murder.

Fifteen minutes later, Southern Lane and the park had been closed to the public. Toby looked anxiously towards Waterside, waiting for SOCO to arrive. Today was going horribly wrong.

Fred called him over. 'Toby, take a look at this.'

Fred was leaning over the wall, looking down at Lizzie Birchwood's body. 'Why is she wearing her nightclothes? What on earth brought her out here in the middle of the night?'

'I know, I've been wondering that. There doesn't appear to be anything wrong with her.'

'Apart from the fact she's dead, you mean,' said Fred.

'No, even from here it's obvious she was strangled but look at her wrists. There are no marks on them to indicate she was tied up. There's no bruising to her face. If she was forced here, I can't see how.'

'I hear you but that's a big call. Let's wait until SOCO and Alf Butcher get here.'

'Do you know who's coming?'

'Christine and Simon. I asked for then specifically.'

Toby nodded with relief. They were the best SOCO team in Warwickshire and they had worked on all of the murders in this case.

Fred stood up and stepped back from the wall. 'You still think it's Oliver Lawrence?'

'Yeah, I do.'

'But Lizzie Birchwood wasn't around Sir Morris and the company when Oliver was sacked. It doesn't fit with the revenge theory.'

'Maybe it's not just revenge any more,' said Toby. 'It may have started out that way but what if he is expanding his plan to people he has clashed with in the past, settling all his old scores?'

Fred thought about it for a moment. 'I don't like the sound of that. If he's going to go after everyone he's fallen out with, we're going to need a new list, a bigger list. Imagine if I decided to kill everyone I had ever argued with!'

Toby couldn't imagine it. Most of the Warwickshire police force would be dead and about twenty per cent of the population of Stratford too.

'This doesn't change anything, boss. All the people we thought were at risk are still at risk, only now we have to start looking at any professional disagreements he had.'

Fred nodded in the direction of Lizzie Birchwood's body. 'What about her?'

'They worked together. Oliver was Romeo in one of her first big hits, the year before everything went wrong for him. I'm going to need to speak to some members of the cast to see if there were any problems behind the scenes.'

Fred pulled a face. 'They're a bunch of luvvies, of course there were problems behind the scenes.'

When SOCO arrived, Toby left Fred to brief them and went over to interview Dick Mayrick and his estranged wife. He knew Dick a little, he often popped into the Dirty Duck after work. They were standing together chatting; for a separated couple they seemed pretty friendly. As he approached, they turned to him.

'This is a bad do, Toby,' said Dick. The colour was returning to his cheeks now.

'Yes, it's awful,' Toby took out his notebook. 'Can you tell who found her?'

'It was me,' said Dick. 'It must have been about ten past eight. I usually take Chris out for a walk before breakfast. I'd been round the church and come through the riverside gate from the graveyard into the park. Chris is getting on a bit now so I don't go too far.'

'Chris?'

'That's the dog.'

'Unusual name for a dog,' said Toby.

'I named him after an old mate of mine,' said Dick.

Toby decided not to dig into that one any further. 'So how did you find the body?'

'That was Chris. As we walked up the path, he went to the gate at the top of the passage and started to bark. I called him but he wouldn't come, so I went to fetch him and I saw her.' He started to go pale.

'And you didn't go down the passage to get a closer look?'

Dick's features wrinkled up in revulsion. 'God, no. I could see Lizzie was dead from the gate.'

'Lizzie? You knew the victim?'

Dick nodded. 'I did, she was a regular. Most of the actors and staff at the RSC tend to come into the pub at some time or other.'

Toby knew that was true. He had seen the after-show dash down Southern Lane by thirsty actors many times. He had been surprised by just how quickly some of them could move.

He turned to Dick's wife. 'Can I ask your name, please?'

'Julia.'

'Julia what?'

She glanced at Dick. 'Bouquet,' she answered.

Toby noticed she sounded a little terse. 'Can I take it that you two are happily married?'

'Do I look happy,' snapped Julia.

Dick grinned. 'I am.'

This interview was getting away from him. 'Can I ask you what you saw please, Mrs Mayrick?'

'It's Bouquet, just call me Julia.'

'Very well. Can you tell me what you saw, Julia?'

'I was on my morning run.'

'You do that most mornings?'

'I did before all these murders started. I only started back today, I thought it was all over.'

'And what did you see?'

Julia nodded towards Dick. 'Him. On all fours, chundering. Always did have a weak constitution.'

'Did you see anything else suspicious?'

'What, apart from the body?'

'Yes.'

'No, just the usual suspects. Dog walkers, joggers. Postmen who can't afford long trousers. Oh, and there was a man in the trees, watching.'

'Are you sure?'

'Yes, I saw him too,' agreed Dick. 'Standing in the shadow of the trees, just watching. Dead creepy.'

'Did you speak to him?' asked Toby, trying to keep the excitement out of his voice.

'No. I think he realised we had seen him and he disappeared into the shadows.'

'He was a big bloke, at least six foot and he looked like a rugby player, powerful,' said Julia.

'I'm a rugby player,' said Dick.

'He was nothing like you,' said Julia dismissively.

'I'm going to need to take a statement from both of you and I'm going to ask you to try and describe him to one of our artists.'

'His face was in shadow.'

'Doesn't matter, just give us as much as you can, it's more than we've got now.'

'I can't hang around for an artist, I've got things to do.'

'I'm sorry, Mrs Mayrick?'

'It's Julia Bouquet,' she snapped. 'I'm using my maiden name these days.'

'There's a dead woman over there and we need to catch her killer so your social life is just going to have to wait for a little, do you understand?'

Julia narrowed her eyes and nodded resentfully.

Toby continued. 'Did either of you go down the passage to the body?'

They both shook their heads. 'We knew she was dead, so we didn't want to mess with the scene.'

'Thank you, that was very helpful. I'm going to get a plain-clothed police officer to come and take a full statement from you in a few minutes.

'How long will that take? I'm doing an early lunch with a couple of girlfriends at eleven thirty,' said Julia.

'I'm sorry if you are delayed a little, Mrs—'

'Julia,' she snapped.

'Sorry, Julia. But we are investigating a murder.'

'Well, I didn't bloody kill her.'

Dick and Toby's eyes met; they understood instantly that appeasement was the best policy. Before Toby could go any further, Fred came to his rescue.

'Have you got a moment? Alf Butcher's here and he's got a couple of interesting observations.'

Toby nodded and turned back to the happy couple. 'If you could both just wait here for a few minutes, I'll get an officer to come and take your details.'

'Make it quick, please, officer. I'm still in my running gear.'

Toby gave Julia a sickly grin and headed back to the scene of the crime. Alf was in the passage crouching by the body. When Toby appeared at the top of the passage, he beckoned him down.

'Morning, Toby, we can't go on meeting like this. It's about time our killer found a different venue. This is the third one in this little corner of Eden.'

'Four if you count the one by the bandstand,' said Fred.

'Better arrest the park keeper then,' said Alf, winking as he did so.

He pulled back Lizzie Birchwood's left foot. 'There's a bit of rigor here so she's probably been dead for at least two to three hours, that's going to put death at about five a.m., maybe four. I'll take the temperatures and that should confirm it. My guess is about four a.m. It's starting to get light by five and our killer wouldn't have wanted to put himself on display in the daylight. Not his MO at all.'

Toby nodded. 'That makes sense, Alf. Got any theories you

want to share?'

Alf looked down at Lizzie's body and then gazed up the slope of the passage.

'I think she was lured here, from her bed.'

'Lured?'

Alf nodded. 'I know, sounds crazy doesn't it? But she's wearing pyjamas and she's got nothing on her feet. Her attire would suggest a kidnapping but there are no signs of a struggle. She hasn't been tied, punched or dragged. So how does she arrive here, in the middle of the night?'

Alf had a point. Toby turned to Fred. 'Do we know where Lizzie was staying?'

'No, I can find out though. I'll send one of the lads to the theatre, they'll have her address.'

Toby was staring at Lizzie again. What if Alf was right and someone had lured her from her bed? Charmed her into the night with promises, and then killed her. Oliver Lawrence could. He was a great actor, capable of portraying huge emotional depth. He could do it with that silken voice of his. But, if he had, why?

Just three hundred yards away, Phil Townsend knocked on the door of Lizzie Birchwood's room. The door wasn't even on the latch; it was ajar. He stood and watched the door slowly swing wide. When it stopped, he could see Lizzie's bed was empty.

He went back onto the landing and called out her name. Quietly to begin with, and then, sensing something was amiss, louder. There was no answer. He ran down the stairs and into the kitchen. She wasn't there. This wasn't right; Lizzie wasn't an early riser and she had specifically asked for a full English at nine-thirty. As he pondered what to do next, he heard a police siren come rapidly down Church Road. There was a squeal of tyres as the car turned a corner and drove down towards Holy Trinity. He had a horrible feeling that something was wrong, very wrong.

Chapter 26
Old Dog, New Tricks

Felix Richards sat in the cabin of his boat; it was rocking gently as the Avon floated past on its way to meet the River Severn at Tewkesbury. The events of the morning had shaken him. He knew Oliver was a great actor, but to witness the way he had charmed Lizzie Birchwood from her bed and out into the night … It had been beguiling. On the table before him, he had his journal open at a fresh page, he titled it:

Entry 2
Lizzie Birchwood

Lizzie Birchwood is dead, she died in the early hours of this morning. Summoned from her sleep by Oliver. First, he shocked her with his own words, then he wooed with Shakespeare's verse. Had I not witnessed it, I would never have believed it. He spoke with the voice of an angel, his warm inviting tones appealing to her every desire. She came to the window and, like Oberon, he stood before her in the moonlight.

'I know a bank where the wild thyme blows.
Where the oxlips and the nodding violet grows.'

His words spilled like the golden threads of a spider's web, drawing her into the dream he was creating. It was as if he were hypnotising her. I watched from the safety of Hall's Croft, peering over the wall as he worked his dark magic. He was the flame, and she the moth. I could have stopped it, I should have stopped it but, like Lizzie, I too was beguiled. I followed, unable to look away from the scene he was creating, a silent scream ringing in my head. A warning on my lips that I would never issue. Lizzie was doomed and all I could do was watch.

We followed the path around the back of the theatre and out across Southern Street. As they moved through the shadows of the park a light appeared from the graveyard, coming through the gateway in the wall. Oliver froze for a moment and then dragged Lizzie into the undergrowth as I dove into the hedgerow. The light came from a policeman's torch, the beam passed through the bushes in which I was hiding, but he failed to spot me. I held my breath as he walked away. If Oliver had been ten seconds earlier, he and Lizzie would have walked right into him as he came through the gate. It had been close. On such moments of fate hang a man's destiny.

Slowly, Lizzie had begun to realise that this was no dream and she ran for her life. She may have made it too, but the fates were not with her. She ran down the passageway that goes under Southern Lane. If the gate had opened, she could have escaped into the gardens beyond and been free …but the gate was locked, there was no escape. I crept to the edge of the wall and watched as Oliver opened the gate at the top of the passage. His athletic frame just a dark shadow in the moonlight, blocking all means of escape. He smiled like a wolf that had cornered its prey and slowly descended the slope that led to the tunnel entrance where she stood, trapped. He paused and pulled on some gloves; only then did I realise how he was going to kill poor Lizzie.

'Let me live one more night, she pleaded. That made Oliver smile. Desdemona to Othello, just the way he had wanted. I can't bring myself to describe the rest, it was revolting … and yet, I witnessed it all. I watched as the last remnants of life drained from her body. I listened as he wove his twisted verse.

'There is no place where the wild thyme blows,
There is no place where the oxlips and the nodding violet grows,
There is just darkness, where you must go.'

He let her body fall from his hands and stood over her for several seconds, gazing on the dreadful sculpture he had created. When he finally looked up,

he smiled. 'Did you hear her, Felix? She begged me for one more night."
I nodded. 'She did.'

I turned and walked away, ignoring his calls. I had seen enough for one night. Oliver had been magnificent, terrible, malignant. There was no beauty in that death because there was no revenge. Lizzie Birchwood did not deserve to die. The monster I have created is now beyond my control and I am beyond help.

Felix put down his pen and gazed down the river towards Stratford. Old Town would be swarming with police and press by now. All looking for clues and evidence that would one day bring them to his door.

Chapter 27
Beeching Goes Ballistic

The incident room at Guild Street nick was a hive of activity. The return of the killer, while expected, had shocked everyone and killed the tiny flame of hope that had flickered across those brief few weeks.

'Gather round, everyone.' Fred was standing beside the incident board. He held up a picture of an attractive woman in her forties. 'This is Lizzie Birchwood. Last night, she became victim number five of our murderer.' A loud murmur of voices flowed around the room. Fred pinned her photo up on the incident board and turned back to the assembled squad. 'Her name may be unfamiliar to you, she wasn't on our watch list, in fact, she has never worked with Sir Morris and his company.'

'What does that mean then, sir?' asked Kinky Berstein, looking as confused as the rest of the squad. 'I thought it was just actors and journalists who had contributed to Sir Morris. The ones that helped destroy Lawrence's career.'

Toby stepped forward. 'Lizzie Birchwood did work with Oliver in 1956, the year before his breakdown, so there is a connection.'

'*Romeo and Juliet*, wasn't it?'

'That's right, Ginger.'

'But that was critically acclaimed.'

'It was, but Oliver and Lizzie famously clashed. She wanted him to play Romeo as an angry young man who discovered his true love was actually a lesbian.'

Ginger nodded. 'Yeah, I can see how that would be disappointing.'

There were a few chuckles from the gathered murder squad.

Toby held up a hand to quiet the room. 'Surely Oliver would have no reason to kill her if she helped to make him a star. It doesn't make sense.'

Kinky looked around the assembled squad. 'Am I the only one beginning to wonder if Oliver Lawrence might not be our man?'

'No, Oliver Lawrence is still our man,' said Toby. 'But now we have to consider that it's not just Sir Morris and his company that he is going after. He's going after anyone he has a grievance against.'

'Basically,' said Fred, 'I think our boy has just got a bit kill happy, I've seen it before. Get away with it a couple of times and they get the taste for it, think it's easy.'

'So you think it's the same madman, only a bit madder.'

The room went silent for a moment. The idea that the killer of four, now five, innocent theatre people had taken a darker turn was not a comforting one.

Toby looked at Fred. 'If you're right we are going to have to increase our surveillance to anyone who ever worked with Oliver Lawrence.'

'Yes, I think we will. We can't rule out anyone who had contact with him during his career at Stratford.'

'How do we find that out?'

Fred sighed. 'We're going to have to interview everyone who is linked to the theatre and was working here during the three seasons Oliver was performing.'

'That could double the size of our list. How are we supposed to watch that many people with the team we have?'

'That I haven't worked out, it may mean bringing in some more bodies from Coventry.'

There was a deep sigh from the gathered officers; the idea of the Coventry force flooding the streets of their town was not appealing.

Fred held up a hand. 'I know, I don't want them here either.

It's our case and we want to solve it ourselves but we can't risk more victims because we don't want head office plods on our patch. We don't have a choice.'

They all knew that Fred was right, even if they didn't like it.

'I'll speak to Mel Townsend,' said Toby.

'I bet you will,' said Fred, unable to disguise the disappointment in his voice.

Toby glanced at him. 'Would you like to do it, boss?'

'No, Toby, I think that's a job for you now.'

Fred turned back to the assembled officers. 'The murder of Lizzie Birchwood will throw an even bigger spotlight on the town. For a few weeks we have faded down the news agenda. After last night, everything's going to change. Fleet Street will put us back on the front page and folks in town are going to be scared. We have a killer on our streets and we're no nearer to catching him now than we were two months ago. Inspector Beeching is on the way in. He'll be on the warpath. All I ask of you is that you keep to the plan, follow the leads and try to look like you know what you're doing. Watch everyone, question everyone and follow every lead. Sooner or later his luck will run out, we need to be there when it does.'

There was a screech of tyres from the car park and Toby glanced out to see Beeching's car come skidding to a halt. 'Looks like Beeching's heard the news.'

Fred sighed. 'Buckle up, boys and girls, the ride's about to get a bit bumpy.'

Twenty seconds later, Inspector Beeching burst into the incident room like a man who could see his career prospects disappearing over the horizon. He slammed the door behind him, strode up to the incident board and glared at Fred and Toby, then turned to the rest of the squad.

'How do I explain this to Chief Constable Wilson?' He was met with silence and a room full of blank stares. 'We've let this monster kill another victim, right under our noses. I'm going to be the laughing stock of Scotland Yard.' He turned to Fred. 'What the hell's going on?'

'Lizzie Birchwood wasn't on our watch-list. She'd never worked with Sir Morris. Nobody thought she was at risk.'

'Well she's pretty bloody dead for someone who's not at risk.'

Fred shrugged, there wasn't much he could say to that comment.

Beeching glared around the incident room. 'Do any of you have a slightest idea of how this will make us look as a force?'

The room fell silent.

'A laughing stock. There's going to be jokes about us in every cop station in the UK.'

'I'm sure there will be some understanding from the press and public, sir, they know we are doing everything we can to catch him.'

Beeching scowled. 'Well it's not working, is it, Toby.'

Nobody said a word; most of the officers looked at their shoes rather than try and hold the withering stare of Inspector Beeching.

'In a strange way this may help, sir,' said Toby.

'Help?' screamed Beeching. 'How does being dead help Lizzie Birchwood? It's not going to be much help when the BBC start interviewing Pierre Corridor, is it?'

'Terry Corridor I think you mean, sir.'

'No, DC Marlowe, I meant Pierre Corridor, Terry's big brother. He's back in charge at the RSC and, if that wasn't bad enough, he was a close friend of Lizzie Birchwood. Be assured that he will soon be arriving in Stratford to pontificate on her tragic loss and that will highlight our shortcomings.'

Fred glanced at Toby. If the more famous of the Corridor brothers did turn up, the press would be ravenous for a quote from him.

'I think Fred and I should speak to him and give him an outline of what we are doing, get him onside first.'

'Providing you can, DC Marlowe. I'm not being filled with confidence by the performance of this lot.' He waved his hand dismissively at the gathered officers. As a motivational talk it left a lot to be desired, but as a demonstration of Beeching's ambition it spoke volumes. Any slight support the team had felt for him dissipated with his words. As Beeching stared at the sullen faces looking back at him, he realised he had gone too far. He turned to Fred and Toby. 'My office. Now.'

They watched him go, then Toby turned to the team. 'You all know what you have to do, get back on observation and watch like a hawk. When we are done with the inspector, we'll alert you to any changes in the operating procedure.' Toby and Fred tried to give their team a reassuring smile; it didn't work. The team filed out of the incident room and back onto the streets of Stratford thoroughly demoralised. In two short minutes, Beeching had destroyed any enthusiasm that was left in the squad. Oliver's job had just got a bit easier.

'Shut the door,' snapped Beeching as Toby followed Fred into the inspector's office. 'What the hell do you think—'

'Why don't you just shut your mouth, Beeching.'

Both Beeching and Toby were stunned into silence.

'You have just destroyed the morale of my team with your stupid defeatist comments. You're supposed to be a leader. Lead!' The last word was shouted.

Beeching's mouth lolled open like a beached tuna; he'd never been spoken to like that before. 'I, I—'

He didn't get chance to say anything else before Fred was on him again.

'I, I, I. It's always about you, isn't it, sir. Well, this time it's not. It's about us trying to catch a killer. You can either be part of it or you can lock yourself in the office and keep out of the way.' Fred straightened to his full height. 'What's it going to be?'

Standing beside Fred, Toby could see the blood vessels at his temple pulsing and the muscles around his jaw clenching; he'd never seen Fred so angry.

Beeching stood with his mouth open while Fred continued. 'You care more about getting into the Met than you do about the victims of our killer and the well-being of the officers under your command. Why don't you stop playing politics and have a go at being a policeman, that's assuming that you can even remember what that is. "Facta Non Verba."'

Beeching looked confused.

'It's Latin, sir,' said Toby. '"Deeds Not Words."'

Beeching still looked confused.

'It's the motto of the police force. You know, the one in which you are a senior officer, sir.'

'Um, sir, that's the motto of London, Canada … never mind, not the time,' muttered Toby.

Fred looked back at Beeching and shook his head slowly, unable to hide his disgust.

Beeching tried to recover. 'Of course I knew that.'

'Did you?'

'Of course, it was your pronunciation that threw me.'

Fred stepped closer to Beeching. 'I'd like to throw you out of that window, sir.'

'I think what Fred is trying to say, sir, is that you need to unite the team.'

'He knows what I was saying, Toby,' said Fred.

Beeching slumped down onto his chair. 'This is a disaster.'

'Who for, you or the victims,' snapped Fred.

'Both,' said Beeching. 'I thought it was over. I thought he had gone.'

'Why would he go, he hasn't finished. There were twelve names on that list, now there could be another twelve, we just don't know.'

Beeching sat in his chair staring at his hands as they clenched and unclenched.

'Well, sir, how do you want us to proceed?'

Beeching looked up at Fred and slowly shook his head. 'I really don't know, Fred. I thought you were on the right track but this …' He hesitated.

'Lizzie Birchwood, sir,' said Toby.

'Yes, her. She never worked with Sir Morris, did she?'

'No, sir, but she worked with Oliver Lawrence and we know that they clashed on *Romeo and Juliet*, despite it being a huge success.'

Toby's explanation didn't appear to register with Beeching. 'What does that mean?'

'It means that anyone who worked with Oliver is possibly at risk.'

'He can't have fallen out with all of them.'

'We are dealing with a very unstable killer, sir. He is clearly very disturbed, look what he's done. With a mind that tormented, even the slightest disagreement could have grown into something darker. Fifteen years since he disappeared, that's a long time for bitterness to stew.'

Fred and Beeching had listened carefully to every word Toby said, his words seemed to have a sobering effect on Beeching and a calming effect on Fred. Beeching took a deep breath. 'I spoke hastily,' he looked up at Fred. 'I apologise, I was out of order. You're a bloody good officer.'

Fred nodded. 'Fair enough, sir, I apologise too.'

Beeching nodded. 'Shall we move on.'

'I think we should, sir. There's a killer out there and we don't even know who he's after.'

'We need to get more manpower. I suppose I'm going to have to call Wilson.'

'No need, sir, Toby can call DI Townsend, she'll help us out.'

Toby glanced at Fred. 'Don't you want to do it, boss?'

Fred smiled wistfully. 'No, son, the baton has been passed. You do it.'

Beeching stood up, straightened his tie and looked at them both. 'Very well, gentlemen. Let's co-ordinate with Coventry, get the extra boots on the ground. And make a list of everyone at the RSC that ever had contact with Oliver Lawrence, prioritise the ones still working there. Put that in motion and then report back to me. Once that's underway, we can put together a statement for the press. Fred, you and I will do a press conference at two p.m.'

Beeching was all business now, Fred's outburst had shocked him out of his self-pity and he was finally thinking like the senior officer he was.

When Fred and Toby came back into the incident room only Kinky and Ginger were left.

Fred looked at them. 'Did you catch any of that?'

'Every word, sir, but, I don't think either of us remember a thing.' Kinky glanced at Ginger. 'Do we?'

'Heard what?'

'I never heard a thing either,' said Sergeant Frank Whittall as he entered the room.

Fred smiled at his team. 'That's what makes you great officers, I suppose.'

A ripple of laughter went around the room; it was like a pressure release valve being opened. The mood had changed from a negative tension to a lighter, more positive atmosphere.

'Right then, you all know that our killer is back. We still believe that it's Lawrence but now it appears that he has expanded his horizons. We thought that it was only those in Sir Morris' group that were potential targets. With the death of Lizzie Birchwood, we have to assume that anyone who worked with him is a target. Kinky, you and Ginger find out if there's anyone at the theatre today that worked with Lawrence, I don't care how tenuous the link is.'

'Righto, boss. Won't take long.'

'Toby is going to get us some more troops from Coventry, the rest of you get back to watching your assigned person. We can only cover those we think are in danger.' Fred looked at Toby. 'Anything you want to add?'

'Yeah. We know that when Lawrence gets going he doesn't hang around. We should be expecting the next murder at any time. If we are not careful this could run away from us.'

Toby and Fred watched their two best detectives head out, there seemed to be a bit more purpose in their step.

'He's going to kill someone soon, isn't he,' said Fred.

'Course he is, he likes it, gives him a thrill. He already knows who his next victim is.'

Chapter 28
I Need To Find My Agent

Toby was right. Oliver Lawrence was sitting in his kitchen, drinking tea and reflecting on a night's work that had gone completely to plan.

'You want a biscuit?' Oliver looked up; he had forgotten that Felix was there. He had turned up around ten minutes before looking pale and nervous.

'Yeah, don't mind if I do, all this late-night stuff gives me an appetite.'

Felix sighed. 'You're really enjoying this, aren't you?'

Oliver shrugged. 'What if I am. You have to admit that last night was a total triumph.'

'You killed an innocent woman; how can that be a triumph?'

'Now, now, Felix, I think you're getting a little overdramatic there. We established that Lizzie was a loose cannon. Would have ruined my career before it started if I hadn't openly defied her in the way I played Romeo.'

'But that turned into a success.'

'It wouldn't if I hadn't had the courage to ignore her. She even tried to get me sacked, but the reviews, especially for me, spiked her guns. I was allowed to stay but I got understudy parts at the start of the next season despite my reviews.'

Felix sighed. 'OK, I'll admit she damaged you a little, but not for long.'

'Look, I'm not in the game of doing things by halves. If I'm going to make a proper comeback, I have to get rid of anyone that might stand in my way. You understand that, don't you?'

'Listen to yourself, Oliver, you sound crazy. This started out as a revenge mission, payback for the evil done to you and your father. Now you're talking about making a comeback to the stage … but you can't seriously think that's an option.'

'Why isn't it? You've seen me act, I'm still better than anyone at the RSC right now.'

'You are, but that's not the point, is it.'

Oliver was confused. 'I'd have thought that was the exact point.'

'You don't understand, if you appear from nowhere, they won't even look at you.'

'I'm Oliver Lawrence.'

'You may well be but you can't tell them that or you'll be arrested.'

'What if I auditioned?'

'How are you going to get an audition? First question they are going to ask you is, who are you. You can't answer that truthfully so you make up a name. You have no résumé in theatre and nobody's ever heard of you, the chances of you even getting an audition are practically zero.'

'So, what do I do then?'

Felix thought for a moment. 'The only way is to take a job at a small provincial Rep and work your way up. Given your talent, you could probably be back at the RSC in four years.'

'Four years! I can't wait that long.'

'You've already waited fifteen, surely another four won't hurt.'

Oliver knew that Felix was right, this wasn't going to be an easy process. 'But if I kill more of the actors in Sir Morris' company that's going to shorten the odds and speed up my return.'

'You can't kill your way to the top, Oliver!'

Oliver shrugged; he wasn't so sure. He sulked for a moment and then he brightened up. 'Did you see the way I wooed her? I charmed her out of her room and into the night.'

Felix nodded. 'It was intoxicating to watch. Like one of those documentaries where a lion is stalking its prey. You just can't tear your eyes away but you really wish you could. You're hypnotic when the mood is upon you.'

Oliver put down his tea and stood up. 'I'll show you a bank where the wild thyme blows. I'll show you a place where the oxlips grow.' Who could resist?'

Felix could. 'Forget getting back to the RSC any time soon, it's not an option.'

Oliver looked hurt; he wasn't. Just acting a part again. 'Well, that was a bit harsh. I've got feelings, you know. Us artistic types are gentle souls.'

'I haven't seen much of your gentle side recently.'

'What about when I wooed Lizzie last night?'

'It doesn't count if you're only doing it so you can strangle her later. Besides, aren't you forgetting I'd drugged her. That wasn't just you doing that.'

Oliver pursed his lips. 'I suppose you've got a point.'

'You're contemplating something. I hope it isn't another murder. It's too soon. I need a good night's sleep first.'

'Do you remember Bernard Wood?'

'Your old agent?'

'Yes. He was very good at getting me work, why don't I contact him?'

'I can't believe what I am hearing. Are you mad?'

'Very probably, but he was a very good agent and he loved me.'

Felix gazed out of the window onto the sunlit garden. 'This is a new level of crazy, even for you. Your lucky streak can only last for so long. What if he recognises you?'

'Nobody else has, why should he?'

'Because you and he were very close. He's an agent, he took you on because he could see the talent, don't you think, despite your changed appearance, he's going to spot that talent once again. That's what he does for a living.'

'Yeah, you have a point. Does he still live in Stratford?'

'No, his mother died and he started to specialise in musical theatre, spends most of his time in London these days.'

'Musical theatre?' Oliver's face twisted with distain. 'Musical theatre. Did he have a mental breakdown?'

'Don't be such a snob, musicals are a legitimate form of theatre.'

'Say that with a straight face,' snapped Oliver.

'Musical theatre—' Felix didn't get chance to finish his sentence.

'Is for the weak of mind who don't have the mental capacity to follow a proper play.'

'But there is a lot of money in them, they help support straight theatre.'

'I would never do one.'

'I wouldn't worry, you can't sing and you're never going to get the chance to find out, are you?' Felix spoke harshly but his words were true.

'You may be right but I could always have a chat with him. His palate must be so jaded from listening to all that godawful warbling, he probably won't recognise a real actor when he sees me.'

'Well, you aren't going to get the chance to find out because, as I said, he doesn't live here any more. He lives in London.'

'All the time? Bernard loved his Shakespeare, surely he comes back occasionally.'

Felix shrugged. 'I saw him last season for a couple of weeks.'

'Where was he stopping?'

'He still owns his mother's bungalow.'

Oliver looked hard at Felix, waiting for more details.

'It's a bungalow on the other side of the Sanctus bridge.'

'Do you know the number?'

'You can't be turning up on his doorstep, it's too risky.'

'What's the number?' asked Oliver, his tone was no longer friendly.

'It hasn't got a number; it's got a name.'

'Which is?'

'I don't know, it's something twee, like Done Working.'

'Done working, what kind of a name is that.'

Felix rubbed his chin. 'Done … Done … Dunroamin, that's it. Dunroamin!'

'Jesus, I hope I never get old. Dun-bleeding-roamin.'

'There's no accounting for taste.'

All of this planning was thirsty work. Oliver took a long sip of his tea. There was no danger that he would ever get old and, the way things were going, there wasn't much hope that Felix would either.

Chapter 29
Choose Your Friends Carefully

The incident room was quiet. Everyone apart from Fred and Toby had headed out to shadow possible victims.

'You going to give Mel a call?' Fred asked, so quietly it sounded more like an accusation.

'Why me?'

Fred shrugged. 'You know.'

Toby put down his pen and leaned back in his chair. 'This is ridiculous, boss. There is absolutely nothing going on between me and Mel Townsend.'

Fred sighed. 'But there could be.'

'One comment, she made one comment. She was probably joking, playing with me to see how I would react.'

'Mel doesn't play. Like it or not, son, and I don't like it one little bit, you have been chosen.'

'What if I don't want to be chosen?'

Fred gave Toby a disbelieving smile. 'Look me in the face and tell me you wouldn't want to be chosen by her. She was my Helen.'

Toby let Fred's words fall without comment, mainly because he didn't have a clue what he was on about.

Fred looked at him, waiting for an answer, an acknowledgement.

'I'm sorry, boss, who is Helen?'

'Try to keep up, Toby. Mel Townsend is Helen.'

'I thought she was Cassandra to your Apollo?'

Fred shook his head. 'I thought you had a proper education.'

'I did.'

'Well, you should know that there are more than just two Greek gods.'

'I do, but why is she Mel Townsend too.'

'Not literally, symbolically. Mel was my Helen and you are her Paris.'

The light was beginning to dawn in Toby's confusion. 'You're talking Greek mythology.'

'Of course. Don't you see the similarity?'

'Not really. I thought you were supposed to be Apollo to her Cassandra.'

Fred glared at Toby accusingly. 'Helen seemed more apt, given the level of your betrayal.'

'That's not fair boss, what happened to Helen?'

'Helen ran away from Sparta with Paris, leaving poor Menelaus broken-hearted.'

'And I take it you're supposed to be Menelaus in this little scenario?'

'Exactly. The young prince came in and stole her heart, leaving Menelaus behind. When he tried to win her back it started the Trojan War.'

'Well, Coventry isn't Troy.'

Fred couldn't argue with that.

'So maybe, we could ditch all this talk of me running off with your Helen and get on with finding our killer.'

Fred nodded. 'Yeah, I suppose that would be best but I still think you should call her.'

Toby picked up his notes and straightened them. 'You call her, you're the senior officer and I don't fancy starting another Trojan War.'

Fred smiled and picked up his phone.

Chapter 30
Building Up A Thirst

Oliver was enjoying a quiet pint in the garden of the Dirty Duck; the sun warmed his face and he had a great view of the police investigating the scene of Lizzie Birchwood's murder. They say that a killer should never return to the scene of their crimes but, when they were opposite one of your favourite pubs, it was hard not to.

Dick Mayrick wandered out of the bar and gazed sadly over the road at the scene of the crime. He turned to Oliver. 'Terrible, isn't it.'

Oliver nodded. 'Yes, I was hoping to go for a walk in the park today.'

Dick flinched. 'Oh, too soon mate. I found her when I was out walking Chris.'

'Chris?'

'My dog.'

'Of course. Must have been a nasty shock.'

Dick nodded and then stepped over to Oliver's table. 'Mind if I join you?'

'Be my guest.'

Dick slumped down. 'I've had a hell of a morning. First, I find poor Lizzie and then I bump into my wife.'

'Do you think she killed her?'

Dick smiled. 'She's capable of murder, but no, she was out running. She's looking really fit.'

'Getting in shape for her new boyfriend?'

'Steady, chap. A man's got feelings, you know.'

'I'm sorry, I've got a pretty dark sense of humour.' Oliver drained his glass. 'I've got quite a thirst too.'

Dick stood up wearily. 'Then I better get that pint pulled. You want anything to eat yet?'

'No thanks, I never drink on a full stomach.'

Oliver watched Dick disappear into the pub, reached inside his pocket and pulled out a beautiful handkerchief wrapped in some pretty tissue-paper. He had bought it last week and he was here to give it to the woman he felt deserved it: Clarissa Pidgeon.'

Fred took a deep breath, straightened his shirt and dialled his phone.

'DI Townsend.'

'Mel, it's me.'

'Oh, hi Fred.'

On the other end of the phone Fred could hear the disappointment in Mel's voice. 'What can I do for you?'

'We've had another murder.'

Mel sat bolt upright in her chair. 'Do we know who it is.'

'Yes. Lizzie Birchwood, the director.'

'Oliver Lawrence is back then,' she sighed.

'He never left, Mel, but this one has a nasty twist. Lizzie Birchwood never worked with Sir Morris when Oliver was there. She doesn't fit the profile of the other victims.'

'Anything to link her to Lawrence?'

'Oh yes. She directed him in *Romeo and Juliet* and they had artistic differences, big ones!'

'I'm guessing you need more officers then.'

Fred smiled to himself. Mel Townsend never missed a thing. 'We do. We have to find everyone that has ever worked with Oliver at the RSC. Toby and I have been going through all the old programmes from back then, trying to find them.'

'You've cross-referenced them back to anyone who is still working there?'

'Of course,' said Fred.

'How many?'

'Six in total,' he paused for a moment. 'Including Lizzie Birchwood.'

'Just five officers then,' sighed Mel.

'Yeah.'

'I'll get them sorted in the next hour.'

'Thanks Mel, you're a star.'

'I know,' she said.

The phone went dead and Fred sat there listening to the echo of a moment he could not recapture. Helen had gone and Menelaus was left alone once more.

Oliver heard Clarissa before he saw her. Her voice carried down Southern Lane like a siren luring him, the ancient mariner, into deep water. 'Is that you up there, Francis, darling?'

For a moment, he had forgotten the false name he had been using, it didn't sound right coming out of the mouth of someone who had once known him as Oliver. He gave her a wry smile. 'Yes, Clarissa, how are you?'

She bounced up the steps to the patio. 'All the better for seeing you, ducky.' She sat down at his table.

'Would you like to join me.'

'I think I just did,' she said, ignoring the irony in his voice. 'I bet you want to buy me a gin and tonic, don't you?'

Oliver nodded and turned to Dick Mayrick who had reappeared. 'Could you get us a gin and tonic for Clarissa and another pint for me, please.'

'Make it a double will you, I've had a terrible morning.'

Dick nodded sombrely. 'You've heard about Lizzie Birchwood then.'

Clarissa nodded. 'Yes. Dreadful, isn't it? She'd promised me a lead role in a play she was doing next year in the West End. Suppose I'm going to have to audition for the new director now.'

Dick and Oliver exchanged glances. That was callous, even by Clarissa's self-centred standards.

'Dick found her, you know,' said Oliver.

Clarissa put her hand to her mouth. 'Oh, I'm sorry, Dick. That must have been terrible for you.'

'It was, she was a nice lady.' Dick gazed into the distance. 'I've never seen a dead body before.'

'I saw my grannie,' said Clarissa. She turned to Oliver. 'Have you ever seen a dead body, Francis?'

'Yeah, I've seen a few. I used to work in an old folk's home. Get a cold snap and they start dropping like flies.'

Clarissa smiled. 'I wouldn't mind a bed bath from you.'

'Before or after your enema?'

Dick burst out laughing. 'I'll just go and get those drinks for you.'

Clarissa scowled after him. 'He's very over-familiar, isn't he.'

'Oh, don't be so harsh on him. It's not his fault I made him laugh. Have you noticed he always gives you and Suzy personal service? When I'm not with you, I usually have to go and order my drinks at the bar like everyone else.'

Clarissa sighed. 'Yes, I suppose I am being a bit harsh. He's a good bloke, and a looker.'

'You not tempted?'

She shook her head. 'He's a scrum-half.'

'That's a bad thing?'

'I once had an affair with a scrum-half. He insisted on making all the decisions and never stopped telling me how well he was doing. All got a bit wearing. Two big egos constantly butting up against each other does not a happy couple make.'

'You admit you have a big ego then?'

'I'm an actress, darling, that's what I hide behind. The bigger the ego, the easier it gets to ignore bad reviews.'

Oliver was surprised to hear such honesty from Clarissa, who he had always found to be loud and shallow. Her comment showed a vulnerability that he had never thought existed. 'You surprise me, I always thought you were super confident.'

'I am, but …' She looked away for a moment. '"Time's winged

chariot waits for no man, or woman." Another couple of years and I won't be the love interest, I'll be the mother of the love interest.'

'I think you'll be fine for a while,' said Oliver.

Clarissa took it as the compliment it was. She leaned across the table and looked into Oliver's eyes. 'Would you like to take a closer look, Francis?'

Oliver didn't fancy that idea at all, but when you are planning on smothering someone with a pillow, it helps if you can get them into bed first. He was an actor and the role he was playing was Francis Bacon, ex-actor and writer and possible lover. He leaned towards her. 'I'd like that very much.' He reached inside his pocket. 'I bought you a little gift from the market yesterday.'

'Oh really, what is it?'

Oliver pulled the package from his pocket and passed it too her. 'I saw this and thought you might like it.'

Clarissa took it from him and eagerly tore off the tissue-paper to reveal a beautiful silk scarf. She held it up in front of her. It was white with strawberries embroidered on it. 'Oh, it's lovely. Thank you, Francis.' She leaned forward and kissed him full on the lips, lingering there a moment too long.

Oliver fought the temptation to pull away. He had to stay in character.

Just as she let him go, Dick Mayrick appeared with their drinks. 'I see you two are busy building up a thirst.'

Clarissa held up her scarf. 'Look what Francis bought me.'

Dick admired the scarf. 'That's lovely. Just like the scarf that Othello bought for Desdemona.'

Clarissa glanced at Oliver. 'You're not Othello, are you?'

'No, not a jealous bone in my body.'

'Thank goodness for that.'

'I didn't mean it like that,' said Dick, realising what his words had implied. 'I don't think Frank has ever smothered anyone, have you?'

Oliver shrugged and winked. 'Not yet.'

They all laughed, and Clarissa wrapped the scarf around her neck. Oliver watched as she pulled it up around her throat and tried to imagine it getting tighter and tighter. Hearing the gasps and guttural grunts as she tried to force air into her lungs past her constricted windpipe. The look of hopelessness and panic as she realised that she was dying. Knowing that after all this there was nothing, a great dark void that stretched on for forever.

'You OK, Francis? You were miles away,' said Clarissa.

'I know, that scarf took me back years, brought back an old memory.'

'A good one, I hope.'

'For me it was.'

Clarissa laid a hand on his thigh. 'Is this a token of your affection?'

'It's a token of something; I saw it and I thought of you.'

'Well, Frank, I think this could be the start of a beautiful friendship,' said Dick.

'Oh, I think Francis and I will be far more than friends, don't you?' She looked at Oliver, her eyes writing cheques her body could keep, but the name on those cheques would be incorrect. Francis Bacon was not who he appeared to be. Clarissa had fallen for the character Oliver had created and signed her name on a fatal contract.

Chapter 31
Wilson's Last Stand

When DI Mel Townsend arrived at Guild Street, she was not alone. Fred had seen her get out of her car and was about to tell Toby when another car pulled up alongside her. A big black Rover, the type the top brass drive around in. A uniformed officer got out and walked around to the nearside rear door and opened it. Chief Constable Wilson got out.

'Jesus! I wasn't expecting that,' said Fred.

'What is it?'

Fred looked at Toby. 'Mel Townsend's here and she's not alone.'

'I know, she bringing reinforcements.'

'She's brought Wilson.'

Toby jumped up from his desk and joined Fred at the window. Wilson was marching purposefully towards their office, behind him Mel looked up and saw them at the window. She mouthed the word 'Sorry' and followed him into the station. Within a few seconds, Chief Constable Wilson had appeared in the incident room. Fred had already warned Beeching, who was waiting for him at his office door.

Wilson glanced at Fred and Toby. 'Morning, gents, shouldn't you be out trying to catch this killer.'

'We are just trying to track down potential victims, sir,' said Toby.

'Maybe you should be trying to track down the killer, Marlowe.'

Beeching stepped forward. 'Morning, sir, we weren't expecting you. To what do we owe the pleasure?'

Wilson snorted. 'It won't be a pleasure, Beeching. Your office, now!'

It was a direct command and Inspector Beeching treated it as such. Wilson paused and turned back to Fred and Toby. 'You two can get yourselves in here as well.'

They looked to Beeching for guidance and he gave a slight nod of his head. Wilson was clearly on the warpath.

'Shut the door, what I have to say is for your ears only.' Wilson looked from Beeching to Fred, and from Fred to Toby. 'You don't like me, do you?'

None of them bothered to deny it.

Wilson sneered. 'I'll take that as a no.' He looked at them all in turn, seething. 'I've been doing some thinking and I've realised that your blackmailing of me puts you at risk too. Not going to look good if it comes out is it … for any of us! I know you think you have me put away in a little box because I borrowed money off a bookmaker, but that doesn't make me bent. I'm still the chief constable of this force, I'm not going to allow you to sideline me from the biggest serial murder case we've ever had.'

'But—'

'Enough, Beeching, I don't want to hear it. This killer is running rings around you and you're making us all look bad. Either convince me that you have a plan to apprehend him or I'm taking you off the case.'

Beeching didn't have a response to that. Clearly Wilson was no longer afraid of exposure. In that moment, Inspector Beeching realised he couldn't reveal he had been blackmailing Wilson. If Wilson was prepared for the information to come out about his illegal loans, it would take down Beeching too.

'Well, sir, it's not that straightforward.'

'Didn't think it would be,' jeered Wilson.

'Look, sir—'

'No, you look, all of you,' Wilson glared at them. 'Last time I checked, I am still in charge of this force and you're not going to stop me from leading it. Whatever you think you have on me it's not enough to get me sacked. The worst that would happen would be early retirement with full benefits, and no stain on my character. Before that happens, I will ruin all of your careers, don't think I won't. Just taking you off the case for failing to catch the killer would be enough to spike any future promotions.' He turned to Beeching. 'And any hope you had of getting to the Met would be gone forever.'

He let his words sink in, it was clear he had thought his position through. He was a man with his back to the wall and nothing to lose and, as he had said, his pension and reputation were safe.

'Very well, sir, what do you propose?' Beeching's words were conciliatory, clearly Wilson's words had convinced him that the boot was very much on Wilson's foot now.

'What I propose is that I take the lead on this case.' Beeching went to protest but one look from Wilson silenced him. 'It's not going well, is it?' They all shook their heads. 'Let me take the flack; I'm near to retirement, you all still have careers to build.'

They were all taken aback by this apparent burst of altruism, Wilson soon disabused them of that impression. 'This could be good for me. I know that this force has never faced a situation like this before. I've read all the case notes and, for what it's worth, I think your Oliver Lawrence is our killer.'

'Wait a minute, you've read our files?' said Beeching. How did you get hold of them?'

Wilson grinned. 'Mel Townsend works for me, not you.'

Fred turned to Toby, a look of disappointment colouring his features. It had been naïve to think that Mel wouldn't have had to share the information with her boss.

Mel was standing in the incident room; Wilson had excluded her from this meeting deliberately. Now Fred understood why she had mouthed 'Sorry' when she was following Wilson in from the car park.

'The killing of Lizzie Birchwood has made the case more

complicated. It's not just revenge now, is it. There is more to it. It's almost as if he is killing anyone he doesn't like. His mission has changed, we just need to understand why. What do you think, Fred?'

Fred wasn't expecting to be asked. 'Well, er …'

'Speak freely, I need to know what you think.'

'In that case, sir, I think you're right. What started out as a revenge has changed, the murder of Lizzie Birchwood proves it. DC Marlowe and I were just discussing it and we have a theory.'

'Let's hear it then,' said Wilson.

'We think that he is getting rid of anyone who could stand in his way.'

'In what way?'

'It's almost as if he believes he could become an actor again,' said Toby.

'Wow, that's a disturbing turn of events. It would suggest that as well as being a homicidal maniac he's also barking mad.'

'Delusional, sir,' said Toby.

'You want to expand on that, DC Marlowe?'

'So far, he's been very rational, controlled. Killed quickly and quietly and left no trace. We don't know what he looks like, we don't even know for sure that it's him,' said Toby.

'It is though, isn't it.' It wasn't a question, Wilson was agreeing with them.

'Yes, sir, I'd stake my career on it.'

Wilson laughed. 'You may have to, Marlowe.' He glanced through the office partition at Mel. 'Let's take this discussion into the incident room. We need to include DI Townsend in this.'

Wilson walked out of the office leaving Fred, Toby and Beeching to ponder the sudden change of command. Beeching stepped close to them and whispered, 'This may not be a bad thing,' before following Wilson.

Toby glanced at Fred. 'What do you think?'

'I think Helen has betrayed Menelaus for a second time.'

Chapter 32
Bad News Travels Fast

Like a pebble thrown into a pond, the news of Lizzie Birchwood's murder had rippled through time's firmament and found its way to Beatrice Oxford. She had known Lizzie well, hearing it on Radio Four news made her stop dead in her tracks. This was the work of her son, she knew it. He was out of control. Lizzie had not been around when Oliver had been thrown out of Sir Morris' company. There was only one reason for killing Lizzie and it wasn't revenge. Although it's never easy for a parent to reconcile the fact that their child has done something terrible, she wasn't surprised. With the role model she had provided for Oliver, it was probably to be expected. She went to the phone and dialled.

'Hello, Royal Shakespeare Theatre, how can I help you.'

'Hello Margaret, It's Lady Oxford here. I need to speak to Sir Morris.' There was no please or thank you.

'Just putting you through.' Margaret's voice was cold, almost disdainful. Beatrice knew that she wasn't well-liked. In her time at the RSC she had never gone out of her way to be nice to anyone who couldn't help her career. Ambition was myopic, only focused on one thing.

'Hello darling, is everything OK?' asked Sir Morris.

'Why didn't you tell me about Lizzie?' Her words were harsh, accusatory.

'I only heard a couple of hours ago myself. It's terrible, I didn't like her much and her directing was crazy, but still.'

'It was Oliver, I know it.' There was panic in her voice.

'We don't know that, dear.'

'We do, open your bloody eyes. He's going to kill everyone; he's going to kill us.'

Sir Morris tried to calm her. 'Now, now, dear. You don't know anything of the kind.'

'You stupid, stupid man, can't you see it,' she shouted. 'It's Oliver. O'er hasty marriage has undone us.'

Beatrice was clearly losing the plot, hearing her quote from Gertrude sent a shiver down Sir Morris' spine. They had married soon after the death of Oliver's father, but he hadn't taken it badly. At least, he didn't appear to have.

'Beatrice, listen to me, you need to calm down. There are police everywhere. Oliver, or whoever it is, will soon be caught.'

'There is blood on my hands, I smell it still.'

Sir Morris didn't know what to say. He could hear the sobbing of his wife at the other end of the phone; he felt helpless. Was this madness he was hearing, had the stress of the last few weeks become too much?

'Listen, darling, I will be home tomorrow. Stay calm and everything will be fine.'

'My sins are coming back to haunt me, Morris. Each and every one, there is nowhere left to hide. They can smell the blood upon my hands.'

Morris remained silent. Beatrice sounded so disturbed. If he had spoken, Beatrice would not have heard him, she had dropped the phone and gone to the sink and was washing and rewashing hands that would never be clean.

Chapter 33
Hands That Dig Ditches

'She was strangled,' said Alf Butcher.

'We knew that already.'

Alf frowned at Fred. 'Let me finish, it's not quite that simple.'

'Big blue sticky-out tongue, bit of a giveaway, isn't it.'

'Do you want to hear my findings or not?'

Fred nodded.

'Good, don't interrupt me again or you can read the bloody report yourself.' Fred nodded again.

'The killer was immensely strong, clearly he has worked with his hands a lot. He crushed the larynx and fractured the hyoid bone. Now that's not uncommon in cases of strangulation but this guy has hands like a blacksmith. He actually burst blood vessels in her neck with the force he applied. Now most of the actors I've met might be good for a bit of light dusting but I've not met many that could apply this kind of physical force.'

'So, we are looking for a big man,' said Fred.

'Is Brian Blessed at the RSC this year?'

Fred chuckled. 'No, but you reckon the murderer would need to be that big?'

'He'd need to be powerful and the pictures I've seen of this Oliver Lawrence don't seem to match the kind of brute force that would be required to fit the nature of the victim's injuries.'

Fred had a photo of Oliver in the file he was holding. He took it out and showed it to Alf. 'That's the latest picture we have of him, taken about sixteen years ago.'

Alf held it up. 'Look at those forearms, he might win a fight with Widow Twankey but those hands and arms are not from the person who strangled Lizzie Birchwood.'

Fred respected Alf Butcher. He was the best pathologist in Warwickshire; what if he was right? 'Sixteen years is a long time. Couldn't he have got stronger?'

'He could have but you would need to be looking for a man built more like a second row forward than a leading man wearing tights.'

'You're not a lover of the theatre, are you, Alf.'

'No, not really, but you can't say that round here, can you.'

'You can to me.' Fred put the photo back in his file. 'So, if it is Oliver he's going to have changed a fair bit?'

'A lot!'

'Could it be the same person?' asked Fred.

'Yes, it could,' Alf sounded doubtful. 'But he would have had to really bulk up to do it. You can't rule it out but, based on the photo we have, I don't believe it could have been him.'

This was not what Fred wanted to hear. His and Toby's theory placed Oliver Lawrence as their only suspect. 'We believe it's him Alf, so what do you suggest?'

Alf considered Fred's question. 'Do you have a forensic artist on the force?'

'Yeah, I think so.'

'Well give them this photo and ask them to age him fifteen years and put two stone of muscle on him.'

'That's going to give him bigger arms and shoulders but his face won't change much, will it?'

'You'd be surprised. His neck will be thicker and that will be the same with his jawline. If he's in his forties, he has probably put on more than just muscle so his whole face will have filled out somewhat. With a different hairstyle, even his best friends would struggle to recognise him after fifteen years.'

Fred held the old publicity shot in his hand. 'So, what you're saying is that this is worthless.'

Alf nodded. 'Afraid so. That's if we assume that Lizzie Birchwood's killer is Oliver.'

Fred sighed. 'You have any good news for me?'

'That is the good news. You've been chasing the wrong man. The Oliver in that picture, if he strangled Lizzie, looks nothing like that now. You need an updated version, an artist's impression of what Oliver would currently look like. Get that and at least you will have a decent likeness of the man you are actually looking for.'

When Fred returned to Guild Street he, found Toby poring over lists of everyone that was working at the RSC during the 1956/7 season.

He looked up as Fred entered the incident room. 'How did things go with Lizzie's autopsy?'

'Still dead,' said Fred.

'Anything more positive?'

'For Lizzie, no, but Alf did suggest something interesting.'

Toby sat up. 'Go on, I need something, I'm banging my head against a brick wall here. There are so many people who could have worked with Oliver, how are we to know if they liked each other?'

'Guess we will have to ask them.' Fred pointed to the kettle. 'Cuppa?'

'Please.' Toby got up from his chair and followed Fred into the kitchen. 'Well, what did Alf have to say?'

'He said that the person who strangled Lizzie must have had forearms like a blacksmith.'

Toby looked over at the picture of Oliver on the incident board. He looked about as far removed from his image of a blacksmith as it was possible to get. 'What does that mean?'

'It means, young Toby, that either Oliver Lawrence has bulked up like Charles Atlas or it's not him.'

'It is him.'

'I agree, so that means our Oliver has been working out or digging ditches for the last fifteen years.'

'Digging ditches? He's an actor.'

'I know, an actor doing manual labour is a hard concept to get your head around. Our only hope is to do as Alf suggested and get the forensic artist to work up a new image.'

'That's going to alter his appearance a lot.'

'It needs to. We've shown this picture of Oliver to every person in Warwickshire and nobody's recognised him. That should tell us something.'

'Let's get hold of HQ and get the contact details for their artist.'

Fred pulled a face. 'Ah, now that's going to be tricky.'

'Why?'

'When Wilson was trying to trim his budget so that he could pay himself more, one of the things he cut was the police artist.'

Toby couldn't believe what he was hearing. 'What do we do now?'

'My great aunt Doris is pretty good at flowers.'

'We're looking for a killer not a bloody chrysanthemum.'

Fred smiled and clicked off the kettle that had just come to the boil.

Toby, on the other hand, was simmering nicely. 'I don't bloody believe this. We're trying to catch a killer here, what the hell do we do now?'

Fred dropped teabags into two cups and poured in the boiling water. 'I may have a solution.'

'Go on, I'm all ears.'

'Whomper is one hell of an artist.'

'Is he?' Toby looked doubtful.

'Oh yes, well known for his artwork round these parts.'

'What's he paint, oils on canvas?'

'Nah, ink on skin.'

'He's a tattooist?'

'He is. A bloody good one. And his sisters share his gift for drawing.'

Toby shook his head. 'So, you are suggesting that to develop some drawings of a suspected serial killer in the biggest murder hunt in the force's history, we use a part-time tattooist and his weird sisters.'

'I am. Never judge a book by its cover, young Toby. Whomper's clan have hidden depths.'

'I can't wait for the press conference when you show the artist's impression and he's got a dragon's tail and a mermaid behind him.'

Fred passed Toby his mug of tea. 'You are way too cynical for one so young. Let's drink our tea and go and find Whomper.'

'Any idea where he'll be?'

Fred raised his eyebrows. 'And you're supposed to be a detective?'

Chapter 34
Post-Impressionist Whomper

The Green Dragon hadn't changed since their last visit. If anything, the stygian gloom and the clientele had become more dystopian. The atmosphere was similar to that of a London pea-souper, drawn straight from a Sherlock Holmes novel. They made their way through the smoke-filled doorway of what was laughably called The Lounge. The orange glow of a cigarette, followed by a consumptive cough, confirmed that Whomper was indeed in residence.

'Ah, the boys in blue. I've been expecting you.'

Fred and Toby sat down opposite Whomper. 'Technically we're not in blue, being detectives,' said Toby.

Whomper shrugged. 'Semantics. What can I do for you?'

'You've heard about Lizzie Birchwood,' said Toby.

'Of course. Nasty. Strangled by the river.'

'How do you know she was strangled? We haven't announced the cause of death yet,' said Toby.

'Intuition.'

'We're here to ask a favour, Whomper.'

'Well I'd love to but you find me unwell.'

'What's wrong?'

'Dehydration and hypoglycaemia.' Whomper pushed his empty pint glass across the table towards them.

Toby sighed and shook his head. 'What's hypoglycaemia?'

'A sudden drop in the body's blood sugar levels, usually caused by hunger.'

'Is there a cure?'

'Two ploughman's should do it.'

'Two?'

'It's an acute case.'

'There's nothing cute about you, Whomper,' said Fred, taking his glass. 'You want something, Toby?'

'Too early for me, boss.'

'Fair enough,' said Fred before disappearing into the haze, headed for the bar.

Whomper smiled at Toby. 'Tough case this one.'

'Feels like a waking nightmare.'

'So, what can I do for you?'

'We need an artist's impression of Oliver Lawrence.'

'Need to update that out-of-date photo, do you?'

'Yeah, we have to age him fifteen years and, according to the pathologist, we need to add two stone of muscle to him.'

Whomper nodded thoughtfully. 'That means whoever did the strangling had very powerful hands and arms, according to Alf Butcher.'

Toby simply nodded his agreement, he was no longer surprised at Whomper's ability to know virtually everything that was going on in Stratford. 'That's going to change the shape of his face quite a bit.'

'Can you do it?'

Whomper glanced at Toby dismissively. 'Course I can. When do you need it?'

'Yesterday.'

'If only you'd asked me the day before yesterday I could have done it.'

'How about tomorrow?

'Can you get yourself around to my studio this afternoon?'

'You have a studio?'

'Well, it's my shed actually, but it's south facing.'

Toby pulled the photo of a young Oliver out of his pocket and passed it to Whomper. 'When do you think you can get it finished by?'

'That depends on you, son.'

'Why's that?'

'I'm a tattooist, I only work on skin. You don't have a hairy chest, do you?'

Toby stared at Whomper. 'Are you suggesting what I think you're suggesting?'

'I don't know, you're the detective, you tell me.'

'You want to tattoo the image on my chest?'

'Is there another chest available?'

As Toby sat open-mouthed, staring at Whomper, Fred returned with the drinks.

'Stop winding the lad up, Whomper, it's child cruelty.'

A broad smile spread across his features. 'I really think he was considering it.'

'Would have made for an entertaining press conference. Have you seen this man? And in walks a topless Toby.'

'Bugger off, the pair of you.'

Fred and Whomper laughed.

'You want a black and white drawing?'

'Perfect.'

Whomper turned to Toby. 'Get yourself around to my studio tomorrow at ten a.m. and I'll do it for you.'

'That's an early start for you.'

Whomper sighed. 'What choice do I have? The pubs open at eleven-thirty so if I don't get it done early I'm missing valuable thinking time.'

'I think you mispronounced that, Whomper,' said Fred.

'No, I think when I drink. Unlike most men, I am capable of multi-tasking. That's why women love me.'

'But you're not in a relationship.'

'I rest my case.' Whomper looked up at Fred. 'Is the food imminent? I fear I'm fading fast.'

Fred nodded towards Whomper's bulging T-shirt. 'With reserves like that, I reckon you're good for a few weeks yet.'

The food arrived and Toby sat back and watched as Whomper and Fred descended on their lunch. It was like a hyena's tea party, without the tea. Food was consumed with a controlled violence, silent but deadly, the cheese and pickle never stood a chance.

As Whomper finished his second helping, his twin sisters appeared from the far end of The Lounge.

'Hello Fred,' they said in unison.

'Valerie, Denise. How are you both.'

'Disturbed.'

Toby caught Fred's eye. He gave him a faint shake of the head and Toby held in the comment he was about to make.

'What's disturbing you, girls.'

'"By the pricking of our thumbs, something wicked this way comes."'

'I see,' said Fred. 'Can you be more specific?'

'No, we are just empty vessels.'

'You certainly are,' whispered Toby.

Suddenly, Whomper sat bolt upright and when the girls spoke he joined them in unison. The Whomper family Greek chorus was reunited.

'A token of affection will be mislaid; an innocent victim will be slayed.'

Fred glanced at Toby and then back to Whomper. 'What was that all about?'

Whomper shook his head. 'I don't know. A premonition; a warning from the future. All I know is when we get together you had better take notice because the three witches have got nothing on us.'

Toby and Fred left the Green Dragon feeling unsettled. They had heard the three Whomper twins' predictions once before and they had been right.

'So, what do you think that meant, young Toby?'

'I don't know, boss. If it is an innocent victim it's probably someone who isn't on our watch list.'

'That's a disturbing thought. Let's get back to the station so I can keep trawling through those lists, there has to be someone that we've overlooked.'

Sometimes, fate takes a hand and events, seemingly unrelated, can fashion our destiny.

Chapter 35
Fate Is The Hunter

Heather Wilson was in her happy place; shopping. The streets of Stratford provided ample opportunity for a lady with time, and her husband's money, to indulge her every whim. Judging by the two rather exclusive bags she was carrying, Heather had already indulged herself. This, she reasoned, was her compensation for allowing her husband, Chief Constable Wilson, to crawl all over her like a bloated spider. He meant well, poor thing, but he was just a stepping stone to something better. For now, his money and status in the community would have to suffice.

The wedding vows, for her, had meant making her richer and him poorer. He treated her well, he'd literally do anything for her and while his money lasted she was going to make the best of the situation. She crossed the road and there before her was her favourite shop, The Italian Job. It was the best clothes shop in town. She had only been able to go there since she had married Harold Wilson but she had certainly made the most of that time and his money. Julien St Moritz welcomed Heather with open arms.

'Quelle surprise, Heather, how are you today?' For a Frenchman he had a surprisingly strong Birmingham accent. Even Heather wondered if St Moritz was his real name.

'Bonjour, Julien, what do you have for me today?'

Julien spread his arms wide. 'For you, Heather, we have a brand-new summer season range, they have only arrived today.'

He'd been saying that to every customer for the last four weeks, sadly with the murders, the blood-red evening dresses had been sticking, but during the short interlude between the recent resumption of killing, business had been good.

Heather gazed at the array of clothes that surrounded her. Temptation was everywhere and her husband was nowhere to be seen. She had an account, let the games begin!

'Where should I start, Julien, there is so much to choose from.'

Julien smiled coyly. 'Shall we start in the bedroom? I have some lingerie to die for.'

Heather shuddered. 'No, let's not buy anything that will rev up the motor of the old boy. I want him asleep watching the telly after dinner, not chasing me around the bed.'

'If it's not for the husband, it could be for your lover,' Julien winked at her. 'Surely you have one.'

Heather blushed. 'Why, Julien St Moritz, you naughty man. I've not been married long.'

'All the more reason, start how you mean to go on.'

There was another customer in Julien's shop, listening to every word. Clarissa Pidgeon appeared from behind a row of lace basques. 'You should listen to Julien; he knows what he's talking about.'

Heather looked up and saw Clarissa. 'Oh, hello. You're an actress, I've seen you on the telly.'

Clarissa nodded, then stepped towards Heather, her hand outstretched. 'Clarissa Pidgeon.'

Heather took her hand and smiled back at her. 'You're with the RSC this season.'

Clarissa nodded. 'I am. Will you be coming?'

'I will now.'

Clarissa held Heather's hand firmly and ran her thumb gently across the back of it. 'I'd like to see you in that lingerie.'

Heather blushed at Clarissa's directness but she did not pull away.

Julien stood back and watched. He had seen Clarissa do this before, she was a total predator. Men, women, young or middle-aged, Clarissa was ready and willing to bed them all. 'Have you two never met before?'

'Oh no, I would have remembered a beauty like this,' said Clarissa, barely able to conceal her lust.

Heather had never been hit on like this before. She was from Bedworth, a small mining town. Clarissa was like no woman she had ever met. She glanced nervously at Clarissa, who held her in an unblinking stare, she leaned towards her and whispered. 'I'm not one of those.'

Clarissa smiled. 'Neither am I, but I don't mind sharing a bed with a beautiful woman.'

Heather glanced anxiously towards Julien, fearing that he would get the wrong impression of her. He was nowhere to be seen. He had witnessed Clarissa's antics before and, without a word, had discreetly faded to the back of the shop to put on the coffee machine.

Clarissa finally released her hand and turned and picked a basque from the rail. 'Why don't you try this on?'

Heather looked at it, it was a very sexy garment. If she wore this at home it would probably give the chief a heart attack. She shook her head. 'No, it's too suggestive. Harold would get the wrong idea.'

'Don't wear it for him, wear it for me.'

There was no doubting Clarissa's intentions. Heather should have run but she couldn't. For reasons she could not explain, she felt drawn to Clarissa, excited by her. She wanted to try the fruit of the forbidden tree and for that there would be a price, a very high price.

There was a short silence between them and then Julien reappeared from the depths of the fitting room. 'Would you ladies care for a coffee?'

'Is it French?' asked Clarissa.'

'As French as me.'

Clarissa smiled. 'I'll have tea then.'

Clarissa and Heather spent the next hour reducing Chief Constable Wilson's liquidity. The bill, when Julien finally rang it up, was over two hundred pounds. For a moment Heather thought she had gone too far, her father was a miner and he had only earned forty pounds a week. He would have gone ballistic. Her husband earned five times that but she had spent his entire weekly salary in over an hour, he too would go ballistic … unless. Heather turned back to Julien. 'Can I have the basque, please, Julien.'

'Changed your mind?'

'No, but I'm going to have to give my husband some compensation for my spending.'

'He's a lucky man,' grinned Julien.

'A very lucky man,' sighed Clarissa. 'Any chance of me getting to see you in it first?'

Without thinking Heather nodded. 'Yes, I'd like that.'

Clarissa's hungry eyes lit up. 'Excellent, my place is just a short walk from here.'

Poor Chief Wilson would never get to see Heather in her cherry-red basque. Clarissa had found her prey and fate had placed Heather into a scenario that had not been written for her.

Chapter 36
Brothers And Sisters

Phil Townsend was not a happy man. He liked Lizzie Birchwood, she had been a good guest and then become a friend. In the last few days before she died, there was something amiss; she hadn't been herself, it just didn't feel right. He couldn't ignore his misgivings any longer. He picked up the phone and dialled. It rang twice before it was answered.

Phil held the receiver tightly hoping he was doing the right thing.

'Hello Phil?'

'Hi Mel, can you talk.'

'Of course, what about?'

'The murder of Lizzie Birchwood.'

There was silence for a moment at the other end of the line. 'Do you have some information?'

'Not really, but there is something wrong about this. Strange things were happening to Lizzie in the days leading up to her death.'

'What sort of things, Phil?'

'I'd rather not say on the phone, it's going to sound crazy. Could you come to the pub? I can go through it then.'

Mel looked at her watch and then at her diary. 'I could be with you at about six-thirty tonight.'

'Great, you can have dinner at the pub.'

'You got one of your feelings, bruv?'

'Yes.'

Mel's brother had once been one of the best detectives in Birmingham and his instincts were legendary. If Phil Townsend said he had a feeling about a case, she needed to listen. 'OK, see you at six-thirty.'

Mel put down the phone. What the hell had gone on at the Windmill to make her brother so concerned?

If Oliver and Felix had known about the relationship between the landlord at the Windmill and DI Mel Townsend, they would have thought twice about placing the walkie-talkie in the wall. It was another twist of fate that they hadn't seen coming.

Chapter 37
Poetry In Motion

Mel hugged her brother. 'Good to see you, bruv.'

'You too, sis, you want to eat first?'

Mel shook her head. 'No. What's bugging you? I know you wouldn't have called if you didn't think it was serious.'

'It's Lizzie, she was great, always positive … but in the last few days she started having these terrible dreams, thought she heard voices. She woke the whole place up. She was in a terrible state.'

'Did you hear anything?'

Phil started to shake his head, but stopped. 'The night she was killed, I was pretty sleepy but I turned over and I swear I heard someone speaking poetry.'

'Poetry? Can you remember any of it?'

'It was Shakespeare, something about knowing a bank where the wild thyme blows.'

'Where oxlips and the nodding violet grows?'

'That's it, what is it?'

'It's Oberon in *A Midsummer Night's Dream*,' said Mel.

'How did you know that?'

'I did it for O Level.'

'Does it mean anything?'

Mel nodded thoughtfully. 'It does, whoever owns that voice is probably the Shakespeare Murderer.'

'You think the two are connected?'

'I do. Where did the voice come from, was it outside?'

Phil shook his head. 'I don't think so, it seemed to be coming from her room.'

'Really, do you think she had someone in there?'

'No. I saw her go to bed, all the exterior doors were locked by me.'

'Well, someone unlocked the door later because she went out and met her killer.'

'The door could only be unlocked from the inside.'

None of it made any sense to Mel. Lizzie had been locked safely in her room and, despite having had nightmares the previous night, ventured out into the night to meet her killer. What would make her do that?

'Can I see her room, please?'

Phil shrugged. 'It's empty, SOCO took loads of stuff and the local force had a look over it.'

'Did you tell them about the voices?'

'Nah, I was still in a state of shock, never thought.'

There was something nagging at the back of Mel's mind, the voice that her brother had heard had to be connected to the murder. They knew the murderer was influenced by Shakespeare. What had drawn Lizzie Birchwood from the safety of her room to the moonlit streets of Stratford and her death? As she followed her brother up the stairs, she felt a growing sense of foreboding.

Phil opened the door and stood back.

As she entered the room the foreboding increased, someone was dancing a two-step on her grave.

'You OK, sis?'

Mel nodded. 'I am but there's something wrong in here.'

'What are you, a cop or a soothsayer?'

Mel smiled. 'Coppers intuition, I can feel it.' Mel had felt the darkness before, been to places where evil seemed to have left an indelible mark. The walls of the room felt like they were closing in, and she felt a wave of claustrophobia sweep across her. The hairs on the back of her neck all standing to attention, she took a deep breath and forced herself to walk into the centre of the room. She breathed in deeply once again, steadying herself. Her brother watched her silently, not wanting to break her communion with the events that had occurred here.

Mel crossed the room and looked out of the window towards the car park. 'Are you sure that the voice didn't come from outside, someone could have stood just below the window and not been seen.'

Phil shook his head. 'No, the voice was coming from this room, I'm certain of it.'

Mel crouched down and looked under the bed, there was nothing except dust. There was a wardrobe in the corner of the room. She walked over and opened it to be greeted by a row of empty hangers, the skeletons of a life passed by. The clothes that had once hung there were now in sealed bags awaiting forensic investigation, the body they had once adorned now cold.

Mel stood up and looked slowly around the room, there was nothing out of the ordinary, no sign of forced entry. She shook her head. 'I have a bad feeling about this room.'

'It's south facing.'

Mel grinned. 'I'm not a hotel inspector, bruv, the rooms fine but …' Mel trailed off.

'What?'

'You're going to think I'm going crazy.'

'Already do, sis. What is it?'

'I just have a feeling that something's wrong in here.'

Before Phil could answer, a strange blipping sound disturbed the momentary silence of the room.

'Did you hear that?'

Phil looked at his sister. 'Yeah.'

'What was it?'

'I don't know.'

Mel held up her hand and stood very still, waiting. *Blip*. There it was again.

'What is that?'

'Beats me, sounds electrical.' Phil was right. The battery pack attached to the walkie-talkie was finally running out and its death throes were causing little static discharges.

Mel was now staring around the room waiting for another blip. After what seemed like an eternity, it came again. *Blip.*

'There.' Phil pointed at an airbrick near the top of the wall. 'It came from there.'

Mel went over to it and peered at the vent; it had a screw missing and the remaining screws looked like they had been recently removed. The vent had been painted over in the past but the paint had been scraped away where a screw driver had twisted in the screw head. 'You got a screw driver? This needs to come off.'

Phil nodded and hurried from the room. Mel could feel the excitement rising. She took a deep breath; this could be something. A few seconds later, Phil reappeared clutching a screwdriver. Mel took it from him.

'I'll do it.' She stood on the bed and then leaned against the wall with her elbow and started undoing the vent. The first two screws came out easily but the last one was more stubborn, whoever had put it in last had been in a hurry and cross threaded it. Carefully, she turned it until it was finally free. She passed the screws and screwdriver to her brother.

'Let's see what secrets are hidden in here.' She gently eased the vent off and as she pulled it away, she saw it. 'Well, now we know where the voice came from.' She leaned back so that her brother could see into the cavity. 'Some clever sod has put a walkie-talkie in here with a battery pack.'

Phil was visibly shocked. 'How the hell did that get in there?'

'Our killer put it there. This is all part of a pre-meditated murder. Looks like some serious planning went into this.'

'What do we do now?'

'We phone Guild Street and get Toby and Fred up here ASAP!'

Chapter 38
The Wrong Light

'Bugger me, this is creative,' said Fred, as he peered into the cavity where the walkie-talkie sat. 'Looks like he's taped down the receive button and switched it on so that he could broadcast into Lizzie's room whenever he wanted to.'

'And he put the battery pack on to give him a few days to play with. A lot of planning went into this,' said Toby. He turned to Mel Townsend. 'Did you call in SOCO.'

Mel shook her head. 'No, thought you might want to do that, being as your boys missed it.'

'That's out of order, Mel, you only found it because it made a noise,' snapped Fred. 'I suppose you're going to report this to Wilson?'

'No. I thought I would let you do it so you can claim the glory. Might be better coming from Toby though, you and Wilson really don't like each other much, do you?'

Fred shrugged. 'He wouldn't be my first choice for a candle-lit supper.'

'You should tell him, ma'am. You found it.'

'No, Toby, you know what he's like. He'd start in on Beeching about his team having to solve your cases for you. It's best coming from you.'

'I'll call in SOCO then we can put it in our reports to Beeching and Wilson.'

Fred climbed down off the bed. 'I reckon we need to have a trawl around all the local electrical shops to see if we can find where this thing came from.' Fred peered back up at the cavity. 'Think we might be wasting our time though; it looks like an old army-issue one. Could have come from any army and navy stores or even a second-hand shop. It's going to be like trying to find a poor man on the Tiddington Road.'

'There are no poor men on the Tiddington Road,' said Toby.

'I rest my case.' Fred turned back to Mel. 'So, what do you think?'

'I think I need to have a chat with my brother. Someone planted that within the last three or four days. We need to know who has had access to this room.'

They all turned to Phil.

'Apart from Lizzie, who has had access?'

'Well, Sandra, the cleaning lady.'

'I'll need her details; we will have to interview her. Who else?'

'Me, I suppose.'

'I think we can rule you out, sir. You do have other rooms here though, don't you?'

Phil looked at Toby. 'Yes, another three on this floor.'

'We'll need names and addresses of anyone who has stayed here,' said Toby.

Phil looked doubtful. 'Nah, that won't turn up much. The only folks who have been up here are all old customers, I can vouch for them.'

'Someone planted that walkie-talkie in the wall,' said Mel.

Phil looked at his sister. 'I suppose they did.'

'We just have to narrow down a list of everyone who could possibly have had access to this room in the last four days,' said Mel.

'Could be more, we need an expert to tell us how long those batteries could last if they were brand-new and then work back.' Fred turned to Toby. 'Let's assume a week and start from there. Phil, can you do me a list of every guest you've had in the last seven days, any member of staff who has worked during the last week and any workmen who have been in the building. Don't leave anyone out.'

Phil nodded. 'I'll do it now.'

The net was slowly tightening. Not half a mile away from the Windmill, the owner of one of those names was eating a sandwich that Oliver had prepared for him. 'What do you think?'

Felix nodded. 'It's delicious, what is it?'

'It's called a maakouda, it's a fried potato pattie inside a sandwich. It's just potato, flour, eggs and herbs. I learned how to make it in Morocco.'

'I love it.' Felix took another mouthful; it was the first thing he'd eaten since seeing Lizzie die.

Oliver watched his friend and smiled. 'You didn't enjoy the last performance, did you.' He waited for Felix to swallow his food.

'No, I didn't.'

'Was it my delivery?'

'Your delivery was perfect, you know that. You enchanted that poor woman, lured her to her death using Shakespeare's verse like a siren calling sailors to their doom.'

Oliver gave a mock bow. 'Yes, I thought I was rather good myself. Can't understand for the life of me why you didn't like it.'

'Because she was innocent,' snapped Felix. 'You killed an innocent person. This is supposed to be about revenge, harming those who harmed you. What did poor Lizzie do?'

'Bloody hell, Felix, put on another record will you, we've been through this before.'

'It was just her doing her job. She made you a star with that part.'

'Only because I ignored her directions. Her interpretation was ludicrous, Romeo wasn't unsure about his sexuality and Juliet most certainly wasn't a lesbian.'

'So, you killed her for artistic differences?'

Oliver thought about it for a moment and then grinned wolfishly. 'Yes, I suppose I did? Does that make me bad?'

'It makes you the very devil! You really have to reign your

murdering instincts in, it's getting embarrassing.'

Oliver fixed Felix with a long, slow stare. 'Or what?'

Felix squirmed uncomfortably on his chair.

'Are you giving me an ultimatum?' demanded Oliver.

'No, no, never that. It's just—'

'Just what?'

'You're going to get caught.'

'By who,' said Oliver dismissively. 'The local plod isn't bright enough to catch me.'

'They're not fools. That Fred Williams has been around here for a long time, he gets results.'

'If he was any good they would have moved him on somewhere bigger by now. He was here when I was last here.'

Felix knew not to argue with Oliver when he was in this mood, he seemed to think he was invincible. 'Who's next then?' It was a simple question but its implications were far reaching, for someone.'

Oliver smiled. 'The next victim. Yes, I've been thinking about that, I've actually put things in motion.'

'What does that mean?'

'Desdemona has been given her handkerchief.'

Felix looked confused.

'Clarissa has been selected. I gave her a handkerchief.'

'Ah,' Felix nodded. 'She is your Desdemona.'

Oliver nodded.

'Did you ever love her?'

'I had sex with her but I never loved her.' Oliver thought about it for a moment. 'You know, Felix, I don't think I've ever been in love. In lust, I've been there many times, but never in love.'

'But Othello was madly in love with Desdemona, that's why he was so jealous when Iago lied to him, how do you square that circle?'

'I don't have to. Don't forget that in this scenario I'm Iago too.'

'That's a deadly combination.'

'It is, I get to load the bullets and pull the trigger.' Oliver laughed. 'It's the most fun part I've ever had.'

'Remind me, why is Clarissa going to die, she didn't cuckold you.'

'She cuckolded every man she ever slept with, the woman's a sexual predator, nothing with a pulse is safe.'

'She does have an outgoing personality,' observed Felix. 'But does that justify killing her?'

'Not really, but my mind is made up. In the new company that I am going to form there is no place for her. She's second-rate at best. Maybe if she'd taken her limited talent to the TV soaps I wouldn't have to kill her, but could you imagine the scenario where I play Macbeth to her Lady Macbeth?'

Felix tried to imagine it and shuddered. 'Fair enough, when are you going to kill her?'

It was as simple as that, Felix had tried to imagine Clarissa playing the dark lady and suddenly the thought of killing her seemed eminently reasonable.

'Tonight, I know where she's stopping and I've taken the time to pick her lock as a trial run. Took me about thirty seconds.'

'Tonight, isn't that a bit soon?'

'You don't understand, do you? The faster we kill them, the higher the body pile gets and the dear old boys in blue will be drowning in a sea of bad publicity and bodies.'

There was a dark logic to Oliver's argument. The police had been staggered by the speed of the first series of murders. Now, after a break of over six weeks, Oliver was back and hungry for more.

'Can I come?' asked Felix.

Oliver nodded. 'Yeah, sure you want to?'

'Not really, but I'd quite like to see Clarissa's big mouth shut once and for all.'

'Not a fan then.'

'She ruined my relationship with the only woman I ever loved.'

'How did she do that.'

'She slept with me.'

Oliver laughed. 'Doesn't that make it your fault too?'

'Not really, she seduced me.'

'Oh, how dare she, no wonder you don't like her.'

Felix could hear the mocking tone in Oliver's voice but he didn't care. Clarissa had tempted him and then told the whole world about it. To make matters worse, when Felix's girlfriend had found out about it she had dumped him, and then Clarissa dumped him too. There was still an indignant rage burning inside him; he was incapable of acknowledging his own part in his downfall.

'Are you taking your own pillow?'

'What?'

'Are you taking your own pillow?'

Oliver shrugged. 'I'm sure there will be pillows in her room.'

'Feathers or foam infill.'

'Does it make a difference.'

Felix looked at Oliver as if he were crazy. 'Of course. Feather will be denser, fewer air gaps. Foam, on the other hand, will have loads of air cavities. You'd have to use a lot more downward pressure to get a result.'

'I'm guessing, where she's staying, they won't be using cheap foam-filled pillows.'

'And if they do?'

'Then I press harder!'

Chapter 39
To Die Upon A Kiss

Less than half a mile from where Oliver and Felix were discussing her death, Clarissa was busy smothering her own victim. To be fair, Heather Wilson seemed to be enjoying herself. The moans that were coming from beneath the sheets were all in the affirmative.

She had never been with a woman before but Clarissa clearly had. Her firm athletic body was so different from the sweaty lump she had become used to of late. She wasn't missing the appendage that Clarissa so clearly lacked. They had been making love for nearly two hours which was one hour and fifty-seven minutes more than the chief ever managed.

Clarissa fell back and gasped, smiling up at the ceiling. 'Phew, been a while since I did that.'

Heather propped herself up on an elbow. 'You're not just a lesbian then.'

'God no, I like men too much for that. I'm just greedy. Who wants to go to a buffet and only eat the sausage?'

They both laughed. Clarissa looked at her watch. 'Jesus, I need to get moving, I've got a rehearsal tonight.'

She sprang out of bed and Heather went to follow her. Clarissa leaned down and kissed her. 'Stay as long as you like, just pull the door to behind you when you leave.'

She watched Clarissa shrug into her jeans and pull on a T-shirt. She had a great body. She flicked her hair back and glanced in the mirror; a quick application of lippy and she smiled at her reflection. 'Good enough.' She turned back to Heather. 'You want to do this again?' Heather nodded. 'Good, you know where I am.'

She shot her one last smile and headed for the door.

As it clicked shut, Heather sighed; she'd never met anyone like Clarissa. The chief really would have to go. He'd been good to her and she was fond of him but not fond enough. As she lay back on the bed, she noticed Clarissa's beautiful scarf on the pillow next to her. Clarissa had used it to tie her hands; she smiled at the memory. She pulled it towards her and held it to her face, it still smelled of her. She breathed in deeply and fell asleep dreaming of her.

Two hours later, Heather still lay sleeping in Clarissa's bed. She was naked, except for the beautiful handkerchief that lay across her face.

Oliver and Felix stood at the end of the bed looking down on her sleeping form.

'We should cover her, she's going to catch a chill.'

Oliver stared at Felix. 'I'm just about to smother her, I really think that's the least of her worries.'

'When you put it like that.' Felix sighed. 'Clarissa's kept herself in great shape, seems a bit wasteful to kill her. Could we give her another year or two and get her then?'

Oliver shook his head. 'No, she needs killing now.'

He leaned across to a bedside chair where a pillow lay, picked it up and then smiled at Felix. 'Feather, quite dense. This will do the job nicely.'

He stood over her, the handkerchief rose and fell with her breathing and her blonde hair lay spread across the pillow. Clarissa had always had lovely hair.

'You going to remove the handkerchief?' Felix stepped forward but Oliver grabbed hold of his arm and held him back.

'Leave it, I don't want to risk waking her. She can die with my gift covering her cheating face.'

'She didn't cheat on you though,' said Felix.

Oliver cast his eyes around the room at the hastily shed clothes and the two empty wine glasses. 'She's cheated on someone.' He held the pillow above her head and then paused. 'Any last words?'

'Goodbye,' whispered Felix.

Oliver nodded approvingly and then slowly lowered the pillow onto the face beneath the handkerchief. 'Think on thy sins, Clarissa, for that thou diest.' Oliver leaned in and increased the pressure. He had no way of knowing that the beautiful form that lay beneath his deadly force was not Clarissa. To him, the evidence of the handkerchief was confirmation of her unfaithfulness, maybe not to him but to someone.

Beneath the pillow her body began to show the first signs of distress, recognition that all was not well. Her left foot began to twitch, then the right. She was still unconscious but somewhere the neural pathways in her brain were beginning to fire out warning messages to the rest of her body. *Wake up, wake up. Can't breathe, can't … this is not a dream.* Her whole body began to shake and Oliver pressed down harder and harder, struggling to hold the pillow in place as her back arched violently upwards. Felix wanted to look away, but he couldn't. He had seen this performed so many times, a scene upon a stage, but this time it was for real. The true horror of it now bore down on him and yet he could not avert his eyes. Oliver's face was impassive, but in his eyes there glowed a hatred that came from a dark, dark place; a place where there was no love or compassion, just a burning desire for revenge.

The shaking of Heather's body increased. Like the possessed trying to exorcise a devil, she tried to arch and twist her head from beneath the feathered tomb that was smothering the life from her. Her lungs could get no oxygen and the screams in her throat had no air to support them. Suddenly her hands shot up and she tried desperately to wrench the pillow from her face. It was too little, too late. Her remaining strength was not enough to save her.

Oliver had her clamped in his death grip and he would never

let her go. For another minute she struggled on, her efforts gradually diminishing as her brain cells shut down through lack of oxygen. Oliver kept the pressure on, absorbed in the moment.

Felix placed a hand on his shoulder. 'I think you can stop now; Clarissa's gone.'

Oliver looked up at Felix. 'Are you sure?'

'I'm sure.'

Oliver straightened slowly, he winced as his back twinged. 'That was harder than I thought it would be. Clarissa clearly wasn't ready to go.'

The pillow was still in his right hand, he glanced down at it and then dropped it, as if surprised to see it there. With the pillow gone, only the handkerchief remained across her face. Oliver smiled. 'Shall I do the honours?'

Felix moved forward, shaking his head. 'No, I think you've done enough for one day.' He leaned down across the bed and gently slid the handkerchief off Heather's face. The silk slid effortlessly across her soft skin until the moment that Felix could see her complete features once again. The eyes looked back from the past, at a future they could no longer see, and Felix froze.

'No! No, it can't be.' Oliver pulled him aside and looked down. 'Oh, bugger!'

The face that stared back at them was not Clarissa's. Felix stifled a scream. 'What have we done?' He turned to Oliver trembling, his eyes full of tears. 'What have we done?'

Oliver looked unconcerned. 'It appears I've smothered the wrong Desdemona,' he shrugged. 'That's a bit unfortunate.'

'Unfortunate? Unfortunate is when you lose your wallet or break a glass. Murdering the wrong woman is more than unfortunate, it's unforgivable.' The tears began to fall from Felix's eyes.

'Don't cry, my friend. We can always get Clarissa another day.'

Felix turned to Oliver, his face twisted in anger. 'I'm not upset about not killing Clarissa, you monster. Don't you get it? We just killed the wrong woman, an innocent. This is out of control.'

Oliver shook his head and held up the dead woman's left hand. 'She's not that innocent. That's a wedding ring and I'm guessing Clarissa isn't her husband.'

'Stop it, stop it now. This isn't a joke, Oliver, you've just killed the wrong woman, we don't even know who she is. This is terrible.'

'I admit, it's not ideal but—'

'But nothing! This lady is dead, don't you understand. This is not revenge, this is cold-blooded murder, it's irredeemable.'

'Look, I can see you're upset, Felix.'

'Upset! What's wrong with you? Have you lost touch with reality?'

Oliver took Felix firmly by the shoulders and pushed him onto the bedside chair. He fixed him with a cold hard stare. 'You need to get a grip, Felix. This has been a blip on an otherwise faultless journey. Look at her hair, it's just like Clarissa's, look at her body, slim, athletic. Just like Clarissa's. It's a mistake anybody could make. How was I to know that Clarissa had given her handkerchief to a stranger?'

Felix did not respond; this was the end of the road for him. He sat there silently listening to a madman rationalising a murder, the death of an innocent.

'Do you think we should just leave her here or should we get rid of the body.' Oliver's tone was matter of fact, seemingly untouched by what lay before him. 'Maybe it would be better to just dump her somewhere. If she is unconnected to the theatre, the police will be confused about why she has been killed.' Oliver smiled. 'This could be a bit of good luck. Police theories are going to be thrown into confusion. I say we dump her at the back of the theatre, what do you think?'

Felix wasn't thinking anything, he just wanted to get away from this room. Away from the evidence of the life he had just seen taken. He stood up slowly and glanced once more at the lifeless form upon the bed.

'I'm done with this, Oliver, I can't go on.'

'How am I supposed to get her to the back of the theatre alone?'

Felix shook his head. 'I really don't care, I just can't do this any more.'

He walked slowly from the room without looking back, leaving Oliver standing alone. He stood there for some time, his eyes drawn to the evidence of what he had done. He felt no remorse, just a mild irritation. It had all gone so well, what a pity it wasn't Clarissa. There was no way he could move the body to the theatre on his own. She would just have to stay here until Clarissa returned and found her.

He smiled to himself. Clarissa would have some explaining to do, not just to the police but to the husband of the woman. Maybe this wasn't so bad after all. Clarissa would be in an awkward situation. She would also know it should have been her; so would the police. The confusion could only be good for him.

Only one doubt clouded his mind. Should he take the handkerchief? He had given it to Clarissa, just as Othello had given one to Desdemona; if he took it would she suspect him? Or should he leave it? He pondered it for several minutes before deciding to leave it. A guilty man would take it, he was just a friend who had given a present to a woman he admired.

The only thing he was sure of was that his visits to the Dirty Duck would have to stop. Well, at least until he managed to kill Clarissa. He couldn't afford to be questioned about the gift.

He took one last look around the room, making sure there was no evidence of his or Felix's presence. Once he was satisfied, he gazed down at his victim. He stroked her face and gently kissed her cooling forehead. '"I kissed thee ere I killed thee. No way but this, killing myself to die upon a kiss."'

His words fell on unlistening ears that could no longer appreciate the excellence of his Othello. This Othello, however, felt no remorse and had no intention of killing himself. Felix, on the other hand, was a different matter.

Chapter 40
No Comedy, Just Errors

The moment she walked back into her room, Clarissa knew something was wrong. Heather's clothes, which had been cast aside so passionately just hours earlier, still lay where they had landed. Memorials to a moment that had passed, pointers to something terrible.

An awful sense of dread consumed her; Heather should have left hours ago. Clarissa tried to call her name but her throat was suddenly dry. She took the few steps that led her to her bedroom door and there, upon the bed, lay Heather. Dead.

She had seen situations like this in films: there were screams, a desperate dash to the victim's side. Clarissa did neither of these things. She just stood, transfixed by the sight before her, death laid bare. Cold, real and irrefutable.

In that moment, she knew that the body on the bed should have been her. She had no logical reason for this, she just knew. A tear fell from her left eye and trickled slowly down her face; sadness and guilt intertwined with remorse. She had brought Heather here, had led her to the place of her death, and for what? To sate her endless desires, to occupy a few empty hours of her meaningless existence. The revulsion at the sight before her turned into self-loathing, and only then did she begin to scream.

Fred and Toby were at Guild Street when the call came in. Ginger Dalton popped his head around the corner of the incident room.

'There's been another murder, sir.'

Fred glanced at Toby. 'Where?'

'An apartment on the corner of College Street.'

'That's in Old Town. Come on, Toby, let's get down there.'

As Fred grabbed his car keys and headed for the door, he nodded to Ginger. 'I want you and Kinky down there asap, call SOCO and get Alf Butcher down there too. Round up some uniforms and seal off Old Town and College Lane.'

As they raced down High Street, sirens blaring, Toby asked the question neither of them had thought to ask Ginger. 'Who's been murdered? We never asked.'

Fred swore at an elderly cyclist who had decided to ignore the police sirens blaring behind him and cut across him into Sheep Street.

'Jesus wept, is that old bugger deaf.'

'Probably.'

'Well, he'll be dead as well as deaf if he doesn't get out of the way.'

The old boy coasted down Sheep Street, oblivious to his brush with death, and Fred gunned the motor as they swept past the Falcon Hotel. The next few seconds passed in a blur of buildings and multiple expletives from Fred, whose invective reached fever pitch as they took a hard left onto Old Town and then gunned it down to the end of College Street.

'Do we know who is on the scene?'

Toby glanced down at the note Ginger had passed him as they had run from the incident room. 'Ken White, boss.'

'Jesus,' exclaimed Fred in exasperation. DS Ken White was his least favourite officer. Overweight and under-brained, Ken White had been marking time until his retirement from the day he had arrived at Guild Street. He still had another ten years to go. Fred hoped to get him killed in the line of duty before then.

As they pulled up outside the building, Ken White was leaning against the garden wall eating a doughnut. When he saw Fred behind the wheel of the car, he hurriedly shovelled the last remnants into his mouth and licked the sticky jam from his fingers.

Fred marched over to him. 'What the hell do you think you are doing? This is a murder scene, not a bloody picnic.'

DS White shrugged. He couldn't reply, the doughnut prevented it.

Fred leaned in towards him. 'Do you have any idea just how much I hate you, Ken?'

Ken nodded.

'Well however much you think it is, it's more, much more. Have you secured the scene?' Ken nodded again. 'Has the victim been certified dead.' Demonstrating his vast array of nonverbal communication skills, Ken shook his head. 'Male or female,' snapped Fred. Ken cupped imaginary breasts. Fred turned to Toby, shaking his head. 'Tell Marcel Marceau here to stop anybody but SOCO or Alf Butcher coming in, apart from you. Soon as he can talk again, get your ass inside.'

Toby couldn't help but smile. As Fred disappeared through the front door, he turned back to DS White who was masticating for all he was worth. 'I don't think the boss is very happy with you, sir.'

Ken swallowed hard and finally regained his ability to talk. 'Well, he doesn't outrank me.'

'No, sir, he doesn't. But he is in charge of this case and he has asked me to tell you to only allow SOCO and Alf Butcher into the building for now.'

Ken shrugged. 'Suits me. I hate dead bodies, makes me hungry.' He reached into his pocket and pulled out a Marathon Bar. 'You get in there, DC Marlowe and I'll look after everything out here.' He then took a huge bite of the bar rendering himself, once more, speechless.

Toby turned and strode into the building.

'Up here.' Fred's voice came from the first-floor landing.

Toby bounded up the stairs two at a time. Fred was standing on the landing outside the open door to the apartment. He looked shocked.

'Is it bad, sir?'

Fred shook his head. 'No, it's worse than that. It's Chief Constable Wilson's wife.'

Toby heard the words but they made no sense. Chief Wilson's wife wasn't anything to do with the theatre. 'Are you sure, sir?'

Fred nodded. 'Yes, it's definitely his wife. I met her at a police do last year.'

There were so many questions flying through Toby's head that he couldn't think of anything to say.

Fred nodded towards the room. 'Follow me.'

They walked into the hallway and then into a bedroom. There were clothes scattered on the floor and there, on the bed, lay a very beautiful but very dead young woman. Despite the bulging eyes and the blue distended mouth, he recognised her from the photo he had seen in Wilson's office at Coventry HQ. Heather Reddy as was, now the late Mrs Wilson. None of this made any sense.

Fred stared around the room. 'What do you see, Toby.'

Toby looked from the body and down onto the floor, taking in the clothes that lay abandoned en route to the bed. 'She clearly had sex before she died.'

'Very spontaneous by the look of it.'

'Well, we know that Clarissa Pidgeon is known to eat from the fruit of several trees, boss.'

Fred sighed. 'We do, but how do we explain that to Chief Wilson? He strikes me as a man that only has his fruit in a pie.'

'That is going to be a tricky conversation. Is Beeching going to do it?'

Fred sighed again. 'No, I think I'm going to have to. We are going to need Wilson to officially identify the body.'

Toby followed the trail of clothes to the bed and his eyes fell on the silk handkerchief, embroidered with strawberries, that lay on Heather Wilson's shoulder.

'Boss, did you notice the scarf?'

'Course I did. Why?'

'Look at the clothes, sir, it doesn't match.'

Fred looked from the clothes on the floor to the handkerchief and back. Toby was right, it didn't match. 'What's your point?'

'That's not Heather Wilson's scarf, it's Clarissa's.'

'There's no surprise there, this is Clarissa's room. What are you thinking?'

'Mistaken identity?'

The curtains were drawn and night had fallen more than an hour ago. Fred looked around. 'This room faces north-east. With the curtains drawn it's going to be pretty gloomy in here, even in the daytime.'

'According to Clarissa, the curtains were closed when she found Heather,' said Toby.

Fred nodded thoughtfully. 'They have the same athletic figures.'

'And very similar hair. What if—?'

Fred was ahead of Toby. 'What if that handkerchief was covering her face and the killer smothered the wrong victim?'

Toby nodded. 'Makes more sense than the killer suddenly killing victims with no links to his past or the theatre.'

Fred knew that Toby was right. 'He's made his first mistake.'

'And it's a big one, but how does that help us, boss?'

'I don't know, Toby, I really don't know.'

Fred took one last look at Heather's motionless body, the force that had once moved it now long gone. No joy, no hope, no future. Sometimes he hated this job.

Chapter 41
The Lonely Heart

Chief Constable Wilson sat alone in his living room. The TV was on but he was not watching. It was nine p.m. Where was Heather? She had told him she was going to Stratford, shopping, but she should have been back long before he returned from his duties. He wasn't used to being alone. Before he had married Heather, he had been married to Barbara for twenty-six years.

Barbara had always been there, caring for him, supporting him. She had been a good wife but she was just so … boring. It wasn't a crime, for years it had been a comfort, with the constant pressures of his rank it was good to come home to a cooked meal, a comfortable house. Safe in the knowledge that nothing was required of him, she really had put his happiness before her own.

The realisation hit him hard: he had taken her for granted. Her life had revolved around him, making sure his every need was taken care of. Heather fulfilled a very different need. Sitting there alone with just the TV prattling away in the corner of the room he realised, for the first time, that he was lonely.

What he and Heather had wasn't a partnership; it was an arrangement. Heather married him for the finer things in life and he had agreed, trading loyal companionship for the excitement of a much younger, forbidden fruit.

He was a fool; he knew at work they laughed at him behind his back. Old Wilson, marrying a girl young enough to be his daughter. They were right, of course. He had been shallow, too eager to betray the loyalty of his former wife for the passing pleasure of revisiting his youth by proxy. The past was indeed another country and he could not go back.

He looked up at the clock: two minutes past nine. He should call someone, but who? He didn't know who Heather's friends were, she had left her old life behind when she had moved in with him. A cuckoo occupying a new nest. The phone rang. That will be Heather, he thought. He hurried to the hallway and picked up the receiver. 'Wilson residence.' There was silence at the other end of the line and he repeated himself. 'Wilson residence. Is that you, Heather?'

'Hello, sir, its DS Williams from Stratford.'

'What on earth are you calling me at this hour for?' There was silence from the other end of the line. 'Well?'

'Is your wife there, sir?'

It was a simple question. Just five words. But as he heard them, he knew his whole world was about to come crashing down.

'No, she's not.'

There was a momentary silence at the other end of the phone. 'I've sent a car across to your house to pick you up, sir.'

'I can drive myself. What's going on, Williams.'

'I'd rather not say on the phone, sir. Your driver will be with you in a few minutes.'

The cold fear of loss was now running through his body. Wilson tried to calm his breathing. 'What is it Williams, what's happened?'

'There's been another murder, sir!'

Chapter 42
What A Piece Of Work Is A Man!

Felix sat on his boat looking down the river towards the weir. What had begun with a simple notion of revenge – revenge that had burned with a white-hot purity of purpose – had now become something less. Tawdry, sadistic and wrong. He should have run when Lizzie Birchwood was killed, she was an innocent, but no. He had been infected by Oliver's poison, a poison that clouded his conscience, justified the wrong; this though could not be justified. His journal lay open before him and he began to write.

Entry 3: The End of the Story?

I fear this may be the last entry I make. Last night was the final straw, the death of innocence.

I laugh as I read that line. There was no innocence, it died a long time ago. How could I have been such a fool? Killing can never be justified. I loaded the gun and let Oliver pull the trigger, now I can't control who he aims it at or how often he pulls it. I'm attached to a runaway train and, for me, it's run out of rail. But how do I get off? Oliver won't allow it. There is a reckoning coming.

I don't know who he killed last night. The room was dark and she lay upon the bed in the gloom, her face covered by the handkerchief that Oliver had given to Clarissa just a couple of days before. We should have removed it, but what was the point? He intended to smother her, her face would be covered regardless. It was terrible watching that sleeping body slowly realise that it was dying. From a deep, untroubled sleep death slowly roused her. She twitched and then trembled until the moment that she awoke, it was horrible. She fought to live, struggled with every fibre of her being, but Oliver was too strong. He held her head down beneath the pillow. As he applied irresistible force, I looked into his eyes … he was smiling.

I told him last night that I was done with this, I've seen too much, I've done too much. Oliver will soon be knocking at my door and I will have to open it to him: he will enter and he is death. My death. In Oliver's world you are either with him or …? The clock of the remaining hours of my life is ticking. Maybe I should kill him, but then what? Confess what happened to the police … how could I justify my part? I couldn't be in prison for years, I'm not strong enough. No, I must stand my ground and face the music, trusting that Oliver will spare my life. I doubt he will.

Felix put down the pen and closed his journal. What was he writing? A confession? Or was it evidence to be found in the event of his demise? He had never felt so near to death. He sighed, looked up and instantly recognised the figure walking towards him from Lucy's Lock: Oliver.

He hurriedly grabbed the journal and crouched down to a hidden compartment he had requested during the refit. It was meant to be a secret compartment for his valuables. He opened it, slid the journal in and clicked it shut. He stood back up. Oliver was only about fifty yards away now. He stepped over to the kitchen area and filled the kettle. He felt the need to try and act as if everything was fine, in case his life depended upon it.

Oliver reached the boat and tapped on the door. 'Permission to come aboard, skip?'

'You don't need to ask, Oliver. Kettle's on, fancy a cuppa?'

Oliver skipped lightly aboard. Felix noted how graceful, how athletic he was. Should there be a struggle, he knew he could not compete with Oliver.

Oliver smiled and then sat down on one of the two stools that were bolted to the floor by the dining table.

'That's was quite some cock up last night, wasn't it.' He was smiling as he said it.

Felix didn't join him in the expression. 'A bit more than that.'

'Yeah, suppose it was.'

'You know it was,' whispered Felix. 'This has gone too far.'

Oliver fixed him with a stare. 'What does that mean?' An awkward silence fell between them. Felix said nothing and Oliver waited. After twenty seconds, Oliver rephrased his question. 'Are we good, Felix? Can we put the events of last night behind us?'

Felix chose his words carefully. 'Depends what you mean by put behind.'

Oliver nodded. 'I thought you might be suffering a pang of guilt over your boiled eggs this morning, that's why I came around.'

Felix sighed sadly. 'You really think I've been able to eat breakfast after witnessing …' he paused for a moment, trying to find the right words. 'That!'

'Listen, Felix, I admit it was unfortunate. The young lady was in the wrong place at the wrong time but it was an innocent mistake. You were there, you thought it was Clarissa too.'

'Do we even know who it was you killed last night?'

'According to *The Herald*, that DS Williams will be making a statement to the press at nine a.m. I listened to BBC radio this morning and I got the distinct impression that they know who it is.'

'Why do you say that?' Felix couldn't hide the anxiety in his voice.

Oliver noted his comment with satisfaction. Felix was still afraid of being caught. Not the response of a man who was going to sell him out and implicate himself at the same time. 'Just the way they read the script. It was a pre-prepared statement written by someone who knew something big was about to break. I could hear it in their voice.'

'You think it was somebody famous?'

'Famously dead,' laughed Oliver. It was a cold hard laugh that chilled Felix to the bone. 'I've a feeling that our fake Desdemona will be a bit hard to explain so, brace yourself, we could be in for a rough ride.'

'You're saying it like this is a good thing.'

'It is, don't you see? I killed the wrong woman. If she has nothing to do with the theatre or me, how will they explain it?'

'The killer's a psychopath,' said Felix, not trying to hide the disgust in his voice.

'Silver linings, remember. Every cloud has them.'

The kettle began to boil and Felix started to make the tea.

Oliver rose to his feet, watching him. 'Is there something you want to tell me?'

Felix slammed the cup he was holding down onto the work surface. 'I told you last night, I'm out!'

The two men stood looking at each other through the steam that rose from the kettle, the hissing of the boiling water the only sound as they both contemplated their next move.

Felix felt his whole body begin to tense. He recognised the feeling from his acting days, he had tensed like this in the moments before he went on stage. Fight or flight. He knew he would lose this fight, and Oliver was blocking the doorway to the footpath, so he waited.

Oliver sat back down. 'I'm not sure you can quit, old boy, you're in far too deep. We've come too far to let this little …' He eyed Felix as he chose his next word, '… hiccup, stop us.'

'Some hiccup.'

'Events, dear Felix, events. They shape us all and change destinies. Last night may turn out to be a blessing in disguise.'

Felix put down the cup and turned to face Oliver. 'Listen to yourself. Where is your regret, your compassion? I don't think I know you any more.'

'I'm the same Oliver you have always known; just a man.'

'Two men: you kill like Othello and justify it like Iago. You're a parody. Divorced from the plot and making up your own lines. I think you're a little mad.'

Oliver bit his lip and considered his friend's words. 'You really don't like me much any more, do you?'

'I don't think I do.'

'So, what is the remedy? Can I believe that you will just walk away and say nothing, fade quietly into the background while I complete my task.' Oliver opened the drawer next to where he sat and pulled out a carving knife. He hefted it in his hands and then ran his thumb lightly across the blade.

'This is sharp, and weighty. I bet it cuts through meat like a hot knife through butter.'

Felix swallowed hard. 'Are you threatening me, Oliver?'

Oliver smiled. 'No, far from it. I would never threaten you, if I have to kill you, well then, I'll just do it. It's not really a subject that's up for debate.' Oliver spoke with a calm which somehow made his words seem even more chilling.

Felix knew he was in the presence of evil, the mask had fallen and he really didn't like what he saw behind it. 'Stop the killing. We could find a way to get you back into the theatre, it might take a couple of years to get back to Stratford but it could be done.'

'Ahh, Felix, still aiming for a happy ending while we are in the thick of the second act. You know this is a three-act play. Dear Sir Morris, Clarissa and maybe even my dear old mother have yet to die.'

'Your mother?' Felix was genuinely shocked. 'You can't be serious.'

'Deadly. She shacked up with Sir Morris before my father's body was properly cold. I need to know why.'

'You know you can't get away with this.'

Oliver shrugged. 'It's not about winning or losing, Felix, it's about how you play the game.' He ran his finger down the blade again and looked up at Felix; a trickle of blood ran down the blade and fell to the floor. 'I think I play it quite well, don't you?'

'It's not a game though, is it.'

Oliver sucked the blood that was trickling from his finger. 'All I have done is because of you. You wanted this revenge for me. Why draw back now when victory is in sight. I don't understand you, Felix. What must I say to convince you?'

'I demand that you stop.'

Oliver rose slowly to his feet, the knife held firmly in his right hand, his eyes cold. '"Demand me nothing. What you know, you know. From this time forth I never will speak word."'

Felix recognised the words; Iago's last line in *Othello*. This was a final warning from his old friend, the true evil that now occupied his soul was clear for all to see.

Oliver laid down the knife and then looked up at Felix and smiled. 'We won't speak of this again, ever. I know where you stand and you know that my path is set. Do not cross it.'

He smiled and, for a moment, Felix saw a fleeting glimpse of the old Oliver he had loved so much.

'Goodbye, old friend, perhaps we will meet again in happier times.' He turned and walked out through the doorway and off the boat.

Felix watched him until he disappeared in the trees by Lucy's Lock. He felt his knees buckle and grabbed the tabletop for support and then eased himself onto a stool. His whole body was trembling, Oliver's message could not have been clearer: cross him in any way and he would kill him. What had he done?

He saw his face reflected in the mirror on the cabin wall. He looked old, frightened, broken. And then the words of Oliver as a four-year-old boy came to him from somewhere deep in his memory.

'"What a piece of work is a man, how noble in reason, how infinite in faculties, in form and moving how express and admirable; in action how like an angel, in apprehension how like a god: the beauty of the world, the paragon of animals—and yet, to me, what is this quintessence of dust? Man delights not me.'"

And then Felix cried. He cried for a friendship lost, he cried for the death of innocence and he cried for himself. He had made a choice and it had been wrong; now he would have to live with the consequences of that choice for the rest of his days. He didn't think he could.

Chapter 43
A Fool And His Honey

As the door swung open, Fred was confronted with a version of Chief Wilson he had never seen before. He had been dreading this.

'Morning, sir.' Fred's voice echoed down the empty corridor. The next stop was the mortuary; a quiet, sterile, empty space, devoid of all comfort. There was no place in its cold stone walls for hope.

In Wilson's face, Fred could see no optimism, just an acceptance that everything he had hoped for was gone, crumbled to dust. He seemed smaller, shrunken by grief.

'Take me to her, please, Williams.'

'Sir,' Fred turned and led the way down the corridor towards the double doors, on the other side of which lay broken dreams and heartbreak. As they reached the doors, Fred stopped and turned to Chief Wilson. 'Are you ready, sir?'

He shook his head. 'No.'

Fred reached out and lay a hand gently on Wilson's shoulder. 'I'm so sorry, sir.'

He could feel Wilson's body trembling. Without thinking, he pulled Wilson to him and hugged him. For a moment, Wilson stiffened in his arms and then Fred felt his whole body go limp as the tears flowed. Deep sobs that came from a place that no hug could reach.

The door to the mortuary swung open and Alf Butcher stopped dead in his tracks. Fred glanced over Chief Wilson's shoulder and gave Alf the faintest shake of the head. Alf nodded and silently backed into the mortuary, closing the door quietly behind him.

Chapter 44
Friends With Benefits

When Fred returned to Guild Street an hour later, only Toby and Inspector Beeching were in the incident room.

'How'd it go, boss?'

'Terrible. Wilson's a broken man.'

'Did he Identify her?' asked Beeching.

Fred nodded. 'Eventually. Poor chap was beside himself.'

Toby walked over to the incident board, there were pictures of all the victims of the Shakespeare Murderer. Between the pictures were lines connecting each to the other and all back to Oliver Lawrence. To one side of the board was the picture of Heather Wilson.

'How do we connect Heather to the rest of the murders, where's the pattern?'

'I don't know,' said Beeching. 'Maybe it's another killer.'

'No chance, sir. It's Oliver.'

'How can you be so sure?'

'Heather Wilson had been sleeping with Clarissa Pidgeon who is definitely a possible target. Maybe he killed her by mistake.'

'Do you think that's possible?' asked Beeching.

'It is, sir,' said Toby. 'The room was dark. Heather and Clarissa have very similar builds and the same head of fair hair.'

'But they don't have the same face, do they,' snapped Beeching.

'We think there was a silk handkerchief covering her face, it was Clarissa's.'

'Surely if you were about to murder someone you'd check you had the right person first. I know I would.'

Fred and Toby both looked at Beeching.

'If I was a murderer … which I'm not,' he added.

'Good,' said Fred. 'We'll eliminate you from our enquiries then.' He turned back to Toby. 'We think it's mistaken identity, he was after Clarissa.'

'What about the handkerchief, surely he would have checked first?'

'I doubt it, sir. He enters Clarissa's bedroom, it's dark. She's lying on the bed naked, her body is the right size and shape, the hair is the right colour and length. He's planning to smother her with a pillow, why would he risk waking the victim by removing the handkerchief from her face? You'd just place the pillow over her face and get on with it.'

'Even without the handkerchief being over her face, it could have happened. It was dark in there, he was in a hurry and they looked very similar. Besides, he wouldn't be expecting anyone to be in that bed but Clarissa.'

Inspector Beeching looked at the board thoughtfully and scratched his chin. 'Where is Clarissa?'

'We have her in Interview Room One,' said Toby.

'We only have one interview room.'

Fred smiled at Beeching. 'Well, we got the number right then, didn't we, sir.'

Beeching ignored Fred's remark. 'You going to interview her?'

'Yes, sir, Toby and I are going to break the news to her. Let her know that we think it was meant to be her.'

'Good idea, I'll watch from the viewing room.'

Clarissa was sitting at the desk smoking heavily when they entered. She looked tired and shocked. 'I thought you'd forgotten about me.'

'Apologies for the delay, Miss Pidgeon, but we have just been trying to clarify a few details. Can we get you a cup of tea?'

'God no, I've had three already. Any chance of a gin and tonic?'

Toby shook his head. 'I'm terribly sorry, Miss Pidgeon, we are not allowed to have alcohol on the premises.'

The bottle of scotch in Fred Williams' desk was not included in Toby's statement.

Fred pulled up a chair opposite Clarissa. 'My name is DS Williams, Miss Pidgeon. Could you tell me how Mrs Wilson came to be in your bed?'

Clarissa grinned. 'You're kidding.'

'Do I look like I'm kidding.'

'Well, what do you think?'

'I'm hoping I won't have to think, Miss Pidgeon. If you can just give me your explanation, we can move on.'

Clarissa looked from Fred to Toby; neither was smiling. 'She and I had been getting to know each other better.'

Fred nodded. 'Could you expand on that.'

'For God's sake, do I have to spell it out?'

'If you wouldn't mind, miss, just so we can be clear.'

Clarissa sighed. 'We'd been having sex, sergeant.'

Fred nodded. 'And was this a regular occurrence?'

'No, I only met her a few hours before. I bumped into her when I was shopping.'

'Amazing what you can find in the shops these days.'

Clarissa stared at Fred and her face coloured. She was embarrassed but that embarrassment quickly turned to anger. 'Who the hell are you to sit in judgement on me?'

Toby ignored her question. 'We think Mrs Wilson was murdered by a killer who was after you.' Toby had made the statement firmly. It had the desired effect.

The anger drained from Clarissa's face, replaced by a shocked incredulity. 'Why would anyone want to kill me?'

'I don't know if you have noticed, Miss Pidgeon, but we have a serial killer in Stratford who only appears to kill actors and people related to the RSC.' Toby leaned back in his chair as he felt Fred nudge him with his leg.

'Which would put you right in the sights of our killer.'

Clarissa just sat there, clearly trying to comprehend the information she had been given.

'You know Oliver Lawrence, don't you?'

'Oliver Lawrence?'

'Yes, Oliver Lawrence. You acted with him in the fifty-six and fifty-seven season, until he disappeared.'

Clarissa stared at Toby. 'I did, but he was a star by then and I was little more than a spear-carrier with a few lines.'

'Oh, you were far more than that, Miss Pidgeon. You played Celia and Oliver was Jaques. Two fairly meaty roles, your paths must have crossed a lot in that production.'

She shrugged. 'I suppose so.'

'Did you get on?'

'We hardly talked, he was a star and that was the first role where I had got some decent lines. There was no need to talk.'

'Come, come now, Miss Pidgeon. "All the world's a stage and all the men and women are merely players." What part did you play?'

Clarissa pushed back her chair and stood up. 'I've had enough of this. A friend of mine—'

'More an acquaintance than a friend,' stated Fred.

'That's it, I'm leaving. I've had enough of your rudeness.'

Toby stood up, his hands held out in apology. 'I'm very sorry if we've upset you, Miss Pidgeon, but there is a reason we are having to ask these questions. We think your life is in danger and we need to know what connection you have to the killer.'

'You think Oliver Lawrence is the murderer?' She looked from Fred to Toby. 'But he's been dead for fifteen years.'

'Missing,' said Fred. 'No body was ever found.'

'We think he's back in Stratford and looking for revenge.'

Clarissa slumped back down in her chair. 'Revenge for what?'

'Are you forgetting how his career ended, the bad reviews and Sir Morris dropping him from his company?'

Clarissa nodded. 'Yeah. Now you mention it, he did have quite a fall from grace in the fifty-seven season, really went off the boil.' She leaned back in her chair. 'Sir Morris really took against him.'

'Do you know why?'

Clarissa smiled at Toby. 'Why do you think? He was getting too good, just like his father. Sir Morris likes to be the centre of attention.'

Toby and Fred exchanged glances, they were starting to get somewhere but, before they could dig any deeper, they were interrupted by raised voices in the corridor outside. The voices became shouts and then the door to the interview room burst open.

Chief Wilson pushed through the opening, the crushing despair of the loss of his young wife had been replaced by blind rage.

Fred jumped to his feet. 'Sir, you shouldn't be in here.'

'Well, I am in here, Williams, now get out of my way.'

Fred didn't move. 'I can't do that, sir, you know I can't.'

Wilson ignored him and tried to push his way through but Fred grabbed him by the shoulders.

'Get out of my way, Williams.'

'Sir, you know—'

'Unhand me now, Williams, or I will have your badge.'

Fred looked into the eyes of his boss and could see that reason had lost its battle with grief. Short of wrestling Chief Wilson to the ground, there was nothing he could do to stop him.

Beeching was standing at the door and shook his head. Fred took the instruction and stood to one side. Wilson moved to the edge of the table and glared down at Clarissa.

'Who the hell are you?' she demanded.

'I'm the man whose wife got murdered in your place. You tell me why Oliver Lawrence wanted to kill you, right now, or I will lock you up until you do.'

Clarissa's bravado deserted her. 'Look, I'm sorry but—'

'Sorry?' screamed Wilson. 'Sorry? Do you know what you've done? Have you any idea what you have taken from me? Have you?' Wilson leaned on the edge of the desk and his head slumped down. They all saw the tears fall.

Fred moved over to Chief Wilson and put an arm on his shoulder. 'Come on sir, let's go and have a cup of tea, we can continue this later.'

All the fight had gone from Wilson; he was a broken man. He straightened and allowed Fred to guide him towards the door.

As he left, he paused for a moment and looked back at Clarissa. 'She was my world, my everything. You took her like a toy, something you could play with and throw away. Heather didn't matter to you but to me … she was my reason for living.'

He turned away and allowed Fred to lead him out of the room.

Beeching closed the door and sat down next to Toby. 'I'm sorry about that, Miss Pidgeon. Chief Constable Wilson is in shock.'

Clarissa nodded but she couldn't respond, her tears were falling too.

Chapter 45
To Kill Or Not To Kill

Oliver stood on top of Meon Hill. The last twenty-four hours had not gone as he had hoped. For the first time, his murderous plan had been thwarted and he didn't like failure.

Clarissa had been lucky and he had been careless. How could he have smothered the wrong Desdemona? It was unforgivable. He didn't even know who she was. If he had, he may have just got into his Morris Minor and headed back to Morocco. Of more concern to him was the fact that Felix was now an unreliable partner in crime. It was disappointing – you murder one wrong victim and he's out.

What should he do? The safest option would be to kill him but that came with its own problems. He was living in Felix's house, kill him and there would surely be a knock on the door from a relative or solicitor telling him he had to vacate the premises. He didn't want that. No, if he killed Felix, he would have to disappear. The absence of a body would leave things in limbo; the knock on the door would be delayed.

He took a deep breath of the fresh air and looked across the valley towards Bredon Hill and, further west, the Malvern Hills. This was a beautiful place, wide open and lightly populated, plenty of places to hide Felix's body should the need arise. Meon Hill had a dark past.

In 1945, a farm worker had been brutally murdered. Rumours abounded that there had been an element of witchcraft to the murder, and the killers were never found. Perversely, Oliver found this comforting; it was good to know that he wasn't the only murderer in the local vicinity. He was merely continuing a local tradition.

'Morning.' The greeting made Oliver Jump. He spun around and there behind him stood a man the like of which he had never seen before. Half leather-jacketed biker, half Greek wrestler. He carried some weight but he carried it with ease. He moved across the ground with a lightness that belied his bulk.

'Morning, you made me jump. I never heard you coming.'

'I move in mysterious ways,' the stranger winked at him.

His eyes twinkled with an alert intelligence that Oliver found both charming and disturbing. 'What brings you up here?'

The stranger reached into his pocket, pulled out a pack of Gauloises and offered them to Oliver. 'You want one?'

'No thanks, I'm trying to keep fit.'

The stranger flicked one into his mouth. 'I hear you, I used to do this walk an hour quicker before I started smoking these things.'

'You walked far?'

'Depends on how you describe far.'

'How far have you walked?'

'Not as far as I can but less than I should.'

Oliver looked at the stranger; he didn't look like a man that could make it up from the bottom of the hill, and yet, there was something about him that made him feel this stranger could be capable of anything. 'How many miles have you walked?'

The stranger pointed to the south. 'I started at Chipping Campden, that's where I left my Enfield. Then I whomped over to Hidcote Boyce, up and over Illmington and then down the back lane to here.'

Oliver did the maths in his head. 'That's about six miles, and full of hills.'

'Yeah, time was when I would do two laps.'

'Two laps?'

'Running.' Oliver shook his head in disbelief. 'With a forty-pound rucksack on my back.'

Oliver leaned back and smiled. 'You're winding me up.'

The stranger nodded. 'Yeah, it was only twenty pounds.'

Oliver looked into the stranger's eyes and knew that he was telling the truth. 'What were you? SAS?'

'I took the Queen's shilling but I signed the Official Secrets Act so if I told you, well, then I'd have to kill you.'

He smiled at Oliver disarmingly and Oliver knew that he meant this too.

'Dare I ask your name?'

'My name's Whomper, Whomper Smith.'

'Is that a real name?'

'Smith?'

'No. Whomper.'

'Whomper's real but Smith, I made up.'

Oliver just smiled, he really could not read this man. 'So, this a regular walk for you, Whomper?'

He nodded. 'Yeah, I do it every month, twice this month. With all the murders Stratford is becoming a little claustrophobic, don't you think?'

Oliver bit his lip. 'Yeah, but I like the streets quieter.'

'It's like *Hamlet* is being played out on the streets of Stratford for real, bodies everywhere. I've never been in a town with a serial killer before.'

'Doesn't that scare you?'

Whomper smiled. 'Been a while since I wore tights, apparently he only kills theatre luvvies.'

Oliver looked at Whomper questioningly. 'You've acted?'

Whomper bowed theatrically. 'I've trod the boards in my time.'

'Pantomime Dame?'

'How very dare you, sir,' said Whomper, his voice full of mock indignation. 'Shakespeare, dear boy.'

Oliver could not hide the disbelief he was feeling. 'Really.'

'"And, when I am forgotten, as I shall be. And sleep in cold dull marble, where no mention of me no more must be heard of, say, I taught thee. Say, Wolsey, that once trod the ways of glory, and sounded all the depths and shoals of honour.'" Whomper finished and bowed once more. His delivery of the lines had been deep and resonant. Full of the emotion of a man whose ambition had exceeded his grasp.

'You've played Cardinal Wolsey in Henry the Eighth?'

'Amongst others.'

'At Stratford?'

'All over. Only amateur, mind.'

'You sounded professional.'

'Oh, I could have gone down that route but it wasn't my first love.'

'What was?'

'Motorbikes. More specifically, going fast on them.'

'How fast?'

'Well, I did the TT several times.'

'The Tourist Trophy! How did you do?'

'I have eight silver replicas sitting on my shelf at home.'

'Wow, you were fast then.'

'Fast enough to live, but not to win. Maybe I just thought too much. Imagination,' Whomper tapped his head. 'It can play tricks on you, take your edge away. I bet you've got a vivid imagination.'

Oliver looked up at him and he felt Whomper's eyes probing into his innermost thoughts. 'Why do you say that?' asked Oliver, sounding more nervous than he would have wanted.

'Because you carry secrets, you're weighed down with them, like a brick filled rucksack. Time for you to unburden yourself, my friend.'

Oliver stood motionless, rooted to the spot by Whomper's words, he forced a smile.

'Considering we've only just met, you're making a lot of assumptions.'

Whomper stepped right up into Oliver's face and spoke in a

voice that seemed to come from a different time and place.

'Macbeth shall never vanquished be, till great Bernard Wood shall come to Dunroamin.'

Oliver just stared at Whomper. He recognised the misquoted speech but why was this weirdo talking about Bernard Wood? 'What the hell are you on about?'

Whomper held up a hand. 'Seek to know no more.' He turned and moved off down the hill without looking back.

Oliver watched him until he disappeared, headed in the direction of Mickleton. Had he just been warned by one of the three witches from the Scottish play? He shook his head. Coming for a walk on Meon Hill had failed to clear his mind. If anything, he was more confused than ever.

To kill Felix or not to kill Felix, that was the question. He turned and headed back towards Quinton, hoping that he wasn't going to be murdered in some black magic ritual on the way.

Chapter 46
Farewell Content

In Guild Street, Chief Wilson stood gazing at the incident board. He hadn't spoken for several minutes and Toby, Fred and Inspector Beeching stood in respectful silence behind him. He turned to face them.

He pointed to the incident board. 'Six murders and this is all you have?'

There was an uncomfortable silence. Beeching nudged Fred.

'The killer's like a ghost, we haven't even managed a sighting of him yet, sir.'

'Then why do you think it's this Oliver Lawrence?' He nodded his head towards Oliver's old photo at the top of the board.

'He's the only one with a motive; the killer knows the theatre and has a knowledge of Shakespeare's plays.'

'But he's been missing presumed dead for over fifteen years, what makes you think he's alive?'

'No body was ever found, sir, so we have to assume that he is.'

Wilson didn't look happy. 'You have a picture of him, Stratford isn't a big town. How hard can it be to find him?' There was anger in Wilson's voice.

'We don't think he looks like that now, sir,' said Toby.

'What do you think he looks like then?'

'Fifteen years older, sir. We've had an artist draw a picture aging him from that photograph. It's been distributed to every shop, household and pub in Stratford. It's been on local TV too.'

'And?'

'Nothing, sir.'

'So, what do we learn from that, DC Marlowe?'

Toby shifted uncomfortably from foot to foot. 'Er … it doesn't look like him, sir.'

'It doesn't look like him. So, let's get this straight. You have a suspect who has killed six victims, including my wife. You think it's a dead man and you don't know what he looks like. Is that a fair summation of your investigation to date?'

Inspector Beeching stepped forward. 'I know it doesn't sound good when you put it like that, sir.'

'It wouldn't sound good if I sang it.' He shook his head in disgust. 'I was under the apprehension that you actually knew what you were doing here, Beeching. Clearly I was wrong.'

Beeching started to protest but Chief Wilson was in no mood to be interrupted. 'I've been looking at this board for twenty minutes now and something has become glaringly obvious. I can't believe that none of you have seen it.'

Fred looked uncomfortably towards Toby. Had they missed something?

'What's that, sir?'

Chief Wilson pointed at the board. 'Look at all the deaths, all in and around Old Town, so the killer must live in the vicinity.'

'That's a dangerous assumption, sir, the killer could be travelling in and out of town,' said Fred.

'We'd spot him!'

'How? As you just pointed out, we don't really know what he looks like and this town has hundreds of thousands of visitors every year, from all over the world.'

Wilson ignored him. 'That's as may be but surely with the murders that have occurred in the early hours of the morning the killer wouldn't risk driving into Stratford, he'd stand out like a sore thumb.'

'Or she, sir,' said Fred.

'She? Lizzie Birchwood was strangled, my wife was smothered, that takes strength. We are dealing with a male killer here.' Wilson turned and pointed to the board. 'And that brings me to my point.

Lizzie Birchwood was stopping at the Windmill. We only have the landlord's word that she had left her room in the night.'

Toby looked at Fred and then back to Chief Wilson. 'What are you suggesting, sir?'

'The landlord lives in Old Town. Lizzie Birchwood was staying there. My wife was murdered within two hundred yards of the Windmill. Why haven't we had the landlord in for questioning?'

'Because he's not a suspect, sir.'

'Why not, Williams? He had the opportunity and he is a copper who had to leave the force in disgrace.'

Inspector Beeching looked confused. 'Are you suggesting that Phil Townsend is under suspicion, sir?'

'I am.'

'But he was a copper.'

Chief Wilson shook his head. 'Why should that concern me when he had the opportunity and the motive?'

Beeching looked at Fred. 'Motive? I don't understand, sir.'

'Phil Townsend has a record, a violent record.'

'Are you sure, sir?'

'Of course I'm sure, Beeching. I arrested him myself over twenty years ago. He was arrested for fighting in the Hope and Anchor in Leamington. He got fined and a suspended sentence. There was a woman injured in the brawl as well.'

This was all news to Fred, Toby and Inspector Beeching. Toby was the first to react.

'That was twenty years ago, sir and a pub fight is hardly comparable to multiple murder.'

'Stepping stones, DC Marlowe, stepping stones. He has clearly been building up to this for years. He was in the right place at the right time, has a history of violent crime and is a convicted felon. He looks good for it to me.'

'With due respect, sir,' began Toby, but Chief Wilson cut him dead.

'I don't want your respect, Marlowe, I want the killer of my wife arrested. Issue a warrant for his arrest now.'

Chief Wilson's grief had turned to a simmering rage which threatened to overwhelm him. He pointed an accusatory finger at all three of the officers standing in front of him. 'You've all dropped the ball, now go and get Townsend in here so that I can charge him.'

'You do know that Phil is DI Mel Townsend's brother don't you, sir?'

Judging by his reaction, Wilson clearly didn't know this. There was a moment of doubt and then the rage overruled it. 'I don't care if he is married to your mother … if you're a suspect, you're a suspect. Now go and get him, bring him back here and let me question him.'

Beeching held up a hand. 'I don't think that's a good idea, sir. You are too close to this one, you need to step back and let us get on with it.'

'Like you've been doing for the last three months.' His response was withering; all three officers were rendered silent. 'Go and get me Townsend now!'

Fred glanced at Beeching and he gave him a nod, there was no arguing with Chief Wilson. His judgement was suspect at the best of times, but consumed by grief, he was making rash decisions.

Fred turned to Toby. 'Come on, DC Marlowe, let's go and arrest Mister Townsend.'

Two minutes later they were in the car travelling down Rother Street.

'Poor old Wilson's lost it,' said Toby.

'Has he?' Fred didn't sound so sure.

'You can't seriously think that Phil Townsend is the killer. He used to be a top detective.'

Fred shook his head. 'Of course I don't. I've known Phil for years, he's a good bloke, but listening to Wilson made me think.

We really don't have anything, do we? We think it's Oliver but we don't have any real proof. We're chasing a ghost that we have created.' He turned to Toby. 'What if we're wrong?'

It was an uncomfortable question.

'We're not wrong, boss. It's Oliver, I know it is.'

'Based on what?' Another uncomfortable question.

'Everything points to it being him, there is no other logical killer.'

Fred shrugged. 'I agree, and I bloody hope we're right.'

Chapter 47
Intuition: When You Know, You Know

Fred and Toby arrived back at Guild Street with Phil Townsend shortly after Mel Townsend arrived. Fred had called her from the pay phone in the Windmill before they had arrested her brother. The conversation had been strained.

'This is a wind up, isn't it?'

Fred shook his head, which didn't really work on the phone. 'No, Mel, Wilson is in shock. He's looking for a culprit and, right now, it's Phil.'

'You can't arrest him, you know he's innocent.'

'I know, but Wilson is our boss, he's the chief constable of Warwickshire. Until he's put on compassionate leave …'

'Or sectioned,' spat Mel.

'Or that,' agreed Fred. 'Until one of those things happens, we can't overrule him. How long will it take you to get to Guild Street?'

'Forty minutes.'

'OK. Me and Toby will have something to eat here with Phil and then ask him to come down to the station to make a statement. That will give you time to get there before we arrive.'

'Thanks, Fred, I appreciate it.'

'No problem, Mel, it's a tricky situation all round.' The phone went dead. 'Well, she's on her way. Going to be an interesting afternoon in the station.'

'Can I stay here, boss?'

Fred raised an eyebrow. 'No chance. Get the beers in and I'll have a ploughman's.' As if by magic, Whomper burst through the door of the bar. 'Did somebody say ploughman's?'

For the first time that day, Fred smiled.

'Jesus Christ, Whomper, do you have a cheese and pickle radar!'

'I do have a hunger, but I also have information.'

'What've you got?' asked Fred.

'All will be revealed.'

'After food and beer?'

Whomper smiled at Fred. 'You know me so well.'

Toby had been listening and added Whomper's order to theirs. Fifteen minutes later they were sitting over the remains of their lunch and Whomper was on his third pint.

'So, what have you got for us, Whomper?'

Whomper smiled at them both. 'I think I met your killer today.'

'Go on,' said Fred.

'I was out for my regular walk over Meon Hill.'

This was news to Fred and Toby, who were not even aware of the fact that Whomper could walk.

'That's quite a walk, Whomper. Are you sure you didn't dream it?'

'Look, I may give the impression of indolence but beneath this fulsome figure lurks the body of Achilles.'

Fred didn't look convinced. 'Go on.'

'There was a man at the top just staring out across the vale towards Bredon. I think he was our killer.'

Fred and Toby exchanged a glance.

Whomper continued. 'There was something about him, he was carrying secrets.'

'What did he look like?'

'Athletic, early forties, blond hair and tanned skin.'

'Well the age is about right,' said Fred.

'And if he'd been in Morocco, he would be tanned,' added

Toby.

'That's all true but something happened up there.'

Fred and Toby said nothing.

'You know that I have a gift.' They nodded. 'Well, when I was talking to this stranger, I suddenly found myself taken over with one of my predictions.'

'Were your sisters there?' asked Fred.

'On top of Meon Hill? In stilettos? I think not.'

'Not the full Greek chorus then.'

'No, just me.'

'Can you remember what you said?'

'I can,' Whomper sat upright. '"Macbeth shall never vanquished be until great Bernard Wood shall come to Dunroamin."'

Fred shook his head. 'What the hell does that mean?'

'It's the warning from the three witches,' said Toby.

'I know that, but who the hell is Bernard Wood?'

Whomper raised his hand. 'I know.'

'Enlighten us.'

'Bernard Wood was Oliver Lawrence's agent, his mother lived in a bungalow on Sanctus Road. He still owns it.'

'How do you know that?' asked Toby.

Whomper shrugged. 'You know me, gents, I know stuff.'

'So what does it mean?'

'It means that Oliver Lawrence is your killer, he's back and I know what he looks like.'

And just like that everything had changed. All Fred and Toby had to do was convince Chief Wilson that an overweight biker with a penchant for beer and Greek mythology had identified the killer while in a prophetic trance. That wasn't going to be hard at all.

Chapter 48
A House Divided

Fred and Toby had omitted to inform Phil Townsend that he wasn't really going to Guild Street to make a statement. As he walked through the door into the station, behind Fred, Chief Wilson was waiting.

'Townsend,' he bellowed. 'Why isn't he in cuffs, he's a suspect in a murder inquiry.'

Phil Townsend looked startled by the revelation. 'I don't think so, mate.'

'Mate! I'm no mate of yours, Townsend. Cuff him and take him to Interrogation Room One.'

The rage within Chief Wilson was beginning to boil over. Fred nodded to Toby to cuff Townsend and then walked over to Chief Wilson.

'Look, sir, we really don't think that Mr Townsend is a suspect in this case.'

'Of course you don't, Williams, your only suspect is a man who appears to have been dead for fifteen years. Now get him into the interview room so I can interrogate him.'

'I really don't think that's a good idea, sir. You're too close to this case.'

'I don't give a damn what you think, Williams. He killed my wife and I'm going to get a confession out of him.'

'You can't, sir, it's not ethical.'

'Ethical? My wife is dead and you're talking about ethics.'

'That's exactly my point, sir. The interview would get thrown out of court because you wouldn't be impartial.'

'I may not be, but you will, Williams.'

'Me, sir? I want no part in this.'

'Tough. I'm your commanding officer, you don't have a choice.'

Fred looked up at Inspector Beeching who was standing by the custody desk, pleading for help with his eyes.

'I think Fred's right, sir.'

Chief Wilson spun around to Beeching. 'Oh, you do, do you. Well maybe you'd like to be in there too?'

Beeching shook his head. He wanted no part of a miscarriage of justice, which was surprising for someone who wanted to work at the Met.

'I thought not.' He turned back to the prisoner and was pleased to see Toby had put the cuffs on him. 'Get him in the interview room, now.'

Toby did as he was told and led Phil Townsend down the corridor. Fred followed reluctantly.

Two minutes later, Fred and Chief Wilson were seated at the desk opposite Phil Townsend.

'Don't I get a phone call?' asked Phil.

'This isn't Dixon of Dock Green, Townsend, you haven't got any rights unless I say so.'

'That can't be right.'

'I think you'll find that as long as I'm in charge you're guilty until proven otherwise.'

'Don't you mean innocent.'

'I know what I mean, Townsend,' growled Wilson.

'Shall I read him his rights, sir?'

Wilson shook his head. 'Far as I'm concerned, he's got none.'

'I'll take notes then.'

Fred reached for his pad but Wilson pushed it off the desk with a sweep of his arm. 'No notes, not until we've had a chat.' Wilson got up and started to unbutton his jacket.

Fred didn't like the look of how events were shaping up. 'We've had some new information this afternoon, sir, evidence that would put Mister Townsend in the clear.'

Wilson looked surprised. 'What evidence?'

Fred thought for a moment about what Whomper had said. Telling an angry, grief-stricken Chief Wilson that, "Macbeth shall not vanquished be until Bernard Wood shall come to Dunroamin," might not have the effect he was hoping for.

'Well?' asked Wilson impatiently.

'Er, someone thinks they saw Lawrence, we have a new description.'

Wilson waved it away. 'Well, we have the murderer here,' he grinned mirthlessly at Townsend. 'So, I think we are top trumps.'

Fred nodded silently.

'Look here—'

Wilson turned on Townsend. 'No, you look here. I don't like you, Townsend, I never have. With your snake hips and sexy smile, you think you're every girl's dream, don't you.'

Townsend nodded. 'Yeah.'

'It was a rhetorical question, but I do have a question you can answer.'

'What's that, then?'

'Why did you kill Lizzie Birchwood?'

Townsend started to laugh. Wilson was still stood up, his jacket was off and he was rolling his shirt sleeves up. Fred knew exactly where this interview was headed, he had been there before, only he had confined himself to those he knew to be guilty.

'You can laugh now, Townsend, but you won't be laughing for long.' Wilson finished rolling up his sleeves and then stepped forward and hit Townsend hard across the face, his chair rocked back but didn't go over.

'Still finding it funny, are we,' spat Wilson. His face was red and spittle rested on his chin.

Fred grabbed Wilson's arm. 'You can't do that, sir.'

Wilson looked at Fred and laughed. 'Fred Williams telling me I can't beat a confession out of a suspect. You have to smile at irony like that, don't you.' He pulled his arm back to take another swing but this time Fred was up and got between him and Townsend.

'Sir, this has to stop.'

'I'll tell you when it has to stop. This monster killed Lizzie Birchwood and then he killed my wife.'

'We don't know that, sir.'

'Then let me find out.'

He tried to push past but Fred was too big and too strong. 'I'm sorry, sir, but I can't let you.'

'I'll have your badge, Williams!'

'That's up to you, sir. But for your own good, and for the protection of the suspect, I can't let this go any further.'

Wilson shook free of Fred's grasp and took a couple of paces back. He looked like he was about to charge at Fred when the door of the interview room burst open.

'What the hell do you think you are doing, sir?' Mel Townsend stood in the doorway and she didn't look happy.

Wilson stared at her. The anger that had enraged him seemed to surge for a moment and then drain from him like a slowly deflating soufflé.

'I've got some questions for your brother.'

'Have you cautioned him?'

Wilson shook his head.

'Don't you think you should, sir? He's an ex-copper, he knows his rights.' Wilson nodded; he seemed more like a naughty schoolboy now. 'He killed my wife, Mel,' there was a quiver in his voice. 'He killed my wife.'

Mel moved over to him and put an arm around his shoulder. 'I'm so sorry about Heather, sir, but this isn't the way. Let Fred and DC Marlowe question my brother. You and I can go and have a cuppa. If my brother's guilty, they'll get it out of him.'

Phil looked up at his sister. 'If?'

Mel shrugged. 'Due process. If you've done nothing wrong,

you have nothing to fear.'

She led Wilson out of the room. He made no eye contact with anyone as he left. Fred and Phil watched him go.

'Poor sod,' said Phil.

Fred turned back to him. 'I'm sorry about that, Phil. This whole thing has made it a bit awkward for your sister. She can't really tell Wilson to let you go, we've got to follow due process.'

Phil shrugged. 'No problem, I'd have probably done the same thing in his place.'

Toby entered the room.

'Get those cuffs off,' said Fred.

Toby nodded and walked over to where Phil was sitting. As he undid the cuffs he looked at the red welt on the side of Phil Townsend's face. 'That's going to be black tomorrow.'

Phil shrugged. 'You've met my sister; I'm used to police brutality.'

They all laughed; it seemed like a long time since there had been anything to laugh about.

Fred sat down wearily across the desk from Phil. 'Look, we know you didn't do this but we have to eliminate you from our enquiries. Do you have an alibi for the time of Heather Wilson's murder?'

'What time was she murdered?'

Fred glanced at the file on the table and pulled out Alf Butcher's preliminary report. 'Our pathologist puts death at between six to eight p.m. yesterday.'

Phil smiled.

Fred recognised the look. 'Were you with a lady friend?'

'Yes.'

'I'll need her name and address.'

'Addresses,' said Phil.

Fred looked at Toby. 'No wonder he didn't resist arrest.' He turned back to Phil. 'I'll need the names and addresses.'

'Lou and Carol, I think.'

'You think?'

Phil shrugged. 'It was all sort of spur of the moment, you know how it is.'

Fred didn't know how it was. 'Let's get this straight, your alibi is that you were having sex with two strangers whose names and addresses you don't know?'

'I do know. It was definitely Lou and Carol,' he hesitated. 'Or was it, Louise and Karen.'

Fred put down his pen. 'For God's sake, Phil, we're trying to help you here. You've got to give us something more than this.'

'They're Americans, I think.'

'You think?'

'Or Australians, I'm always mixing those two up.'

Fred leaned back in his chair. 'DC Marlowe, would you like to summarise Mister Townsend's alibi, please.'

'It's crap, boss.'

'It is indeed.' Fred picked up his pen and began to write, repeating what he was writing out loud. 'So, you were having sex with two ladies that were either called Lou and Carol or Louise and Karen. They came from either the United States of America or Australia. Have I got their information correct?'

Phil nodded. 'Yeah, I think so.'

'So how are we supposed to track these two … or four, ladies down.'

Phil grinned. 'Easy, they're stopping at my pub.'

Fred threw down his pen again. 'Is this how you treat all your guests?'

'Look, Fred, I just showed them up to their room and one thing led to another. If anything, I'm the victim here.'

'How's that then?'

'It's going to make it very awkward when I give them the bill at the end of their stay.'

'Put it down as room service!'

An hour later, Kinky Bernstein knocked on the door of the interview room.

'In,' bellowed Fred.

Kinky entered.

'Well, does Mister Townsend's alibi stack up.'

'Sort of.'

'What does that mean?'

'Well, there were two ladies.'

'Lou and Carol,' said Toby. Kinky shook his head.

'Louise and Karen,' offered Fred.

'Laura and Christine,' said Kinky.

Fred sighed. 'Were they American or Australian?'

'Canadian,' said Kinky.

'That's pretty close,' said Phil.

Fred held up a hand to silence him. 'Did the ladies confirm Mister Townsend's alibi?'

'Yes, said they were with him all night.'

'Good,' Fred shoved the notepad over to Toby. 'You can write this one up, I don't think my imagination is up to it.'

Chapter 49
The Sky Is Falling

Lady Beatrice Oxford stood alone on the stage of the Royal Shakespeare Theatre. The theatre was empty but she felt claustrophobic. Events were gathering pace and she had no control over them. Oliver was back and everything she had taken years to build was threatened by collapse. Each carefully placed brick of her ambition was being undermined, the walls were falling down and the sky would surely follow. She felt hopeless.

'Afternoon, Lady Oxford.'

Beatrice spun around. 'Oh, hello, Mister Morris.'

She smiled at Alan Morris; she had always liked him. He was in charge of the stage sets that had outacted her on many occasions. He walked to the centre of the stage and looked out at the empty auditorium.

'Are you planning a comeback?'

She smiled sadly. 'We both know that's never going to happen, don't we.'

He nodded. 'Well, I suppose you're too busy with your charity work to tread the boards again.'

'I am busy but I think we both know that I wasn't a very good actress, Alan.'

Alan shook his head. 'I'm not so sure, I think you were miscast.'

'Really?'

Alan nodded. 'I watch a lot of performances from the wings and Sir Morris always cast you as the dramatic heroine. Juliet, Lady Macbeth, Ophelia. That's not you.'

'Sir Morris wanted me to play opposite him.'

'And you could, but not in those plays, you have a talent for comedy.'

'You think?'

'I'm sure of it. I have seen you perform and I know that as Puck you would shine. Rosalind in *As You Like It* was made for you. You have a cheeky charm that you have tried to mask with a gravitas you don't possess. You need to let your comic side free. You'd be great.'

Beatrice was dumbfounded. She had always thought this but Sir Morris had badgered her to play the big tragic roles; it just wasn't her. What could she do? He was the head of the company and she needed him.

'How come you could see that, Alan, but not Sir Morris.'

'Objectivity. I'm not married to you. Tell him that you want to come back to play the comic parts. We're doing *The Dream* in the autumn, you'd make a great Puck.'

Her heart gave a skip; could he be right. 'Not the tragedies then?'

Alan shook his head and pulled a strained expression. 'Nah, really not your forte.'

'You don't pull your punches, do you!'

'What's the point. I spend months getting the sets right, last thing I want is some ugly acting making them look bad. You're a comic actor, Lady Oxford, take my word for it.'

'Are you sure?'

Alan turned to her. 'If something doesn't work, change it.'

'I did, I gave up.'

'That's not change, that's quitting. I don't think you're a quitter.'

Beatrice thought for a moment. 'I'm not a quitter, Alan, I'm just not very good.'

'I'm not very good at ballet, that's why I don't do it. I am very good at set building and design. Now you, clearly, can't do tragedy but you could do comedy.'

'You really think so?'

'I do.'

Beatrice stepped forward and gave him a big hug. 'Thanks, Alan, I needed to hear that.'

'Let me ask you this. If a tree falls in a forest and there's nobody there to hear it, does it make a sound?'

Beatrice scrunched up her face in thought. 'I should know this one, shouldn't I.'

Alan looked back knowingly at her. 'Well?'

She shook her head. 'I don't know.'

'Nobody does, we assume it does but if there's nobody there to hear it we will never know. If you don't give comedy a go, we'll never know.' Alan smiled at her. 'I have to go now, got to see a man about some wood glue.'

'Thanks, Alan.'

'My pleasure, see you in the autumn.'

She watched him walk off stage. He was a nice man. She never had a lot to do with him in previous years, but they had always got on well when they had spoken. Maybe because he had nothing to do with acting so she hadn't felt threatened by him. Her normal self-defence mechanisms were held in check, whatever it was, she trusted his judgement. For the first time in months she felt the sky might just be turning blue and the clouds that threatened to engulf her were lifting. She was wrong.

'Darling, so good to see you back where you belong.'

Beatrice recognised the voice; she set her face in a smile and turned to greet its owner. 'I heard you were back too, Pierre, I thought we'd lost you to Hollywood.'

Pierre Corridor smiled. 'Films are for money; theatre is for the soul.'

'Didn't go well in LA then?'

Pierre shook his long dark hair. 'No, they hated me. Apparently, I shouldn't complain about unrealistic plots and dialogue so wooden it needed staining.'

'Well, Hollywood's loss is Stratford's gain.'

'Do you mean that?'

Beatrice shrugged. 'Surprisingly, yes.'

They both smiled.

'What brings you back here.' Pierre paused for a moment. A worried look crossed his face. 'Sir Morris hasn't cast you in *Othello*, has he?'

'Don't panic, Pierre, he wouldn't do that to you. The only thing he wants in *Othello* is the leading role. He wouldn't want me ruining Desdemona.'

'Don't be so hard on yourself.'

'Why not, you were.'

Pierre couldn't deny it. He had made no secret during his last tenure as artistic director that Beatrice was best seen and not heard. 'I may have been a little harsh.'

'You were right, I can't play serious drama.'

Pierre agreed completely with her statement but said nothing, he didn't want to be upsetting Sir Morris Oxford's wife on his first week back. Beatrice could see his discomfort and enjoyed it for a moment. 'Can I ask you something, Pierre?'

'Of course, anything.'

Beatrice stared seriously into his face. 'I want your honest answer, I won't be offended.'

He grinned nervously. 'They all say that, and then take offence.'

'I won't.'

Pierre nodded. 'Very well, ask away.'

'Do you think I could play comedy?'

Pierre went to answer, but paused. 'I've never seen you play comedy.'

'Exactly. Both Richard and Morris always cast me against them in the bloody tragedies, I can't do them.'

'I agree.'

'But I used to play comedy when I was at RADA. I could make people laugh, be myself.'

Pierre Corridor stroked his beard. 'You know, I do believe you could.'

For the first time in a long time, Beatrice Oxford's smile reached her eyes. Alan had been right.

'Why don't you read Puck for me.'

'Do you mean it?'

'Surprisingly, yes. I really think you could do it. Can't think how I never saw it.'

Beatrice ran over to him and gave him a big hug, it was as if the weight of the world had been lifted off her shoulders.

From the back of the stage, Alan smiled to himself. They should have put him in charge of everything, not just the sets. He turned and headed for his appointment with the wood glue man.

Chapter 50
A Chippy On His Shoulder

As Alan Morris walked down Southern Street, headed for the RSC workshops in Old Town, he was unaware that he was being watched.

Oliver Lawrence was sitting in the shelter in the Memorial Gardens. He recognised the man in charge of the main sets, Big Al Morris. Nobody dared call him that, years spent on the tools had given him forearms like Popeye. Oliver recognised him the second he saw him.

Big Al had been in charge of the sets in the main house for over twenty years. He was good at his job and everybody liked him, they also feared him, just a little. He took no nonsense. Oliver remembered bumping into the set on a dress rehearsal. He had come running on too fast, adrenalin pumping, missed his mark and banged into the wall beneath Juliet's balcony. He had been stunned and fallen down. The rehearsal was stopped while everyone rushed to Oliver's aid. Big Al had wandered over to the scene of the impact and looked at the mark Oliver had made with his head. He turned to the crowd tending to Oliver.

'It's OK, no real damage done. A spot of paint will sort it.'

He'd started to walk offstage when Sir Morris had called to him. 'What about poor Oliver?'

Big Al nodded. 'Should be enough in the tin to do him too.' And with that, he had disappeared into the back of the set.

Oliver smiled at the memory. Two nights into the run, Oliver had been waiting in the wings to go on and Big Al had appeared at his side.

'Good luck.'

'Thanks.'

'If you're going to bump into something tonight, make it Juliet. There's a replacement for her.'

After imparting those few words of wisdom, Big Al had slipped once more into the shadows, leaving Oliver laughing quietly and almost missing his cue.

Oliver decided to follow him; he knew where he was headed. A plan was starting to form in his mind. What if the battlements that Sir Morris would be standing on in the next production were sabotaged? Killing off the old boy in front of a full house would be a real coup. Oliver followed discreetly and watched Big Alan turn in to the workshops through the open doors.

'Morning, Alan.'

'Morning, Julian, are we still on schedule?'

'Yeah, but we're having trouble with the mech on that folding arch.'

'Thought you might, let's take a look at it.'

The two men disappeared into the back of the workshop and Oliver crept over, opened the doors and peered in. This was where the sets were made by a small team of very skilled carpenters and artists. Their standards were extremely high and Oliver knew anything that left this workshop would be checked and double checked. He needed to do his sabotage in the theatre between shows. He heard voices coming his way and ducked behind a panel that had been painted to look like part of a forest.

'Think that will do it?'

'Yes, put a heavy-duty hinge on top and that will cantilever the weight better and take the load off the castors, they won't stick then.' The voice was Big Al's.

'You got time for a cuppa?'

'Are there biscuits?'

'Of course.'

'Then you have your answer.'

Big Al and Julian headed off towards the kitchen, and Oliver appeared from the west side of Birnam Wood. It would be a shame to sabotage the excellent work of the set team but it would be a hell of a way to send Sir Morris off into the underworld.

Oliver slowly backed out of the workshop and headed back down to Trinity Street. He needed to formulate a plan to sabotage the set. All he had to do now was make sure that it would only be Sir Morris who was affected. He needed to go and watch the play to discover the perfect place onstage to enact his deadly plan. The idea of watching Sir Morris' demise from the stalls filled him with pleasure. How to bring it about, that was the question. He wanted to kill Sir Morris without actually killing Sir Morris.

Sabotaging a major piece of scenery would be almost impossible but there was another way. Caesar gets stabbed to death on the way to the Senate. What if one of those retractable blades didn't retract? It was so simple it was brilliant. Big Al wouldn't be responsible for that; Shelagh Fergusson was the set designer and he'd never liked her. If one of her retractable blades failed to retract, well, whose fault would that be?

Chapter 51
A Change Of Heart

Sir Morris Oxford walked into the lounge at the White Swan Hotel to be greeted by something he hadn't been expecting: his wife was smiling.

The smile brightened as she saw him. 'Morris, darling,' she held her arms open.

He hesitated for a moment. Was this a trap? Beatrice hadn't been this pleased to see him in years. Throwing caution to the wind, he moved into her arms and she embraced him. 'Oh, Morris, I have great news.'

'You do?'

'Yes, darling, after all these years it's like a dark cloud has lifted.'

Sir Morris smiled back at her; she really was a beautiful woman when she smiled. 'And what is this good news, my love?'

Beatrice turned back to the bar and picked up two glasses of champagne. She offered one to him.

'Pol Roger, your favourite.'

He took the offered glass. 'So, what are we celebrating?'

'Me, darling, I'm coming back to the stage.'

The glass ceased its journey towards Sir Morris' mouth. 'Sorry, my love, didn't quite catch that.'

'I'm going to start acting again.'

Sir Morris took a huge swallow of his Pol Roger while he tried to think what to say. 'That's nice, dear.'

It wasn't the ringing endorsement that Beatrice had been hoping for but, in her state of excitement, she didn't really notice his lack of enthusiasm. 'I had a road to Damascus moment today.'

Sir Morris raised an eyebrow. 'Planning a holiday?'

'No, silly, a proper Damascene moment. I was standing on the main stage looking out into the auditorium and that nice Mister Morris turned up.'

'Big Al, the chippy?'

'He's a lot more than a chippy, dear, he's in charge of all the sets.'

'Did he tell you how to put up a shelf,' said Sir Morris.

'No, he did not. He told me I should act again.'

Sir Morris drained his glass while he tried to think of a suitable response.

'That's nice, dear. What reason did he give?'

'He thinks I have been miscast my whole career.'

'Well, he must have seen a lot of plays in his time.'

'Yes, dear, he has, and his opinion was that I should play comic roles. He said I don't have the gravitas for the dramatic stuff.'

Sir Morris couldn't disagree regarding the dramatic roles but the comic suggestion made him think. 'You know, dear, I don't think I've ever seen you in a comic role.'

'No, because you always cast me in the tragedies.'

'I did, didn't I.' Morris proffered his empty glass to his wife. 'Any chance of a refill, dear?'

Beatrice pulled the bottle from the ice bucket and poured him another glass. 'So, what do you think?'

'It's a bit late in the day for that.'

'Why?'

'You retired, dear, you have all your charity work.'

'But I want to act, I want to play comic roles. Hear the laughter echoing around the theatre.'

'Oh, they'll be laughing.'

Beatrice put down her glass. She looked furious. 'You patronising sod! Is that all you have to say? You're not even going to consider it.'

Sir Morris realised that he had been way too honest for his own good and tried to back pedal furiously.

'I'm sorry, darling, I thought you were joking so I played along.'

'I wasn't joking,' she snapped.

'Listen,' Sir Morris held up his hand as a brilliant excuse entered his mind. 'The real reason is I don't want to put you at risk.'

'What of, a bad review?'

'No, dear, of being murdered. There's a killer out there and he's killing actors.'

For a few brief hours, Beatrice had forgotten about the killings; pushed her fears about her son being responsible to the back of her mind. Her husband's words brought reality crashing down on her like a collapsing wave. Sir Morris watched the hope drain from her face.

'I'm sorry to be so negative but your safety is my first concern.'

Beatrice nodded slowly, she looked totally defeated. Sir Morris tried to give her hope.

'Tell you what, darling, as soon as the killer is under lock and key we will get you in a comedy, how does that sound?'

It should have sounded good but Beatrice didn't smile and looked sadly at her husband. 'Do you think we will still be alive? The killer's after us too.'

'We don't know that.'

'Oh, we do.' Beatrice picked up her glass and took a long gulp. 'It's Oliver, you know it and I know it.'

Sir Morris made to protest but Beatrice shook her head. 'Don't say it. I'm his mother, I know it's him. His father was crazy and he's crazy too. We finished him as an actor and he wants revenge. He will only be stopped by death.'

Sir Morris stared at his wife. He heard the words but didn't want to understand them. He had treated Oliver like his own son, he had loved him.

'Nobody's going to kill him.'

'Somebody needs to.' Her eyes narrowed and became hard.

'It's him or us, darling, no middle ground, kill or be killed.'

For once in his long and privileged life, Sir Morris was speechless. Was his wife advocating killing her own son? He couldn't think of anything to say.

His wife said it for him. 'We betrayed him, Morris, and he's come back to settle old scores. Deep down we both know it. The way I see it, we either fight back or die. The police won't ever catch him, he's too clever.'

Sir Morris shook his head. 'Even if you're right, the police will catch him.'

'They haven't got anywhere close yet,' she scoffed. She leaned in close to her husband and spoke in a harsh whisper that made Sir Morris' blood run cold. '"Screw your courage to the sticking place and we'll not fail!"'

Sir Morris recognised the quote from Lady Macbeth. 'He's our son.'

'My son,' she whispered bitterly. 'You were just good old Uncle Morris. So good you ruined his father and then years later you ruined him too.'

Anger flashed in Sir Morris' eyes but he held it in check. 'I raised him as my own.'

'Guilty conscience. You just wanted me and he was part of the package.'

'It wasn't like that.'

'It was exactly like that. Our relationship was never love; it was a transaction.' Beatrice took a vicious swig of her champagne, draining the glass. 'And you got what you wanted.'

'So did you dear, don't forget that.'

They glared at each other as the open bottle of champagne slowly went flat, just like their marriage. If Oliver had been watching, he would have been delighted by the toll his actions had taken on their relationship. He wanted to destroy them and the pressure was doing that for him. Neither said a word, they turned away from each other and stared into the distance trying to figure out where it had all gone so wrong.

Chapter 52
All's Well That Ends Well, For Phil

Fred and Toby sat with Phil and Mel in the bar at the Windmill. Phil raised a glass. 'Here's to me not being the Shakespeare Murderer.'

'More like the Stratford Shagger,' suggested Fred.

Phil grinned. 'If the world gives you lemons, make lemonade.'

His sister held her head in mock despair. 'You have to stop this, Phil, you could have been in real trouble. If those two young ladies hadn't been stopping here, you'd have had no alibi.'

'And now I have two, so I reckon that makes a good case for going the extra mile.'

'Maybe we should lock him up for the protection of all women in Stratford,' said Toby.

'Nah, there can't be that many gullible ones left.' Fred turned to Phil. 'Seriously, Phil, lie low for a while … on your own. The chief is hurting and may still do something rash.'

'You think so,' said Mel, sounding dubious. 'Wilson's a broken man.'

'He is,' agreed Fred. 'But that devastation can turn to hopelessness and that can turn to anger. I've seen the fury of loss and the violence that can bring. You need to keep an eye on him. He's a ticking time bomb.'

Mel looked doubtful. 'No, Wilson would never do anything like that.'

'You think not? In case it escaped your notice, he was just about to beat a confession out of your brother when Kinky came in with the alibi. Anybody can crack given the right set of circumstances.'

Mel looked at Toby. 'What do you think?'

'I think the boss is right. Wilson had lost it; he could lose it again. I can't imagine how he must be feeling. If it was me, I would want to find the killer and batter him.'

'But that's not what we do, is it, Toby? We have to let the law run its course.'

Mel smirked at Fred. 'Like you did in the past.'

Fred shrugged. 'Horses for courses. Sometimes the horse needs a kick up the arse to get it to the finish. In this case, we just need to make sure that our chief doesn't let his grief get in the way of a result.'

'You still think your killer is Oliver Lawrence?' asked Phil.

'Unless you want to confess?'

Phil gave Fred a sickly smile. 'I don't think I'd do well in prison.'

'Stratford would be a safer place for female tourists though.'

'Ease up, Toby. I can't help it if the ladies find me fascinating,' grinned Phil.

'I think the fact that you own a pub with rooms is the bit they find fascinating, you're just the baggage that comes with it, mate.'

Phil chuckled. 'That may be a factor.'

Chapter 53
The Madness Of Grief

On the outskirts of Warwick, Chief Wilson sat in his living room staring into the fire place. There was no fire burning; like his future, it was cold and empty. He was alone. The harsh reality of Heather's murder was sinking in. He was still in a state of shock, but he could see past that now. Like staring down a long, dark, empty corridor, with nothing at the end of it. That would be his life now. He had no future, just the knowledge that passing down that corridor, towards the inevitable, he would be alone, totally alone.

His children were not there to comfort him, they had taken Barbara's side when he had run off with Heather, family friends had done the same. Even Heather's family hadn't made contact. They blamed him for her death; if she hadn't married him, she wouldn't have died. It wasn't fair, but there it was: grief isn't rational.

He was full of regret for what he had lost, the life that had been stolen from him. The house was cold, silent, empty. He knew the phone would not ring and the doorbell would remain silent. He had marooned himself on an island of his own making. How could he have been so foolish?

He had based his entire future on one person: Heather. Forsaken his family and friends to be with her, he had invested all his hopes in just one person, and now she was gone. Murdered. The killer had to pay. He didn't buy the alibi from the girls that Phil Townsend had come up with, he'd seen straight through it. Fred and Mel were protecting him.

The room was cold but Chief Wilson was burning with a fire of all-consuming hate, hate that prevented logic. He would find Townsend, get his confession and end him. For the first time since Heather had died, Wilson smiled. It wasn't a warm smile, just an acknowledgement that he was taking back control of his life.

He was on what they laughingly called compassionate leave. Not much compassion dumping him off in an empty house surrounded by no one. But that gave him one very precious thing: time. Time to plan, time to plot. Time to find Phil Townsend and make him pay.

Chief Wilson got up and hurried to his garage. He grabbed a holdall and into it he shoved a crowbar, gaffer tape, gloves and some rope. He stared at the contents of the bag; there was something missing. Yes, a hammer; always useful when trying to get a confession. Toes first, then fingers. He saw the Stanley knife on the worktop, that could come in handy. He remembered using it to cut in the floor tiles in the kitchen, better put a new blade in.

It hadn't been a long journey, just a few hours of heartbreaking, soul-crushing grief. It's a short walk from sanity to madness and Chief Wilson was on his way. If his life was over, he was going to take Phil Townsend with him. Oliver was about to have some competition.

Chapter 54
Friends Reunited?

Felix sat on his boat in the Marina at Welford. It was only five miles from Stratford, six by river, but it felt a million miles away. There was a dark cloud hanging over those ancient streets that had once more fallen quiet; fear stalked the quiet passageways.

After Oliver's visit, it felt safer to put some distance between them. Tomorrow he would push on down the Avon to Pershore. He had no hard plans, he just wanted to put even more distance between him and Oliver. It had been a surprise when Oliver didn't kill him; when he had boarded the boat, he was sure he would. He had started something that he could no longer control. Oliver had got a taste for killing. It was his fault, he should have known that revenge has momentum. Like an avalanche, it had started with a tiny crack which had then gained pace. Instead of killing specific targets it was now just mowing down anyone that got in its way, including him. He was on borrowed time.

Felix leaned back and took a swig of wine. It was peaceful here, he would eat at The Four Alls pub tonight and move off in the morning. He took another sip of his wine and watched three young boys fishing by the bridge. It reminded him of his own carefree days of youth. Innocence that was gone forever. His hands were covered in the blood of others; like Lady Macbeth, he could not rid himself of the stain.

In the distance, he could see a runner moving steadily up the towpath towards the marina. He moved smoothly, easily, his gait showed no sign of effort; clearly the man was an athlete. He watched, enjoying the ease of movement and the graceful pace. As the runner got nearer a feeling of unease began to make itself felt; there was something familiar about him. He held the glass of wine to his lips but could not swallow, his throat had begun to tighten with fear. He knew now who the runner was: Oliver.

Like a rabbit caught in the headlights, Felix watched, motionless, as Oliver reached the bow of his boat. Every fibre of his being was telling him to move, but he couldn't. Oliver was a fate he couldn't outrun.

The boat swayed as Oliver stepped onto the gang plank. 'Permission to come aboard, captain.'

He sounded cheerful, as if he didn't have a care in the world. Felix nodded and Oliver hopped into the cabin.

'I thought I might find you up here.'

'You thought right,' said Felix, sounding more confident than he felt. 'To what do I owe the pleasure, have you come to kill me?'

Oliver looked hurt. 'Why would I kill you, you're my friend.'

'Then why are you here.'

Oliver sat down on a stool opposite Felix. 'I've been thinking about what you said.' He pointed at the open wine bottle. 'May I, it's six miles up that towpath to here.'

Felix pushed the bottle towards him. 'Help yourself.'

Oliver poured himself a glass and took a long sip. 'I think l may have been a little unreasonable the last time we talked. Lizzie Birchwood was a mistake. She was a bloody terrible director, but I didn't need to kill her.'

'You didn't,' agreed Felix.

'I know, I just got caught up in the purity of the mission. I wanted to cleanse everything that was wrong with the theatre. Make it perfect for the future. In my … enthusiasm, I may have got a bit carried away.' Oliver took a sip of wine and smiled. 'Still, no real harm done.'

'Try telling Lizzie that.'

There was bitterness and anger in Felix's reply, and Oliver knew it was justified. 'Look, Felix, I'm trying to say sorry here. We started this together and I don't want to fall out over one little error.'

'Some error! You also killed another innocent woman.'

'I know, I know, that really was unfortunate.' He paused for a moment. 'But Lizzie, she wasn't a very good director, was she.' Oliver saw the anger rise in Felix's face. 'Sorry, bad choice of words. Her directing was an acquired taste; it gave me indigestion. She would have been a disaster for the new company.'

'What new company?'

'The one we will form to replace Sir Morris'.'

'I think Sir Morris will have something to say about that.'

'No, he won't.'

Felix raised an eyebrow. 'Is there something you want to tell me?'

'Yes, it's time to get back on track. I came here looking for revenge and I got side tracked. The killings were just so … enjoyable.' He saw the look on Felix's face. 'From an acting point of view, you understand.'

Felix did understand. When Oliver killed it was a performance, the greatest theatre he had ever seen. He smiled. 'I do. When you kill it's like watching your father in his prime. There is something primal, untamed in your performance. It's utterly compelling.'

Oliver chuckled.

'What's so funny?'

'Listen to yourself, Felix, that could have been straight out of *The Sunday Times* review. "When Lawrence kills it is primal, untamed and utterly compelling."'

Felix smiled too. 'Quite a flowery way to describe a murder.'

Oliver drained his glass. 'If I ever get caught, nobody is ever going to understand what this was really all about. The wrongs that were done to my father and then to me. My only chance is to keep my revenge to those that were actually complicit in the plan to ruin me.'

'Does that mean that Clarissa is safe?'

'No, she was there when it happened and she went along with Sir Morris. She even fed me some wrong lines at his instruction.

I'm just going to have to be more careful when I kill her. I can't afford to kill the wrong person again.'

'Do you regret that?'

Oliver shrugged. 'I regret that it wasn't Clarissa.'

'That poor young lady you killed, she had nothing to do with the theatre.'

'I know, I feel bad, but we could all be hit by a tidal wave tomorrow.'

'We live in Stratford,' observed Felix.

'I was being metaphorical. It's fate, isn't it. Fate decreed that the girl would be drawn into Clarissa's bed and that the scarf I gave to Clarissa would be draped across her face. I just assumed that the person under that scarf was Clarissa. It's a mistake any serial killer could make.'

'I don't hear much regret in your voice, Oliver. You killed an innocent young woman.'

Oliver sighed. 'I do regret it, but I can't undo what's been done. All I can do is be more careful.'

'So, what are you here for?' It was a good question.

Oliver pointed at the bottle. 'Can I have another glass?'

'Help yourself.'

Oliver poured. 'I want to get back on to ground we can agree on, focus on finishing what we started. If I do that, will you help me?'

Oliver saw the doubt in Felix's eyes. 'Please, I won't get it wrong again.'

'Only if we agree the targets beforehand; I'll not have another Lizzie Birchwood.'

Oliver nodded. 'Fair enough. Let's draw up a list.'

Felix shuddered. 'No, I'm not doing that any more, it's too clinical.'

'It's only a bit of paperwork. We don't want any more mistakes, do we.'

'Give me the names, and then I'll tell you whether I'm going to help you or not.'

Oliver took a long gulp of his wine. 'Fair enough, Felix, that's a reasonable request.' Oliver cocked his head to one side and gazed into the distance. His actions were meant to convey deep thought, but in reality his mind was already made up. 'Clarissa, is the next one for the chop.'

Felix slammed his fist down on the table. 'Are you crazy? You just tried to kill her, and failed. The police will be guarding her like the Crown Jewels.'

'Ah, but will they?'

'Yes,' said Felix, unable to hide the incredulity in his voice. 'They will have realised by now that the young woman you killed was mistaken for Clarissa. Only a madman would go back after her so soon.'

'I do have a possible distraction planned.' He winked at Felix, his features twisted into a wolf-like grin. 'When I said the next person I kill will be Clarissa, I failed to mention that there will be another victim before her, who I won't be killing.'

'I don't understand,' said Felix. 'If you're not killing the next victim, who is?'

'Oh, that's the clever bit. I don't know either.'

Felix poured himself another glass of wine and then looked at Oliver. 'You're going to need to spell it out because what you're saying makes no sense.'

'Do you remember Big Al, the chippy?'

'You mean Alan Morris?'

'That's the one.'

'Course I do and he's not a chippy, he's in charge of all the sets in the main house.'

Oliver shrugged. 'Whatever, you know who he is.'

'Everyone at the RSC knows Big Al, he's a legend.'

'He is loved and respected. Now I had a rather clever idea today. I thought I could sneak into the workshops in Old Town and sabotage the battlements for *Hamlet*, so that when Sir Morris leans against the ramparts they give way and he falls to his death.'

'That won't work, they'll find your sabotage when they install the set.'

Oliver grinned. 'I know, that's why I changed my plan.'

'Go on,' said Felix.

'Can you remember what play is on in the main house?'

'Of course, it's *Julius Caesar*.'

'Well done, Felix. How does Caesar die?'

'He was stabbed on his way to the Senate.'

'Correct. Do you know how many times?'

Felix shrugged. 'Ten?'

'Twenty-three, according to the historians.'

'What's your point?'

'My point is, do you know how many actors stab him onstage during the performance?'

'Six or seven.'

'Seven in this performance and they all use stage knives with spring loaded retractable blades, it's a prop that Shelagh Fergusson has provided for the scene. I thought these would be much easier to sabotage.'

Felix put down his glass and began to really listen. 'How would you sabotage them?'

'Do you play the clarinet?'

Felix looked confused. 'No.'

'Neither do I, but for some reason I found a pack of reeds in the middle drawer in your kitchen.'

'This is all very interesting, but why are you telling me this?'

Oliver looked triumphant. 'Because, my friend, I'm going to use two of those thin wooden reeds to jam the blades of two stage knives. When Caesar is stabbed on the steps of the Senate, it will be for real. I'm getting two of the RSC's finest to do my job for me. Talk about life imitating art! Old Sir Morris, like Julius Caesar, has overstayed his welcome. It's rather poetic, don't you think?

The angry mob actually doing him in.'

Felix couldn't help nodding his approval. 'That's actually rather brilliant, Oliver.'

'I know.'

'One slight problem though.'

'What's that?'

'Big Al, he will check everything before the performance, he's very thorough.'

Oliver's smile didn't fade. 'I've thought of that. He checks the set and props every morning, he's usually in the workshop in Old Town in the afternoon and then home for his tea at five. He gets back to the theatre about thirty minutes before curtain up. That gives me a chance to slip in mid-afternoon and do my stuff.'

'Are you sure about his movements?'

'Yes, I've followed him a few times. I had this idea weeks back. There's a part of me that wants to shove the knife into him myself.'

'What part?'

'Pretty much all of me,' admitted Oliver.

Felix chuckled, he couldn't help himself. 'I like it. I like it a lot.'

'You're back on the team then?' asked Oliver hopefully.

'To kill Sir Morris? Most definitely. When's he for the chop?'

'There is a performance tomorrow but if I don't get it done before then there is another performance the day after.'

'And Clarissa?'

'Well, hard to say really. If I get Sir Morris tomorrow, there will be such an uproar it will take the focus off Clarissa, maybe give me a chance to pop round and put out her light.'

Felix shuddered. 'Do you have to put it so crudely.'

'Yes, I do. I'm still annoyed about killing the wrong Desdemona, do we know who she was?'

'I'm afraid I do,' said Felix. 'They gave her name out on the radio about an hour ago.'

Oliver held up his hand. 'Don't tell me, I'd rather not know.'

'I'm afraid you don't have much choice, it will be all over the papers tomorrow.'

Oliver could sense something was wrong. 'Was she someone important?'

'Everyone's important to someone but Heather Wilson was very important to someone who's been looking for you.'

Oliver was confused. 'Looking for me? Surely only the police are looking for me?'

'Exactly. The young lady you smothered was the wife of the chief constable of Warwickshire, Harold Wilson.'

'Oh, bugger,' sighed Oliver. 'He's not going to be happy.'

Felix shook his head slowly. 'Far from it. Chief Wilson had not long married her, had to divorce his wife of over thirty years to do it and all for a woman who was younger than his own daughter. He lost everything to be with her. His marriage, his children, most of their friends and virtually all of his savings paying his first wife off. Now you've killed the only person he loved that was still talking to him. I would imagine he's pretty annoyed with you.'

Oliver bit his lip. 'Yeah,' he sighed. 'In his place, I'd be pretty annoyed too.'

At his home outside of Warwick, Chief Wilson was more than "pretty annoyed." He had loaded his bag of tools into the boot of his car. He burned with a hatred that would only be sated when he had killed the murderer of poor Heather. Phil Townsend must die, slowly and horribly, at his hand.

Hunger gnawed at him but he could think of only one thing: revenge. He knew that if he did this his career would be over, his freedom would be taken. Everything he had worked for would be lost, and yet, he knew he would do it. Without Heather, he had no life. She was his lifeboat, the only vessel that could save him from drowning, and now she was gone. Somebody had to pay and he knew who that somebody was. The clock chimed the hour. He couldn't just sit here, listening to time ticking away the ever-decreasing hours of his life. A life which was over, it had ended with Heather's last breath. The only reason he had left to live was to avenge her, and avenge her he would.

Chapter 55
Divided Duty

The incident room was full, except for Inspector Beeching. After the murder of Heather Wilson, he had taken to his office and not come out.

'Is he all right?' asked Toby, inclining his head towards the door of Beeching's office.

Fred shook his head. 'No, I don't think he is. He doesn't like Chief Wilson much but seeing him like that … It's affected him.'

'Ruined his chance of getting to the Met, allowing the boss' wife to get murdered. Not going to look good on his CV, is it.'

'My, haven't you become hardened and cynical. That usually takes years, you seem to have achieved it in a couple of months.'

Toby shrugged. 'I had a good teacher.'

Fred leaned towards Toby. 'None of us are out of the woods yet, can you imagine what this looks like to any other force? All these murders and no real leads, we must look like a joke. My career's going nowhere but yours could be ruined before it even gets started if we don't catch this killer. Guilt by association sticks, and right now failure is sticking to us like a flasher's Mac on a rainy day.'

Toby smiled. 'Beautiful image, boss. I'll treasure it always.'

Fred ignored Toby's remark and pointed at the whiteboard. 'This is Heather Wilson.' The assembled detectives looked at the board. 'This case is now personal. Chief Wilson's wife has been killed. I don't need to tell you all how bad that is and how bad it looks. I don't need to tell you that the people of Stratford are beginning to lose faith in us, hell, I'm losing faith in us. But we're close. The killer has made a huge mistake; he meant to kill Clarissa Pidgeon, so we know who his next victim is.'

At the back of the room, Mel Townsend wasn't so sure. 'We know who his next victim was supposed to be. What if he's looking elsewhere? He knows we'll be watching Clarissa like a hawk. Do you think he's just going to wait for us to relax?'

'No, I don't,' said Fred. 'He's clever, he will just move on to his next victim hoping that we are preoccupied with Clarissa. We just need to make him believe that we are.'

Ginger Dalton nodded. 'So who do you think is next, boss?'

Fred pointed at the picture of Sir Morris Oxford. 'Him.'

There was silence in the room. You could have heard a pin drop as slowly, very slowly, Fred's finger moved across the board.

'Or her.' He was pointing at a photo of Lady Beatrice Oxford. His finger began to move once more and came to rest on the picture of Theo Cumberbatch. 'Or him.'

The assembled officers looked at each other in confusion.

Mel Townsend spoke for them all. 'Well, that's narrowed it down.'

'That's my point, Mel. We don't know for sure who he will be going after next, we've been one step behind him since he started. We have to assume that each of these three are potential targets.'

'I don't think Cumberbatch is under real threat, boss. He and Oliver were friendly.'

'Were you there, Toby? Do you really know what their relationship was like? Theo said they were close but we've only his word for that. We have to assume that they are all under threat. We need to watch them round the clock. Oliver Lawrence is a man intent on revenge.'

From the back of the room came a raised hand. Fred acknowledged it. 'Go on, Kinky.'

'What if it's not Lawrence?'

'It is.'

There was an uncomfortable silence for a few moments.

'But what if it's not.'

Fred stared unblinkingly at Kinky. He had considered this

question many times during the past weeks. It had kept him awake late into the morning hours. The doubt had nagged away at the back of his mind: were they chasing a shadow?

'We have eliminated every other possible suspect. There is only one man that ties all of these victims together. Only one man who fits the profile perfectly. Oliver Lawrence. He didn't die, he just ran away. Now he's back and settling old scores.' Toby's words seemed to calm the room. 'We've had two possible sightings. One by Dick Mayrick and his wife, and one by Whomper Smith. We need to re-interview all of them now and try and get an up-to-date picture done.'

Fred nodded. 'Kinky, you and Ginger go and find the Mayricks and get them back here, me and Toby will go and see Whomper. The rest of you have your assignments. Don't let your targets out of sight, even if it means blowing your cover. I would rather frighten Lawrence off than see another victim getting hurt.' Fred looked around the room and most of his team seemed to be nodding in agreement. 'Good, now let's get back on the streets and find this sod.'

Mel Townsend sat at the back of the room watching the officers disappear. She waited until there was just the three of them left. 'You know that Scotland Yard will soon be imposing a team on you, don't you?'

Fred nodded, he knew that all too well. He had been brought onto other force's cases a couple of times when they were failing. It always brought resentment.

'They may, but we have to follow our hunches, it's all we have.'

'It's not much.'

Fred looked at Mel. 'You think I'm wrong?'

She shook her head. 'No, I think you're right, and that's what worries me.'

Fred and Toby peered into the stygian gloom inside the Green Dragon.

'It doesn't look like he's in here,' said Fred.

'How can you tell; a miner wouldn't bring a Canary in here.'

'Very true, it would probably end up on the menu, smoked!'

Fred thought for a moment. 'What does Whomper like more than beer?'

'Nothing.'

'Come on Toby, think.'

Toby did think. Whomper liked food, but nowhere near as much as beer. He shrugged. 'I don't know, boss, I'm struggling to think of anything he would put ahead of his love for beer.'

'What about his children.'

'He has children?'

'I would imagine he has many little Whompers strolling around, he strikes me as a man who is profligate in many ways. He does have one passion that would appear to be as important to him as his beer.'

'Motorbikes!' exclaimed Toby.

'Motorbikes,' agreed Fred.

As they pulled up outside the Monumental Stonemasons on Sanctus Street, Toby thought Fred had come to the wrong place.

'What are we doing here, boss? Whomper's not looking for a headstone.'

'Have you seen him ride?'

'Fair point, boss,' agreed Toby; he had only seen Whomper ride once, but that had been enough.

'The bike shop is around the back. Old man Clifford lets Franco rent one of his outbuildings.'

They walked round the back into the yard and there, outside an outbuilding that was little more than an overgrown shed, was a row of second-hand motorbikes. None of them had the sparkle of youth. Fred saw the look on Toby's face.

'Franco specialises in used bikes. It's like a care home for bikes awaiting the scrapyard. Don't be fooled by appearances though,

Franco is a great mechanic, all these little beauties will go like the clappers.'

As they walked towards the display, a figure appeared from between a BSA C15 and a Suzuki GT250. He had long dark hair, and a single grimy smear of oil running across his forehead and down the left-hand side of his face.

'Hello Franco.'

Hello Fred, what brings you here? Thinking of getting another bike?'

'Maybe.'

'How about this little beauty, GT250, goes like the clappers.'

'It's a bloody two stroke,' snarled Fred. 'I'm not a hairdresser, I want a proper bike.'

'It is a proper bike, bet you it's quicker than your 500 Triumph Tiger.'

'Don't be soft, it's a bloody hair dryer with wheels.'

Franco laughed. 'You need to get with the times, Fred. These Japanese two strokes are the future, twice the power with much less weight.'

Fred took a long look at it. 'Suppose I could give it a test ride.' He turned back to Franco. 'But I'm not here about bikes, Franco.'

'He's here to see me.' Whomper emerged from the shadows of Franco's garage, a large mug of tea in one hand and a fag in the other. 'I do perceive a divided duty. Are you here about the case or here to buy a motorbike. Or both?'

'What do you think, Whomper? I've got six bodies and no killer.'

Whomper sat down on the old sofa that was shoved against the outside of the garage. He took a drag of his fag and then a large gulp of his tea. 'Who said men can't multi-task.'

'Every woman I've ever met,' sighed Fred.

'That's because you don't know how to fascinate a woman.'

Toby and Fred looked Whomper up and down. Long hair, unkempt beard, clothes that looked like a tramp had slept in them.

'Fascinate,' said Toby, clearly struggling to combine the statement with the creature seated before him.

'When I'm with a woman, I'm really with her. Not in a sexual way, that comes later.'

'After you've fascinated her.'

'Obviously. I listen to every word she has to say. I take an interest in the ironing. Sometimes I even do the food shopping with her and then I explode the fascination bomb.'

'What's that when it's at home?'

'I treat her as an equal.' Whomper put down his tea, put his hands to his head and then threw them outwards as if his head had blown up. 'Blows their minds, and then—'

'They realise you're a scruffy, scrounging git and kick you out on your arse.'

Whomper smiled at Fred reproachfully. 'Not at all. You see, there is no pretence. I really do listen and I really do treat any woman as my equal. You boys need to wake up and smell the coffee. It's 1972, women aren't going to take being treated like second-class citizens any more. I'm ahead of the curve.'

Fred nodded approvingly. 'That's pretty radical thinking. It's nothing like that in the force, but it should be.'

'Exactly, Fred, you see it. Do you, young Toby?'

'I think so. DI Townsend is as good as any male DI, better than some.'

'Good lad, you'll go far.'

Fred walked over to where Whomper was sitting. 'Much as I would like to talk about your fascinating relationships with the opposite sex, Whomper, I've got more important fish to fry.'

'I'm listening.'

'That bloke you saw on Meon Hill; you still think it's our killer?'

He nodded. 'Yeah, he was giving off this aura. It was all around him, shimmering like a rainbow of death.'

'Could we just say he looked like Oliver Lawrence.'

'He did.'

'Great. We have a local couple who saw someone after Lizzie Birchwood's murder. I want them to take a look at your sketch of the man you saw, see if they think it's the same person.'

'You want me to do it again with a rainbow of death. I could make it Dali-esque.'

'I don't think that's required, Whomper, not everyone has your … gifts.'

'Fair enough.' Whomper turned to Toby. 'You ride, son?'

'Used to, before I became a copper.'

'You should start again, that little Suzuki would suit you fine.'

'Don't be encouraging the lad onto that two-stroke crap, he needs a nice single like that BSA, it's the SS80 with the overhead cam.'

Whomper looked at Toby. 'Ignore Fred, he's a dinosaur. That SS80 will rattle out your fillings and spray oil all over your shiny shoes, it'll also leak on your mum's drive and she won't like that at all. Plus, with the Suzuki, you get the added bonus of a two-stroke.'

'What's that?'

'Castrol R, the women love it. It's like catnip.'

Toby stared at the GT250. 'It does look nice.'

'Ah, I do perceive here a divided duty.'

'Thank you, Desdemona, but Toby's got work to do.'

'You can have a test ride now if you like,' said Franco.

'No, he bloody can't, we've got a killer to catch.' Fred turned and headed back to the car. 'Come into the station in the morning, Whomper.'

'What for?'

'To help the police with their enquiries.'

'Why did you call him Desdemona?'

'*Othello*, Act 1, Scene 3. Whomper's a big fan of the Bard.'

Toby followed Fred. Not for the first time recently, he didn't feel like the smartest person in the room.

Chapter 56
Altered Image

Dick Mayrick sat quietly sipping his coffee in Interview Room One at Guild Street. He had been there for nearly half an hour when Kinky Bernstein and Ginger Dalton walked in.

'Sorry to keep you waiting, Dick, but we are trying to locate your wife.'

'Good luck with that. I never could when we were married.'

'But you are still married, aren't you,' said Ginger.

'Define still.'

'Not divorced.'

Dick nodded sadly. 'No, that small mercy has yet to be granted.'

'Do you love her?'

Dick looked at Ginger. 'Is that really relevant to this inquiry, I thought you were looking for a killer.'

'We are, but we haven't caught him—'

'Or her,' added Kinky.

'Yet!'

'You're not suggesting that we are suspects, are you?'

'No, but we need to get a better picture of the man you spotted in the trees when you found Lizzie Birchwood's body. You both saw him.'

'Yeah we did, he was in the shade of the tree so we couldn't see his face clearly.'

'From what you could see, are you certain it was a man?'

'Oh, it was definitely a man. Broad shoulders, big thighs, thick neck.'

'Sounds like one of DC Bernstein's girlfriends.'

'Sod off,' said Kinky, failing to hide a smile. 'What can I say, I like a strong woman.'

There was a knock on the door.

'Come,' said Ginger.

The door opened and Sergeant Frank Whittall's oversized head appeared around the door. 'We've got Mrs Mayrick, Ginger, and she's not very happy.'

'That's her normal state,' said Dick.

'No, it's more than that. She was having her nails done at the time and we had to insist that she came down to the station as instructed.'

'Is that a problem?'

'Apparently so, she's like a de-clawed lioness,' sighed Frank.

'She can still bite though,' sighed Dick.

Ginger breathed in. 'Show her in please, Frank.'

Frank was barely out of the door before Julia came sweeping in. She held up a hand that had no false finger nails, then the other that did. Neither had been painted.

'What am I supposed to do with these?'

The three men looked at each other.'

'Answers on a postcard,' suggested Dick.

'Why have I been virtually arrested at my beauticians to come down here? I'm not a criminal.'

'No, Mrs Mayrick.'

'Call me Julia,' she snapped.

'Sorry, Julia,' said Ginger. 'We need you to give us a description of the figure you saw in the trees on the morning you found Lizzie Birchwood's body.'

Julia did not look impressed. 'I told you back then that we couldn't see his face because he was in the shadow of the trees.'

'I told them that,' agreed Dick.

'We understand that, but what *can* you tell us.'

Julia paused for a moment. 'He was over six foot and he was built.' Julia held up her hands to illustrate the width of his shoulders.

'He could have been a rugby player like me,' said Dick.

'He was nothing like you,' snapped Julia. 'He looked like a proper man.'

Ginger and Kinky turned to Dick, who seemed totally unfazed by the attack on his physique.

'My wife—'

'Ex-wife!'

'Doesn't really understand the nuances of rugby. The grunts in the pack take their orders from the likes of me, the on-field general. My physique may not be as large but my brain is, and I can tie shoelaces, chew gum and walk in a straight line at the same time.'

Ginger and Kinky nodded in unison. 'Thanks for clarifying that, sir,' said Ginger. 'So, could I summarise that you both agree he was over six foot, and built powerfully.'

'Sexily,' suggested Julia.

Ginger paused. 'That's not really a description though, is it, Mrs … Julia.'

'Well, it is where I come from. For instance, if I was looking for a sexy man, I could rule you two out.' She turned and nodded towards Dick. 'And him.'

Kinky added a comment to his notes. *Possible lesbian.*

Ginger glanced at his notebook and nodded his approval. 'That would explain it,' he whispered.

'What colour was his hair?'

Dick and Julia looked at each other. 'Blond, I think,' said Dick.

'Kind of like the blond hair you get by being out in the sea and the sunshine,' suggested Ginger.

'Bleached, but natural looking,' agreed Julia.

'This is great,' said Ginger. 'We are starting to build a picture,'

They were, but in the bathroom at Trinity Street that picture had just changed. Oliver looked in the mirror; his once blond hair was now a dark chestnut brown; the dye had taken well. He'd also shortened his hair using the clippers Felix had given him.

His reflection in the mirror made him smile, he looked a different person. His eyebrows had always been thick but when he was still blond they faded into the background on his face. Now they stood out like a couple of caterpillars at rest. He had removed the contact lenses to reveal the natural brown of his eyes. This would never do, he thought. In the old days folks had commentated on his beautiful brown eyes. He opened the plastic container and picked up the first lens, gingerly easing back his eyelid and slipping it into place. He blinked a few times and then opened his eyelids to reveal stunningly green eyes, it made him look even less like the picture the police were busy compiling in Guild Street. His final flourish was a pair of brown tortoiseshell glasses which he'd bought from a street vendor in Casablanca. He had assured him they were genuine Yves Saint Lauren; the price clearly didn't reflect this, nor did the lenses which turned out to be clear glass. Oliver didn't mind, they looked smart and made him look cool … different, and different was what he wanted right now.

The police artist finished his sketch and handed it to Ginger Dalton. He turned it to show the Mayricks.

'Does this look right?'

They nodded approvingly.

'Yep, that's what we could make out,' said Dick.

'And you can see what I mean by sexy, can't you,' added Julia.

Dick took another look at the sketch. 'If you like that kind of thing,' said Dick grudgingly.

Ginger looked at Kinky and winked before turning back to the Mayricks.

'Thanks for your help. Can we give you a lift back to the beauticians, Julia?'

'No, it's all right,' said Dick. 'I can do that.' He turned to his wife. 'Do you have any plans for tonight?'

'No, not really.'

'In that case why don't I take you and your new nails out for a meal at The Vintner.'

Julia paused for a moment, surprised by the unexpected nature of the invite. 'Really?'

'Really,' said Dick. 'It's been nice to see you again. He paused for a moment. 'I've missed you.'

Julia's face coloured. 'I guess I've missed you too,' she admitted.

'Steak and Kidney pie tonight, I think.'

'With suet pudding,'

'Is there any other way?'

'I'd love to,' replied Julia.

Ginger smiled. Julia had taken her time realising that she had agreed to a date with her ex … and she didn't really seem to mind.

Ginger watched Kinky escort the newly-united couple from the interview room and marvelled about the human condition. Somehow, a strangled woman and a killer in the trees had reunited an estranged couple. Who needed marriage guidance counsellors?

Chapter 57
The Sleep Of Reason

As the rays of sunlight lengthened with the day, Chief Wilson slid his Rover quietly onto the kerb in Mill Lane. Behind him the imposing outline of Holy Trinity Church stood basking in the golden glow of the late evening. That beauty was lost on him now, everything in his world had become dark. The only light in his life had been extinguished and someone had to pay. He knew who that someone was.

He got out of the car and looked up and down the quiet lane. There was no through traffic, it was a dead end. There was a couple walking away through the graveyard headed for town. Apart from that, he was alone.

From here it was a short walk to the river and the Lucy's Mill footbridge.

He opened the boot and pulled his tool bag towards him; he would find what he needed in there. He picked up the chisel; it felt good in his hand, he could inflict real pain with it. But he didn't want to inflict pain, only death would fill the void in his heart.

He looked at the axe: that would be too messy and uncertain. He had seen evidence of axe attacks in his career and often the axe had got jammed in a bone and the attacker hadn't managed to retrieve it. No, he needed something heavy, something that would crush a skull with one blow. Blunt trauma, rendering the victim helpless.

He saw the hammer; it was heavy with a sturdy wooden handle. There was no claw, just a small ball of hardened steel. He would use the big flat head of the other end of the hammer to administer his retribution.

He had done his research. Townsend had a dog which he liked to walk along the riverside on the Rec. From the location of the pub, the logical route would be down to the end of Church Street and then left onto Old Town. This would bring him down to Mill Lane and the footpath to Lucy's Mill footbridge. Logic had played a major part in Chief Wilson's life. Tonight, hopefully, it would be his ally.

He picked up the hammer. It felt good in his hand; solid, deadly. He slipped it inside his jacket. It was a heavy-duty tweed but the weight of the hammer still made it pull to one side. He decided to place it, head down, in his left-hand side pocket where he could let his arm hang down and conceal it. It would also be easy for him to reach across his body and pull it out with his right hand when the time came. He patted the hammer in his pocket and headed down the quiet lane towards the footpath that led to the bridge.

Just a few hundred yards away, Phil Townsend was putting the lead on his bulldog, Chris. He'd got good staff and he always liked to take Chris out for a stroll before the Windmill got busy. Chris was a good dog but it was always hard to drag him past a pub, he just loved the smell of beer. Left to his own devices, he would have visited every bar in Stratford.

'I'm just taking Chris out,' called Phil. 'Be back in twenty minutes.'

Out on the street, Phil turned left on Church Street and then left onto Old Town; logic was indeed dictating that he was headed for a meeting with Chief Wilson on Lucy's Mill footbridge.

Wilson stood in the middle of the bridge looking back down the river towards the weir. It was quiet now. The old railway bridge, crossing the river behind him, was silent, and there was nobody walking up the riverbank towards the bridge. If Phil Townsend was coming this way, he would never return.

Chief Wilson wasn't quite right about him being alone. Behind him, in the shadows beneath the bridge, was a fisherman. Had he turned away from the town and peered into the shadows beneath the old railway bridge, he would have spotted an ample figure watching him.

Whomper had seen Chief Wilson make his way to the middle of the footbridge some ten minutes ago. He had wondered what the hell he was doing there, just gazing upriver. For a moment, he thought that he may be about to jump, but then he spotted him pull a hammer from his jacket and practice three heavy downward sweeps. There was no doubt what he was rehearsing.

Whomper wound in his illegally cast line, he was fishing in the shadows because he didn't have a licence for this part of the river. The perch he was seeking usually fed at this time of night, and in the shadows, but for the last hour, nothing, not even a nibble. He laid his rod down; he was planning on making a much bigger catch.

As Phil made his way down Mill Lane, he thought about the events of the last two days. Lizzie's murder, the hidden walkie-talkie in her room, and then being questioned about her murder by Chief Constable Wilson. The poor man had been convinced of his guilt and there had been moments when he had feared for his safety. Thank God Fred had been there. He couldn't help feeling sorry for the chief. To lose his wife in such a terrible way had clearly been too much to bear. He breathed in the warm evening air and followed Chris onto the shaded footpath that led to Lucy's Mill bridge.

Chief Wilson saw the dog first. Chris was off the lead and sticking his nose into everything, his shaggy long hair making him look a lot wilder than his temperament. Wilson hoped the dog wouldn't attack him when he killed his master. He was slightly annoyed that he hadn't considered that possibility before.

Chris was a mongrel that appeared to have been crossed with just about everything; judging by the way he was sniffing around it was a trait he had inherited from his lineage. There appeared to be Afghan, poodle, Labrador and several other breeds he couldn't name mixed up in his genepool.

He was a big dog but seemed placid. He hoped that would continue to be the case when he buried his hammer into Phil Townsend's skull. Chris made his way up the steep steps onto the footbridge and Chief Wilson leaned back on the bridge rail, moving his right hand onto the handle of his hammer as he did so.

From beneath the bridge, Whomper could see the situation developing; if he didn't do something now, he was going to be the witness to a murder.

'Chris, heel boy. Chris.'

He recognised the voice and when its owner strolled into view, any doubt was gone. Phil Townsend. He knew Phil from his many visits to the Windmill, and he also knew that he had been questioned in relation to the murder of Chief Wilson's wife.

All of Whomper's synapses were firing as he put everything together in a moment of absolute clarity. As Phil started up the steps, Whomper ran from the shade of the old railway bridge and took the stairs two at a time on the east side of the bridge.

Wilson was looking the other way, intent on his victim, hatred burning a hole in his reason. Phil reached the top of the bridge as Whomper was halfway up the far steps. He wasn't going to make it. Chief Wilson had bent down to pet Chris, hiding his face from Phil and putting him in a position to surprise Phil when it was too late for him to escape.

As Phil walked towards the crouching figure, he spoke. 'Lovely evening.'

The stranger slowly stood up and smiled at him. 'Not for you.'

Phil recognised Chief Wilson immediately but, in his confusion, he didn't run. He saw Wilson pull the long hammer from his pocket and swing it back in a fatal arc.

'No!' cried Whomper as he charged towards Wilson. Wilson's arm was just starting to swing downwards, but Whomper's shouted warning caught him off balance as he half turned to see where the call had come from. The hammer swung down past Phil's face, missing it by inches. Momentum is an irrefutable fact of physics and Chief Wilson's hammer had developed a great deal of it. The huge force, fuelled by hate, had failed to find its target and the fatal metal lump swung out across the bridge safety rail and into the void.

Wilson followed it and, colliding with the rail, failed to keep his balance as the swinging weapon still sought the victim it had missed. He hit the rail hard. There was a crack as a rib broke and he rode up on the rail, still clinging onto the hammer.

For a moment he balanced on the rail like a broken seesaw and then momentum and gravity triumphed as he toppled over and fell into the dark waters of the Avon below.

Whomper watched him fall, paralysed for a moment by his inability to do anything. As he fell, Chief Wilson's eyes looked into his; there was no fear, just a vague look of surprise. He didn't scream and hit the water head first, disappearing beneath the waters rapidly and leaving only expanding ripples to mark his passing.

Whomper ran to the spot he had disappeared and watched, waiting, hoping that Chief Wilson would emerge. He never did. There had been heavy rain the previous night and the river was in full flow.

Phil Townsend just stood there, too shocked to move.

Whomper looked at him. 'You OK, Phil?'

Phil nodded. 'I'm not sure. Did he just try to kill me?'

'Well, unless he thought you were a nail, I'd say so.'

Phil joined Whomper and they both gazed over the bridge into the dark waters below.

'Shouldn't we dive in after him?'

Whomper shrugged. 'Not in these jeans, they're not pre-shrunk.'

Phil started to clamber over the rail but Whomper pulled him back.

'Leave it, Phil, the water's deep and the currents run strong under the old railway bridge, you could end up drowning yourself.'

It was dark and cold in the waters of the Avon. Chief Wilson bumped across the riverbed with no thought of trying to escape. What was there to live for? Everything he had loved was gone. He had failed to kill Heather's murderer and even if he did survive, his career wouldn't. All he ever was and everything he would be was over. He breathed in, taking the water of the Avon deep into his lungs. There were no tears, no cries, just a growing darkness that enveloped his despair.

Chapter 58
The King Is Dead

At dawn the next morning, Fred and Toby stood on the Lucy's Mill bridge looking down at the waters that had claimed their chief constable.

'Poor sod couldn't even attack the right person.'

Toby nodded. 'Chief Wilson wasn't the best detective, was he.'

'His kind never are, it's all about climbing the corporate ladder. Crime is just something they read reports about.' Fred turned away. 'Still, can't help feeling sorry for the old boy. He was a broken man when he left Guild Street.'

'He's left a big gap.'

Fred chuckled. 'Just watch Beeching try and fill it, he'll be in there like a rat up a drain pipe.'

'You think so?'

Fred scowled. 'He's a career policeman, there's no quick route to the Met after what's happened in Stratford. Becoming chief constable in Warwickshire is the next best thing. Birmingham is the second city, not a bad place to cool his heels while this blows over.'

'You're getting cynical, boss. I'm sure Beeching isn't that bad.'

'I've been doing this a long time, Toby. Getting to the top is about claiming credit for the good things others have done and placing the blame on others for bad things you've done. Pretty much sums up every senior officer I've ever worked for.'

'That why you're still a DS?'

'Yep, just can't stand the bullshit. Give me a criminal to hit and a nice bacon butty and I'm happy.'

Toby nodded down at the river. 'You reckon he survived?'

Fred shook his head. 'He didn't want to survive. The frogmen will find him somewhere round the back of the racecourse near Stannals Bridge, that's where the bodies usually wash up when the river's running high.'

'So how do we report it then?'

'Just how Whomper and Phil told us.'

'You don't believe he jumped,' said Toby.

'Course he didn't. He was trying to kill Phil but he couldn't even get that right.'

'So why are Whomper and Phil saying he jumped? We both know that isn't true.'

Fred sighed. 'What good will it do branding the poor sod as a failed murderer? Phil and Whomper know the score. Poor chap had suffered enough and Phil doesn't want his very active sex life being broadcast by the tabloids. It'd ruin his reputation.'

'But—'

'Drop it, Toby. Sometimes you just have to leave things be. There's no point ruining the reputation of the chief now he's dead. What do we gain?'

Toby shook his head. 'It doesn't feel right.'

'Sometimes you just have to let sleeping dogs lie.'

'The king is dead, long live the king?'

'Pretty much, young Toby, and the new king won't take long to claim his throne. Beeching will be trying to replace Wilson before we bury him.'

As Fred and Toby stood watching the river flow towards the place where Chief Wilson had finished his journey, they became aware of a figure running down the path towards the bridge.

'Brace yourself,' said Fred. 'Here comes the heir apparent to the throne of Warwickshire.'

Toby glanced behind him just in time to see Beeching bounding up the steps towards them. Clearly the rowing had kept him in good shape.

They both turned to face him.

'Morning, sir.'

Beeching ignored Toby's greeting. 'Is it true?'

'Is what true, sir?'

'Wilson. Is he dead?'

'Too early to say, sir. We have two witnesses who saw him go in last night at dusk and, so far, he doesn't appear to have resurfaced.'

'He's dead then?'

'Unless,' Fred glanced at his watch, 'he can hold his breath for ten hours.'

Beeching shook his head. 'What happened?'

Fred looked at Toby, he turned away. 'According to our witnesses, he jumped from the bridge. He didn't scream or struggle, just hit the water and disappeared without a murmur.'

'He killed himself? It doesn't seem like the kind of thing he would do.'

Toby looked uncomfortably downstream, trying to distance himself from the conversation, unwilling to be part of the lie. Fred had no such qualms.

'Grief's a funny thing, sir, how would you react if your wife had just been murdered?'

A smile flickered across Beeching's face which he rapidly extinguished. 'Ironic that one of the witnesses who saw him die was Phil Townsend. Are we sure that his statement is correct?' He looked at Toby who in turn looked to Fred.

'We have a statement from the other witness that confirms it.'

'Whomper Smith,' chuckled Beeching. 'What were the chances of Whomper being not in a pub but out in the fresh air.'

'There's more to Whomper than you think, sir. He's a lot fitter and cleverer than he looks.'

'He'd have to be.' Beeching turned back and gazed at the old railway bridge. 'My uncle closed that, you know.'

'Lord Beeching was your uncle?'

Beeching nodded. 'Afraid so, he was a good man but he was

told that there had to be massive cuts made in the railway system to save money.'

'By ministers who had big shares in the companies supplying concrete to the motorway builders,' said Fred.

'Yep, no conflict of interest there. It was supposed to be progress but it certainly doesn't feel like it to folk that can't afford a car.' Beeching gazed down at the river. 'How deep is it here, Fred?'

'It's about eight feet under the arches. The heavy winter rains really deepened the channel but further down it's not so deep. Apart from the main channel, you could probably wade out.'

'He could still be alive then?'

'No, he's dead. Could have knocked himself out when he fell but both Townsend and Whomper said he jumped, didn't scream and never resurfaced. Sounds like a man that wanted to die to me.'

'What do you think, Toby?' Toby hesitated. 'Do you think Fred is right?'

'I don't have to think, sir, we have two witnesses who saw what happened.'

'One who Wilson had wrongly accused of murder and attacked the day before and the other who is … well, Whomper!'

There was an uncomfortable silence and then Beeching slowly straightened and stood back from the rail. 'You know what I think?'

'No, sir, but I'm sure you're going to tell us.'

'I am Fred. I think that Chief Wilson came here to kill the man he thought killed his wife. I think he cocked it up, fell in and drowned himself. How am I doing, Fred?'

'Not what the witness statements say, sir.'

'True, but I'm pretty sure that once you had explained to Phil that he wouldn't come out too well in the tabloids … The gigolo about town who had been having sex with just about every other woman in Stratford except, ironically, Wilson's wife.'

'And Whomper?'

'Whomper doesn't want to appear in a court case; it will get in the way of his nefarious activities.' Beeching wagged a finger at both Toby and Fred. 'I think what you boys did is persuade Townsend and Whomper that it would be much better if Chief Wilson had died from a broken heart. Looks better than the commander-in-chief of the force dying in a botched attempt at murder. It would have made the force look bad and ruined the old boy's reputation. Have I got it right?'

Fred nodded. 'It was my idea, sir. Toby had no choice.'

Beeching clapped his hands in applause. 'Bravo, Fred, you did the right thing.'

Toby couldn't disguise his surprise. 'But—'

'But nothing, Toby. There is no upside to letting the world know that the chief, in his grief, tried to kill Townsend. He's dead and the whole sorry tale is best left to die with him. The force will get sympathy from the press, as will Wilson, and it will take the focus off our murderer for a short time. It was the right thing to do. Sometimes telling the complete truth isn't the right option.'

'Glad you see it that way, sir. I didn't want to burden you with the full story.'

Beeching smiled at Fred. 'You mean you didn't expect me to work it out.'

'That too, sir.'

Beeching looked back down at the river. 'Well, unless we hear different, the king is dead. Long live the king!'

'You, sir?'

Beeching nodded. 'Who else, Fred, who else.'

Chapter 59
Lies For A loved One

Sir Morris sat in Pierre Corridor's office at the RSC. It was their first proper meeting since Pierre had returned from the USA.

'You've heard the terrible rumours?'

Pierre nodded. 'Another death last night. Awful.'

'Not the murders, my wife,' said Sir Morris. 'She wants to come back to the theatre. To act.'

The pained expression on Sir Morris' face said it all. Pierre sympathised. He had been unlucky enough to direct Beatrice in *Romeo and Juliet* some years back, an experience he had described as, 'Like trying to milk a bull. No matter how hard I tried, nothing came out.'

'Apparently, Big Al Morris has put the idea into her head that she could play comedy.'

'Alan the chippy?'

'Oh, he's much more than that these days, Pierre, he's in charge of all the sets.'

'He knows a lot about all things wooden then.'

'Including my wife's acting,' sighed Sir Morris. 'How do we stop this? I don't like to tell her she can't act.'

Pierre considered the problem for a moment. He didn't want to admit to Sir Morris that he was encouraging Beatrice to play comedy. 'Neither you or I want to make a decision like this, so why don't we pass it on down the line.'

'I like the sound of that, Pierre. Who do you think is dumb enough to volunteer?'

Pierre winked at him. 'I think I have just the man for the job.'

'Who?'

'Someone I managed to convince that a brief return to the

stage would give his film career a solid boost.'

'Who is it?' demanded Sir Morris.

Pierre Corridor leaned back in his chair and a huge grin spread across his features. 'Hugh Pitt.'

'Huge Pitt!' cried Sir Morris, his features twisted in distaste. 'I thought we'd managed to lose him to Hollywood forever.'

'Sadly not. Bernie Rothstein has convinced him that doing Shakespeare at the RSC will add gravitas to his CV, especially if he directs it.'

'Isn't Rothstein the head of Reynard Films?'

'He is, and that makes him one of the most powerful players in Hollywood. I don't think Hugh had much choice in the matter.'

'I'm not sure I like the idea of that little snake coming back to Stratford and trying to steal my thunder.'

Pierre chuckled, he could practically feel Morris' hackles rising. 'You have nothing to fear, Morris, he wants to star in and direct it.'

This came as a horrible shock to Sir Morris who hadn't starred in and directed a play at the RSC in years. 'This is terrible news, what if he's good?'

Pierre grinned. 'He won't be.'

'What makes you so sure?'

'We gave him *Much Ado*.'

They looked at each other and started to giggle. As poisoned chalices go, this one was right up there.

'Much ado about bugger all, you clever sod.'

'Yes, I am, Morris. I could make sure Beatrice gets a part too if you like. Let her go down with the ship.'

'If you weren't so ugly I'd kiss you,' said Sir Morris. He was on his feet and doing a jig. 'There are no decent speeches in the play, nothing happens and the plot is thinner than my mother's soup, it'll be a disaster.'

'That's why I'm going to put it on at The Other Place and only give it a tiny budget. I can easily disclaim it there saying it was thrust upon us by Hollywood. Do you mind Beatrice being attached to such a vehicle?'

Sir Morris shook his head. 'Not at all, I welcome it. The sooner she realises something's wrong, the sooner she's going to come back to me to help her. And I will help her.'

'How are you going to do that?'

'By pointing out what a shitshow the play was and that her career would be best served by those that don't actually remember it. Beatrice has this aura about her, she's beautiful and linked to greatness. Richard, who was on the way to greatness, and then me. If you dug beneath the surface, her lack of major roles would soon become apparent.'

Pierre nodded. 'Yes, the line that Beatrice gave it all up to be a wife and mother sits a lot better with history.' He leaned back in his chair and looked thoughtfully out of the window. The waters of the Avon ran deep, as did Pierre Corridor's cunning. 'There is one thing that I think you should consider.'

'What's that?'

'Big Al could be right. I remember seeing Beatrice in a performance of The Dream. It was a matinee at Oxford Playhouse. She played Puck and, quite frankly, she was brilliant.'

'Oh yes, I vaguely recall it. I didn't think she was all that.'

'Really? I remember thinking that she had a real flair for comedy. How come she never played one again?'

Sir Morris shrugged. 'I don't really know. By the time I was aware of her, she was already married to Richard, and then pregnant with Oliver before you could say cross your legs.'

'What about when you two became a couple?'

Sir Morris considered the question. 'You know, Pierre, I don't think I ever gave her the chance. I like the serious stuff. The tragedies, the historicals, comedy just isn't my forte. She was in my company so she just ended up playing serious stuff.' Sir Morris sat back in his chair. 'I suppose I'm to blame.'

'There's no blame attached, Morris, it's just life. Sometimes though, life gives us a second chance, so why not give Beatrice a second chance? What have you got to lose? If she fails, she fails, and if she succeeds, everyone wins. What do you say?'

Sir Morris looked at Pierre's smiling face and, after a moment, nodded.

'Fair enough, let's get her into *Much Ado* and see what happens.'

Pierre smiled contentedly. Somehow, he had managed to get Sir Morris to agree to his wife being back on the boards. He would make sure that *Much Ado* was a success; he had a good feeling about Beatrice.

Big Al, totally unaware of what he had started, was walking down Southern Street. He had just checked over the set for tonight's performance of *Julius Caesar*. He was, as always, thorough. He'd even checked the knives to make sure that all the blades retracted when they were pushed into something, the last thing he needed was an actual stabbing live onstage. As he crossed the road and entered the Memorial Garden on Old Town, a well-built, dark-haired man came out of the garden and held open the gate for him.

'Thanks,' said Big Al. The stranger smiled. There was something familiar about him, like a voice calling from the past. A moment of déjà vu swept over him. He stopped. 'Do I know you?'

The stranger shrugged. 'I get that a lot; guess I've got one of those faces.' He shot Big Al that smile again and turned and walked away.

Al watched him go and, as he did so, a feeling of dread began to overwhelm him.

Oliver hurried down Southern Street towards the theatre. That had been close; he had known Big Al Morris well in his days at the RSC. The fact that he hadn't identified him was good, they were virtually touching. But there could be no mistaking the fact that Big Al felt he knew him from somewhere. His cloak of invisibility would not last forever.

As he neared the stage door, he took out the contractor's pass that Felix had nicked for him. He walked confidently up to the door and pulled it open.

There was a member of staff at the counter, he looked up as Oliver entered. 'Can I help you?'

Oliver held up his badge. 'Just here to check the locking mech on the steps of the Senate. Apparently, they're a bit stiff. We don't want them locking and leaving the cast no place to stab Caesar now, do we.'

They both laughed and Oliver was through. He didn't waste time, he knew the backstage area like the back of his hand and nothing had really changed in the last few years.

He made his way quickly to the wings of the main stage and there were the steps of the Senate, waiting for the moment when they would be wheeled onto stage later that evening. To one side was a box of props. He rummaged around but found no daggers. He paused and listened, making sure that he was still alone. The auditorium was silent. Where could the daggers be? They had to be here somewhere but the clock was ticking, he wouldn't be alone for long.

Then he saw it, a metal tool box placed behind the Senate steps. It had to be. He crossed over and bent down; it wasn't locked. Breathing a sigh of relief, he began to open it. The metal lid creaked like a pensioner's hip and the sound echoed around the empty auditorium. He held his breath and waited for footsteps … They never came. Breathing deeply, the sound of his heartbeat pounding in his ears, he opened the lid. He smiled: was this a dagger he saw before him? It was several. He picked one up and tested the blade against his leg. As he pushed, the blade retracted, giving the impression that it had buried itself deep into his thigh. Working rapidly, he pulled the clarinet reed, wrapped in tin foil, from his pocket. He had already cut two small sections from it. He took the first section and jammed it into the tiny opening at the side of the blade. As soon as it was in place, he reached deeper into his pocket and brought out the tiny tube of super glue. Removing the top, he gently squeezed the glue into the opening and watched it trickle down and around the sliver of clarinet reed. The glue ran smoothly and cleanly into the opening. He put down the knife and picked up another and repeated the process. Within two minutes both knives were prepared. As he replaced them, he pressed the blades into the palm of his hand. The blades did not retract and he could feel the sharp metal beginning to break the surface of his skin. He closed the box and replaced it behind the Senate steps before making his way out of the wings and back to the corridor that ran down to the stage door.

When he reached the counter, the staff member looked up. 'Everything OK?'

'Yes, the steps are working perfectly. Caesar won't have to die in the car park tonight.'

They both laughed as Oliver made his way back out onto the street. Tonight's performance would be one to remember and he had a front row seat. Felix was in for a big surprise, but not as big as Sir Morris.

Chapter 60
Deep Waters

Toby and Fred stood on Stannals Bridge. The train tracks on the Honeybourne line were quiet but Fred glanced anxiously over his shoulder.

'There's not one due for another hour.'

'I don't care, be just my luck to be run down by a train that was actually early,' said Fred.

Below them there was a crew of police supporting the frogmen's search for the body of Chief Wilson. The local water bailiff had advised them that, considering the height of the river, and where Wilson had entered it, they should start their search at Stannals Bridge. He had been correct. A frogman broke the surface, his right arm held aloft.

'Looks like the fish are biting today,' sighed Fred. 'We'd better get down there.'

Toby nodded sadly. 'Shall I call SOCO?'

'Nah, let's make sure it's Wilson first.'

They made their way from the bridge and down the river bank as the body of Wilson surfaced, supported by a number of inflatables. The frogman guided the body to the water's edge, where three policemen in waders eased it out of the river.

Fred was first on the scene. He gazed down at the face of Chief Wilson. Looking at the empty husk of what once had been his boss, he felt emotion flood through him. Wilson had died alone. No family to hold his hand as he left this world. That could be him in a few years, slowly slipping away with no one to mourn his passing.

'You OK, boss?'

'No, Toby, I'm not OK. I just saw my future and I don't like it.'

'You think you're going to drown?'

'No, but I will die alone.' Fred paused for a moment. 'Unless I change my ways.' He knelt down and gently closed Wilson's eyes.

'Should you do that, boss?'

'We know the cause of death, giving the chief a little bit of dignity isn't going to affect anything. Get Alf Butcher out here. Now we know it's Wilson, we need to get this sorted.' Fred stood up but kept his gaze on his old boss. 'Goodbye, sir, and flights of angels sing thee to thy rest.' He turned away and Toby could see a tear rolling down his cheek. 'Come on, Toby, we still have a killer to catch.'

Toby followed his boss up the bank and back to the bridge. He'd never seen him like this before. Wilson's death had clearly made him consider his own mortality.

As they walked back down the tracks towards the road, Toby turned to Fred.

'You all right, boss?'

Fred nodded his head almost imperceptibly. 'I will be, Toby, but this has made me think.'

'About death?'

'No. About life. It's time I seized the day. Are you and DI Townsend an item?'

The question took Toby by surprise. 'No, boss, we flirted a bit but it's never going to happen.'

'Why not, she's a good-looking woman and she clearly fancies you.'

Toby laughed. 'She was playing with me, boss. Having a bit of fun at my expense.'

'And if she wasn't playing?'

'Well, she's a senior officer and I'm just a DC. It would never work.'

'That your only reservation?'

'No.'

'So, what is it?'

Toby's features twisted with discomfort. 'The other day I heard her singing a song that my mum always sings. Made me think, you know. She's old enough to be my mum.'

Fred laughed. 'Well, young Toby, if you can't get past the age gap and her seniority, take a step back and let me have a go. It's about time I told DI Townsend how I really feel.'

'Like you said, sir, you've got to "Seize the DI."'

Chapter 61
Dead Man's Shoes

Inspector Beeching had taken the confirmation of Chief Constable Wilson's death in his stride. He was a man possessed. He called Fred into his office and shut the door. 'The chief's death will only buy us a couple of days breathing space before the press start banging on about our killer again. We need to move fast.'

'We're doing everything we can. All the possible victims are being watched, we have extra patrols in town. Short of bringing the Army in or putting a curfew in place, there is nothing more we can do.'

Beeching pointed to the chair opposite his desk. 'Sit down, Fred.' Fred sat. 'I don't think you understand the context here. When I said we need to move fast, I wasn't talking about catching our killer. This is our chance to suggest to the press that now Wilson is gone the case will have more chance of a successful conclusion.' Beeching cocked his head and stared at Fred. 'Do you get my drift?'

Fred did. 'The man's only been dead a few hours and you want to blame him for us not catching the killer. That's disgusting.'

'It's expedient. Wilson's dead, it's over for him. His wife is dead, and the wife and family he divorced are all estranged from him. It's perfect. We imply that the late, great chief was a wonderful man but some of his methods were a bit dated. His loss is regrettable but a younger leader with new ideas may just be able to give the inquiry a boost. We've got to be careful how we do it or we could be admitting incompetence—'

'Who's this "we" you keep referring to?' said Fred, not bothering to hide the anger in his voice.

'Well, us. You talk about what you think I will bring to the role as the new commander-in-chief.'

Fred stood up. 'There is no "we". I'll have nothing to do with this. If you want to blacken Chief Wilson's reputation, you can do it on your own.'

Fred shook his head and walked from the room, ignoring the calls from Beeching to sit back down.

As Fred walked into the incident room, Toby was looking at the images on the board. 'My car. Now,' said Fred, grabbing the keys from his desk and heading for the car park.

His words required no response so Toby just grabbed his jacket and followed.

Fred had the motor running. When Toby got into the car, he gunned it off the car park and onto Guild Street.

'What's going on, boss?'

Fred gripped the wheel tightly and Toby could see that all his knuckles were white.

'Remember I told you that Beeching would be after Wilson's crown?' Toby nodded. 'He's already started.'

'Jeez, he could have given it a bit more time, out of respect.'

'Respect, he doesn't know the meaning of the word. He wants me to imply in the press conference that Wilson was leading the manhunt for Oliver Lawrence and his dated methods have been holding us back. How's that for a quick rewriting of history.'

Toby shook his head in disbelief. 'That man has no shame. The chief isn't even cold yet.'

'He is after a night in the river, trust me.'

'What are you going to do, boss?'

'My job,' snapped Fred. 'I'm going to find our killer and I won't be bothering Beeching again until I've caught the bugger.'

Fred turned left and headed towards Rother Street. 'I think we need to speak to Sir Morris and Lady Oxford.'

They drove past the American monument and pulled up outside the White Swan Hotel. 'Come on.' Fred climbed out and headed for the entrance without pause. 'Leave the talking to me.'

Toby followed without comment, he hadn't got a clue what Fred was going to ask.

'Can I help you, sir?'

'DS Williams,' Fred showed his warrant card. 'I need to speak to Sir Morris and Lady Oxford, are they in?'

'Yes, sir,' replied the receptionist.

'Well, give them a call then and let them know we are here.' Fred forced a smile but there was no mistaking the hard edge in his voice.

The receptionist looked nervous. 'I'm afraid I can't, officer. Sir Morris is on stage tonight and he doesn't allow any interruptions to his afternoon rest on performance days.'

Fred leaned over the counter. 'Listen, son, I think there's a bit of a misunderstanding here. I'm not making a request, I'm *telling* you we are going to speak to him.'

'But—'

Fred didn't let him finish. 'Do you know what obstructing an officer in the course of his duties is?'

The receptionist shook his head.

'It's deep shit, son, the kind of shit you don't ever want to step in. Now be a good lad and tell Sir Morris that we are coming up before I have to arrest you.'

The receptionist picked up the phone and dialled.

'What is it,' boomed a voice from the receiver. Fred and Toby could hear Sir Morris' irritation, despite the phone being clamped to the poor chap's ear. He flinched.

'It's the police, Sir Morris, they want to speak to you.'

Fred reached over and took the receiver from his hand. 'DS Williams here. Would you and Lady Oxford like to come down to reception or shall we come up to your room.'

It wasn't a question. There was a moment's silence before Fred handed the phone back to Raymond. 'They'll be down in ten minutes. We'll be in the lounge; nice pot of tea and some biscuits wouldn't go amiss.'

'I'm afraid we only do that for residents.'

'It's a pot of tea for four. Sir Morris and Lady Oxford can't be expected to come down here for a chat and not have some tea and biscuits now can they.'

The conversation was over and Fred stalked off into the lounge. Toby gave Raymond a weak smile and followed.

Fred wasted no time finding a wingback armchair and dropping into it. 'Always liked this place. They make their own shortbread biscuits, you know.'

Toby sat down opposite him. 'Why are we here, boss?'

'Why do you think?'

'Because you fancy some biscuits?'

Fred nodded. 'Can't deny it, but that's not the reason.'

'What is?'

'Look at the list of victims, it's all leading in one direction.'

Toby said nothing, waiting for Fred to expand his theory.

'Sir Morris is next, who else is there to kill from the old company?'

'Theo Cumberbatch.'

'Oliver won't kill Theo, he was friends with him and, as far as we know, Theo didn't take part in the plan to end his career. I think Sir Morris is next or pretty near the top of the list.'

'What about Lady Oxford?'

Fred rubbed his chin. 'I think she's at risk too. She shacked up with Sir Morris pretty quickly after her husband died. Can't think that when Oliver became a teenager he wouldn't resent that, even a little bit.'

'He was close to his father.'

'He worshipped him. Richard Jenkins was on his way to becoming one of the greats. Imagine how you would feel if your mum shacked up with someone she worked with a couple of months after your father died. You wouldn't like it, would you.

That must have festered inside him for years and then, when he became an actor himself and could see the chemistry between them, he would have known. He must have known.'

Toby nodded. 'You think they were having an affair before Richard died.'

'Is the Pope a Catholic?'

Before Toby could answer, Sir Morris came bustling into the lounge; he was red in the face, flustered.

Fred glanced at Toby and smiled. He stood up and held out his hand. 'Good to see you again, Sir Morris.'

'I hope this is important, DS Williams, I've got a play to do tonight.'

'I appreciate that, sir, but we have a serial killer to catch. I think that trumps your afternoon nap!'

It was a cutting remark and Sir Morris bridled. Toby watched as his face flushed with anger but he said nothing. There was a tense silence. The three of them stood there eyeing each other, like cowboys in a B-movie shoot out. Before anyone could draw, Raymond arrived with the tea and biscuits. There was a large plate of home baked shortbread.

Fred eyed them and winked at Toby. 'I took the trouble of ordering some refreshments.'

'I'll take some tea but I never eat anything in the afternoon before a show, sits on the stomach and affects the diaphragm.'

Fred's smile broadened and Toby knew that the extra shortbreads would soon be taken into custody.

Sir Morris sat down. 'I'm very sorry to hear about Chief Wilson, it must have been a shock.'

'It was, sir. He was a good man. The murder of his wife hit him hard, they hadn't been married long.'

'So I understand. Running off with a younger woman seldom works out.' Sir Morris sighed, his face now full of sadness. 'No fool like an old fool, eh?'

'I wouldn't know, sir. I'm single,' said Fred.

'Keep it that way, makes life so much easier.'

Fred and Toby had not been expecting such candour. Fred seized on it. 'But isn't Lady Oxford a lot younger than you?'

Sir Morris nodded slowly. 'She is, and it's worked out well over the years, but with all this going on …' He gesticulated with his hands. 'I can't help thinking that our relationship could have something to do with it.'

'You mean, if our killer is Oliver,' said Fred.

Sir Morris nodded sadly. 'My wife is convinced that it's him.'

'And you?'

'I'm not sure.'

'If not Oliver, who?' Fred's question was short and to the point.

'I don't know,' sighed Sir Morris. 'It's getting harder to imagine it could be anyone else now. I loved that young man, treated him as my own son …' he trailed off and sat there silently, his head bowed.

'But all he saw was betrayal. You got rid of his father, moved in with his mother and then sacked him from your company when he became an actor. When he disappeared, you married his mother the second he was out of sight. That's bound to make him resentful, don't you think?'

Toby cringed. Fred's line of questioning was blunt and direct but Sir Morris didn't seem to be taking offence. It was as if the mask had been removed from his face. Gone was the bluster and certainty; doubt had now replaced it and it made him look smaller, vulnerable. He seemed to be shrinking before their eyes, a slowly deflating ego.

'I never claimed to be perfect. Becoming a surrogate father wasn't easy. Oliver was … tricky. He had his father's genius, no doubt about that, but he also had the madness. There was an edge to him. I always felt like I was walking a tightrope, one misplaced step and …' he shrugged. 'You know.'

'Actually, I don't,' said Fred. 'Why don't you spell it out for me.'

Sir Morris poured himself a cup of tea and took a sip.

'I could never say this in front of his mother but I think the boy was a little crazy. Schizophrenic.'

'Was he diagnosed?' asked Toby.

'No, his mother would never have allowed that.'

'Schizophrenics can believe that they hear and see things that aren't there, see things that aren't real,' said Toby.

'Sounds like an actor,' observed Fred.

Surprisingly, Sir Morris chuckled. 'Touché, DS Williams, we do make things up for a living. With Oliver it was something more. He imagined slights that were never given, he was always looking to be offended.'

'But, you did undermine him, didn't you.' It wasn't a question, Fred was making an accusation. 'You and your friends actively plotted to ruin Oliver's career. He was a threat, a very talented one. He was trouble and you didn't want that in your cosy little company.'

Sir Morris' cup had paused on the way to his mouth and now he lowered it slowly, menacingly.

'What are you trying to infer, DS Williams?'

'Isn't it obvious? You got rid of Oliver because he was trouble. He was too good as an actor; a clear threat to your crown, just like his father. And he was too close to his mother. You wanted her all to yourself.'

If Sir Morris had been a kettle there would have been steam coming out of his ears. He slammed his cup and saucer down onto the table. Before he could erupt, another voice spoke.

'It wasn't like that.'

They all turned and there, in the doorway of the lounge, stood Lady Beatrice Oxford. She walked into the room and sat on an empty chair next to Sir Morris. 'Oliver was paranoid about his father. He felt that by killing himself he had taken the decision to leave us both behind. He believed that Richard deserted us.'

'He was three when his father died, bit young to feel like that.'

Lady Oxford smiled. 'You don't have children, do you, DS Williams.'

He shook his head.

'He was almost four. At that age, they feel it all, they just can't express it. Oliver harboured that resentment, then as he grew he got to hear all these wonderful tales about his father and realised that he was something of a legend.' Lady Oxford looked away. Sir Morris reached for her hand and squeezed it. 'He felt robbed!'

'And then he would have discovered that his father had been sacked and that you started having an affair with Sir Morris,' said Fred.

'We did not,' snapped Sir Morris.

Fred held up his hands. 'I'm not sitting in judgement, it's just how it appears to me. All I'm trying to do is find out why Oliver is doing this and who is in danger. That's all I care about. Your relationship and when it started is of no concern to me.'

Sir Morris and Beatrice looked at each other. The wall they had built between the truth and the lie they had constructed began to crumble.

'It was a difficult situation. Richard was out of control, drinking a lot,' said Sir Morris. 'He could be a monster at times.'

'One you helped to create,' said Fred.

'I'm not playing this game,' snapped Beatrice. 'You have no authority to make moral judgements about our relationship.'

'I'm not making any, all I want to do is catch a murderer and I think we all believe it's your son. I just want to try and figure out who is left on his hit list. What do you think, DC Marlowe?'

Fred's question took Toby by surprise. 'Me, er … I think Sir Morris is in danger.'

'What about Lady Oxford?'

'I think she will be OK. She's his mother, it's not easy to kill your mother.'

'Maybe not, but it happens.' Fred turned to Beatrice. 'What do you think, Lady Oxford, does Oliver have a reason to kill you?'

Her voice was a whisper. 'No.'

'You sure about that?' Fred would not let it go and Toby had no wish to intervene.

'My relationship with Oliver was … strained. As he became a teenager and began to act, a distance grew between us. It was almost as if he had rejected me.'

'Did he approve of your relationship with Sir Morris?'

'I don't know, I never asked him. Morris was good to him, treated him like a son.'

'But he wasn't, was he. Sir Morris had replaced his father and young Oliver felt pushed out, resented his replacement in your affections.'

'Hold on, old chap. I think you're reading a bit too much into this. Oliver was a happy young man until—'

'Until you pushed him out.' Fred's words hung in the air; an accusation. Sir Morris' face reddened with anger and then subsided in sadness. 'It may appear that way but it wasn't like that.'

'What exactly was it like then?'

'Why are you asking all these questions? We all think Oliver is the killer, does it matter what his childhood was like. He's holding a grudge against all of us that were around when his career went bad, look at the list of victims. None of those helped to bring him up, and yet they're dead.'

'I'm just trying to establish if you are both at risk.'

'Just assume we are and then we can get on with our day. I don't know about you, officer, but I'm busy.' Beatrice spoke with a haughty dismissive air, almost as if she was irritated by having to be there.

Fred nodded. 'Fair enough, Lady Oxford. Let's assume, for now, that you are both at risk and I will arrange protection for you.'

'Good luck with that.'

'We know what we are doing,' said Fred.

'So how have you allowed six murders to happen under your nose and still not caught the murderer?'

'He's clever.'

'And lucky,' added Toby.

'And that's all you have to say. Seems to me that the killer is just wandering around killing whenever he feels like it. Why isn't the town shut down with a curfew imposed?'

'Because we live in a democracy, Lady Oxford. If this was a police state, we would have had him by now.'

'That will be a big comfort to the dead, I'm sure.'

'Lady Oxford.'

She turned to Toby. 'Yes?'

'Do you think your son has a reason to kill you?'

It was a hard question for any mother to consider but Beatrice seemed unfazed. 'Did he have a reason to kill any of the other victims? He got sacked because he wasn't performing. Lots of people lose their jobs but they don't return years later and start killing everyone in the company. This isn't the reaction of a rational man. So, yes. If it is Oliver, and he's this crazy, I believe he could kill me.'

'Oh, it's Oliver, we're sure of that.'

Beatrice forced a smile that was gone in an instant. 'You had better go and catch him then, DC Marlowe. I've got a play to rehearse.'

Sir Morris looked at his wife in surprise. 'You do?'

'Yes, dear. Pierre Corridor has offered me a part in *Much Ado* for the new season. Seems he also believes I can play comedy.'

'Well that's marvellous, dear.'

'Don't sound so surprised, darling, he told me he had discussed it with you.'

The smile on Sir Morris' face flickered for a moment: what if he had also told her that he didn't think his wife could do it?

'He told me it was your idea, is that true?'

Sir Morris hesitated for a moment, desperately trying to

answer her without actually lying.

'Well, after what you told me about Big Al's comments, it got me thinking.'

She stepped forward and hugged him. 'Thank you, darling, this means everything to me.'

As the couple hugged, Toby turned to Fred. 'Two of them on the stage. How do we protect them there?'

Fred shrugged. 'I'm not sure we can.'

Fred didn't know it, but he had never spoken a truer word.

Chapter 62
Beware The Ides Of March, Again

'You looking forward to the show, Felix?'

Felix sat across from Oliver in the kitchen at Trinity Street. 'Yes, it's one of my favourite plays. Didn't expect you to want to see it with Sir Morris poncing about as Caesar.'

Oliver took a sip of his gin and tonic. 'Not my first choice, I have to admit but, on the upside, he gets killed in Act Three, so a happy ending.'

Felix stared at Oliver. 'Am I missing something here?'

'Like what?'

There was a mischievous air to Oliver; Felix could sense it.

'What, it's happening tonight? I can't be sitting with you if that's going to happen.'

Oliver laughed and put a reassuring hand on his friend's arm. 'Relax, Felix, I'm not going to kill anyone tonight. I promise.'

'I'm not sure I believe you.'

Oliver put down his glass. 'I swear on Suzy Tench's life that I am not going to kill anyone in the theatre tonight.'

Felix relaxed a little, he knew that Oliver had feelings for Suzy. Surely he would never swear on her life if he didn't mean it. 'So, why are we going?'

'You know, I'm not sure. Let's call it curiosity, I haven't seen the old windbag act in over fifteen years. I guess I want to see if he's as panto as I remember.'

'He's not that bad, a little overly dramatic maybe.'

'Let's wait and see. I'm really looking forward to seeing Theo's

Brutus, he's a fine actor.'

'He is,' agreed Felix. 'It's a shame he won't be around Stratford next year.'

'Why?'

'Apparently, he's been offered a role in a big TV series, playing an English version of Shaft. Sounds horrendous.'

That's a shame, I was looking forward to acting with Theo. He deserves a break though, he's been trapped in the shadow of Sir Morris and the late Desmond for too long. With Desmond dead there won't be another series of *Coffee and Cream.* You think British TV is ready for a Black actor leading a TV series?'

'Why not, he's already popular and he's definitely good enough.'

'I agree, Felix, but I just don't think the TV execs are ready for that step yet. They do a nice line in token gestures … but a starring role? I'll believe it when I see it.'

'Times are changing, Oliver, you've been away a long time. Oswald Mosley and his blackshirts are long gone.'

'They may be but I read about Enoch Powell's Rivers of Blood speech. Doesn't look good when a member of the ruling government makes a speech as racist as that now, does it.'

'You have been paying attention. I suppose you've heard about the National Front as well.'

'We can get British newspapers in Casablanca. I think there's a real race issue going on here right now. Maybe not in Stratford, but in the big cities it's there for sure.'

Felix couldn't disagree with his friend. 'Why don't you kill some of them too, I could definitely get behind that.'

An amused look crossed Oliver's face. 'And I could definitely do that; the only problem is that would be diluting the mission. I'm here for revenge, to put the record straight. Much as I'd like to, I can't go around killing a bunch of racists for fun.'

Felix took a sip of his gin. 'So, we are just going to the theatre to watch the play, no ulterior motives.'

Oliver smiled reassuringly at Felix. 'I just want to see *Julius Caesar* one more time, it's one of my favourite plays.'

'Yeah, mine too. Always liked the histories.' Felix drained his glass.

'God, I'd love to be up there tonight.' Oliver gazed off into the garden, remembering being on the main stage on a night with a full house. He could taste the atmosphere; it was like no other. If all went well tonight there would be yet another vacancy on the actor's list tomorrow. 'I love it when he ignores the warning of the soothsayer. "Beware the ides of March." Silly old sod thought he was invincible.'

'I think you've proved that nobody is invincible, Oliver.'

'Caesar certainly won't be,' he grinned.

Seconds passed as Felix looked at Oliver. 'What do you know that I don't?'

Oliver shrugged. 'It's live theatre, Felix, you never know what could happen, that's why we love it. It's a living breathing thing with a life of its own. Once it starts, there is no stopping it until the end. All the actors are merely players and have to play their part.'

'"All the world's a stage, and all the men and women merely players. They have their exits and their entrances."'

Oliver nodded his approval. 'Exactly.'

'Who is making an exit tonight?' There was a nervous quiver in Felix's voice. 'You promised me you wouldn't do anything tonight.'

'I won't, I promise. We will sit there and try to enjoy the play. It won't be easy with the bingo caller taking centre stage, but let's just do our best.' Oliver put down his glass. 'Right then, time we got ready for the theatre.'

In his dressing room at the RSC, Sir Morris Oxford felt strangely apprehensive. He had performed this play many times before, but tonight he felt nervous. He gazed into the mirror; the face that looked back at him was old. The lines had deepened and gravity was taking its toll.

He had passed the point of romantic lead many years ago and was now looking at playing King Lear, Henry VI and Friar Lawrence. These roles were still good but he found it hard to accept that his time as undisputed king of the Shakespearian stage was drawing to a close.

Julius Caesar had been fifty-five when he died, fifteen years younger than he was. Time and the ticking of the clock were against him. It would be hard to let go, relinquish his crown, he had fought so long and hard to retain it. His grip was slipping, soon the king would be dead and voices would cry, "Long live the king." And there would be a new king but it wouldn't be him. The end of his reign.

Maybe he should anoint his successor, pass the crown to his chosen heir. Abdicate and curry favour with the new king, thus ensuring he remained at the top table. Be the Svengali who pulls the strings. It was a lot to consider but tonight, for the first time, he did. He stared into the mirror again, looking past the reflection that confronted him, peeling back the layers that time had wrought. Searching for that young man who had grasped the crown so many years ago and held on to it for so long.

Defiance filled his eyes and a quiet rage filled his soul. He spoke to the image in his mirror. 'I am Sir Morris Oxford, the greatest Shakespearian actor that ever lived. This is my stage, my company and I am its king. Anyone that wants to try and take it from me will have to pull the crown from my cold dead hand.'

He roared like a wounded lion and the years fell from him; a renewed energy filled him and he rose from his chair. Tonight, he would show them, tonight he would be a Caesar they would never forget.

He would be right on both counts.

Chapter 63
Then Fall, Caesar

'Tell me again why on God's Earth we are meeting Whomper here.'

'He's taking us to the theatre,' said Toby, thrusting a pint of bitter into Fred's hand.

Fred looked at Toby like he had gone mad. 'Why?'

'He didn't explain, boss, he just said it was important that we are there tonight.'

'It's not going to look good, is it?'

'What isn't?'

'If members of the public recognise two leading detectives in the hunt for the crazed Shakespeare Murderer out for a night on the town.'

Fred did have a point but the arrival of Whomper seemed to drive that from his thoughts. 'What the bloody hell are you wearing?'

'This is my theatre-going outfit,' grinned Whomper. He was wearing a pair of pristine white trainers, and a red tracksuit with a white stripe that ran down the outside of both arms and legs. 'It's one hundred per cent cotton, breathable and very comfortable for when you are sitting around for several hours.'

Toby nodded. 'Makes sense.'

'Did you hear about the sports shop being robbed last month, Whomper?'

Whomper shook his head. 'No, didn't hear about that, Fred. What did they take?'

'Oh, cricket bats, couple of tennis rackets. Some Birmingham City football kits.'

'They won't be able to give those away,' observed Whomper.

'And some tracksuits, some of them red.'

'Good colour,' said Whomper.

Fred looked him up and down. 'And some white trainers. You got a receipt for that lot?'

'Me? No, I've had these ages, just been waiting for the right opportunity to wear them. I thought *Julius Caesar* would be the perfect occasion.'

'I can see why you would think that.'

'Really?'

'No.' Fred took another gulp of his pint.

'Why are we here, Whomper?' asked Toby.

'Me and my sisters warned Sir Morris to beware the ides of March and he has ignored us.'

'But it's late July,' said Fred.

'Not in the play, we think something is going to happen to Sir Morris tonight.'

'Based on the warning that you and your sisters gave him?'

'Exactly.'

Toby glanced at Fred, who was doing his best to ignore everything but his pint. 'I know that you and your sisters have had some success with your … predictions in the past, but what are you suggesting? We can't just stop the show. Not without real evidence that Sir Morris is at risk.'

'I understand that. That's why the three of us have front row tickets in the stalls for tonight, in case anything goes off.'

'That's why you're wearing the tracksuit is it, so you can leap onto the stage like David Hemery and rescue Sir Morris.'

Whomper nodded. 'I'm sensing a little sarcasm, Fred. You think I'm wrong.'

'I'm trying not to think at all, Whomper, I find it helps with police work sometimes.' Fred refocused his attention on his pint.

'What do you think is going to happen?'

Whomper shook his head. 'I don't know, Toby, but I've got a terrible feeling that something nasty is in the offing. I've felt it for a while. I just think we should be there.'

Toby looked from Whomper to Fred; their demeanours couldn't have been more different. Whomper looked taut, worried. Fred looked indifferent.

'OK, I'm prepared to believe you,' said Toby.

'Really,' exclaimed Fred. 'No offence, Whomper's been very helpful in the past but this really is flying a bit of a kite, even by your standards.'

Whomper shook his head. 'Something's wrong, Fred, you've got to believe me.'

There was a strange desperation in Whomper's voice.

Fred drained his glass. 'OK, we'll buy it.'

'Great,' said Whomper. 'I love *Julius Caesar*.'

Two minutes later, they were walking down Southern Street towards the theatre. It was a warm evening and, despite the recent deaths, the streets were busy.

Children played on the grass and eager theatregoers made their way to the entrance of the RSC. As on most nights, the show was sold out. They made their way into the entrance and then showed their tickets to gain entry to the stalls.

Toby looked around, awestruck. He loved theatres, the memories they held, the moments they had captured, all live and never to be repeated. A special kind of magic and, of all the theatres, he loved this one the best. The Royal Shakespeare Theatre in Stratford. All the greats of the stage had played here, and their voices still echoed in the memories of those that had seen them. The sinusoidal waves of speeches, long since spoken, that had penetrated the very fabric of the building and left a scar that time could not erase. All you had to do was listen, remember and imagine, and you could enter the time machine of past performances, held forever in one place.

'Toby. Toby.'

Toby shook his head. 'Sorry?'

'Our seats are down here.'

He nodded at Whomper. For a moment he had been lost in the past, caught up in the voices whose words still vibrated silently around them.

'Sorry, I was miles away.'

Whomper gave him a knowing smile. 'Vibrations from the past, I feel them too. A soundwave never dies, it just becomes quieter, bouncing on forever between the walls of where it was spoken.'

'I thought it was just me.'

'No, if you open yourself to it, it's there. It's always there.'

Fred sat down and looked disappointedly at his fellow theatregoers. 'Have you two quite finished with your vibrations and voices from the past? I'm going to have enough trouble staying awake with just the voices of tonight.'

'Philistine,' said Toby.

'I don't think anyone will be sleeping through this production,' said Whomper, unable to hide the warning tone in his voice. 'I have a bad feeling.'

They sat down and a short time later the lights went down.

For a few moments the theatre was dark and then the stage was bathed in light as several commoners walked onto the imaginary street in Rome. Two Roman Tribunes appeared.

'"Home, you idle creatures, get you home. Is this a holiday? What, know you not. Being mechanical, you ought not walk upon a labouring day without the sign of your profession. Speak, what trade art thou?"'

In the seat next to him, Toby heard Fred whisper, '"Why, sir, a carpenter."'

Toby smiled to himself, Fred was not the cultural desert he pretended to be.

As the play proceeded, he lost himself in the story and the reason for his being there was forgotten.

Whomper had not forgotten; his fear and foreboding grew like mushrooms in the dark. Something was wrong, very wrong.

Further along the front row, Oliver had no such foreboding; excitement tingled through him. The moment he had so long dreamed of would soon arrive, delivered by the hand of those Sir Morris trusted most: his company members. To him it would seem, like Caesar, he had been betrayed.

When those blades failed to retract and went into his body, he would taste the cold steel of pent up revenge.

Who would hold the two doctored knives? Oliver had no way of knowing. He hoped one would be Theo, he had been held down by Sir Morris for too long. He had found out that Hugh Pitt was also in the cast playing Casca. He would be the first to stab Caesar; how he hoped that he too would have a faulty knife. Their dislike was well known; the press would have a field day. Oliver loved the theatre but had never felt anticipation like this.

Sitting next to him, Felix just felt scared. Oliver was happy, excited, this was not a good thing. These days the only thing that seemed to excite him was murder. What would he do if Oliver jumped onto the stage to attack Sir Morris? Would he, could he, try to stop him? He had feared something terrible was going to happen tonight and had made an entry in his journal, just in case he never returned to his boat.

Something is wrong. Oliver is taking me to see Sir Morris play Caesar tonight. He hates Sir Morris' acting, and yet, he seems excited to be going. This is not right. If I do not survive this night, it means that Oliver has completed his mission and I have been deemed too dangerous to remain alive. When you light a fire, you sometimes get burned. I have ignited an inferno and I fear the flames will consume me.

Felix decided there was nothing he could do, he would just sit there and let it play out. He was a mere bystander, a witness to history held in place by his actions which had trapped him on what now seemed the wrong side of the story. All he could cling to was Oliver's promise that he would not kill Sir Morris tonight.

Onstage, the story moved along, relentless as a river flowing towards its conclusion. Each line, every scene moving inexorably towards … What? A murder, a miracle. The thought of failure crossed Oliver's mind. Had he pushed the reeds into the side of the retractable blades far enough? Had he put enough glue in to ensure they stuck? Sir Morris was a big man but that torso was hard, packed with the muscle required to provide a voice that could fill an auditorium. An actor's diaphragm would be twice as strong as a non-actor's, one needed those muscles to project one's voice. What if the muscle was so strong that the glue failed or the reed popped loose and the blade slid helplessly back into the handle?

Oliver shook his head and breathed deeply. What will be, will be. For now, he had done all he could. He would wait, watch the show and hope. Hope that the years of waiting were over, that his father was finally revenged and that he would, once more, have the chance to tread again on the boards he had loved so much.

Act 1, Scene 3 was under way. The stage was illuminated by a flash of lightning and thunder boomed around the auditorium. Cicero arrived to persuade Casca to join the conspiracy to kill Caesar.

"'Good even, Casca. Brought you Caesar home?'"

Casca shook his head and gazed up at the storm. "'Are you not moved, when all the sway of earth shakes like a thing unfirm?'"

Whomper was shaking. The vision he had seen was now becoming clear: Caesar lay, bloody, upon the steps of the Senate, and Caesar wore Sir Morris Oxford's face. He touched Toby's arm. 'It's going to happen.'

'What?'

'Sir Morris is going to die.'

'Of course he is, he's playing Caesar.'

Before Whomper could respond, a voice from behind demanded they be quiet. Toby turned away from Whomper; he had no wish to break the etiquette of the theatre or miss a word of the play.

To his left, Toby could hear Fred speaking quietly under his breath.

'"I believe these are omens regarding what will happen in the place where they occur, right here in Rome."'

Whomper heard Fred too and he knew the omens were correct and Rome was here, on the stage at Stratford. He sat there powerless to respond to something he could not fully comprehend; fearing and knowing were two sides of the same coin. He had flipped the coin in his head but, until it landed, he could do nothing. He was an observer of history and unable to influence its outcome.

In his seat on the front row, Oliver had no such fear, just an excited tingle of anticipation. He was rather enjoying the play. It was a fine production, even Sir Morris had impressed; his stentorian delivery was well-suited to the tyrannical role of Caesar. This was a hectoring, bullying role of a man clinging to power by the force of his personality, a mirror image of Sir Morris. The climax of the show was approaching, although only he knew it.

Out of the corner of his eye, he saw Felix relax. His pep-talk must have done the trick; he really did seem to be enjoying the show. It was a shame that it wouldn't last.

Oliver felt his grip tighten on his programme: Act 3, Scene 1 had arrived.

Caesar: - (to the Soothsayer) The ides of March are come.
Soothsayer: - Ay Caesar, but not gone

As the assassination of Caesar approached, Whomper moved to the edge of his seat, as if ready to spring onto the stage.

Fred noticed him and followed suit, sitting up straight and paying close attention to the action taking place on the stage.

Oliver also moved to the edge of his seat, but he was not coiled and ready to spring, he just wanted to be nearer to the stage. Close enough to hear the thud of blade against ribcage, the cry of pain and the screams as real blood splattered across the stage. This scene would be the greatest ever played in Stratford.

Caesar: - Doth not Brutus bootless kneel?
Casca: - (Moving forward) Speak hands for me!

Casca stabbed Caesar and he cried out in pain. It was a fine cry, but unrealistic; Sir Morris was acting. Then the others stepped up and stabbed Caesar. The third blow extracted a sound that was not scripted.

Fred looked at Whomper and they knew. Before they could move, Brutus thrust his dagger deep into Caesar's back.

Sir Morris' scream echoed around the theatre like the howl of a wounded animal. Blood spurted from two wounds; it pulsed upwards to the rhythm of Sir Morris' heart and Fred knew that this was real. The actors onstage were beginning to realise that there was something very wrong. Sir Morris did not utter the immortal words, "Et tu, Brute?" He had fallen to the stage, screaming for help.

Fred headed towards him, followed by Whomper. They pushed the actors out of the way and crouched down next to Sir Morris: there was a wound to his back and one to his side. They glanced at each other and began applying pressure to the wounds, desperately trying to stem the flow of blood.

Toby leaped onto the stage. 'Is there a doctor in the house, please?' Two hands went up and Toby beckoned them up to the stage. 'He's been stabbed. Please, do what you can.'

The stage manager ran to the middle of the stage.

'Call an ambulance,' demanded Toby. The stage manager hesitated. 'Now!' roared Toby.

In the front row, Oliver turned to Felix. '"Then fall Caesar."'

Felix looked from Oliver's smiling face to the stage where Sir Morris lay bleeding and moaning. Oliver had been as good as his word. He hadn't killed Sir Morris tonight, some of the cast had.

Oliver got up and, without looking back, made his way out of the theatre. Felix watched him go. This then was the end of Oliver's second act. There was only one to come: *Macbeth*. The Scottish play.

Felix knew that neither he nor Oliver would escape from that with their lives or freedom intact. He looked around him: Oliver had gone, left him behind to see the outcome. The uproar in the auditorium seemed to be growing louder by the second. Sir Morris was dying and soon Oliver's revenge would be complete. The final curtain was about to fall.

The End

Acknowledgements

I went a lot darker in this book and a big thanks to my wonderful editor Samantha Brownley for going there with me. I think we kept the tone just right, darker but still retaining that line of humour.

Again, a big thankyou to Will Templeton for his proofreading and fantastic setting out, immaculate as always.

Another great cover from the legend that is Pete Adlington and a big thank you to Laura Lees for her PR support and endless charm.

Thanks to Dave Brownley for his constant work on promoting the book on all sales platforms.

And finally to the lovely Lou, the boss! Always giving me the space and time to write, even when she has jobs for me. What a girl!

Coming soon…

Read on for an extract from

Sleep No More

the next book in **The Shakespeare Murders** series

Chapter 1
Then Fall, Caesar

Felix sat motionless, rooted to his seat. Before him on the stage lay Sir Morris Oxford; like a giant felled oak, its majesty lost. The stage was raked. Two rivulets of blood ran down its slope towards him; he watched in horrified fascination. It was the blood of someone he had once considered a friend; it seemed inconceivable that this scene had been partly his doing. The two daggers that Oliver Lawrence had tampered with were mixed in with the others, strewn across the stage. The blades had failed to retract and the stabbing of Caesar had been real.

Sir Morris had stopped moaning now. He was lying between two doctors from the audience that were fighting desperately to save him. His skin had taken on a deathly pallor. The rivulets of blood had worked their way to the edge of the stage and now began to pool at Felix's feet, as though Sir Morris was pointing accusing fingers at him. Was this finally the end; would Oliver now be satisfied?

He didn't know, but for Felix the mission had reached its conclusion. How much blood could one man bathe in before it drowned his soul, destroyed his mind. He was done. He turned and hurried away from the awful scene.

Caesar lay upon the steps of the Senate, his life force flowing like the River Styx. Charon, the ferryman, would be waiting to carry his soul to Hades, and he was certain that he and Oliver would be joining him there before too long.

Outside the theatre there was total chaos. Shocked audience members were milling around, chatting, crying, disbelief etched across their faces:

'A terrible accident … right in front of me!'
'There must have been a mix-up with the props.'
'Sir Morris was bleeding, howling – how could this happen?'

Felix knew. Oliver had doctored two of the knives so they wouldn't retract; it wouldn't take long for the police to work out that this was no accident. He needed to get away from the theatre. As he walked down the steps onto Waterside, two ambulances came screaming towards him, sirens blazing. Sir Morris was a big chap, but two ambulances? That was overkill.

Chapter 2
Brutus Makes Tea

As Felix made his way down the river path to Holy Trinity, the sound of the chaos that reverberated around the theatre receded. It felt like walking away from madness. He could hear it in the distance but it no longer possessed him; neither did Sir Morris. As he walked through the graveyard a calm slowly descended. It was over. With the death of Sir Morris, it had to be, didn't it?

When he reached the house on Trinity Street the door was on the latch. He pushed it open, entered and locked the door behind him.

Oliver had wasted no time. He looked at him cheerfully. 'Well, that went better than I expected.' He offered Felix the biscuit tin. 'There's some of your favourites in there.'

Felix opened it and took two. He bit into the first one without speaking. It felt familiar, reassuring. As he munched he stared at Oliver, which seemed to amuse him.

'Watching the old boy flap about given you an appetite?'

Felix nodded and then shoved the other half of the biscuit into his mouth, preventing any reply.

Oliver reached into the cupboard, pulled out another pack and put them next to the tin. 'Just in case one packet isn't enough.' He laughed and turned back to making the tea.

It took five biscuits before Felix had clarified his thoughts. By this time there was a mug of tea steaming beside him on the table. He took a sip and then looked at Oliver. 'Is that it then, are we done?'

'Not sure.'

'But you've got him, what else is there?'

Oliver looked doubtful. 'We don't actually know if Sir Morris is dead, do we?'

'He looked pretty close to it when I left.' Felix stared at the strawberry jam filling the Jammie Dodger he was holding. 'I didn't realise how much blood was inside a body. It ran down the stage and over the edge. A person can't lose that much and survive, can they?'

'Morris isn't a normal human being though, is he. He has an ego the size of a small English county. That on its own should guarantee another couple of hours before the blood loss takes him.'

Felix said nothing.

'What's on your mind,' asked Oliver.

'Wiltshire, I was thinking about Wiltshire.'

'I think you'll find that's a large English county, that's why the army drive their tanks all over it.'

Felix nodded. 'Bad example.' He took a sip from his mug and then looked up. 'Let's assume he's going to die, what then. Are we done?'

Oliver shrugged. 'If it is fatal, we may be. Just depends, there are loose ends to attend to.'

'Such as?'

Oliver leaned back in his chair. 'Well, Clarissa Pidgeon for starters. Let's not forget I accidently strangled Chief Wilson's wife in her place.'

'How could I forget,' sighed Felix.

'That was Clarissa's fault. If she hadn't been bisexual it would never have happened.'

'Maybe if you hadn't tried to strangle her it would never have happened,' snapped Felix.

'Let's not play semantics, dead is dead. Clarissa's immoral behaviour caused the problem. I am blameless in this unfortunate incident.'

Oliver's rationale was not that of a sane individual, and yet there was a weird logic to it. The death of poor Heather Wilson was an unfortunate case of wrong lesbian in the right place. They weren't to know that Clarissa swung both ways, or that the naked form lying before them in that darkened room, her face covered with a strawberry-patterned handkerchief, was not the victim they sought.

'You still want to kill Clarissa then, even after Sir Morris is dead?'

Oliver considered Felix's question for a moment. 'It's a question of unfinished business. I can't envisage a future where I have to share the same stage with her. She is bound to botch a scene and leave me regretting not having killed her. I want a completely fresh start, clear the slate.'

Felix couldn't believe it: Oliver still thought a return to the stage at Stratford was possible. 'Let's assume Sir Morris dies and you kill Clarissa, will that be it?'

Oliver grinned at Felix. 'My, my, Felix, you sound like you're not enjoying this.'

'I'm not. Maybe to start with but it's become—'

'Real?'

'Nasty. Vindictive.'

Oliver shrugged. 'Collateral damage. I wanted revenge but then I thought of all the other hangers-on that fed off the monster. When I cut his head off, I don't want them attaching themselves to me. I want them gone.'

'You didn't answer my question.'

'No, Felix, I didn't, did I.' Oliver thought for a moment and then, without looking up, whispered. 'It may be time to kill my mother!'